"I WISH TO INTRODUCE YOU TO MY SERVANT CREKKID."

Keprose extended his hand. Something silvery writhed upon the palm. A length of undulating metallic substance reared itself. A tiny head turned toward Relian. Two ruby eyes examined him minutely. The mouth opened, a silver tongue flickered and Crekkid hissed.

"An automaton?" Relian inquired.

"My Crekkid is a steel serpent—part steel, part flesh, and partaking of the nature of both substances."

"You're asking me to believe that this metal thing is alive?"

"I ask nothing," Keprose returned tranquilly. "I advise you to observe and to form your own conclusions."

"I observe a finely-crafted steel mechanism capable of very lifelike movement. It is cleverly executed, and I must admire the Seigneur's ingenuity."

"Ssstupid." The voice was thin, shrill, and piercing. Crekkid's gleaming tongue winked. "Ssstupid, ssstupid, ssstupid."

"Manners, my Crekkid," Keprose admonished. Then he smiled at Relian. "Be so good as to approach and bow your head."

Relian did not move. "May I ask why?"

"That I may loop Crekkid about your neck, of course," Keprose explained.

Crekkid hissed eagerly.

Ace Fantasy books by Paula Volsky

THE SORCERER'S LADY
THE LUCK OF RELIAN KRU

THE LUCK OF RELIAN KRU

PAULA VOLSKY

ACE FANTASY BOOKS
NEW YORK

This book is an Ace Fantasy original edition,
and has never been previously published.

THE LUCK OF RELIAN KRU

An Ace Fantasy Book/published by arrangement with
the author

PRINTING HISTORY
Ace Fantasy edition/June 1987

ISBN: 0-441-83816-2

Ace Fantasy Books are published by The Berkley Publishing Group,
200 Madison Avenue, New York, New York 10016.
PRINTED IN THE UNITED STATES OF AMERICA

To Aline Volsky, with love.

"My young gentleman was born under an unlucky star. That's a fact," the lackey Trince announced. "Or else he's the victim of a curse. It's one or t'other, without a doubt. Poor Master Relian!" He took a swig of ale. His broad, shrewd face bore an expression of regret.

"A curse?" one of the young cookmaids echoed in flattering wonder. "Your master is accursed? *Really?*"

"It's true, sweetheart, every word. Master Relian must be the unluckiest man alive. Fate's plaything, that's what he is."

"Oh, what's Fate done to him?"

"Nearly everything. But that's a long story. I'm only a visitor here in Neraunce and I wouldn't want to impose on the patience and hospitality of you good folk," Trince replied with spurious modesty. He took another swallow of ale and covertly studied his audience of fellow-servants. His inborn showman's instinct assured him that they were hooked, each and every one of them.

The servants sat around a wooden table in the kitchen of Gornilardo, the famous Dhreve of Neraunce. The warm, low-ceilinged room was circular in shape—a common feature of the regional architecture. The natives were wont to inhabit round stone towers of dizzying altitude. It was claimed that these structures represented a visual embodiment of the Neraunci quest for spiritual enlightenment. A more realistic explanation might have cited Gornilardo's quest for personal glory, but such excessive accuracy was customarily eschewed. The palace of the Dhreve consisted of no less than fifteen towers of varied height joined by ornate aerial walkways of extraordinary beauty and insubstantiality. At the top of the Mauve/Garnet Tower was the suite of rooms occupied by the Divine Vhanaizha, Gornilardo's current mistress; and there a reception was in progress. Down below in the kitchen, the servants idled and gossiped. As a stranger and a traveler, Trince would have been the center of attention at any time. His flair for narration, however, added immeasurably to his glamour. Trince was enjoying every minute of it.

"Tell us about the curse," the little cookmaid coaxed. "Who did it to him, and why?" Trince winked at her.

"Yes indeed, friend Trince," one of the footmen urged. "Why should anyone wish to curse your master? I saw him as the two of you were riding in and he seems a likely young fellow, except maybe for those odd-looking white hands of his—"

"That's right," the cookmaid agreed. "I saw him too, and he's a mighty handsome gentleman but for those *hands*. They're so long, and white like a corpse's, and the fingers look like they've got no bones in them, and they're just so—so—*strange*."

"Well, there you have it," Trince sighed. "Being stuck with those hands is just the beginning of the bad luck that's plagued poor Master Relian and those around him all of his life. You should know, since you're interested, that my young gentleman and I are Travornish by birth. Master Relian is a person of quality, being born twenty-one years ago to Squire Berlian Kru of Hillheather Manor over in West Greding, near the Porpol. That's a fine name in those parts of Travorn. Of course Squire Berlian and his lady were overjoyed to have a son, but their pleasure didn't last long. Shortly after the arrival of Relian, things went pretty sour. The crops failed, taxes went up, and the tenantry got sullen. There was an epidemic of the Shivers among the cows, and some loony started setting fire to folks' barns at night. And all that before Relian was past the age of two!"

"Well that's all very sad, I'm sure," the cook observed. "But I don't see how anyone could say that it had anything to do with the boy."

"Very true, but keep listening. Time went by and things

got worse at the manor. Lady Jemanthey—Master Relian's mother, that is—took a tumble from her horse and broke her arm. It never healed proper. Squire Berlian developed gout and the temper of a rabid wolf. They discovered that Meb the Steward was pilfering, and Meb had to be turned out without a reference. Without Meb around, the records of the estate got in a muddle and money was lost. The Squire had to sell a parcel of land at a big loss. He drank brandy, raved and smashed crockery for three days running, and was never the same thereafter. Then Lady Jemanthey's mother came to Hillheather Manor to stay and the old lady started suffering spells when she'd throw off her clothes and run out into the garden at night to dance naked in the light of the moon. She claimed to carouse with the fairies, and may have spoke the truth for aught I know, for somehow the old lady was got with child. Then Meb came sneaking back one night to poison the well, and—''

'' 'Tis untrue and unjust to blame the boy for all this,'' the cook interrupted.

''You think so, eh? During this time,'' Trince continued, ''Master Relian was getting bigger. He was as bright, hand-some and good-natured a child as you'd ever care to see, but already he wore bad luck like a garment cut to his measure. In the first place there was the matter of his hands, as you've already noticed. Those hands were peculiar from the first, and the children of the gentry all over the countryside took to sniggering and calling Master Relian 'Wormfingers.' That was hard on the lad, but it wasn't the worst of it. It seemed that nothing went right for him from the very first, and it was never his fault. He caught every ailment of childhood you can think of and some you can't imagine. Who ever heard of a Travornish boy falling sick of the Gangeloid Spasms? Or the Foaming Heaves? The Strellian Scabies or the Seven Week Mucosity? Well, Master Relian had 'em all. And that meant the whole household caught 'em—Squire, Lady, retainers— everyone. Glymbelt the kitchen boy never did get over the Mucosity, and Master Relian felt terrible about it.

''Then,'' Trince went on, ''there were the tutors. My young gentleman applied himself faithfully to his studies, but things went bad there too. There was the doctor of natural philosophy who came to demonstrate his experiments, mixed the wrong powders and got burned in the explosion. There was the dancing-master who tried to demonstrate the Maquirvian

Prance, tripped and broke his head. Then there was the
fencing-master who impaled himself. And the riding-instructor
who got trampled. As for Relian himself—he didn't get off
easy, neither. Why, I think he broke near every bone in his
body at some time or other. The lad went through a dozen
tutors within the space of a couple of years and mind you, the
accidents and tragedies were never his doing. He didn't complain much, but things were telling on him, you could see.
And so it went," Trince continued, "all through Master
Relian's childhood. He grew up at last, and things got no
better. If I told you about the times he's gone a-courting—but
no, those stories are too sad. Enough to say that Squire
Vorpiu's second daughter had it all wrong when she claimed
that Master Relian did it to her on purpose. And as for the
other one—the young Lady Dajanett, that was—well, the
physicians believe that the scars on her face will fade, in
time. I still maintain it wasn't my young gentleman's fault.
But it's all soured his nature a bit, as you may well imagine.

"Finally," Trince went on, "Master Relian's studies were
finished and the young gentleman set forth on his travels.
They say 'tis meant to complete his education, but truth is,
the family really wanted to get 'im out of the way. Squire
Berlian and Lady Jemanthey were delighted to see him go,
and to my mind they'll be glad if he never comes back home.
And Master Relian, he don't even want to go back before
he's found some way of ending his run of bad luck—and
maybe not even then. So we've been traveling now for six
months and wherever we go, misfortune follows. When we
visited Ferille, the floods came with us. While we were in
Wherautin, fire destroyed the ducal palace. When we visited
the court of Xasxin, the old king was taken with fits. In
Auswesl, Master Relian paid his addresses to a veiled lady
who turned out to be the wife of the Dorbidadur, and we had
to flee for our lives. We were declared persona non grata in
the Low Hetz and we've been banished on pain of death from
Beruze. Now we've come to Neraunce, and who can say
what will happen? There'll be something, though—on that
you may rely, my friends. So you see," Trince concluded,
"that this life-long run of bad luck isn't natural. The most
likely explanation that *I* can see is a curse. I don't know
who's done it to my poor master or why it was done, but
there it is. And where it will all end, I could not say."

The servants regarded Trince with mingled interest and commiseration.

"Pretty hard on your master," a footman observed.

"Pretty hard on anyone who comes anywhere near your master," said the cook.

"Why, he must have lay in a cradle of black-and-tawny!" a potboy exclaimed.

"Eh?" Trince looked blank.

"Black and tawny together signify the Dedication to Disaster," the potboy explained. "Add a green stripe and you have the Dedication to Disaster with Emphasis."

"Oh."

"Aren't you afraid?" the cookmaid inquired.

"Afraid, sweetheart?" Trince smiled indulgently.

"Yes, aren't you afraid that something terrible will happen to *you* if you don't leave the unlucky gentleman's service?"

"Oh, I've already had my arm broke twice, and a case of the Grinning Jerks, and I've stood in the stocks in Wherautin and I've had my pocket picked three times, since I entered Master Relian's service. But these are only trifles and you may be certain I do not *fear* them. I'm not so easily affrighted as that, I warrant you. When Bendo Trince enters a gentleman's service, he's not to be frightened off by curses. He spits upon all such impertinent knaveries! Aye, Bendo Trince laughs them to scorn!"

"If there's really a curse on your master, then why don't he seek out a magician or sorcerer to take it off again?" asked the cook.

"Sorcerers? Magicians? Bah—where should we find such creatures?"

"Oh, they live as great lords over in Nidroon, in the town of Vale Jevaint."

"Foolery," Trince opined. "Carnival mountebanks and rogues, I doubt not."

"Not so, friend Trince. The sorcerer Keprose Gavyne is the hereditary seigneur of Vale Jevaint."

"He practices magic openly?"

"So I'm told," the footman answered.

"Then why don't they burn 'im at the stake?" Trince inquired.

"How are they going to do that?" the cook countered. "A sorcerer isn't about to let himself be burned, is he? Not a *real* sorcerer. The ones that get burnt—I'll stake my money they aren't the real thing."

"That may be so," Trince conceded. "But I'm still a long way from believing that such a one could help my young gentleman."

" 'Tis natural that you should be a skeptic." The cookmaid suppressed a giggle. "Your colors signify as much."

"How's that, sweetheart?"

"You wear dark blue and gray, with brass buttons on your jacket."

"Aye—the Kru livery."

"Well, dark blue, charcoal and brass convey the Specific Incredulity in the Second Degree of Intensity."

"Is that a fact, now? You've different notions from the people at home, that's certain. And what do your colors say, sweetheart? Let's see—red, orange, brown and buff stripes, black rosettes, gold buttons, blue eyes, pink cheeks—shall I take a guess what they might mean?"

"No need to guess," the girl replied. "They signify the Potential Ferocity in Defense of Virtue."

The kitchen door banged open and another of the Dhreve's servitors came scurrying in. The fellow was flushed and excited. "There's going to be bloodshed before long," he announced. "Scrivvulch the Stick will be busy tonight, I can tell you."

Trince instantly lost his audience.

"What are you talking about, Guz?" the potboy demanded.

"It's the stranger, the young Travornish gentleman. You'll hardly believe me when I tell you what he's done. But I'll swear it's true!"

"What's he done?"

"Listen to this. The Travorner is wearing a dark green coat with gold embroidery. Green breeches, black waistcoat with gray trim. White cravat and stockings. And a ring with a great stone of blue!"

"Why, the young noddy!"

"If he thinks Gornilardo will suffer this, then he doesn't know our Dhreve!"

"Scrivvulch will make quick work of him, I shouldn't wonder."

"The young gentleman's a stranger," the little cookmaid reminded them. "Perhaps he just don't know any better?"

"Perhaps, but that won't matter a pyte's worth to Scrivvulch the Stick."

"Here now, wait a bit." Trince thrust his way into the excited conversation. "What are you saying here? You're talking about my master Relian Kru. What concerns Master Relian concerns Bendo Trince."

"Friend Trince, after tonight you may need to seek new employment," one of the footmen observed. " 'Tis no great matter. A stout fellow such as yourself should have no trouble—"

"Enough!" Trince exclaimed. "My present employment suits me fine and I've no ambition to change it. Now what's all this about Master Relian? Are you saying he's done something wrong?"

"Well, if you call offering a mortal insult to the Dhreve something wrong, then he's done it," Guz replied.

"That I cannot believe. Master Relian was brought up proper and there's nothing wrong with his manners. He wouldn't insult anyone, I can attest to it."

"It's his clothes," said Guz.

"What's wrong with 'em? That green suit of his is brand new and the tailor swears it's a masterpiece for fit and cut."

"It's *those colors*. The Dhreve must be boiling."

"Look here," Trince argued. "I've seen that you Neraunci set a lot of store by color. But it ought to be pretty plain that my Master Relian is a stranger here. He don't know your ways and if he's caused offense, 'tis accidental—"

"Perhaps that's so. Aye, there could be something to that," Guz admitted. "You see, we're reasonable people and we're willing to be fair. Scrivvulch is reasonable too, but Scrivvulch will always follow the Dhreve's orders. And the Dhreve—well now, sometimes he's a bit hot and he never *will* forgive an insult. So I'm afraid your young gentleman has run into some serious bad luck—"

"Hold on," Trince demanded. "Who's this 'Scrivvulch' blackguard you keep talking about?"

"Perhaps 'tis unjust to call Scrivvulch a blackguard—" suggested the potboy.

"No it isn't," the cookmaid declared. "That wicked, crafty gray-poll!" She shuddered.

"—But Scrivvulch is very serious about his work and won't let anything or anybody get in the way of it. He's mighty proud of his position—"

"And what position might that be?" asked Trince.

"High Court Assassin."

"Wait." Trince took a deep breath. "I can't be understanding you right. You don't mean—you can't be saying—that your Dhreve Gornilardo is a-plotting to *assassinate* my innocent master? That's not what you mean, is it?"

"Alas, friend Trince," a footman sighed. " 'Tis most probable. Our Dhreve is a lofty man that will not abide an insult without taking his revenge. If I don't mistake the matter, Scrivvulch would already be spying out your young gentleman."

"He is," said Guz. "I was up there in Madam Vhanaizha's suite and I saw it. You may be sure Scrivvulch is making his plans."

"Well *you* may be sure that your Dhreve Gornilardo is a devil!" Trince exclaimed. "Like it or not and I don't care who hears me say it! What kind of a black-hearted, sneaking, treacherous, blood-drinking savage would kill a guest under his own roof? Take it as you will, here's what I think of your Dhreve!" Trince spat upon the floor.

The servants evinced surprisingly little perturbation. Clearly their devotion to their employer was not all it might have been.

"The Dhreve is a fire-breather and no mistake," the cook conceded. "In all fairness though, the offense is considerable. Your gentleman's combination of green, gold, gray, black and white with the Blue Point—you don't understand what that means."

"And I don't care overmuch," Trince replied. "All right, what does it mean, then?"

The reply was enlightening.

*   *   *

In the silken suite of the Divine Vhanaizha, Relian Kru stood alone. His complete isolation in the midst of a festive crowd was acutely noticeable and disturbing. Relian was a too-thin young man with well-cut features and an expression of habitual, somewhat embittered unhappiness, lightened by a humorous twist of the lips. A very pale complexion bespoke ill health. Slightly shaggy black hair emphasized the unusual pallor of the face. His large, dark eyes were melancholic at the best of times and nearly black with gloom now. The young man stood with his shoulders slightly hunched as if braced to receive the bloody stripes of Fortune, his hands buried in his pockets. It was a characteristic pose enabling him to conceal the long, luminously white hands that had earned him the despised childhood nickname of "Worm-fingers."

Relian wandered over to the buffet and poured himself a goblet of wine. A perfumed, curled and pomaded notable of Neraunce stood nearby. "The Lady Vhanaizha's hospitality is lavish—" Relian began, but got no further. The notable flashed a glare of icy contempt, deliberately turned his back and walked away. These courtiers of Neraunce were an unfriendly lot! Certainly he had done nothing, said nothing, to give offense? He and Trince had only arrived that very afternoon. During that brief stay, what social blunder could he possibly have committed?

At the far end of the buffet stood the Divine Vhanaizha herself, tropically lush in her turquoise satin and cloth-of-gold. The Divine One picked avidly at a plate of oysters; perhaps she searched for hidden pearls. Relian approached and addressed her with caution. "Madam, permit me to express my appreciation of your kindness in—"

Vhanaizha flirted her fan violently, turned a haughty shoulder and walked away, gilded curls bouncing.

Relian sighed, took a sip of wine and surveyed the apartment thoughtfully. The warm light of a thousand candles set in crystal chandeliers illuminated a curiously appointed chamber. The walls were covered with smoke gray damask, the windows hung with great swags of charcoal silk, and polished black marble lay underfoot. The furnishings were scanty, consisting of nothing more than the buffet and a battery of small, ornate chairs of carven ebony, with seats upholstered in gray silk. The somber setting seemed designed to emphasize the brilliant costumes of the titled guests; a gaudy, fatiguing brilliance. The Neraunci nobility favored the strongest of colors in the most unsettling of combinations: silver, lemon yellow and mahogany; burgundy, peacock and vermilion; one reckless soul flaunted rose, bottle green and carnelian. The general effect was dizzying, and in that overheated atmosphere, almost sickening. Relian shook his head. It was not his business as a visitor to pass judgment on the tastes and customs of his hosts, and yet . . . Clusters of courtiers were scattered throughout the room, and conversation seemed particularly lively. From time to time he caught glances thrown in his direction—glances of unmistakable indignation, hostility, even hatred; and instinct informed Relian that he himself was the object of discussion. *Why?* The young man wandered away from the buffet and seated himself in one of the uncomfortable chairs. Neighboring seats were promptly vacated. One bejeweled beldame withdrew herself with an audible grunt of disgust. Relian leaned back and considered the situation. In view of his lifelong, never-failing bad luck, it was only reasonable to assume that he had inadvertently committed a serious offense. But how could he make amends if he didn't know his error, and how could he learn it if nobody would speak to him? One thing only was quite clear—his sojourn in Neraunce would be brief. On the morrow he would express his gratitude to the Dhreve Gornilardo and depart. Relian's eyes automatically sought out the Dhreve. Gornilardo, who sat on the far side of the room, resembled nothing so much as a volcano in full eruption, with his massive bulk swathed in crimson, orange and purple; his carrot-colored hair and his fleshy face scarlet with rage. The heat of his anger could be felt clear across the room. Frequently he gestured in Relian's direction.

Relian watched curiously. The Dhreve was deep in conversation with a long-shanked, gaunt and gangling gentleman of refreshingly conservative appearance. The man was attired in a suit of sober brown and he carried a polished walking stick. A quantity of very fine, light hair fluffed around his head like the down of some silvery gosling. The cast of his bony face was mild and almost foolishly gentle. He might have been a pedagogue, perhaps a scholar or divine. Relian liked the unworldly look of him. After a time, the conservative gentleman detached himself from Gornilardo, bumbled his way through the gorgeous mob and seated himself at Relian's side. Relian's brows arched inquisitively.

"Master Relian Kru of Travorn?" the newcomer asked with a shy smile. Relian nodded. "I hope I do not intrude?"

"Not at all." Relian smiled in return, grateful for the companionship of a civilized, amiable Neraunci. His ostracism was not to be total after all.

"Delighted. Delighted. Permit me to introduce myself. I am Scrivvulch, known to certain wags as 'the Stick.' The sobriquet is hardly flattering, but seems preferable to total anonymity. In this bustling world, a modest man is destined for near invisibility, and the plodding mortal who makes no impression for good or ill upon his fellow creatures can hardly be said to have lived.''

"I can't agree with you," Relian replied, amused by the other's comical solemnity. "There are worse things than anonymity, and infamy is one of them. In the matter of sobriquets, I'd be only too happy to forego mine."

"Which is—?"

"It's 'Wormfingers.' " He did not ordinarily reveal as much, but the stranger's manner somehow invited confidences.

Scrivvulch appeared sympathetic. "Oh my. Oh my, that is unfortunate. I must concede the point. How did you happen to come by so unflattering an appellation?"

Relian mutely displayed his hands. Scrivvulch surveyed them attentively. "That's interesting. Very interesting indeed. Are you aware of the implications—" he broke off. "Perhaps you are one of those favored beings whose native abilities snare the eyes of the world?" He posed the question as if he imagined the answer might be significant.

"Not to my knowledge. But I seemed to have snared the eyes of Neraunce, and the regard is disapproving." Relian's face lapsed into its customary expression of melancholy. "I'm a stranger here and I don't know your customs. It's plain I've offended the Dhreve. I'd be willing enough to apologize for my error, if you'd be so good as to tell me what it is."

Scrivvulch wagged a reassuring finger. "Do not trouble yourself, sir. It must be confessed that the citizens of Neraunce are wary of strangers, reserved even to the point of coolness. It's possible that our naturally warm hearts haven't as yet manifested themselves to you."

Relian was diplomatically silent.

"Had you truly given cause for offense, even unwittingly, the blade of mortal vengeance would strike so swiftly as to leave you little time to suffer the hostility and contempt attendant upon your blunder. Therefore be at ease."

Relian pondered the meaning of this remark and arrived at no satisfactory conclusion. "And you, sir," he inquired at last, for want of anything better to say. "Why, if I might ask, are you known as 'the Stick?' "

"Partly for that I'm a gaunt, desiccated old body, hardly a fit object to appear at a pretty woman's soiree," Scrivvulch replied with disarming self-deprecation. "And partly for the sake of my cane, which serves as an aid to locomotion as well as a personal trademark. Its uses are manifold."

"I see." Relian examined his companion, noted the air of kindliness, and asked, "Sir, will you forgive the ignorance of a stranger? You spoke just now of 'the mortal blow of vengeance' that strikes offenders. What did you mean by that?"

"Enemies of his Dhreveship are wont to encounter the High Court Assassin," replied Scrivvulch the Stick.

For a moment, Relian was speechless. *Different customs,* the young man reminded himself. *Your journeying was meant to broaden your mind. This should certainly do it.* Aloud he inquired somewhat inanely, "High Court Assassin? You mean it's an official position?" Scrivvulch inclined his downy head. "A recent innovation?"

"On the contrary, an ancient tradition of Neraunce. The present Assassin has held his office nearly twenty years now. How time flies by!"

"The incumbent enjoys his work?"

"He has striven to realize the full potential of his office—and I believe, not without success."

"How did he happen to attain his present eminence, Master Scrivvulch?"

"He strangled his predecessor, thus demonstrating his superior qualifications in a more or less unmistakable manner."

Relian could not bring himself to express the admiration obviously called for, hence the remark was almost unanswerable. But the young man was of a naturally curious turn of mind. *Here is a society,* he reflected, *that legitimizes, even glorifies the stealthy killer. When shall I have another such opportunity to learn of foreign mysteries?* Aloud he remarked, "I'm eager for instruction. What means of assassination does this man employ?"

"His own blade, for choice. But he regards himself as a master of death and has been known to use a variety of methods—steel, fire, the cord, the wire, the hot poisons, the caustic ices, Sentient Darts, the carnivorous insects, Noerbelm's Vapors, the False Apoplexy, Dedennowd's Abrupt Descent—in short, whatever comes most readily to hand. Versatility is essential to success in his profession, and our Court Assassin has acquired proficiency in many arts."

"The customs of Neraunce are exotic. Ordinarily, the state establishes a judicial system of some kind or other to inflict justice—or vengeance if you will—upon malefactors. There are courts, tribunals wherein the accused is given an opportunity to—''

''Clumsy, lumbering, cumbersome anachronisms,'' Scrivvulch interrupted. He leaned forward in his chair and spoke with feeling. ''What is a trial but the creaking tumbril that bears a criminal to his death at the agonizing pace of a snail? Think of the time wasted, lost! Consider the pointless delay, the empty formality! The entire protracted procedure surely represents the ultimate victory of form over substance. But the truly advanced state has passed beyond the need for courts, prisons and public executions—those sorry relics of a primitive age! Imagine if you will our modern Neraunci system wherein justice is administered swiftly, mercifully, infallibly—to the benefit of all. This happy result is achieved naturally and inevitably by means of the High Court Assassin, whose greatest qualities are his dedication to his work, his pride in craftsmanship, his absolute determination to succeed. The Assassin, who may be regarded as a veritable sword of justice, receives the instructions of his ruler, notes the victim, chooses the appropriate weapon. The deed is performed within hours, and behold!—justice is served. You observe that the perfection of this concept lies in its extreme simplicity. There is no recourse to the humiliating arrest and accusation; the vulgar tribunal, fit only for the common herd; the noisome oubliette, the incompetent headsman. There is only the brief flash of a skillful blade. Tell me, my dear Relian, were you condemned, would *you* not prefer it so?''

''Perhaps, but only if my death were a foregone conclusion.''

''A legitimate reservation, but minor. Essentially we are in agreement.''

Relian did not answer directly, as a statement of his true opinion would have alienated the only Neraunci present willing to speak to him at all. He observed only, ''You pique my interest. Shall I be introduced to your famous Assassin?''

''At the earliest opportunity. I give you my word.''

''Are my questions apt to cause offense?''

''I believe not. Our Assassin is of a retiring nature, but I see no reason why your curiosity should not be satisfied. It seems a small thing to ask.''

''Excellent! I'll look forward to the introduction.''

''No more than I, my friend. No more than I.''

Shortly thereafter Relian bade good night to the sociable Scrivvulch, fled the hostile ambiance of the Divine One's apartment and sought the sanctuary of his allotted chamber. There he found Trince awaiting him.

"Master Relian, you must leave Neraunce at once," the lackey announced without preamble.

"I agree. The climate is damp, the architecture atrocious, the people are barbarous and their ruler doesn't wash. As far as I'm concerned, we can leave tomorrow."

"You must leave tonight, Master Relian. Right now, in fact."

"Now? You can't be serious. It's far too late to travel, it's been dark for hours. We may not like this place, but another night of it won't kill us—"

"It will kill you! That's just what it will do, Master Relian!"

Relian studied his servant. "What have you found out, Trince?"

"Now you're coming upon it. What I've found out is, you're in the stew. If you don't get out of here tonight, you'll be dead before morning. Murdered, sir."

"Neraunci version of hospitality?"

"I'm not joking, sir. Believe me."

"I can believe you, all right. I learned this very night that the Dhreve employs an official assassin. Think of it—so careless is Gornilardo of the blood let beneath his roof that he openly acknowledges his hired killer."

"Aye, Master Relian, I've already heard about Scrivvulch the Stick."

"What's Scrivvulch got to do with it? I met him this evening. Funny old bird, has some wrongheaded ideas, certainly knows how to talk—"

"Scrivvulch the Stick a funny old bird? Sir, he's the one! He's the Dhreve's handpicked assassin! That's the kind of funny old bird he is. Think about it."

Relian thought about it. "How do you know this?"

"The Dhreve's servants gave warning. When all's told, they're not so bad as their masters. They told me about the Stick and they told me something more. Scrivvulch is set on cutting your throat before sunrise."

"Yet he was expounding his peculiar philosophy to me not a quarter of an hour ago."

"They say he likes to acquaint himself a bit with his victims before he does 'em. The human side of his work, perhaps, sir."

"Perhaps. But why me?" Relian's frown was more thoughtful than fearful. A lifetime of ill luck had taught him fortitude. "What can I have done to enrage Gornilardo?"

"From what I hear, it don't take much to enrage Gornilardo. But this time I happen to know the answer. It's your clothes, sir. You've probably already noticed that the Neraunci have their own language of colors, as it were. Well, your green jacket and all the rest of your rig-out, it's all shouting something the Dhreve don't like to hear."

"Is that all? It should be easy enough to set things right, then. I'll go to Gornilardo and explain—"

"No you won't, sir! The Dhreve won't hear a word from you, he's that angry." Relian looked skeptical and the lackey inquired, "Would you like to know what your colors mean?"

Relian assented cautiously.

"They convey the Taunt Doubly Contemptuous of Matriarchal Liaison With Diseased Goat. So you see, sir, you'd better go. Fast."

"I think you're right."

"I've got a bag packed for you, and you can tip the undergroom and get a horse out of the stable easy enough."

"We'll need two."

"No, sir. I've thought about that. It's best you go alone for now. Now you hear me out," he pleaded as Relian began to protest. "For one thing, you'll attract less attention on your own. Get away easier, see. Secondly, I've still got to pack up the rest of your gear. Third, if I stay here, then the Dhreve's man will think you're still somewhere around the palace, and that way you can get a good head start with no one the wiser. By the time they see you're away, 'twill be too late. As for me, I'm in no danger at all, for no one's out for *my* blood. So you see, 'tis the best course by far."

"You should have been a scholar, you argue so prettily," Relian conceded with reluctance. "Very well, I'll go on condition that you follow at the break of dawn. We must decide on a place to meet. The Nidroonish border's not far off."

"Aye, sir. Follow the Northerly Way, and just over the border you'll find the town of Vale Jevaint, where I'm told that the Bearded Moon Tavern serves the finest ale this side of the Bhorphins. What's more, the seigneur of the place is one Keprose Gavyne, a sorcerer. It may be this Keprose can break your curse of ill-fortune—"

"Trince, you know my opinion of these sorcerous charlatans. I've consulted a dozen of them and it's been a waste of money and time."

"Oh aye, sir. I won't argue with you—although it may be that you just haven't met up with the real article yet. Forget the wizard then and think of the ale."

"The Bearded Moon Tavern in Vale Jevaint it is. Tomorrow night."

"I'll be there without fail. Here's your traveling coat and cloak. Better give me the green velvet."

"I don't like leaving you here."

"Worry about yourself, not me, Master Relian. It's you they're after. Here's your bag, sir. Better make tracks."

"I'm off. Until tomorrow night, then." Relian quickly changed garments, accepted the proffered bag and exited. He made his way through Gornilardo's luridly ornate towers without mishap. Only once did he lose his way, and soon found a footman to direct him.

The young man slipped out a side door, nodding as he went to the indifferent sentry. Outside the air was crisp, the sky overhead clear and starry. The courtyard was deserted. Far above, strains of cloying music dripped like honey from the open window of Vhanaizha's apartment. In the midst of that tranquillity, it was difficult for Relian to believe that an assassin sought his life. On the other hand, it was exactly his luck.

Not far away a lantern burned above the stable door. Relian approached, entered and paid the sleepy groom. As Trince had predicted, he obtained a horse without difficulty. The groom was able to provide directions and, for an additional coin, guaranteed silence. Relian guided his horse past the sentry box and out of the courtyard, through the quiet park where grotesquely painted statuary blighted the moonlit landscape, on as far as the great outer gate. The guards on duty there were bored and amiable. They opened the portal without argument. That, Relian reflected, was the great benefit of the Neraunci system of justice. Since executions were carried out in secret, no guard had received instructions to detain him. He passed through the gate, out into the streets of Flugeln, the Dhreve's capital. The roads were as the groom had described, and Relian soon found himself upon the Northerly Way. He urged his fresh horse to a smart trot and pressed on with confidence. Now that he was clear of the palace there seemed little reason to fear pursuit, but it would not do to tarry. The young man had learned long ago to base every action on the expectation that the worst of all possibilities would inevitably come to pass. In his particular case, it was generally the correct assumption. He kicked the horse to a canter and maintained the pace until he had left the Dhreve's abode some distance behind him. Only then did he permit the animal to rest a time before pressing on toward Vale Jevaint and its tavern with the peerless ale.

*   *   *

It was well past two o'clock when the chamber door swung silently open. Trince had been waiting for hours. A tall, gaunt, knobby figure hovered upon the threshold like a poorly-strung marionette. The visitor was garbed in brown and he carried an ebony cane. Trince recognized him at once, but kept his face carefully empty. ''Sir?'' he inquired, and yawned as if just awakened.

''I've a message of importance for Master Relian Kru,'' the newcomer announced mildly. ''Great importance.''

''Master Relian isn't here now.''

''Oh my, that is unfortunate. Where might I find him?''

''How should I say, sir? He's somewhere about the palace, I daresay. Maybe here, maybe there. You might look anywhere. Maybe the young gentleman's made an assignation, if he's lucky.''

''But the young gentleman seems far from lucky. Poor lad!'' replied the man in brown. ''You've packed up all his belongings, I observe.''

''Why yes, sir. Truth to say, Master Relian plans to make an early start of it in the morning.''

''Indeed.'' Trince's visitor entered the room, walked to the small leather trunk that sat in the corner and casually lifted the lid. A green velvet coat lay folded within.

''Here now! You can't do that, sir!'' the lackey protested. ''That's my master's property!''

''Why yes, I recognize some of it. This coat, for example. He was wearing it this evening. Can you explain why he's not wearing it now?''

''What's to explain, sir?'' Trince inquired blankly. ''He came in here awhile ago, changed his clothes and went out again. That's all. I think he did it because he had some notion that the great folk here didn't care for the rig-out he was wearing, but I wouldn't know anything about that. Me, I don't set such store by clothes as all that. But a wise man don't question the doings of his betters, does he?''

"And I perceive that you are a wise man. Tell me—what is young Kru wearing now? Traveling clothes, perhaps?''

"Shouldn't think so, sir. We're not leaving until tomorrow. Didn't I tell you?''

"But I wonder if you might not be in error? Could it be that your master has departed tonight?''

"Travel in the middle of the night, sir?'' Trince inquired in amazement. "Sounds uncomfortable. What would he want to do a thing like that for?''

"Young gentlemen are often prey to reckless impulses. The matter demands investigation and I must forego your company in favor of the stable grooms'. Their conversation is apt to prove less enjoyable, but more informative.'' He turned to go.

"Not so fast, Master Scrivvulch.'' Trince's air of stupidity vanished. He deliberately interposed his bulky self between his companion and the door.

Scrivvulch paused. "Ah, you know my name?''

"Aye, your name and a lot more besides. I know who you are, what you are, and what you're after.''

"Of course. I've a message from the Dhreve for young Kru—''

"That you do, and I know what kind of a message it is. Fortunately, Master Relian's not around to receive it. The bird's flown, Scrivvulch. You'll have to go back to your blood-drinking Dhreve empty-handed this time. But you're not going anywhere for a while. You're going to sit here all night long, until I'm sure that Master Relian is well out of danger. So you'd best make up your mind to it.'' The lackey folded his arms and leaned against the door.

Scrivvulch the Stick studied his muscular gaoler for a moment, ambled over to an armchair and seated himself. His arched brows and the droll set of his mouth expressed amused chagrin. "Well, well, it seems I am in prison, then. May I know the charge? Master Lackey, are you under the impression that I mean your young gentleman harm?''

"It's more than an impression. You're High Court Assassin, aren't you?''

"I am—? Oh my. Friend Trince, did one of the palace servants tell you this?''

"Never mind about that. Enough to say that some Neraunci are still men of conscience."

Scrivvulch could not forbear laughing. "My dear fellow," he inquired at last, "don't you know when you've been the victim of a practical joke? It was unkind of the footmen to use a foreigner as the butt of their humor, but I trust your good nature will permit you to pardon the rogues."

"Listen, Master Stick, I know what you're trying to—"

"I'm sorry, my friend, indeed I am, but you've been mightily abused," Scrivvulch declared. "They told you, did they not, that your master has committed an offense and I'm to punish the lad? Ha, I thought as much. They *will* repeat that foolish tale, the rascals! Stop and look at me. What do you see?"

" 'Tis a question better left unanswered," Trince replied.

"An aging pedant, that's what you see. I, a man of violence? I, a killer? The incongruity is laughable!" Scrivvulch lifted his stick, jabbed the air for emphasis. "Look you, they've played a sorry trick, but you're a stranger and they're a merry crew—"

"Better stop waving that cane around—" Trince directed.

He spoke too late. The cane paused in midair. Scrivvulch pressed a button in the handle. The snap of a powerful spring was heard and a light, triangular blade shot from the end of the stick, flew through the air and buried itself in Trince's breast.

The lackey stiffened, gasped, attempted to cry out. Blood sprayed from his open mouth. Briefly he clawed at the steel in his chest, then crashed to the floor and lay still.

Scrivvulch rose from his chair, crossed the room and bent to his fallen victim. He pulled the triangular blade free, wiped the blood off on Trince's jacket and carefully returned the steel to the cane. The Assassin stood. "So much for the servant," he mused aloud. "And now for the young master, whose allotted span seems so sadly brief. Ah, well—in this woeful world, the man whose life is cut short is spared an infinitude of suffering."

Scrivvulch stepped over Trince's body and walked from the room. Intuition led him to the stables and a groom who wisely did not attempt to withhold information from the High Court Assassin. Scrivvulch was not wont to waste time. Pausing only long enough to check his pockets for certain small belongings, he commandeered the swiftest mount avail-

able. In a matter of minutes he was out of doors beneath a
spangled sky, whipping along the Northerly Way toward the
town of Vale Jevaint.

*   *   *

The distance from Flugeln to Vale Jevaint was not great. The
Northerly Way wound through miles of placid farmlands,
crossed the Flat of Tchine and ran through the heart of North
Yaubin before attaining the River Idwence, which marked the
Nidroonish border. A ferry was there, and the ferryman was
still asleep when Relian Kru arrived at dawn. Relian lured the
sleepy-eyed fellow from his warm hut with the promise of an
extra-generous tip. He was accordingly carried across the
Idwence and found himself in Nidroon, where he breathed
easier.

On the Nidroon side of the river the road continued, but
was now known informally as the Equalists' Run—"Equalist"
being Nidroonish slang for a highwayman. Relian paused to
survey his surroundings. Before him rose the Bhorphins, their
icy peaks touched with the light of the rising sun. The gray
mists of morning still lay thick upon the land, and the first
early frost of autumn hoared the grass. The breezes were raw
and Relian shivered a little beneath the heavy cloak that
Trince had insisted that he wear. Where would he be now, he
wondered, and in what condition, were it not for Trince's
vigilance? Far colder yet, without doubt.

The Equalists' Run arrowed across the quiet fields with
mathematical precision for miles before finally surrendering
to the exigencies of the landscape at the foothills of the
Bhorphins. There, where the terrain rolled, dipped, plunged
and at last erupted into jagged hills, the highway zigzagged
amongst great granite outcroppings. Black-green conifers covered the slopes, and the air was fresh with their tang. The
hills were curiously deserted. No woodsman's cottage, no
lord's hunting-lodge broke the stand of pines.

Relian rode on throughout the day. The sun rose high in a
crystalline sky and the morning mists soon burned away.
Presently the young man's stomach began to growl. He encountered no inn, no cottage, and no fellow travelers. No
berries grew alongside the highway. No laden apple tree
reared itself conveniently among the hemlocks. Relian's wallet was full of good Travornish notes and silver, yet he went

hungry. A curious state of affairs for a civilized man! The thought of the money that he carried put him in mind of the highway's sinister title, and he thought of the silver-mounted pistol he had brought from home. How he wished he had it now! And perhaps he did. The bag that Trince had packed lay strapped to the saddle. Relian had not opened it throughout the night. Now he reached around behind him, undid the strap and buckle, felt within the bag. He encountered linen, wool, leather; then his hand closed on the pistol butt. He withdrew the weapon, ascertained that it was loaded and primed, and replaced it within easy reach. Now he need fear no Equalists. The hours passed and his hunger did not abate. It occurred to him from time to time to wonder if he had been pursued. But no—surely these quiet woods sheltered no predators, human or otherwise.

The hills grew steeper and the way more difficult. Relian paused to rest the horse and himself. Dismounting, he sank to the ground beneath a huge old tree, tossed his hat aside, leaned back against the trunk, extended his legs and filled his lungs with the pine-scented air. There was something more than pine in the air—a faint acridity that he could not identify. He sniffed experimentally and his nose tingled. His sinuses itched and he sneezed. Further experimentation provoked additional sneezes and he soon abandoned his efforts. The scent was elusive and distinctly unpleasant. Decomposing meat? No—something reminiscent of the vapors that had risen just an instant before the explosion during the visit to Hillheather Manor of the ill-fated doctor of natural philosophy, so many years ago. Fulminates? Corrosives? Tincture of Yellow Mordancy?

Relian remounted and rode north. He grew accustomed to the odor and dismissed it from his mind, but his nose continued to itch and he sneezed periodically. His horse seemed similarly afflicted. The animal snorted, tossed its head, and proceeded with obvious reluctance. The sun was setting and Relian was ravenous by the time he topped the crest of a hill and beheld the town of Vale Jevaint spread out below him. The sight was startling. In the midst of that isolation it was only natural to expect a community of rustic simplicity, but Vale Jevaint was no such thing. The town lay in a wide valley bounded by peaks of uncompromising verticality. The streets were numerous and most of them were paved. The buildings were constructed of the local honey-colored stone, and the architecture was eccentric. A profusion of domes lent Vale Jevaint the semblance of a cauldron frozen at rolling boil. Most of the domes bore spiked cupolas, often adorned with pennants whose varied colors probably were of some significance to the residents. A few stone towers of ornate construction reared themselves above the level of the surrounding structures—whether they were public edifices or private dwellings of the grandest citizens, Relian could not judge. It was a community of altogether greater size and sophistication than he would have expected to find in such a locale. Clearly the town was prosperous, wealthy in fact.

Beyond Vale Jevaint stretched a forest, a great expanse of trees that occupied at least half the valley. Although the day had been clear, a kind of haze lay over the forest—a thick effluvium that trapped and held the red light of the setting sun. The ruddy glow on the distant foliage was peculiar, almost ominous, and Relian looked on with interest. A wind swept the valley and with it came the corrosive breath of those woods. The horse snorted and Relian sneezed. His gaze wandered to the surrounding hills and encountered a great granite fortress that hulked like a mindless titan atop a distant cliff. The fortress, a huge and graceless structure of great antiquity, held Relian's attention for a while. Clearly it was the abode of the local seigneur, whose family had probably ruled Vale Jevaint since the founding of the town. Trince had told him something about the seigneur, something that Relian had instantly dismissed. What was it? *Sorcery.* Trince had said that the lord, whose name was Gravane or something of the sort, claimed mastery of magic. Nonsense, of course. Local superstitions, fears, misunderstandings and rumors magnified beyond all semblance of reality. No doubt this Gravane was a man of breeding whose level of education placed him far beyond the ken of the local peasantry, who viewed the incomprehensible as supernatural. Or Gravane might be an eccentric, an earnest crackpot, even a madman cherishing delusions of power. He might be a deliberate fraud, adopting the trappings of the magician in order to impress his subjects. The one thing he was not likely to be was a genuine adept. It was too much to hope for; and miserable experience had taught Relian the folly of extravagant hopes. *But what if it's different this time?* All the conscious pessimism in the world could not suppress the question. Hope rose once again like an incompetent wrestler unwilling to admit defeat. *What if he's actually*

*got power? Could he help me? Would he be willing to? My
life might be very different.* For a few moments Relian in-
dulged in the luxury of speculation. An end to his constant
ill-luck . . . no more unlikely illnesses, improbable accidents,
ridicule . . . no more impossible disasters befalling those
around him . . . the chance of a happy home, tranquillity,
family. . . . Such thoughts were dangerous, conducive to
self-pity and paralytic gloom. Nonetheless, they *would* invade
his mind from time to time.

His reverie ended abruptly. An explosive crash reverber-
ated through the hills and Relian automatically glanced at the
sky in search of storm clouds. But the heavens were clear and
the sanguinity of the setting sun promised fair weather. The
ground underfoot shook slightly. Relian's horse whinnied in
dismay, plunged and shied. As the young man struggled to
control the frightened animal, another crash sounded and the
hills themselves rumbled in protest. Earthquake? Volcanic
eruption? Relian wondered if his mere presence might induce
seismic convulsions. Hubristic perhaps, and yet—there had
been the quake that had destroyed several of the outbuildings
of Hillheather Manor when he was four years old. And then
there was the time he'd called upon his cousins in the South
Greding. The ground had quivered every night during the
course of his visit and the hens had unanimously refused to
lay. They'd sent him home in short order.

His horse quieted and Relian's eyes turned back to the fortress. As he watched, a radiant bolt of scarlet lightning shot
from a tower window, sped high above the town, clear across
the valley, and vanished amidst the thick mists that veiled the
opposing peaks. A dull booming sound reached his ears as the
bolt presumably struck its unseen target. Relian caught his
breath. Had he actually seen—? A second glowing missile put
his doubts to rest. The crimson lightning streaked overhead
and disappeared into the mists. Distant thunder as it struck—
something. The fog that sheathed the far side of the valley
was thick, extraordinarily so in view of the clear weather.
The peak directly opposite the granite fortress appeared to be
packed in cotton wool. Whatever lay beyond the nebulous
barrier clearly possessed power of its own. A moment later,
a blue thunderbolt blazed out of the mists, arced through
space, struck at the fortress like a winged viper. And missed.

The blue bolt slowed as it neared its target, lost momentum and plunged to earth well short of the granite walls.

Relian watched in fascination, but the inimical exchange was not repeated. The sun had sunk behind the hills and the atmosphere was uniformly gray. The wind out of the Bhorphins was cold. Down below in the town, lights began to appear in the windows. Similarly, several windows in the fortress glowed yellow. But no light fought its way through the fog blanketing the far peaks. Whatever lurked in the mists remained concealed.

The horse had recovered its equanimity and now stood idly cropping the grass. A knife-edged breeze sliced along the Equalists' Run and Relian shivered in response. Simultaneously his stomach growled. No point, no point at all in loitering out on the highway at dusk within shouting distance of a tavern reputed to serve the finest ale this side of the Bhorphins. He cast a final doubtful glance up at the fortress. The windows were alight and all seemed tranquil. Could he have imagined that barrage of colored lightning? No. He had not imagined it. Relian set heels to his horse and rode down the slope into the town of Vale Jevaint.

On closer inspection, the signs of civic prosperity were very evident. The cobbled streets were wide and clean. The lead-sheathed domes were imposing. There were no beggars to be seen. *Wrong*—on the far side of the square stood a beggar, a blind man with a cup, his face disfigured with the marks of burning. Around his neck he wore a purple kerchief, incongruously bright . against the rest of his shabby attire. Lanterns bloomed golden along a thoroughfare still alive at that hour of the evening with pedestrians, sedan chairs, and a few surprisingly fine carriages. The merchants were just shutting up for the night. The merchandise displayed in the bow windows of their shops was fine. The garb of the customers was expensively eccentric. The men of Vale Jevaint favored saffron-colored stockings with gold-embroidered clocks, multicaped redingotes, bagwigs and plumed quadri-cornered hats. The women endured tight lacing, high-heeled slippers, and non-functional lace gloves. Their long, dome-shaped skirts deliberately echoed the lines of the local architecture. Many women were masked. Both sexes carried small bouquets of scented artificial flowers in which noses were frequently buried.

Relian besought information and was directed to the Bearded Moon Tavern. Along the way he passed through residential neighborhoods of well-ordered prosperity. Prosperity, however, could not banish the peculiar, distinctive odor that hung over Vale Jevaint. He recognized it easily enough as the scent he had encountered earlier in the day, the scent that tickled and burned his sinuses. The wind was blowing from the head of the valley, where the woods were. Relian recalled the haze that hung over the woods—very likely, the source of the odor. *Why have these wealthy people built a town in this strange spot?* he wondered. *The land hereabout's no good for farming, and surely it's no market town, and never was.*

On his right-hand side loomed a charred and gutted ruin. Evidently a fire had occurred not long ago and somebody's home had been destroyed. Piles of debris were strewn about the blackened walls, and the entire area was cordoned off with makeshift barriers from which fluttered rags tinted the same shade of purple as the blind beggar's kerchief.

Relian rode on past the stone houses, the gardens, parks and a vacant lot, apparently the site of another fire. At the center of the square of scorched earth stood a pole from which depended a purple pennant. Presently he came upon the tavern he sought, easily recognizable by its sign of a fat-cheeked, curly-bearded moon. The windows were invitingly alight. The place looked clean and phlegmatically respectable. Relian entered the courtyard and entrusted his mount to an overfed ostler. The illusion of universal prosperity was belied only by the presence of a crippled beggar stationed at the tavern door. The unfortunate had lost a leg. Both his hands were covered with the scars of a severe burning. Around his neck he wore a purple kerchief. Relian deposited coins in the beggar's cup, and entered the Bearded Moon. The interior of the tavern was in keeping with his expectations, being well-scrubbed, well-appointed and well-frequented. A generous sea-coal fire warmed the common room, threw red glints on the terra cotta tiled floor, the diamond-paned leaded windows, the rows of pewter tankards and dishes that lined the shelves. Close beside the fireplace stood a couple of leather wing chairs occupied by what must have been the establishment's most esteemed customers—Councilmen, by the consequential look of them. Other customers, less exalted, sat at small tables scattered about the room. Behind a counter stood the innkeeper, a beer-bellied, fat-cheeked, bearded old cherub who bore a ludicrous resemblance to the sign above the inn door. The innkeeper, Relian had already been informed, was known to would-be wits as the Man in the Moon, or Moon for short. His real name was forgotten or ignored.

Relian seated himself at the counter, ordered dinner and a pint of the celebrated ale, and bespoke a chamber for the night. A slice of beef pie with pickled lorbers, frolloberries in sour cream and a tankard soon appeared before him. The ale was deserving of its reputation: dark as garden loam and equipped with a head of foam built to last the night. Relian removed his gloves and the innkeeper stared at the elongated, double-jointed hands. Moon seemed caught by the young guest's tentacular fingers and melancholy mien. Perhaps he sensed an interesting history, for he waxed friendly and garrulous. "Going to be with us long, sir?"

"Perhaps a few days. I've not decided yet."

"Traveling for pleasure, sir?"

"Theoretically." Relian's expression suggested that his journeying had been far from pleasurable.

"Ah, the delights of youth! You'll find much to keep you entertained in Vale Jevaint, sir. There are the shops, the parks and Basale's Tower. There's Dingel's Incredible Rock. There's the Egg House, of course. You could visit the house of Clym Stipper, Master Gatherer, and for twenty pytes he'll let you see the three-armed baby. There's the Great Abscess not far off. You could hire a guide to take you into the Miasm to see the ferns, but you'd need to rent the proper gear for that, and it would cost you something. But you can see, there's no end of jollification here in Vale Jevaint!"

"What's the Miasm?" Relian asked.

"Oh, it's a wonder, sir!" Moon's round face glowed with civic pride. "A deadly source of life! A vital fount of death!"

"And a source of rhetorical inspiration, it would seem."

"That too, sir. And there's been poems as well. There's the *Ode to a Venomous Fern*, for example. That one was inspired by the poisonous ferns of the Miasm. I'll recite it for you. I don't want to sound too prideful, but I must confess to you, sir—'tis my own composition, and very poetical."

"I'm sure it is," Relian replied. "But there's really no need to—"

He was too late. Moon struck an attitude and declaimed,

"Mine eyes are captive to thy fatal grace.
Delicious venom hath o'ercharg'd my soul.

O sweetly poisoned siren! Green embrace!
Thy verdant lure exacts a fearsome toll.

Thy perfum'd breath wafts death and chlorophyll,
And yet my vanquish'd heart is foolish-fond.
Sweet subjugation brings me more of ill.
Thou art my love, my fate, my foe, my frond.

What tongue can sing the beauty of thy being,
The wonder of thy fiddleheads and spores?
Desire's heat hath set cold Reason fleeing,
As Appetite with just Discretion wars.

O Sorceress, thou hast enslaved my senses!
Thy fell enchantment drowns my will in flame.
My walls are breach'd and sunder'd my defenses.
This is the love that dares not speak its name!''

"That's very nice," Relian interrupted.

"There's lots more, sir, and I'm still working on it—"

"Not a married man, are you, Master Moon?"

"Not I, sir. Never met a woman that took my fancy, as it were. Never met one who could share my feeling for the ferns, either."

"I understand."

"I sort of come right out and say it flat in the next verse—"

"What *is* the Miasm, Master Moon?"

"Why, it's the great Forest of Miasm, sir. Vale Jevaint is built as close to the forest as man may safely build. And even as it is, when the wind's wrong people here have had their faces blistered for them, which is why our ladies go vizarded more often than not. The Forest of Miasm is poison, sir. Notwithstanding but that it's a wonderful place, it's all poison. Every stick, every leaf, flower and fern, the dirt, the rocks, the water, the bugs, beasts and birds—most particularly the birds—the whole works. And mind you, I don't mean you have to *swallow* anything there to get the ill of it. The whole place gives off noxious fumes and vapors that kill you if you breathe 'em, and burn your flesh if you linger under the trees. Bad business, sir. Very bad."

"I see." Relian was much interested. This was the sort of novelty he had traveled to find. "Are the fumes of this forest responsible for the unusual odor that permeates this town?"

"That's it, sir. But there's little cause for worry. What we get here isn't enough to harm a flea except, as I told you, once in awhile when the wind's blowing the wrong way."

"Still, it can't be pleasant. Why do people choose to live and build their homes in the shadow of a poisoned forest?"

"Because it's not all bad, by any means. The Miasm is a source of all that makes life truly sweet. In short—prosperity," Moon responded with spirit. "You've doubtless noted that we of Vale Jevaint are mighty grand and imposing folk. You might expect that a town so much out of the common way would be filled with bumpkins, and thus a visitor such as yourself is bound to be astonished and maybe abashed by our splendor." Relian's brows lifted a trifle and Moon continued kindly, "Ah, I see it's so. Well, it's all thanks to the Miasm. You've heard of the famous Wingbane eggs, of course?"

Relian had to think a moment. "Why yes, I believe so. The physicians claim that Wingbane eggs possess marvelous curative properties. But the eggs are costly and very difficult to obtain."

"Correct, young sir, correct! That's because there's but one happy refuge in all the world wherein the Black Wingbanes build their nests and lay their precious eggs. That place is the Forest of Miasm. We of Vale Jevaint depend upon the sale of these eggs for our livelihood. Our Master Gatherers collect the ovoid treasure. The eggs are transported and vended to foreign merchants. Fifty percent of the proceeds are turned over to the Lord Keprose Gavyne. And the rest is profit, sir, pure and glorious profit!" Moon concluded on a note of exaltation.

"Fifty percent to Lord Keprose, eh?" Relian mused. "Sounds rather a lot. Keprose Gavyne is your local seigneur, I've been told. The town is quite content to meet his demands?"

"Quite content, sir."

"Out of a sense of duty, loyalty, affection, I suppose?"

"Yes, sir, all of that. Also out of a desire to avoid incineration. Our seigneur has sort of—a way with lightning, you might say. His talents are most apt to manifest themselves when the Lord Keprose has been thwarted in any way. Perhaps you've already noticed certain lightning-struck architectural ruins scattered about the town. They are marked with purple flags. In them you see the tangible results of Lord Keprose's displeasure."

"I've also noticed certain lightning-struck human ruins

scattered about the town," Relian replied. "They are marked with purple kerchiefs. Additional results of Lord Keprose's displeasure?"

"Ah yes," the Man in the Moon sighed. "Those unfortunates who saw fit to question the Lord Keprose's seigneurial right to his fifty percent. Behold the fruits of their ingratitude!"

"It would appear that your Lord Keprose possesses the powers of a true sorcerer," Relian suggested.

"Let us say that he is a seigneur of unusual and unquestionable abilities, sir."

"His temper, however, is uncertain?"

"He is kindness itself, as long as he is not crossed."

"And yet I noted evidence of seigneurial irritability as I approached Vale Jevaint," Relian observed. "Scarlet lightning issued from the fortress overlooking the town. It would seem that the Lord Keprose is aggrieved."

"Indeed, sir. But not with us, his devoted servants," Moon protested. "Since the blasting of Councilman Gyf Fynok's mansion two weeks ago, the Lord Keprose has had no reason whatever to doubt the loyalty of the townsfolk. No, young sir, the lightning that you saw was undoubtedly aimed at the Tyrant of Mists."

"Who's the Tyrant of Mists?"

"What, not who. The Tyrant of Mists is the name of the fortification high up on the peaks, directly across the valley from Fortress Gavyne. The building can't be seen, 'tis shrouded perpetually in fog. No citizen can supply information concerning the Tyrant of Mists, for those who climb the hills to reconnoiter don't come back again. All that's definitely known is that the Tyrant of Mists houses a race of sorcerous adepts—ancient, hereditary enemies of the lords of Gavyne. For generations the lords of Gavyne have bombarded the Tyrant of Mists without discernible results. The present chatelaine, one Vanalisse the Unseen, of whom little is known, has seen fit to respond in kind. Evidently a woman of spirit. For the last two years lightning has flown from fortress to fortress, and it may be assumed that eventually one or the other will be destroyed. The citizens of our town are wont to take odds upon the ultimate outcome—as I mentioned earlier, there is no lack of jollification here in Vale Jevaint! I myself have wagered two hundred silver trilbins upon the triumph of Lord Keprose Gavyne. Perhaps you too would like to wager, sir?"

"Not yet, Master Moon," Relian responded politely. "I

need more information concerning the relative abilities of the contestants. Is there any chance I might meet this Keprose Gavyne?"

"He doesn't ordinarily receive visitors, but I think he might make an exception in your case," Moon replied, with a quick glance at Relian's hands. "In fact, I'm almost sure of it."

The young man ordered a second pint. Moon served it, but his duties demanded his attention and the colloquy ended. Relian examined his fellow customers. The common room was crowded. The Bearded Moon was understandably popular. The clientele was generally of a settled and repectable-appearing sort, with the possible exception of three muscle-bound, pinkish-haired young louts of repellent aspect who sat drinking at one of the corner tables. Master Moon served the ill-favored trio with unusual solicitude. There was no sign as yet of Trince. It was possible that the lackey might not arrive for hours, perhaps not until morning. Relian found himself yawning. He drew the watch from his pocket and checked the time. It was still early, but he was inordinately tired. Perhaps the famous ale was more potent than he had realized. The young man settled his reckoning and ascended the stairs to his chamber, whose furnishings he scarcely noted. He threw himself down upon the bed and fell asleep within seconds.

Time passed. Only one candle still guttered in the wall sconce when a quiet knock sounded on the chamber door. Relian, anticipating such a knock, awakened at once. It would seem that Trince had arrived. The young man dragged himself from bed, stumbled to the door, unbolted and opened it. His grogginess vanished. He beheld a familiar gaunt and gangling figure, all spindle shanks and elbows. Relian took an involuntary step backward.

"Well, young Master Kru, you've led me quite a chase." Scrivvulch the Stick spoke with an air of humorous reproach. "I've ridden for more hours than I care to think of and these aging bones are no longer fit for such exertion. I'm quite exhausted. By your leave—" He entered and shut the door; drew a chair before the door and seated himself with a sigh. "Ah, that's better." Carefully he laid his walking stick across his knees.

Relian was now wide awake. "The Dhreve's servants are more diligent than I'd realized," he remarked, not without bitterness. "Fortunate is Gornilardo to inspire such devotion."

"Gornilardo—inspire devotion? Not a bit of it, young Kru. As we both know, his Dhreveship is a distinctly disagreeable animal, incapable of inspiring a dog's devotion."

"Yet you serve him zealously."

"Say rather that I serve an ideal. To perform my duties flawlessly—to attain preeminence in my chosen field—to strive for perfection—these are admirable ambitions, do you not agree, my friend?"

"Oh, admirable in themselves." Relian recalled that Scrivvulch liked to talk. "But I must question whether it is possible that idealistic actions performed on behalf of an ignoble patron, whose own motives are dishonorable, may be regarded as praiseworthy? Does not the baseness of the patron's intentions negate the deed's virtue?"

Scrivvulch tilted back on two legs of his chair to consider the problem. "That's an interesting question. Very interesting indeed." He withdrew a chased snuffbox from his pocket and toyed with it frowningly. "What you suggest possesses a certain specious logic, and yet it should be noted that—"

Relian lost the thread of the other's conversation. He thought of the pistol that lay in the traveling bag he had dropped on the floor beside the bed. It should be an easy matter to reach the weapon while Scrivvulch was busy talking. And then? Could he shoot Scrivvulch? Relian considered his visitor's pacific aspect—the mild expression, the pedantic speech. And no sign of a weapon. Scrivvulch probably wouldn't know how to use a weapon. Was it not likely that Trince had been mistaken about this man? Well, there would be time enough to think about that as soon as he knew he was safe. Relian edged toward the open traveling bag.

Scrivvulch was still talking. ". . . and thus it follows that each action must be judged absolutely independently of the standards and intentions of all but the active participants. If the matter is considered in that light . . ." The voice droned on and on. Scrivvulch appeared wholly lost in the discussion. His hands, empty of all save a harmless snuffbox, chopped the air in gestures of awkward sincerity.

Relian began to relax. He was all but certain that this man had been misrepresented. Trince had been the victim of a hoax. Still, best to be safe. Once he had the pistol safely in his possession, the matter could be examined at leisure. He was now almost within grabbing range of the bag.

Scrivvulch paused in his discourse. "If you'll allow me a

small indulgence, Master Kru," he remarked half-apologetically. "I find that a pinch of snuff clears my mind wonderfully well. A filthy habit, some would say, yet in this cold and sterile world, it is man's most trivial solaces that paradoxically yield the deepest consolation. Will you join me? No? Permit me." Scrivvulch snapped open the lid of the box, which contained no snuff but rather, a collection of small, spherical pellets. Relian caught no more than a quick glimpse of them. Scrivvulch picked a pellet out of the box and flung it to the floor, where it shattered at Relian's feet. A dense black cloud of vapor arose. Relian was enveloped, blinded, suffocated. He opened his mouth to speak and the noxious fumes plunged down into his lungs. He choked spasmodically. His eyes were burning. He could see nothing and the pain was intense. *Trince was right.* He staggered blindly backwards, tripped over something and fell, striking his head against the bedstead as he went down. For a moment he lay still, semi-dazed. Then dizziness and pain receded somewhat, but he remained sightless. The world was a black void. Relian heard a creak, a footstep, and realized that Scrivvulch had risen from his chair, was approaching. He groped frantically and encountered the traveling bag over which he had tripped. His hands closed on the pistol. He withdrew the weapon, clutched it uselessly. His vision remained totally obscured. *"What have you done?"*

"You have encountered Bewbigo's Final Shadow, my friend." Scrivvulch's reply came equably out of the dark. "I'm told that the inventor considered it a major triumph, representing a tremendous advance over Bewbigo's Initial Shadow, which induced vocal paralysis as well as blindness. Bewbigo's Ameliorated Shadow induced blindness only, but the effects were permanent. The effects of the Final Shadow are quite transitory, but I fear that you'll have to take my word for that."

His meaning was all too clear. Relian aimed at the voice, squeezed the trigger, and the pistol went off with a roar, startlingly loud in the confines of the small room. Surely it could be heard downstairs? The reverberations died away and there was silence. Relian listened intently but heard no cry, no footstep, no sound of breathing—nothing, nothing at all. Could his blindly-fired bullet actually have struck its target? Had fortune favored him, for once?

A blow descended on the blind man's wrist. Scrivvulch's

walking stick thwacked on bone. Relian gasped in pain. The pistol flew from his grasp and skidded out of reach.

"I admire your spirit, young Master Kru," Scrivvulch observed. "In fact, all things considered, I think I may say I like you."

"You've an odd way of showing it."

"Ah—the tyrannies of one's profession. I'm sure you understand."

"I don't understand why a man of your intelligence chose such a profession."

"Better and better! Do you know that you are only the third person in twenty years with the wit to ask that? Ordinarily all I hear are pleas and threats, which exert a cumulatively depressing effect. Well, in answer to your question, my choice of profession stems from my belief in the social significance of the function performed by the Court Assassin. Beyond that, my work provides great variety, travel, excellent financial rewards and genuine personal satisfaction. In short, young Kru, I enjoy it."

"I understand, Master Scrivvulch. You mention financial rewards. Should I ride out of Vale Jevaint tomorrow morning in good health, your financial reward is bound to be considerable. It goes without saying that his Dhreveship of Neraunce is unlikely to learn of my departure."

"Young Kru—is it possible that I understand you correctly? Are you attempting to bribe the Court Assassin?"

"Generously," Relian agreed.

"Oh my. Oh my, you do disappoint me. What do you take me for? Do I look like a brigand? Do I look like a bandit?"

"Impossible for me to judge at the moment," Relian replied.

"Then know here and now that the Court Assassin of Neraunce is a man of unimpeachable integrity." Scrivvulch pressed one of the buttons in the handle of his cane. An interior lock clicked open.

"What was that?" asked Relian, straining his sightless eyes.

"Do not alarm yourself, young Kru. The mechanism of my stick wants oiling, that is all." Scrivvulch removed the lower portion of the cane, thus uncovering a thin, needle-pointed spike. "And now, have you anything more to ask me? I promised to satisfy your curiosity concerning the nature of the Court Assassin, and I am a man of my word. If you have any questions, ask them now."

"Many questions. I'll need time to collect my thoughts—several minutes at least." *Trince might turn up,* Relian thought. *Unlikely, but not impossible. Start thinking of questions.* Whereupon his mind went blank.

"Certainly, my friend. Certainly. All the time you require, within reason."

Relian sat in midnight silence for a time. No queries suggested themselves, and the sweat broke out on his brow. Presently he felt a gentle prodding at his chest and started nervously. "What's that?"

"Do not concern yourself, young Kru. It occurred to me that you might be wearing an undergarment of steel mesh, or some similar protective appurtenance. I wished only to investigate."

"I'm not wearing anything like that."

"So I perceive. Excellent. Questions?"

Relian thought of one at last. "Aren't you concerned that your activities will draw the attention of the innkeeper?"

"I doubt it. Master Moon appears to be a reasonable man with a well-developed sense of self-preservation. More questions?"

Relian was silent and the prodding resumed. He lifted his hand and encountered the steel spike. Instinctively he sidled away from it and soon collided with the wall. The shock of pain disoriented him. With hands outstretched, he groped in desperation.

"Calm yourself, young Kru. Your distress saddens me. In order to spare you additional suffering, I feel obligated to bring this interview to a close—"

Relian heard a footstep, felt the bite of the spike at his throat. "Wait!" he cried.

"Yes, my boy?"

Relian grabbed the spike with both hands and attempted to wrest the cane from Scrivvulch. The effort was unsuccessful and the steel was drawn easily from his grasp.

"As I said, young Kru, I admire your spirit. And now—"

What happened next was utterly confusing. Relian heard the chamber door bang open, heard the tramp of heavy footsteps, scuffling and the scrape of metal along the floor. "Trince?" he cried. "Is that you?"

"There he is. That's the one," came an unfamiliar voice. "Take him."

"Gentlemen, this is not the common room," Scrivvulch reproved. "I must ask you to withdraw."

"Get out of the way, you old beanpole!"

"Who's there?" Relian appealed. "Who is it?"

"I said get out of the way!" A thud and a grunt. More footsteps, as of several men. An indeterminate number of invaders moiled about the room.

"Young sirs, your intrusion is unwelcome." Scrivvulch's tone was admonitory. "I must insist that you—"

"Hold your jaw, scarecrow." It was yet another voice, coarse and youthful. "And don't meddle, if you know what's good for you."

Hard hands grasped Relian under the arms and hoisted him to his feet. "Who are you? I can't see—"

"Bring him along."

"Look out for the old man!" someone warned. "Careful, Pruke!"

"He's stuck me!"

A sharp cry of pain, a muttered curse, and the grip on Relian relaxed abruptly. The blind man staggered. Someone grabbed him from behind and locked an arm around his neck. He struggled uselessly.

Relian heard a snarl of rage, a blow, the thud of a body hitting the floor.

"You've killed him, Vazm!"

"I hardly touched him. Anyway, the old fool was asking for it. Look what he did to Pruke."

"He stuck me! Look—I'm *bleeding!*"

"See? It wasn't *my* fault!"

"Uncle won't be pleased."

"I had no choice. It wasn't *my* fault!"

"Is he dead?"

"What have you done? Who are you?" Relian demanded.

Nobody answered him. Shuffling footsteps, heavy breathing. "The old man's still alive. He'll be right enough."

"No thanks to your bungling."

"Here now, Druveen—"

"All right, let's go." Druveen, who seemed to be the leader of the group, spoke directly to Relian. "You—move. What are you standing there for? You hear me? Move!"

"Move where?" Relian inquired. "Who are you and what do you want?"

"No questions or it's the worse for you. Look—you see this knife? Well, do you?"

Relian was silent.

"Druveen—" Vazm spoke up. "I don't think he sees anything. I think maybe he's blind."

There was a shocked silence, then Druveen asked, "Is that true? Are you blind?"

"Yes," Relian admitted.

"Oh, wonderful, just wonderful. We go through all this and he turns out to be *blind*. I'll wring Moon's neck for this trick."

"Uncle won't be pleased."

"We didn't know. It wasn't our fault," observed Vazm.

"Well, what shall we do about it? Leave him here?"

"No," Druveen decided. "We'll take him. Blind or not, he's got the hands. Maybe Uncle can find some use for him."

"What do you want?" Relian repeated.

"You'll find out soon enough. Right now, you're coming with us."

"To meet Uncle," Pruke explained.

"I'm not going anywhere with—" Relian's protest broke off suddenly. A gag was thrust between his teeth. He struck out at blackness and encountered anonymous flesh. Someone nearby grunted in outraged agony. "You mangy bat, I'll kill you—"

"Wait, Vazm! Put that down—"

Vazm did not obey. A blow descended upon Relian's skull. A split second's astonishing pain preceded complete unconsciousness.

* * *

"Dearest children, your Uncle will be proud of you." It was a woman's voice.

"You really think so, Mum?"

"I'm sure of it. Your courage, your initiative, your devotion to your Uncle's interests—make no mistake, they'll not go unappreciated. Oh boys, you've made me very happy! Pruke, come here and let me kiss you."

"Not now, Mum. I'll get blood all over your dress."

"My wounded darling, Mother doesn't care! Come here."

"Oh, all right."

Reluctant footsteps and the sound of lips smacking. Relian

opened his eyes and found himself peering through fog. His eyes smarted and his vision was blurred, but he could see. As Scrivvulch had promised, the effects of Bewbigo's Final Shadow were transitory. The thought of Scrivvulch brought back full recollection of the events of the preceding twenty-four hours and Relian sat up abruptly, only to subside with a moan. He was weak, dizzy, and his head was splitting. For a moment he lay still, then raised himself with care. He sat on the stone floor of an unfamiliar hall whose ribbed and vaulted ceiling suggested great antiquity. Relian gazed about in muzzy bewilderment. At the far end of the room a thronelike chair sat atop a dais. Off to the right, a short flight of steps led to an arched doorway. Not far away his kidnappers clustered dutifully around their mother. He examined the young men and his confusion deepened. He beheld a triple image: three low-browed, heavily freckled countenances; three broad, snub noses; three receding chins; three heads of pinkish ringlets; three muscular bodies of similar height and breadth; and six vacant blue eyes. Relian rubbed his own bedeviled orbs and his vision cleared, but the image did not change. Vazm, Pruke and Druveen could only be identical triplets. *One would have been more than sufficient,* he thought, but wisely kept the opinion to himself. The mother was a stunted, frizzle-haired female with a taste for improbable furbelows. Like her sons, she possessed a receding chin. In her case the unfortunate condition was emphasized by a mouthful of protruding rodential teeth.

Relian spoke with deliberate restraint. "Who are you and what do you want with me?"

"Oh look, he's awake. Pruke, my love, go inform your Uncle at once."

"Why *me*? Why not call one of the servants?" Pruke complained. "I'm wounded, remember. I lost a lot of blood when that old scarecrow stuck me. I ought to save my strength. Make someone else go."

"You're quite right, my brave darling. Vazm, go fetch your Uncle."

"Why pick on *me*?" Vazm demanded. "It wasn't *my* fault that Pruke got stuck. If he'd kept his eyes open—"

"Naughty boy, don't argue with your mother!"

"Oh all right, I'll go then. But it's not fair." Vazm slouched from the room.

"Why have you brought me here?" Relian asked.

"Mum," Druveen inquired, "if Uncle is pleased with what we've brought him, d'you think he might increase my allowance? I lost at Deebo the other night and I haven't a pyte to my name."

"Gambling again? Oh, Druveen, Druveen—"

"What do you want of me?" Relian dragged himself painfully to his feet. His eyes burned and watered. "What place is this?"

"Oh, don't fuss, Mum! I don't want to listen!" Druveen fretted. "I need some cash to cover my debts, that's all. I shouldn't have to beg for it, neither. Begging's beneath me," he concluded.

"Dru's right," Pruke agreed. "We both need more money if we're to live as befits our quality. Won't you drop a word in Uncle's ear? The old boy will listen to you. Please, Mum."

"We *need* it, Mum!"

Relian's jaw clenched. His head throbbed. "Gentlemen— Madam—if you will be so good—"

"My precious lads, I desire your happiness above all things. But you must understand my reluctance to trouble your Uncle with trifling requests at this time. Your Uncle is engaged in a great and glorious enterprise—nothing less than the complete development of his native supranormal abilities," the woman explained. "Such abilities are rare indeed, my darlings—rarer than sun-emeralds, rarer than shernivus. Not one in a thousand possesses the supranormal Vision. Not one in ten thousand owns the supranormal Tactility. Manifestation of the Collective Recollection is even less frequent. Yet your Uncle possesses all of these abilities. Think of it—all! His gifts are immense and his nature noble. It is his conviction that genius carries its own responsibility—"

"Responsibility to what?" Pruke interrupted.

"To itself," his Mother replied. "Natural genius is at once self-perpetuating and self-consuming. It carries tremendous obligation to itself and thus, self-expression may be regarded as a moral duty."

"What are you talking about, Mum?"

"Your Uncle could explain it better than I. He, after all, is the genius in question. Suffice it to say that my brother has undertaken to fulfill his responsibility by developing his powers to a level never before attained by another human being. Always he strives for perfection! It is a magnificent endeavor, and all of us should be glad and proud to render him such

assistance as we can. May roses ever strew his path! The rest
of us must dedicate ourselves to his service and thereby
consider ourselves privileged. Do you understand, children?''

"Yes, Mum.''

"Anything you say, Mum.''

"Good boys.''

Relian shrugged, turned and lurched toward the doorway.
In so doing, he finally caught the attention of his hosts.

"Here—where d'you think you're going?'' Druveen demanded.

"You just stay where you are, if you know what's good
for you,'' Pruke directed.

Relian paused. He was in no condition to take on his two
vigorous kidnappers and he knew it. "Who are you and why
have you brought me here?'' he asked once again.

"You'll find out soon enough,'' Druveen replied.

"All in good time,'' Pruke concurred. "In the meantime,
you just stay put where we can keep an eye on you.''

"Is it your intention to hold me for ransom?''

"Ransom?'' Druveen was insulted. "Why you meaching
boggler, I ought to break your head for that. We're gentlemen, not criminals.''

"Watch your mouth,'' Pruke advised.

"Really, young man, I must protest your choice of words,''
the mother objected. "Your confusion is understandable, but
there's no excuse for discourtesy.''

Relian inclined his aching head. "No discourtesy was intended, Madam. I merely seek information. Under the circumstances, I'm sure you'll agree I'm entitled to—''

"You're entitled to exactly nothing,'' Druveen informed
him. "So keep your mouth shut.''

"We didn't bring you here to chatter,'' said Pruke.

"What *did* you bring me here for?'' Relian demanded,
heedless of the threat of Druveen's brawny fists. "Whatever
your reasons, you've saved my life and I'm not ungrateful—''

"Eh?'' Druveen grunted.

"You saved my life,'' Relian repeated. "The elderly gentleman was on the point of dispatching me when you arrived.''

"Pah—that old stick didn't look like he could kill a flea,''
scoffed Druveen.

"Don't be so sure. Remember, the old devil stuck me,''
Pruke observed. "He's dangerous.''

"Only because you were stupid.'' Ignoring his sibling's

scowl, Druveen turned back to Relian. A thought surfaced slowly. "But then, I don't suppose you could do much to defend yourself, being blind and all—"

"Are you sure, my darling?" the mother inquired. "This young man doesn't look at all blind to me."

"Well he said he was, Mum—"

"I don't believe he is, dear."

"I'll take my oath he *was*, Mum." Druveen addressed Relian truculently. "Answer straight, and no tricks. Are you blind or are you not?"

"It wore off," Relian confessed.

"Are you trying to be funny?" Druveen glared. "Because if you are, maybe you should try harder."

"My darling boys must curb their high spirits. This is neither the time nor the place for quarreling. I want you both to promise me that this stranger will not be damaged in any way until your Uncle has had a chance to inspect him."

"But Mum—"

"If your Uncle has a use for him, then he must be left intact."

"What sort of use?" Relian demanded. "What does this Uncle want with me? *Who is Uncle?*"

"I am, young man. I am he."

Relian wheeled at the sound of the voice to behold an overwhelming figure poised in the archway at the head of the stairs. Uncle was a tall man whose monumental girth was emphasized rather than concealed by a voluminous black gown. He possessed the pinkish curls and receding chin characteristic of his family. If he had a neck, it was invisible. His broad, pendulous cheeks appeared to rest upon his shoulders. The meaty cheeks framed a tiny cupid's bow mouth. Uncle's face shone with moisture, although the atmosphere was not warm. His eyes were the same china blue shade as those of his nephews but there the resemblance ended, for the older man's eyes were alight with complacent intelligence. Behind him stood Vazm and a brace of resigned-looking footboys.

"I will introduce myself. Attend." Uncle swept down the steps like a thunderhead riding the wind. "I am Keprose Gavyne, hereditary seigneur of Vale Jevaint, lord of Fortress Gavyne, master of the supranormal arts. This—" he indicated the squirrelish woman, "is my sister the Lady Fribanni, and these are her three regrettable whelps whom I must call nephews. I bid you welcome to my house. My hand, sir." He extended a lordly hand of greeting which Relian ignored.

"Are you aware," Relian inquired coldly, "that your three nephews attacked me without provocation in a public inn, overpowered me and carried me to this place against my will? I am Relian Kru, a traveler from Travorn. I've committed no offense within your jurisdiction, done nothing to warrant such treatment. I request an explanation."

"Your manner, dress and bearing denote a person of quality, your foreign barbarities notwithstanding," replied Keprose. "As such, I assume you possess some rudimentary learning together with a measure of that tolerant flexibility characteristic of the educated intellect. Let us hope so. In any event, you will overlook the peccadilloes of my kinsmen. They are young and exuberant."

"They are young and criminally inclined." Relian's eyes rested briefly upon the glowering triplets. "A period of incarceration might prove morally instructive."

"Keprose, I won't have this man tormenting my boys," Fribanni complained.

"If you don't stop his mouth then I will, Uncle," Druveen promised. "With my fist."

"We will have no talk of violence here. We are civilized people, are we not? We are capable of magnanimity, are we not? Let us overlook past offenses. It is my desire that we make our peace. Accept the hand of friendship, sir," Keprose commanded.

"Friendship must be built upon a firm foundation if it is to endure," Relian replied. "In this case such a foundation requires an apology and your assurance that I'm free to leave this place."

"Leave?" Keprose's roseate brows arched in polite astonishment. "The suggestion is unacceptable. You are my honored guest, and you have only just arrived. It is no time to contemplate departure."

"But," Relian replied carefully, "I wish to leave. At once."

"Impossible. You will remain to enjoy the hospitality of Fortress Gavyne. I insist."

"I have pressing engagements elsewhere."

"Cancel them, then. Cancel them all. They will wait."

"How long shall they wait, Seigneur?"

"How long?" Keprose's mountainous shoulders sketched a

shrug. "How long? Prognostications of such a nature are the hallmark of the superficial mentality. It is my fervent hope that your visit will be an extended one."

"Extended—?"

"Indefinitely. Let us not fix a time limit upon it. Why limit the possibilities of the situation?"

"The Seigneur Keprose is remarkably lavish of hospitality," Relian responded with the stoicism that a life of adversity had taught him. "May I ask why he confers such favor upon a total stranger?"

"You express yourself amusingly, young man," Keprose observed. "Living as I do in rural isolation, in the company of dolts and clods—" his eyes flicked his sister and nephews, "conversation with a person of verbal dexterity is as a draught of wine, and I shall therefore tolerate your impertinences, up to a point. Your own qualities are in themselves almost sufficient to stimulate my desire for your company. But there is another reason, as you may perhaps have surmised."

"I may perhaps have surmised," Relian agreed dryly. "What is it?"

"I shall explain. But first we will clasp hands in friendship."

Relian did not glance at his host's proffered hand. "First, an explanation. After that we'll speak of friendship—perhaps."

"Possibly you have failed to understand my wishes, young man."

"Uncle wants you to take his hand," Druveen explained.

"It would be a good idea to do it," Pruke suggested.

"Now," said Vazm.

"I have no intention—" Relian began, and got no further.

"You heard what your Uncle said, children. Make yourselves useful!" Fribanni commanded.

The triplets wasted no time. With one accord they hurled themselves upon Relian, who was too dizzy and too astounded to resist. Druveen seized Relian's wrist, dragged the arm forward and presented the member to the inspection of Keprose Gavyne. Keprose's attention seemed fixed upon Relian's long, pallid right hand. "Yes," the Seigneur muttered. "So."

"You see, Uncle Keprose?" Vazm inquired. "Didn't I tell you? He's got it, hasn't he?"

"Yes," Keprose nodded. "He has indeed. Let me see . . ." He bent close to examine the double-jointed fingers, wiggled the thumb experimentally.

Relian recoiled at the unwelcome contact. "What are you doing? What do you want?"

"Extraordinary," Keprose mused. "Remarkable development." He easily bent Relian's ring finger backward until the finger curved like a bow to touch the wristbone. "Marvelous. The flexibility rivals my own."

At that, Relian glanced for the first time at the other's hands, which were slender, delicate, and quite unsuited to their owner's massive body. The fingers were long, mushroom-white, tentacular. Like Relian, Keprose Gavyne possessed "Wormfingers."

"What do you think of your nephews now, Brother?" Fribanni inquired proudly.

"I am pleasantly surprised." Keprose carefully bent Relian's index finger backward to a ninety degree angle at the middle joint. Relian strove unsuccessfully to withdraw the hand. "I am pleased, Nephews."

Fribanni beamed. "That is all we ask, dear Keprose. Your approbation."

"Your approbation and maybe a bigger allowance," Druveen suggested.

Keprose removed a bodkin from one of the pockets of his robe and jabbed experimentally into the ball of Relian's thumb. Blood spurted. Relian could stand no more and with a violent effort managed to pull free of his captors. He threw a quick and desperate glance around him. Five people stood between him and the exit. At the head of the stairs the two footboys still loitered in the doorway. There was no point in trying to run. Relian withdrew several paces, took a deep breath and spoke with what dignity he could muster. "Seigneur Keprose. Enough of this, it's pointless. Tell me what you want of me. It's possible I'll comply willingly."

"That is a surprisingly sensible attitude, young man. I'm glad to find you so reasonable. It bodes well for the future of our association, which I trust will prove enduring and mutually profitable. Ah, I see by your face that you do not understand me. Yet you are curious, inquisitive—an encouraging sign suggesting that your mind has hitherto escaped total stagnation. I am pleased. But perhaps you wonder why my nephews brought you here tonight?"

Relian nodded. He did not trust himself to speak.

"I shall enlighten you." Keprose glided to the great chair, sat and disposed his bulk comfortably. "If, as I hope, you possess a modicum of intelligence, you have realized by now that you are here because of your hands. Naturally we are all well aware of the significance of such hands. In Vale Jevaint your extreme hyperdigitation was noted by the master of the Bearded Moon Tavern. The innkeeper, who is loyal to his seigneur, informed my nephews and thus you were brought to Fortress Gavyne. A rare and glorious opportunity now presents itself to you. I, the Seigneur Keprose Gavyne, consent to permit you to assist me in my supranormal investigations. My supranormal abilities are of an extraordinary order. In allying yourself with me, your own powers will be enhanced a hundredfold, a thousandfold. If your abilities fulfill the promise of your hands, then our supranormal synchrony will lend us illimitable power. Young man, we are going to join forces." Keprose paused, evidently awaiting thanks.

Relian decided upon honesty. "Sir, you confuse me. You speak of matters of which I know nothing. In the first place, contrary to your belief, I'm unaware of the significance—if any—of my hands. I've never heard the term 'hyperdigitation' and can only guess at the meaning. I've never heard of 'supranormal powers' and most certainly possess none. You've mistaken me for someone I am not."

Keprose smiled indulgently. "Come, come, young sir. You are pleased to joke with me. Never heard of hyperdigitation, when you yourself exhibit the condition to a remarkable degree? Never heard of supranormal powers when you have surely enjoyed them all your life? Pleasantries may amuse, but they are inappropriate at present. This is a serious matter."

"I assure you I'm not joking, Seigneur. I hardly understand you."

"Is it possible?" Keprose regarded his prisoner minutely. What he saw gave him pause and he shook his head in wonder. "To think such ignorance exists! Can it be true?"

"It's true, Seigneur. And therefore, as I clearly fail to meet your expectations, there's no reason to prevent me from leaving Fortress Gavyne this very night—"

"It's not what I had expected." Keprose seemed to speak to himself. "But all may not be lost. The talent is surely present, the hands prove it. With adequate training, much may be accomplished. There are endless possibilities here." To Relian he said, "You disappoint me, young man. Most men disappoint me and you are no exception, but I feel there is still hope for you. Education overcomes many natural deficiencies. I am willing to undertake your education in exchange for your loyalty and obedience. You appear confused. The expression does not suit you. Listen carefully to what I say, for the information I am about to impart is of importance. The term 'supranormal' refers to those mental and physical abilities that lend certain favored individuals power over their surroundings and ascendancy over their fellowmen. There is the Vision that grants knowledge of distant or invisible events. There is the Tactility which permits unusual manipulation of physical objects, the senses and the mind-stuff of human beings. There are other powers as well, and you will learn of them in due course. In short, 'supranormal' describes the abilities that the ignorant call magical. I dislike the expression 'magic,' which carries any number of grotesque and absurd connotations. I do not permit the word to be used within my house. You will remember that. There is much misunderstanding among the vulgar concerning the origin and supposed acquisition of supranormal powers. One does not acquire such rare powers, however. One is born with them or one is not, and they are bestowed in widely varying quantities. It is possible—indeed necessary—to work, to study, to strive in order to develop inborn abilities. It has been argued that no man ever developed his supranormal talents to their fullest potential. If so, I shall be the first. Much may be done to augment the powers, provided they are present at birth. Who are the fortunate, so richly gifted? No one knows, but it is an observed fact that the powers are apt to recur within families. It is therefore my conclusion that they are transmitted through the blood, or possibly by way of shared eating utensils. An outward manifestation of inherent supranormal ability is the condition known as hyperdigitation— that is, possession of very long, flexible, double-jointed fingers similar to yours. Hands such as yours, young man, are a sure sign of the presence of supranormal power. That you have ignored its existence throughout the brief course of your life suggests atrophied powers of observation. We shall remedy that defect, together with any others you may happen to own. You will reside at Fortress Gavyne, you will study and work indefatigably. Under my tutelage you will discover the use and extent of your talent, and much else besides. Come sir, what do you say?"

I say you're as loony as a rabid bat, Relian thought. Aloud he replied, "I am dazzled, overwhelmed by the generosity of the Seigneur's offer. Yet honesty compels me to confess that although the circumstances of my life have been somewhat unusual, they haven't indicated the existence of uncommon powers over men or events. Quite the contrary, in fact—too often have I found myself at the mercy of forces beyond my control. The present instance is a perfect case in point. It's doubtful indeed that I'll fulfill your hopes. In addition, despite the explanation you've provided, one essential point yet eludes me. You've expressed willingness to assist in the development of my so-called supranormal powers, but you've neglected to explain your reason for doing so. Presumably the Seigneur Keprose's time is valuable. Whence arises his prodigality with so precious a commodity?''

"In despite of your glum expression you exhibit an unbecoming tendency toward flippancy, young man," Keprose observed. "No matter, such tendencies are correctable. Your question reveals a failure to grasp one of the essential aspects of supranormalcy, which is this—its most potent manifestations are always the result of collective effort. Consider. If a single supranormalist is able to perform wonders, then how much more might not be accomplished by two such men working in synchrony? The power of each is more than doubled and the whole is much greater than the sum of its parts. That being the case, what might be the result if three adepts were to join forces? Or four? The supranormal potential thus generated would be awesome, the possibilities almost infinite. I intend to investigate.

"I see." Relian studied the floor, the walls, the faces of his captors. "Then you simply scheme to increase your own powers by making use of mine—such as they are."

"A bald and ungracious explanation, but essentially correct," Keprose replied.

"Wouldn't it save you time and effort to enlist the services of supranormalists who have already succeeded in refining their own abilities?"

"Such was my original intent, but supranormalists of talent are rarely encountered. Moreover, such men are prone to arrogance, independence, insensate individualism. I should not receive the unquestioning cooperation I require. You, however, are as clay in the hands of the sculptor, ready to be shaped according to my will. I think I need anticipate no serious opposition, and in that light your present incomprehension may be regarded as less of a misfortune than I had initially supposed. Yes. When your instruction has been completed, I do not doubt that I shall be able to rely upon your perfect compliance.''

You will also be in a position to enforce it, Relian thought.

''When you have been adequately trained, you will assist me in my endeavors.''

''Specifically what endeavors?''

''That will be explained in due course.''

Relian took a guess. ''You want me to help you destroy the fortress on the far side of the valley.''

''Not the fortress, young man, merely its owner. I've no objection to leaving the building intact if possible. In fact I'd prefer to do so, as the Tyrant of Mists doubtless contains many marvels, many objects of virtu with which to adorn my collection. But the chatelaine Vanalisse the Unseen Hag must die. Her death will not be easy to effect, as the Hag is armed with some trifling supranormal powers of her own—''

''Trifling? I watched her blue lightning strike at your fortress as I rode into Vale Jevaint.''

''You have seen. The Hag attacks, I must defend myself and my family against aggression, as I'm sure you'll agree.''

''I'd be far more apt to agree had I not seen the red lightning fly from your tower window. It appears to me that you were the one to initiate hostilities.''

''Young man, your every word betrays abysmal ignorance. I would advise you not to pontificate on matters of which you know nothing.''

''Enlighten me,'' Relian suggested dryly. ''What is your quarrel with this Vanalisse woman?''

''Vanalisse the Unseen Hag is a member of the House of Maveel. Surely that intelligence clarifies all.''

''Afraid not.''

''You are not acquainted with the perfidy of the House of Maveel?'' Keprose inquired. ''The quality of education these days is deplorable. My generation has sired a population of illiterate young boors. That description is somewhat less applicable to you than to my loutish nephews, but you are sadly lacking nonetheless. I will explain briefly since I must, but I will say this only once, as I do not relish squandering my time upon remedial history lessons for the unschooled.''

Relian stirred resentfully.

''As all the world must surely know, the lords of Gavyne are the hereditary seigneurs of Vale Jevaint. By right of birth and of supranormal powers we are rulers here. However, in the second age following the fall of Nurunul the Tippler, one Honas Gavyne-Maveel appeared out of nowhere. This man, apparently a member of a collateral branch of our family, had the temerity to claim seigneurship on the basis of some absurd technicality involving descent of title through a female Gavyne married off to a lord of Maveel during the reign of Unyo. His was clearly an untenable position. Title can descend through a female only in the complete absence of male heirs and in this case a male heir existed—the Lord Gavyne's bastard son, begotten upon a kitchen wench and declared legitimate for purposes of inheritance. Honas Gavyne-Maveel dared to deny the legality of the legitimization and asserted his own right to seigneurship. My ancestor, the Lord Jexard Gavyne, very rightly declared Honas an outlaw and ordered the pretender braised to death in the blood of his wife and sons. The sentence was duly executed. Unfortunately the warrant did not include Honas Gavyne-Maveel's daughter, who conceived a vicious, irrational hatred of Jexard Gavyne and all his immediate kin. The Maveel female possessed supranormalcy to an immoderate degree. She constructed the fortress Tyrant of Mists and there retired to dwell in solitude and brood on vengeance. In time she gave birth to a daughter—''

''You said she dwelt in solitude,'' Relian objected.

''I also said she possessed supranormal powers. Perhaps you did not hear me? In solitude she delivered herself of a daughter, and imbued the supranormal little slut with a thirst for vengeance equal to her own. Having done so she died, thus ridding the world of at least one shadow. Alas, the daughter throve and her life was a reprise of her cursed mother's. Solitary she walked the Tyrant of Mists, hidden from all eyes behind her walls of stone and fog. She wreaked what harm she could upon my ancestors and foiled all men's efforts to bring her to justice. Eventually she too bore a daughter and died. The daughter continued the feud. And so it has gone on throughout the years,'' Keprose concluded. ''Always there is a fatherless Maveel chatelaine and always she seeks to reduce our state and usurp our place. It is my firm resolve, however, that this Vanalisse the Unseen Hag shall be the last of all her unnatural line. I am determined to destroy her. It is my duty and my pleasure. You, young man, will assist me.''

''Have you ever considered the possibility of making your peace with Vanalisse?'' Relian inquired.

"You have failed to grasp the sense of my narrative. Are you quite devoid of understanding? I do not wish to make my peace with Vanalisse. Her existence is a threat as well as a personal affront. With you now here to aid me, this irritant will be removed once and for all. That accomplished, I shall proceed to activities of infinitely greater import in which you will play your part. Come sir, don't stand there gaping. Do you comprehend the significance of what I offer? I trust you are eager to begin."

Better humor this madman, Relian thought. *Else there's no telling what he and his incredible family might do.* "Once again I find myself at a loss for words," he confessed modestly. "The nature of my own fortunes never ceases to amaze me. You have given me much to think upon. I must have time to consider before I can frame an adequate reply."

Keprose lifted his chins. "I am displeased. This is not the reaction I anticipated. I expected gratitude, appreciation, enthusiasm—but you are lukewarm at best. The tepidity of your response is not gratifying."

"Oh do not call it tepidity, Seigneur. Think of it rather as a natural hesitation, the pause that lends the astonished intellect time to absorb, weigh and contemplate a host of startling new possibilities."

"Possibilities. Ah. Yes, I see. Your intelligence is not of the swiftest nor is your spirit of the boldest, but we shall make allowances for that. Not all of us can be blessed with the courage, the vision that enables a man to seize the flying moment. Such vision is an attribute of greatness and greatness is necessarily rare. Well sir, you shall have time to reflect. You may retire to a bedchamber, there to rest, refresh yourself and examine the matter at leisure. Tomorrow we will talk again."

"I shall look forward to our next meeting, Seigneur." *Preferably about fifty years hence. If there's a window in my bedchamber, I'm off. Better not return to town, though. Can't trust anyone there. But if I don't return to the Bearded Moon, how will I ever find Trince? Never mind. Think about it when I'm safely out of this place. If worst comes to worst and we lose one another, Trince will simply return to Hillheather Manor.* "And now, as I'm very weary and have much to consider, if you'll permit me to retire—"

"Certainly, young man."

"Uncle—" Druveen protested, "You're not going to let

this fellow go wandering about the fortress at will, are you? Let me tie him up or at least lock him up.''

''Nephew, such is not the hospitality of the Gavynes,'' Keprose reproved. ''You shame me. This young man—what did he say his name was?—is our guest. Certainly he is free to move about as he chooses. I shall simply appoint a servant to conduct him to his chamber, and there he will be left to his own devices.''

''But *Uncle*—''

''I am honored by the Seigneur Keprose's confidence,'' Relian murmured.

''Uncle, you don't know what you're—''

''Peace, Nephew,'' Keprose commanded. ''All is well. You will see.'' He reached into the pocket of his mammoth robe to withdraw something long, flexible and glittering. A faint hissing sound could be heard. Keprose held the object coiled loosely in his hand. ''Come closer,'' he invited Relian. ''This will interest you.''

Relian edged a few inches nearer. ''What is it?'' he demanded.

''You can hardly see it from there. Will you not come closer? No? Where is the ardent courage of youth—all sicklied over with the pale cast of thought? It was not so in my day. No matter. My fainthearted guest, I wish to introduce you to my servant Crekkid.'' Keprose extended his hand. Something silvery writhed upon the palm. A length of undulating metallic substance reared itself. A tiny head turned toward Relian. Two ruby eyes examined him minutely. The mouth opened, a silver tongue flickered and Crekkid hissed.

''An automaton?'' Relian inquired.

''Nothing so crude as that,'' Keprose informed him. ''My Crekkid is a steel serpent—part steel, part flesh, and partaking of the nature of both substances. He is my faithful servant, my serpente-servente if you will, and one of the few in whom I genuinely trust. Owing to the dualism of his nature, he is immune to temptation and equally immune to rust. He is my own creation, a masterpiece of nature and of supranormalcy.''

Relian gazed into the faceted ruby eyes with their translucent lids. The steel snake stared back unwaveringly. ''You're asking me to believe that this metal thing is alive?''

''I ask nothing,'' Keprose returned tranquilly. ''I advise you to observe and to form your own conclusions.''

"I observe a finely-crafted steel mechanism capable of very lifelike movement. It is cleverly executed, and I must admire the Seigneur's ingenuity."

"Ssstupid." The voice was thin, shrill and piercing, like the sound produced by a cheap tin whistle. Crekkid's gleaming tongue winked. "Ssstupid, ssstupid, ssstupid."

Relian could not repress a start of surprise.

"Manners, my Crekkid," Keprose admonished playfully. "Manners. Our guest is unaccustomed to creatures of your sort. Observe the young fellow's expression of amazement amounting to stupefaction."

Fribanni tittered at the witticism and the triplets guffawed.

"Note the air of vacant confusion," Keprose continued jovially. "The blank incomprehension of the undisciplined mind confronted for the first time with the reality of the unexpected."

"Ssstupid. Ssstupid."

"Regard him well, my Crekkid, and consider the remarkably dull—"

Relian found his voice. "Can it say more?"

"Assuredly. My Crekkid is not devoid of intelligence. Are you, Crekkid?"

"Crekkid isss not ssstupid."

"Of course not. Is Crekkid hungry?" Keprose inquired.

"Yesss. Hungry. Yesss."

"And what does Crekkid like?"

"Mice. Frogsss. Beetlesss. Blood. And oil."

"What else does Crekkid like? Whom does Crekkid love?"

"Massster. Massster. Massster."

"Just so. Well, young man—" Keprose arched expectant brows. "Are you convinced? What do you think of my work?"

"I'm convinced and astounded," Relian answered truthfully.

"Appropriately so." Keprose appeared gratified. "Thus your education commences. However, my purpose in introducing the steel serpent is not purely pedagogical. Crekkid will conduct you to the chamber wherein you may contemplate my offer at leisure."

Couldn't one of the footboys have done as much? Relian wondered. *The sorcerer likes to show off. Humor him. And as soon as you get the chance, run for your life.* He nodded graciously.

Keprose smiled with equal graciousness. "Be so good as to approach and bow your head."

Relian did not move. "May I ask why?"

"That I may loop Crekkid about your neck. He will then guide you to your chamber," Keprose explained. Crekkid hissed eagerly.

Relian took a step backward. "Unnecessary, surely? Crekkid will lead and I'll walk behind him."

"Impossible, young man. Such an arrangement would confuse and intimidate my poor servant. The little fellow possesses delicate sensibilities."

"I see. In that case, I'll carry him in my hand. Or else he may twine about my wrist."

"Out of the question. My Crekkid is a creature of habit and he is rather set in his ways. How do you ride a man, Crekkid?"

"Around neck," the serpent replied. "Like noossse."

"Exactly. You have heard, young man. Now approach and bow your head."

"I'd rather not."

Keprose frowned. "Is my every request to be met with argument and contradiction? Must I be thwarted at every turn? Are you unaware that a guest customarily accedes to the wishes of his host? Your inflexibility is a serious character flaw. Did they teach you nothing of the most ordinary forms of courtesy in that sinkhole of barbarity from whence you've sprung? Neraunce, was it?"

"Travorn."

"Even worse. A population of savages. My time is valuable, young man. I do not intend to waste it in argument. Come here at once." Relian did not move and Keprose's jowls quivered like custard. "Nephews," he commanded shortly.

Instantly the triplets flung themselves upon the prisoner, secured his arms and bore him forward. Relian found himself staring into Keprose's blue eyes from a distance of some eighteen inches. Someone grasped a handful of his hair and violently jerked his head down. For a moment Relian regarded the stone floor. Keprose bent forward. There was a faint hiss. Relian felt the cold touch of steel at his throat and shuddered. Quite slowly the metallic circle closed around him. It was neither tight nor heavy, but it was horribly cold. At a sign from their Uncle, the triplets loosed their hold. Relian straightened and his hands flew to his neck. His jaw was clenched, his face as white as his fingers.

The triplets evidently found his appearance comical, for

they laughed without restraint. "He looks like his eyes will pop right out of his skull!" Druveen choked at last.

"If Crekkid gives a good squeeze, that may happen," Pruke replied amidst gasps of merriment.

"Children," Fribanni reproved fastidiously.

Relian yanked at the living collar, but his efforts were useless—slender Crekkid possessed the strength of steel. Relian slid his fingers along the metal scales until he encountered a slight bulge. His hand closed over Crekkid's head and he twisted with all his power.

"Ssstop," the serpent hissed.

Relian ignored the implied warning. Small jaws gaped and a pair of steel fangs plunged into his flesh. He gasped and snatched his hand away. The palm was bleeding.

"Ssstupid. Ssstupid. Good blood. Blood. Massster?"

"No, Crekkid. Manners," Keprose replied. "Do not provoke him," the supranormalist advised his captive. "Crekkid is aware that you are my valued guest, but his temper is uncertain and his appetite is almost uncontrollable. You have been warned. You understand me?"

Relian nodded mutely.

"In that case I shall give you leave to retire. You appear somewhat enervated—evidently the vitality of today's youth is in a state of sad decline, no doubt the result of excessive self-indulgence. In order to build your strength, I would recommend a diet enriched with quantities of raw liver and bullock's blood, combined with a daily program of several hours of rigorous exercise followed by a plunge in an icy mountain stream. Happily, such a stream is to be found not far from the fortress. But we may discuss these details tomorrow, unless you are eager to settle all matters here and now. Nothing to say? I understand. You are prey to conflicting emotions and you desire solitude. Crekkid will now conduct you to your chamber. I wish you good night, young man. Sleep well."

Relian did not attempt reply.

"Upssstairsss. Through door. Turn left. Move," Crekkid directed. "Move. Move. Move. Move."

The unlucky young man obeyed and found himself in a deserted stone corridor where he paused, eyes wandering in search of an escape route.

"Go forward. Go. Move. Move. Move. Move." A nip of steely fangs punctuated the last command.

Relian clapped a hand to the side of his neck and the hand was promptly bitten. The puncture wounds were tiny but sharply painful. A quiet curse escaped him and he resumed walking. The corridors were cold and there was scarcely a servant to be seen. Evidently Keprose maintained a skeleton staff. Perhaps few townsmen cared to serve the Seigneur?

"Turn right. Turn right. Turn. Turn. Turn. Turn."

Relian allowed himself to be guided by the shrill-voiced commands. At last he came upon a featureless door opening off an anonymous hallway.

"Ssstop. Here. Ssstay here. Here. Here. Here. Here," Crekkid announced.

Relian entered, shutting the door behind him, and beheld a cheerless but adequately comfortable bedchamber. The furnishings consisted of a narrow bed, a table and chair of unfinished wood with a single rushlight upon the table, a large wooden chest and a cupboard-washstand equipped with a pitcher, basin and shaving implements. The fireplace was dark, the atmosphere chill. Evidently the Seigneur Keprose numbered frugality among his virtues. The chamber possessed one large window, deep-set in the massive stone wall. Relian pulled back the shutters, admitting the cold night air. In the absence of a fire, it scarcely mattered. He stared thoughtfully out into the moonlit garden. *A room on the ground floor—that's fortunate. Astonishingly fortunate, in fact. Surely it can't be as easy as that? Well, we shall see.* He settled himself to wait.

Relian managed to control his impatience for two endless hours, during which time he paced, fidgeted, pondered blackly, paced some more and watched the moon creep across the heavens. At last, in the very dead of night, he judged it safe to assume that the denizens of Fortress Gavyne slept. It was time.

He paused, listening intently, and heard not a sound. Once again he wondered, *Surely it can't be as easy as that?* Relian was halfway out the window when Crekkid spoke. "Ssstop. You ssstay."

The young man swung his legs out the window and dropped to the ground. He gasped as the tiny steel fangs sank into his neck.

"Ssstop. Go back. Go back," Crekkid commanded.

"I'm leaving and there's nothing you or your lunatic creator can do to stop me," Relian replied in a goaded undertone.

"Ssstop. Ssstupid. Go back. Crekkid bite." Crekkid did so.

"Bite away, you unspeakable little abomination. I can stand it. Your teeth are too small to do any real damage."

"You think? Ssstupid. Sssoft flesssh. Weak. Ssstupid. You ssstay while Massster want. You ssstay."

Relian did not bother to reply. He cast a quick glance around him. Before him lay an expanse of trees, hedges and ornamental shrubbery. Beyond the garden rose the great outer wall of the fortress.

"Go back. Inssside. Inssside. Inssside. Or Crekkid angry." Again Crekkid's fangs pierced flesh.

Ignoring the attack, Reilan headed for the wall. He stopped abruptly when the steel coils tightened around his throat, cutting off his breath. No pain that Crekkid had hitherto inflicted remotely approached this new agony of suffocation. For a few seconds he tore fiercely at the thing that was choking him, but the small tormentor was not to be dislodged. Relian's eyes bulged and his face swiftly purpled. His mouth was wide open, the tongue protruding as he fought desperately for air. Presently his struggles grew weaker, he tottered and fell to his knees; whereupon the pressure on his windpipe eased.

Relian collapsed face down in the dirt and lay there gasping. For a time he was conscious of nothing but the joy of pain's surcease, the acute pleasure of unobstructed breathing. It was only gradually that he began to perceive the helplessness and near hopelessness of his own situation. Shrill syllables and hisses tickled his ears. He became aware that Crekkid was addressing him.

"Get up. Get up." The steel coil tightened subtly.

Relian obeyed with difficulty.

"Go in now. Go in now. Go in now. Go in now."

He dragged himself wearily back through the window and stood once again within the confines of his allotted chamber. His head was bowed, his mind uncharacteristically inactive.

"You sssee?" Crekkid's hiss somehow conveyed triumph. "Crekkid sssaid. Sssaid. Sssaid, but you do not lisssten. Ssstupid. Now you know you ssstay here. You ssstay here. You ssstay, ssstay, ssstay, ssstay, ssstay, ssstay, ssstay, ssstay, ssstay, ssstay, sssssss, sssss, sssss . . ."

* * *

Morning sunlight streamed into the common room of the Bearded Moon. Master Moon, alone in the room, sat hunched over the counter. His account books lay open before him. The innkeeper's face glowed with satisfaction, for the neat columnar figures bespoke profit, pure and glorious profit. Presently his joy overflowed its bounds, finding outlet in poetic effusion. Moon pushed the ledger aside and took up the thick notebook labeled *Ode to a Venomous Fern;* turned to a blank page, dipped his quill in ink and wrote:

Canto the Twenty-third

LXII

The lover swears that he is seldom dealt hurts
When Mind and Heart agree upon love's fashion.
But all is chaos and incessant Weltschmerz
When Man falls prey to vegetative passion.

LXIII

The wound of passion festers, swells with grief,
Despite all recourse to the surgeon's function.
Death is the soothing balm that brings relief,
But who resorts to so extreme an unction?

Composition was interrupted by the sound of footsteps descending the stairs. Moon glanced up to behold one of his guests of the previous night: the downy-haired gentleman with the mild manner and the ebony walking stick. The gentleman wasn't looking too chipper, Moon decided. His face was gray and haggard, his eyes bloodshot—the classic signs of riotous dissipation. And yet the guest didn't have the look of a hard drinker. The sober brown suit was faultless and the walking stick was grasped in a perfectly steady hand.

"Lovely morning, sir," Moon observed.

"Lovely," the visitor agreed. His eyes fell upon the open notebook and he scanned the poetic contents swiftly.

"Perfect weather for growing things—bracken, toadstools, ferns . . ."

"Yes, indeed."

"Feeling well this morning, sir?"

"No. But I do not complain. For in this brief and transitory world, mere continuity of existence must be accounted a victory," replied Scrivvulch the Stick.

"If you say so, sir."

"Master Moon, there are three things I require of you without delay. First, a cup of chocolate. Second, a cold, wet cloth. Last—information."

"What's the cloth for, sir?"

Scrivvulch appeared deaf.

"Well, first things first, then. Would you like a dollop of brandy in that chocolate, sir?" Moon inquired, taking note of his guest's lackluster aspect. "Settle your stomach a bit, eh?"

"Brandy? Indeed no. My tastes are not so liberal as to countenance consumption of alcohol at this time of the morning."

"Of course. Sorry, sir." Moon mentally categorized his customer as a straight-laced old codger of a moral rectitude verging on holiness. The innkeeper poured and served the chocolate and shortly thereafter produced a damp cloth. Scrivvulch gingerly applied the cloth to the back of his neck, wincing a little in pain as he did so. Moon looked on attentively. "Had a lively night of it, sir?"

"Quite the contrary. I've slept very deeply indeed all through the night. It was only a short time ago that I awoke to find myself upon the floor of your upstairs chamber."

Moon forbore to inquire whether the bed would not have been more comfortable, for long association with the general public had taught him discretion. "That so, sir?"

"That is so." Scrivvulch folded his hands precisely. "And now, Master Moon, comes the interrogation."

"Interrogation? You've an odd way of putting things, sir. You're a professor over at th'University, perhaps?"

"No."

"Doctor-at-law, perhaps?"

"No, but you're getting closer. I am Scrivvulch, Accredited Agent of his Dhreveship Gornilardo of Neraunce. If you wish, you may examine my papers of identity and my letters of introduction. Would you care to see them at this time?" From an inner pocket of his coat Scrivvulch brought forth a leather wallet. He withdrew a packet of documents and presented them to Moon, who read curiously. The identification was as Scrivvulch had described. Moon returned the packet, eyeing his guest with newfound respect. "You have heard of the Dhreve Gornilardo, I doubt not. All the world has surely

heard of Gornilardo, wisest and most temperate of rulers."
Scrivvulch's lips curled whimsically. "I am his Dhreveship's
representative abroad. I am empowered to speak and to act on
behalf of the state of Neraunce." He paused to allow his
companion opportunity to appreciate the significance of this
disclosure. "I have come to Vale Jevaint upon a mission of
some urgency, and I require your assistance in order to ensure
a successful outcome."

"Is that a fact, sir?" Master Moon enjoyed the flattering
illusion that he participated in great events. "And what mission might that be? Something secret, is it?"

"No, Master Moon, not secret. In fact, the more of your
compatriots made aware of the danger in your midst, the
greater the chance that justice may be served."

"How, sir—justice? And what danger in our midst? Don't
tell me there's another outbreak of the Grinning Jerks?"

"No disease, but something nearly as virulent. I speak of
the notorious felon Black Relian Kru."

Moon appeared disappointed. "Never heard of him."

"What? Never heard of Black Relian Kru, *alias* Captain
Kru, *alias* Gentleman Relly, *alias* Heartbreaker Relian, *alias*
Wormfingers? Why man, 'tis a famous rogue, feared from
Dysfindel to Travorn! Black Relian is surely the most blood-
thirsty, desperate Equalist ever to haunt the highway."

"Never heard of him," Moon repeated.

"I am astounded. Never heard of Captain Kru who robbed
the Flugeln coach, slaughtered the driver, three guards, and
four passengers, and escaped with ten gold ingots and five
thousand trilbins of silver?"

Moon shook his head.

"Never heard of the Gentleman Relly who, posing as a
Travornish traveler, gained entry to the home of the Lord
Mayor of Rendendil; murdered the Mayor and seven servants;
ravished the Lady Mayoress—a gentlewoman of five-and-
seventy winters and famed for her charitable works, sir; fired
the mansion and escaped with a fortune in silver, notes and
jewelry?"

"Sounds like a bad lot, sir." Moon was beginning to look
impressed.

"Oh, I've scarcely begun to name his offenses. Have you
never heard of the time that Black Relian, in order to evade
pursuit, set torch to the Belbin Forest, thus igniting a conflagration that consumed a vast tract of woodland and adjacent

farmland, resulting in the death of at least thirty human beings and the destruction of countless trees, shrubs and ferns?''

"Oh, he didn't, sir! He didn't!''

"I assure you it's true.'' Scrivvulch took a grave sip of chocolate.

"And you say this heartless devil has come to Vale Jevaint?''

"Not only to Vale Jevaint, Master Moon, but here, yes *here,* to this very tavern.''

"You don't mean to say, sir—?''

"I do, Master Moon. The guest that I inquired about last night—the pale-complexioned, black-haired, black-eyed young scoundrel with the peculiar fingers—that was Black Relian Kru himself. Following his violent escape from the condemned cells of the Dhreve, young Kru fled from Neraunce to Nidroon. I followed his trail of blood. As of yesterday evening, I had tracked him to this tavern. I was on the point of placing him under arrest, preparatory to a return to the justice of Neraunce and the hanging he so richly deserves, when I was forestalled, overpowered and struck unconscious by a trio of identical pink-haired ruffians—Kru's confederates, no doubt—who managed to effect the prisoner's escape. Now, Master Moon. In my official capacity as Agent to the Dhreve I must inquire—are those three hooligans known to you?''

"Ah—that's a kind of a delicate question, sir—''

"Delicate in what way? Come, come, man—you appear uneasy and I promise there is no cause, provided I receive your cooperation.''

"That's all you know about it.''

"You are afraid to speak?''

The innkeeper was silent.

"There is nothing to fear. Be assured our conversation is entirely confidential. Moreover, you may rest secure in the knowledge that you enjoy the personal protection of the Dhreve's Accredited Agent.''

"Well naturally that makes me feel a lot better sir, but—''

"Master Moon, you do not wish to obstruct justice, do you? In Neraunce, Obstructionism is a criminal offense, an offense particularly abhorrent to his Dhreveship.''

"Well maybe, but I'm not one of the Dhreve's subjects—''

"To be sure you are not. And yet, so powerful is great Gornilardo's love of justice that he has not infrequently been known to institute extradition proceedings against foreign malefactors. His Dhreveship enjoys excellent relations with your King of Nidroon, as I'm sure you realize. But I tell you all this purely by way of increasing your store of knowledge. For in this gross, materialistic world, 'tis Man's store of knowledge that constitutes his truest wealth. Do you agree, Master Moon, or am I too much the idealist?''

"Well sir, actually I—''

"Who were young Kru's pink-haired friends, Master Moon? Answer, if you please. You will thus avoid prosecution, serve justice and simultaneously earn yourself thirty pytes.'' Scrivvulch waited with an air at once self-effacing and imperative.

Moon found himself talking. "Well, sir, I guess there's no real reason not to tell you. Why not, especially if that's the way to serve justice? But I'll feel happier if you promise that no one will know that the information came from me.'' He waited for Scrivvulch to nod before continuing. "The pink-haired triplets that you ran into last night—those are the nephews of our Seigneur Keprose Gavyne.''

"Gavyne . . . Gavyne . . . surely I've heard that name before.''

"Well I shouldn't wonder, sir. The Seigneur Keprose Gavyne is a great sorcerer, famed far and wide. He's a mighty powerful and irascible lord. And when he's displeased, the whole town knows about it, you may be sure. That's the reason it's a sticky thing for me to be the one to tell you that the lads you want are members of the Seigneur's own family.''

"I see. I see. I appreciate the delicacy of your position, Master Moon. I remain somewhat mystified, however, as to the triplet's motives in rescuing so dangerous an outlaw. Am I to believe that the Seigneur's nephews are personal friends of Black Relian Kru—childhood companions, perhaps? I did not form the impression that the prisoner was acquainted with his deliverers or vice versa. But events moved swiftly, all was confusion, I was not in a position to observe closely, and Black Relian himself was somewhat discommoded at the time. You seem familiar with the habits of the Seigneur's nephews. Perhaps you can shed some light on this matter?''

"I wouldn't say they did it out of friendship, exactly. Truth is, they did it to please their Uncle Keprose. You see, Druveen—he's top nephew—he's been tight for money for some time and he thought Seigneur Keprose might come across with the cash if he got hold of this stranger who arrived last night. The stranger seemed a quiet, polite young gentleman and nobody could have guessed what a devilish character he really is.''

"Nobody ever guesses. Certainly the Lord Mayor of Rendendil did not guess,'' Scrivvulch concurred sadly. "Tell me—why should your Seigneur Keprose be at all interested in Relian Kru?''

"Well, sir, it's because of those hands.''

"They are singular.''

"More than that, sir. Those long, white hands have got something to do with sorcery. I don't know what, but there's a connection.''

"I've read something to that effect. Hyperdigitation.''

"There you are, sir. I don't know if it's true or not, but that's what you hear all the time. Anyway, Pruke and Vazm and Druveen—that's the triplets—figured that their Uncle would want to see anybody with hands like that, so when the young gentleman turned up last night, they broke in and grabbed him. But you already know about that, sir.''

"Only too well.'' Scrivvulch nodded dryly. "And how did the triplets happen to notice Black Relian's hands? By chance, I suppose?''

"That's it, sir. Purely by chance.'' Master Moon's round face was more cherubic than ever.

Scrivvulch sipped his chocolate and studied his companion thoughtfully. Master Moon sustained the regard unmoved. "Then you believe that the triplets have taken Black Relian to their uncle, your Seigneur,'' Scrivvulch said at last. "Where does the Seigneur Keprose reside?''

"At Fortress Gavyne, up atop the cliff overlooking the valley,'' the innkeeper replied. "It was dark when you came in last night else you'd have seen it, sir. Now it's daylight and you can't miss it.''

"Good. Then it's simply a matter of approaching the Seigneur and requesting the surrender of the escaped criminal Relian Kru in the name of his Dhreveship of Neraunce.''

"And I wish you the very best of luck, sir. The very best.''

Something in the innkeeper's tone and expression gave Scrivvulch pause. "Is there some obstacle I have failed to perceive, Master Moon? Is there something you are not telling me?''

"Well you never know, now do you, sir? Maybe you'll

have no trouble at all. It's just that if the Seigneur Keprose has some use for your man Kru, then he might not be so quick to hand him over to you, Dhreve or no Dhreve. If Black Relian is locked up somewhere in Fortress Gavyne and the Seigneur wants him to stay there, then you'll not be seeing him again, sir.''

"What? Even if it is made clear to him that he harbors a wanted criminal? Has your Seigneur no concern for decency, law and social welfare?''

"Oh yes he does, sir. Indeed he does, but he has other concerns as well and sometimes those others take precedence. Often, in fact.''

"I understand. Well, I shall appeal first to the Seigneur's sense of righteousness. Next, to his sense of responsibility. If those don't work—then we shall see. There are various possibilities. And now Master Moon, there are just two more things I require of you and then you shall have your thirty pytes. Firstly—the name of the chief of your local constabulary.''

"Constabulary, sir? In Vale Jevaint?''

"Don't you have any?'' Scrivvulch inquired, and Moon shook his head. "A watch or party of men-at-arms, then?''

"Not here, sir. There's no crime to speak of in Vale Jevaint. The Seigneur won't have it, and anyone who crosses him gets thrashed with lightning. So we don't need a constabulary.''

"A most fortunate community. There are then no armed guards to keep watch over your prized Wingbane eggs?''

"Oh that, well naturally. But that's not a constabulary, sir. Those are private guards in the employ of the Guild of Gatherers. If you want to know more about that, then you'd best go talk to Master Gatherer Clym Stipper. His house is in the Gavyne Square, and for twenty pytes he'll let you see the three-armed baby.''

"That is a tempting prospect, to be sure. I shall give the suggestion the consideration it deserves. Finally, I should like directions to Fortress Gavyne.''

"That's easy, sir. You just carry on straight through the town along the Rising Road, with the Miasm at your back. The Rising Road will take you up the hills the roundabout way. It's a stiff climb, but still the easiest route to the top of the cliff. Of course, you could also go to Noio's and hire yourself a carriage if you want to go in style. That would cost you something, but you appear to be an openhanded gentleman, sir,'' Moon concluded hopefully.

"Money spent in a good cause is money well spent," returned Scrivvulch. "Speaking of which, what is my reckoning for last night?"

"Fifty pytes, sir." Moon neglected to mention that the room had already been paid for by Relian.

"Excellent. Please be so good as to accept an additional thirty pytes for your information and an extra five in appreciation of your cooperation."

"My pleasure, sir," Moon replied, accepting the proffered coins. And it was a pleasure, the innkeeper reflected, to deal with so affable, courteous and generous a customer.

"I bid you adieu for now, Master Moon."

"Good-bye, sir. And good luck. I hope you get your man, sir."

"I shall. In the course of a long and eventful career, it is my special pride that I have never failed. For in this blighted, most imperfect world, the quest for excellence in his chosen career lends purpose to Man's life." So saying, Scrivvulch the Stick bowed and walked out of the inn.

"Well spoken, sir, well spoken!" Moon addressed the empty common room. "I wish I'd said that!" After a moment's reflection he took up quill and notebook and indited:

LXIV

For in this blighted, most imperfect world,
A world replete with misery and strife,
Man's hopes upon a barren strand are hurled,
but fern-green love lends purpose to Man's life.

He paused in his labors. His eye traveled from poem to account ledger, to the pile of silver coins on the counter before him, and Master Moon smiled with a satisfaction that approached euphoria.

* * *

Scrivvulch the Stick did not go to Noio's for a carriage but instead contented himself with the horse that had carried him from Neraunce. As he made his way along the Rising Road, with the Forest of Miasm breathing poison at his back and the great Fortress Gavyne high up on the cliffs before him, the expression on his face was thoughtful and his aspect more than ordinarily professorial. Many a citizen of Vale Jevaint noticed the spindling stranger, for strangers were rare. Most eyed him with favor, for his appearance was neat, orderly, altogether respectable; and his demeanor was kindly.

Scrivvulch observed the town and townsfolk attentively as he rode through, for keen observation was his ingrained habit. He noted the prosperity, the propriety, the eccentric provincial elegance. He saw and marked well the blackened architectural ruins and the maimed human victims of the wrath of the Seigneur Keprose. He noted the turnoff to the Gatherers' Row that led to Gavyne Square and the home of Master Gatherer Clym Stipper. He observed the guarded, heavily-fortified Egg House. And he did not overlook the tall obelisk of black marble, encrusted all over with mournful bas-relief faces, on which was inscribed in letters of gold, "In Memory of the Miasmic Victims." He scrutinized all in his unobtrusive way, and filed his observations away for possible future reference.

Scrivvulch rode on. The buildings were spaced more widely now, and soon he passed beyond the town limits. Ahead of him the Rising Road snaked among the trees and crags to lead the traveler to the summit of the hill by the easiest possible route. Easiest route notwithstanding, it was a long and arduous climb, designed to discourage all but the most resolute of visitors to Fortress Gavyne.

Scrivvulch ascended by stages, pausing periodically to rest his horse and to gaze back at the town spread out below, and beyond the town to the sinister Forest of Miasm. Around the peaks on the far side of the valley, the fog hung in dense, tethered clouds. Scrivvulch watched curiously. The sky was coldly clear, the world was awash in sunshine, and no explanation for the highly localized mists suggested itself. Scrivvulch shrugged and resumed his journey. Above him the fortress brooded in silence. After another hour of riding he emerged from the trees, crossed a wide clearing and arrived at the outer gate. There he paused to reconnoiter. The fortress was obviously impregnable. The granite wall was high and massive. The stones had been set together with such precision as to present an almost perfectly smooth vertical face to the world. There was apparently but one portal, a huge iron-bound affair—closed, barred, and implacable as time. Above the wall, the leaden-roofed turrets were visible. All was silent and appeared deserted. No sentry paced the ramparts and no faces could be glimpsed at the tower windows. Birdsong was hushed and even the rustle of leaves in the wind was muffled here, as if in deference to the acute sensibilities of the Seigneur Gavyne. But Scrivvulch's own acute sensibilities informed him that he was being watched. Closer inspection of the gate revealed a head-sized, nearly-invisible square cut into the oaken timbers at eye level. At the center of the square he discovered a minute peephole nearly lost in the groove between two great planks. He rapped sharply on the door with his stick. After a moment the square panel opened and Scrivvulch found himself gazing into the stone-dull eyes of Keprose Gavyne's porter.

"Good morning. I am Scrivvulch, Accredited Agent of the Dhreve of Neraunce," the assassin announced ceremoniously. "I seek an audience with the Seigneur Keprose."

"Appointment?" the porter inquired.

"Alas no. But I have come a long way on a matter of some urgency, and I am hopeful that the Seigneur will consent to grant me a few moments of his time."

"The Master sees nobody without an appointment," the porter replied.

"Perhaps he will make an exception in my case?"

"The Master sees nobody without an appointment."

"You do not understand. I speak to the Seigneur on behalf of the Dhreve of Neraunce." This disclosure made no visible impression on the porter and Scrivvulch inquired, "You have heard of his Dhreveship?"

A brief pause. "Aye," the porter admitted.

"Do you know what the Dhreve is?"

"Aye."

"He is the ruler of all Neraunce—that is to say, much like a king, although the dignity is not hereditary. He lives in a great palace filled with hundreds of downtrodden servants and fawning courtiers. He clothes himself in tents of crimson satin and cloth-of-gold, with enough gold jewelry to founder a cargo ship. He is intemperate, concupiscent, and he has the appearance, appetites and temper of a boar-pig. So you see, my friend, the Dhreve is almost indistinguishable from a king. As I am his representative, it is as if the Dhreve himself, speaking through my lips, has paid a call upon your Seigneur. Now will you admit me?"

"Appointment?"

"Don't you understand—"

"The Master sees nobody without an appointment."

"I've a message of great importance for your master," Scrivvulch remarked, his courtesy fully intact. "If I am not mistaken, he harbors beneath his roof a fugitive felon, a very dangerous criminal, the perpetrator of numerous crimes of the vilest and most violent sort. Thus the Seigneur unwittingly places himself and all his household in grave danger. He must be warned. I have come to resolve all difficulties by taking the criminal into custody and returning him to the justice of the Dhreve. Now perhaps you will understand the necessity of allowing me an interview with the Seigneur?"

The porter thought it over for a time. The vertical crease between his brows proclaimed the intensity of his mental effort. At last he replied with an air of faint perturbation, "You have no appointment."

"Correct, my friend, but I have just explained—"

"And the Master sees nobody without an appointment," the fellow continued with more assurance. "That's the rules."

"Would it be against the rules," Scrivvulch inquired with apparent sympathy, "to inform your Master that I wait without his gate?"

The porter thought some more. "No," he replied at last. "That wouldn't be against the rules. But it would be a waste of my efforts. Wastefulness is wicked and I'm an honest man."

"No waste if you are compensated, my honest man." And Scrivvulch held up a five-pyte piece invitingly. A hand came through the opening, grasped the coin and withdrew. "Tell the Seigneur who I am and why I have come. Impress upon him the urgency of my mission. No doubt he will grant me an audience at once."

"I'll tell him. You wait." The panel clicked shut.

All was again silent. Scrivvulch retreated to the shadow of a pine where he sat and contemplated the fortress. "And what a great, thick shell of granite must be cracked in order to extract a tiny kernel," he mused aloud. The minutes passed. At last he withdrew a monograph—*Brulyuri's Poisoned Pomade: An Analysis*—from his breast pocket and began to read. The information contained therein was of a useful nature and Scrivvulch failed to note the passage of time. About an hour had passed before he raised his eyes from the pages. He replaced the monograph in his pocket, rose and returned to the door. Once more he rapped smartly with his cane. The panel opened and the porter's face reappeared.

The porter eyed Scrivvulch without apparent recognition. "Yes?" he demanded.

"Well? Am I to see the Seigneur?"

"Appointment?"

"My friend," Scrivvulch inquired gently, "did you inform the Seigneur Keprose of my presence and my status?"

"Oh, yes."

"And of my request for an audience?"

"Certainly."

"His reply?"

"He asked if you had an appointment. And what could I say? I'm an honest man."

"Did you tell him that the guest he shelters is a wanted man who must be returned to Neraunce?"

"Assuredly."

"Did this information appear to affect him in any way?"

"Oh, yes. His eyebrows went up and his lip curled."

"And—?"

"He said he doesn't recognize the authority of the Dhreve himself, much less the Dhreve's flunky. He said he'll keep the visitor for his own purposes as long as he likes. He says that if the Dhreve of Neraunce wants the visitor back, he'll have to send an army. And he questions the Dhreve's military competence. The Seigneur's words were more polished than mine, but that's the sense of 'em."

"I see." Scrivvulch had already gauged the strength of the Seigneur's defenses. Fortress Gavyne could undoubtedly withstand a siege of months' or possibly years' duration. "Did he say anything more?"

"Aye. He said that if you're not off the premises within the hour I'm to set the dogs on you. And—" the porter flashed a downward glance, apparently checking a watch, "you've got about three minutes left."

"The information is appreciated. I shall leave, then. Before I go, there's one last question I must ask. Tell me, my friend—how does one go about making an appointment to see the Seigneur Keprose?"

"How? I couldn't say." The porter mulled it over. "After all, that's not my job, is it?"

Scrivvulch the Stick took his leave. As he departed Fortress Gavyne, his face reflected neither rage nor disappointment. Rather, he wore the thoughtful, moderately amused look of one who has encountered an unexpected and not unwelcome challenge.

Scrivvulch rode at a leisurely pace. There was no need for haste; he would be back in Vale Jevaint long before sundown. His head was bowed and he appeared lost in a pleasant reverie. During the entire course of the return journey, a single dreamy utterance escaped him. "Clym Stipper, Master Gatherer."

* * *

Relian was awakened by a tickling in his ear and the screech of a tiny shrill voice.

"Get up now. Get up now. Get up now. Get up now. Now. Now. Now."

He opened his eyes reluctantly and raised a hand to scratch his ear. The hand was flicked by Crekkid's little forked wire of a tongue, the source of the tickling.

"Get up now. Get up now. Get up now. Get up now."

Relian tossed the covers aside and rose. Save for his bare feet, he was fully clothed. He had been too weary and sick the previous night to undress. Now he donned stockings and shoes.

"Get ready," Crekkid commanded. "Get ready. Now. Now. Now. Now."

"Ready for what?"

"Ready to go. Wasssh. Wasssh. Ssshave face. Ready to go."

"Go where?"

"You sssee. Sssoon."

"Why don't you just tell me now, snake?"

"Not jussst sssnake. Sssnake common. Many sssnakesss. Crekkid different. Ssspecial. Ssspecial. Ssspecial. Crekkid sssteel ssserpent. The only sssteel ssserpent."

"I hope so. All right, Crekkid. Where am I to go, and why?"

"You go where Ssseigneur want. Why? Becaussse you mussst. Yesss, mussst. Now hurry. Hurry. Hurry. Hurry."

"What about something to eat?"

"Maybe yesss. Maybe no. Hurry. Hurry. Hurry. Hurry."

Relian shrugged and performed perfunctory ablutions. Swift though his preparations were, Crekkid was not satisfied.

"Fasssster," the serpent commanded. "You lazy. Go fasssster. Fasssster. Fasssster." The miniature fangs nipped Relian's earlobe.

The young man started, nicked his chin with the razor, and cursed.

"Fassster. Fassster. Go. Go. Go. Go."

"You little mechanical horror, when I get out of this place I'll see to it that you end up as scrap metal." On impulse, Relian applied the razor to Crekkid's coils and sawed vigorously. As he had expected, the blade made no impression upon the steel scales.

Crekkid yammered with metallic laughter. "Ssstupid," he whistled at last. "Ssstupid. Ssstupid. Ssstupid."

Stupid? Perhaps I am, if I can't think of some way out of this, Relian mused. *I wonder what might be done with the razor that the Seigneur has been so kind as to give me? Of course, the razor's useless against the snake. And the snake can incapacitate me within seconds. I might manage to wound or kill someone before Crekkid got me, but that would be quite pointless—I'd still be trapped in this place. In any case, I don't want to kill anyone. The Seigneur seems to proceed on the assumption that I'm rational and not vindictive. He happens to be correct. Is he perceptive, or just lucky?*

"Move. Move. Move. Move." The steel coils tightened insistently and Relian gasped. "Through door. Turn left. Turn left. Left. Left. Left. Left."

The young man obeyed. Subsequent commands steered him through a maze of corridors, up a winding flight of stairs, and brought him at last to the summit of the Cloudmaster, greatest and tallest of Fortress Gavyne's many towers. The stairs ended in a small landing. The way was blocked by an iron-strapped door.

"Through door. Go. Go. Go. Go," Crekkid ordered.

Relian tried the door. It was unlocked. He walked through and found himself in what could only have been the workroom of Keprose Gavyne.

The workroom was a huge, high-ceilinged, hexagonal chamber with a great arched window set into each of its walls. The windows admitted a flood of intense sunlight and permitted observation of the surrounding countryside. A hexagonal table equipped with six chairs of polished dark wood occupied the center of the room. The tabletop was cluttered with papers, notebooks, scrolls, tablets, unrecognizable instruments of unknown function, sealed canisters, half-consumed boxes of bonbons and the remains of various meals. Evidently this was one of the Seigneur's favorite haunts. Bookcases lined the walls and banks of low cabinets bulged with a king's ransom in arcane hardware. The most conspicuous feature was a set of three gigantic glass tubes lined up in a row along the eastern face of the room. Each tube stood half again the height of a man. They were thick of wall, vast of circumference, and brimming with cloudy violet fluid. Relian approached for a closer look. Floating in each tube, suspended midway between the floor and the surface, was an amorphous blob of solid matter. He pressed his nose to a glass wall and peered into the murky depths. The blob was white, shapeless, subtly translucent. It looked as if the consistency might be gelatinous. Some tiny current swirled the clouded liquid and the blob quivered. Relian was forcibly reminded of the quivering of the Seigneur Keprose's jowls. The recollection was unpleasant and he turned away from the tubes. He wandered over to one of the windows, stood gazing down at the town of Vale Jevaint with its bubbling domes and its broad clean streets. Somewhere near the middle of the town stood the Bearded Moon Tavern. *Trince must have arrived by now. How long will it take him to find out where I'm imprisoned?*

And when he does, what can he do about it? He could get himself killed trying to help me. The safest thing to do would be to send to my father. But I'm not at all sure the Squire would be willing to help. Relian's disagreeable reverie was interrupted by voices on the landing outside the workroom.

"Wicked, *ungrateful* girl! Lying hussy!" There was no mistaking that adenoidal soprano. It was the Lady Fribanni.

An unintelligible reply in a youthful feminine contralto.

"It isn't true, Mum! It wasn't *our* fault!" Coarse masculine tones. One of the triplets, probably Vazm.

The workroom door burst open and a young girl ran in. She was slightly disheveled and breathing hard. Behind her came Fribanni and the triplets.

"Wretched, foolish girl!" Fribanni's narrow face was white with indignation. "Trying to run away after all we've done for you! After all the kindness, the *charity* the Seigneur has shown you! Have you no sense of appreciation, no gratitude?"

"Lady Fribanni, I—"

"Don't interrupt me. I won't stand it from you. My brother Keprose is all kindness. He is too magnanimous for his own good, and he is willing to tolerate your insolence. Be assured *I* will not. *I* will not hesitate to remind you of your place,

Miss, as you seem disposed to forget it. Now what have you to say for yourself?''

The girl did not answer at once. She stared in silence as if gauging the collective strength of her foes. Relian took the opportunity to examine her. She was no more than seventeen or eighteen years old, of medium height, very slight and graceful of figure. Her mahogany-colored hair, worn girlishly long, was caught up with a ribbon, the only adornment on her plain costume of a—servant? Greddirswoman? Paid companion? Gray eyes shone with defiance in a delicately pale face. The fragile features were set in an incongruously determined, almost mulish expression. Her hands played nervously over the folds of her skirt and Relian noted that the fingers were long, white and tentacular as his own.

''Well, what do you have to say for yourself?'' Fribanni repeated. ''Were you or were you not trying to run away?''

The girl answered at last. ''I wanted to see what's outside.''

''Oh? And what do you imagine is outside, pray?''

''That is what I want to discover.''

''Very cool, very impudent, aren't you? Well don't take that tone with me, Miss Bold-face. Remember whom you're speaking to. I ask you—what do you think you'll find outside the fortress?''

The girl was silent.

''Cold, hunger, privation. Danger, hardship and suffering. That's what you'll find out there, my girl,'' Fribanni asserted. ''Desperate men who'll use and abuse you; mad experimentalists who blast you with artificial lightning; surgeons who vivisect you; slavers who chain and sell you. Wild beasts and monsters eager to feed upon your flesh. Ghouls, ghosts and demons waiting to twist your mind and snare your spirit. Animate corpses hungry to sate their lusts upon your body. Carnivorous vegetation, poisonous birds, and quicksand underfoot. All that and worse besides.''

Relian opened his mouth to speak, thought better of it, and remained silent.

''*That* is what's out there,'' Fribanni continued, ''and that is what the Seigneur Keprose saved you from! He took pity on you, plucked you from the gutter that was your birthright, fed you, clothed you, preserved you from all dangers, and lavished his affection upon you all these years. And you repay him by trying to run away. You will wound him to the heart. Have you no remorse, you callous baggage?''

The girl's expression of determination intensified. "The books I read," she replied, "suggest that the world outside isn't exactly as you describe."

"Books are filled with dreams, deceit and illusion. Have I not told you so again and again, you silly creature? Books are poetry and fancy."

"That may be. But I'd like to see for myself—"

"Don't believe her, Mum," Druveen advised. "I'll take my oath the chit was trying to run away. Look—" He extended a cloth bundle. "She was carrying this when we caught up with her."

The girl made a motion toward the bundle and Fribanni elbowed her aside. "Open it, my darling," Fribanni commanded.

Druveen complied. The bundle was found to contain a couple of dresses, a few cheap toilet articles, a loaf of bread and three apples.

"See, Mum, she was going to take her things and clear off."

"And she'd have done it, too, if we hadn't caught her," Pruke observed.

"My clever, sharp-eyed lads, once more you've performed a great service for your Uncle."

"Then will you ask him to increase our allowance?"

"We shall see. We must await the propitious moment." Fribanni turned back to the pale-faced girl. "Well, Miss, this is all the evidence I require. You stand revealed as a liar as well as an ingrate. We ought to let you do as you please. We should let you take your paltry belongings—yours only by virtue of my brother's generosity, I might add—and we should let you leave. In fact, we should turn you out. It would serve you right."

The girl's eyes reflected mingled hope and trepidation.

"Yes, it would serve you right, Miss Gadabout. Then, when you find yourself freezing, terrified and starving to death in a ditch or under some roadside hedge—or more likely, caught fast in the grip of one of the forest ghouls, then you'll think of the comforts you threw away and then you'll be sorry. But then, my girl—ah, then it will be too late."

"So how do you like that?" Pruke inquired.

"Well, are you still so determined to brave the perils of the cold outer world? All alone?" Fribanni demanded. "Think carefully."

Despite her air of resolution, Fribanni's lurid descriptions had obviously impressed the girl. She stared at the floor and at last replied in a low voice without raising her eyes, "I won't try to run away if you'll promise—if you'll promise—"

"You presume to impose conditions? Well, what is it, then? If I promise what?"

"To keep your sons away from me," the girl concluded with an effort.

There was a moment's dreadful silence. While Relian looked on in fascination, the girl studied the floor, the triplets fidgeted restively and Fribanni's face darkened to dull crimson. At last Fribanni commanded in tones of careful self-restraint, "You will be so good as to explain that remark."

"Your sons have taken to bothering me. I'm asking you to put a stop to it."

"Bothering you how? In what way?"

The girl's eyes remained fixed on the floor. A faint stain of rose colored her cheeks. "They trouble me, they waylay me in the empty corridors."

"My boys have the right to go where they please. Are you suggesting otherwise? This is their home. They are of the Gavyne blood, which is more than can be said for you."

"They follow me everywhere."

Vazm and Pruke shuffled their feet, while Druveen suppressed a snicker.

"You impudent hussy, do you imagine that the nephews of the Seigneur Keprose would condescend to seek you out?"

"They do more than that." She raised her eyes at last and they were dark with anger and humiliation. "Last night one of them followed me out to the garden, put his arm around my waist and tried to slide his hand down the front of my dress. I escaped with difficulty."

"You—shameless—little—guttersnipe!" Fribanni's hands jerked like the tail of an angry squirrel. "How dare you? How dare you utter these filthy lies? My boys would not soil their hands thus! They would not dream of touching you!"

"One of them more than dreams."

"Liar! Which one do you accuse? Say which one if you dare!"

"I can hardly say which," the girl returned with perceptible disdain. "They all look exactly alike. As for character, there is little to choose among them. That one, I think." She indicated Druveen.

Druveen's reply was instantaneous. "Not I, Mum. I never touched her, I swear."

"I know you did not, my dearest."

"Nor I, Mum," Pruke asserted.

"I'm not about to mess with her," said Vazm. "Uncle wouldn't like it."

"Correct, my wise lad." Her lips pursed in distaste. Fribanni turned back to the girl. "I am convinced of my boys' innocence. However, I wish to be fair, for that is what dear Keprose would wish. Therefore I ask you—have you proof? Is there evidence of any kind to support your outrageous tales? Or do you perhaps expect me to accept your word?"

"Accept it or not as you please, Lady Fribanni."

"I've warned you not to take that tone with me."

"I am telling you the truth."

"Truth? You would like to believe it is the truth, I am sure." Fribanni's eyes narrowed. "You look surprised. Do you suppose you've deceived me for one moment with your innocent airs? I am not blind, girl. Do you think I haven't seen the way you've been dangling after my boys? I see through your sly little artifices, Miss Languishing. I've seen the way you flaunt yourself, I've seen the tricks you play to catch their attention. There's nothing you'd like better than to sink your low, vulgar little claws into one of my lads, is there? I see through you. There's nothing you wouldn't stoop to in order to trap my boys."

"Madam, I don't want your boys. Given the choice between any of your boys and one of the forest ghouls you've so often described, I should be at a loss for a decision."

"Lying, insolent trollop!" Fribanni's jeweled hand lashed out and she smacked the other across the face.

The girl gasped in outrage and raised a hand to her cheek. Her eyes flashed and she took a step toward Fribanni.

The older woman retreated hastily. "Boys!" she appealed.

Druveen obligingly stepped forward and seized the girl's wrist. "Let's see some respect for my Mother here," he advised.

"Take your hands off me." She attempted without success to twist her wrist from his grasp.

"Apologize first." She didn't answer and his grip on her wrist tightened. "Mum's waiting, Mereth."

Mereth aimed a kick at his ankle. Druveen sidestepped without difficulty, while his two brothers whooped and cheered.

"Don't let that vixen loose, my brave boy! Someone go fetch my brother! He'll know what to do with her!"

Mereth ceased struggling. Slowly she lifted her free hand, the hyperdigital fingers weirdly contorted, and spoke in cold menace. "Listen to me. Your Uncle Keprose has taught me much of supranormalcy. If you do not release me immediately, I will use my powers to melt all the fingernails on your right hand. It will be painful and the effects will be permanent. Now let me go."

Druveen howled with laughter in which his brothers joined. "Nice try, but it won't work. Melt my fingernails—why don't you just go ahead and do it if you can? Uncle Keprose may have trained you for years, but everyone knows you're too stupid to learn a thing. And if you believe you can frighten me with your nonsense, you must think I'm even more stupid than you."

Mereth did not reply to the taunt in words. The upraised hand clenched and she drove her fist into her captor's midriff. Druveen grunted explosively, Fribanni screamed, and Mereth managed to wrench herself free. But only for a moment. Druveen's face suffused. He grabbed the girl's shoulders and shook her violently.

Relian, hitherto silent, now spoke without thinking. "Let her go, Druveen." Instantly he regretted his words.

The others turned to stare at him in surprise. The triplets were clearly nonplussed, but did not remain so long. After a moment Druveen inquired, "You think this is any business of yours, Scrawny?"

It was, Relian admitted to himself, a reasonable query. Before he had invented a forceful but safe reply, Druveen spoke again.

"You think you give orders around here, Scrawny?"

"You think your Uncle Keprose would want you to mistreat this lady?" Relian returned equably.

"Lady, indeed!" Fribanni hissed.

Druveen ignored his mother. "I suppose you're planning to tell him about it?" he asked.

"That's not impossible."

"Isn't it?" Druveen released the girl and took a deliberate step toward Relian. His glowering brothers closed ranks behind him. "Then maybe someone should shut your mouth for you." The triplets advanced.

Relian cast about desperately for a weapon. If only he had

his pistol, or even a sword! He had acquired considerable swordsmanship prior to his fencing-master's self-impalement.

"No one goes running to Uncle to tell tales about us," Druveen observed. "You're going to learn that here and now."

There was no weapon to be had. The vigorous triplets were near, the odds were hopeless, the escape route was blocked, and it seemed he was in for a severe beating. Relian decided to go down fighting. Without warning he sprang forward and threw a straight right that connected solidly with Druveen's jaw. Once again Fribanni shrieked. Druveen reeled backward across the workroom, crashed into a glass-fronted cabinet, overturned it and went down amidst a pile of broken glass and priceless, shattered instruments. Without pausing to assess the damage, Relian leaped to the center of the room, grabbed one of the wooden chairs and slung it at Vazm's head. Vazm ducked. The chair hurtled past his ear and slammed into another cabinet. Dozens of glass jars and bottles crashed to the floor. Pruke and Vazm rushed forward with roars of rage.

The fracas was halted by Fribanni's shrill-voiced, almost hysterical command. "Boys! Stop this at once! *At once*, do you hear me?"

The triplets paused reluctantly. Druveen slowly arose from the floor, cradling his bruised jaw. "But *Mum*—" he complained.

"Children, you are destroying your Uncle's property. Dear Keprose will be shocked and grieved. This must stop immediately."

"But, Mum, you saw what that underhanded, sneaking cheat did. You saw the trick he pulled—"

"Dru's right, Mum. We can't let him get away with this!"

"And he's the one who destroyed Uncle's property, not us. It wasn't *our* fault, Mum!"

"Boys, dearest boys, of course I know it wasn't your fault. Mother understands. Nevertheless, this violence must cease. Remember who you are. You mustn't lower yourself to *his* level. Particularly not for the sake of an insignificant, common girl," she added with a glance of dislike at Mereth. Mereth returned the look stonily.

"But, Mum, that fellow needs to be taught a lesson—"

"No doubt he will be, my darling, when your Uncle learns what has transpired. Keprose will know how to deal with these two, never fear. In the meantime, I want my boys to show their breeding. Ignore the brawling bully and the scheming minx. They are unworthy of your notice, and their company is distasteful. Come, let us withdraw. We shall find your Uncle. Come, boys.''

''Oh, all right, Mum.''

The triplets slouched toward the door and Fribanni followed. She paused on the threshold and addressed Relian bleakly. ''You'll start your work now. The girl will tell you what to do. I can only hope that you'll not prove as brainless and inept as she. But I feel it my duty to inform you, young man—you have made a bad beginning. A very bad beginning indeed.'' She exited, leaving Relian and Mereth alone.

Tears now sparkled on Mereth's long lashes and she wiped them away with a furtive hand. Relian seated himself at the table and waited until the girl appeared to have recovered her poise before asking uncomfortably, ''Are you all right?''

''Yes,'' she replied in a voice whose musicality he had not previously noticed. She sat down and scrutinized him for the first time, with apparent incomprehension. ''Thank you for helping me. But you were unwise.''

''You fear the Seigneur will object to the destruction of his workroom property?''

''By the time he's finished listening to his sister and her sons, he'll hold you personally responsible for it.''

''I *am* personally responsible for it.''

''Better not be so quick to admit it, Master—?''

''Kru. Relian Kru. The Seigneur will exact vengeance?''

''It's not easy to predict what he'll do. He'll be displeased, that's certain. He is vindictive, but if you're fortunate he'll hesitate to abuse a fellow supranormalist.''

''I'm no supranormalist. If I were, is it likely the Seigneur could keep me here against my will?''

''You have the hands,'' Mereth observed. She regarded Relian's telltale fingers with curiosity.

''Yours are the same.''

Mereth sighed, shrugged, flipped the long hair off her shoulder with a nervous toss of the head. ''My fingers are liars. The Seigneur has expended much time and trouble on me, but his efforts have been wasted. Despite the years of training and practice, despite the hyperdigitation, I've never displayed the slightest sign of supranormalcy.''

''Then hyperdigitation isn't a certain sign of unusual powers?''

"The Seigneur says that it almost always is."

"What do you think accounts for your difficulties?"

"Presumably my own stupidity," the girl returned matter-of-factly.

Relian looked at her in surprise. Her expression was bleakly resigned. She did not seem to invite compliments. "You don't look at all stupid to me, Mistress Mereth," he told her.

"I don't look at all stupid to me either," she agreed readily. "But then, does anyone ever look stupid to herself? Why am I unable to master even the most rudimentary forms of supranormalcy, despite all my training? Stupidity alone explains it. The Seigneur Keprose is doubtless intelligent, and he's told me all my life that I'm backward. His sister Fribanni agrees and so do the three nephews. Even the Seigneur's creature Crekkid is of a like opinion."

"Ssstupid," Crekkid put in obligingly. "Ssstupid. Ssstupid. Ssstupid."

"You see?" Mereth concluded. "He agrees, as do they all. Surely such unanimity of opinion is suggestive."

"Suggestive yes, but of what? Unanimous agreement isn't necessarily any indication of truth," Relian replied. "In any event, the accord in this case is hardly universal. From what I've seen here, it appears that the Seigneur Keprose regards all human beings as vastly inferior to himself. It's also clear that Keprose exerts inordinate influence upon the beliefs and opinions of his household members. Therefore uniformity of thought within the confines of Fortress Gavyne is hardly to be wondered at. If you desire an unbiased opinion on this or any other topic, you must question folk outside the fortress."

"I'm told that the population out there consists largely of violent criminals, mentally deficient beggars, perverts and homicidal deviants."

"I suspect your fears are somewhat exaggerated."

"Possibly, but the only way to put them to the test is by means of direct observation. And then what becomes of me should it happen that my worst fears are justified?"

"Who put these notions into your head?"

"The Seigneur and his sister."

"They misled you. When were you last in Vale Jevaint?"

"I've never been down to the town, nor met any strangers," she admitted, and the large gray eyes were thoughtful. "In fact, I've never left Fortress Gavyne at all."

"You were born in here?"

"No, but I've never left since I can remember. I know no other place."

"You've been here since earliest childhood. You're related to the Seigneur?"

"No," she said shortly.

"Adopted, then?"

"No."

"An employee?" She had hardly the air of a servant, but he was running out of respectable possibilities.

"More or less a charity case, or so the Lady Fribanni keeps telling me," she explained. "I gather I was found, or purchased, or otherwise acquired as an infant. My hyperdigitation caught the attention of the Seigneur, who hoped to develop my supranormalcy for his own purposes. So far he's been disappointed, for I've shown no ability. It's been different with the other subjects I've studied—history, literature, languages, mathematics, chemistry, philosophy, music and all the rest of it. But I can't learn supranormalcy. Hence the Seigneur's conviction of my stupidity, and often I think he must be right. As I'm neither a supranormalist nor a useful servant, the Lady Fribanni desires my expulsion from the fortress."

"Perhaps that wouldn't be such a bad thing," Relian suggested.

"But what of the demons, monsters, ghouls and carnivorous vegetation that I'll find outside?"

"It's been my experience that such dangers are rarely encountered."

"So I've sometimes suspected, but hardly dared to hope. Lately it's almost seemed worth the risk to—" She broke off with an abrupt shrug. "But why discuss it? The entire question is academic. Unlike his sister, the Seigneur does not wish to turn me out and I'm hardly free to go of my own volition."

"Mistress Mereth, is it your desire, as it is mine, to leave this fortress?"

The girl looked uneasy. "We mustn't speak of it."

"I promise you can trust me. I intend to leave this place at the earliest opportunity. If you'd like to go too—"

"Don't speak of it!" Her eyes were filled with stormclouds and Relian subsided. For a moment he thought she was angry, then perceived her fear. Mereth lifted her hand and silently pointed at Crekkid. Relian nodded his comprehension.

"Well, to work then," she said. "You'll want to start practicing your exercises."

"Exercises?"

"The Lady Fribanni tells me that you've come to Fortress Gavyne in hope of persuading the Seigneur to accept you as a student or assistant. You'll be happy to learn that the Seigneur has consented to do so."

"The Seigneur has *consented*—?"

"So I'm told. You'll need to study and work hard in order to develop your supranormal powers, and much of what you must know in order to begin is contained in those seventy-four introductory volumes on the shelves along the southwest wall." She pointed them out and Relian regarded the massive matched tomes without enthusiasm. From where he sat he could make out some of the titles: *Vol. XX—Two Thousand Greej Patterns; Vol. XII—Kly's Theory of Supravisual Flaccidity; Vol. LXXIV—Index of Temporal Vortices.* "You'll want to read those books carefully and assimilate all their contents before proceeding to more difficult—"

"Have you read the books yourself?" Relian interrupted.

"Several times. Some of them I've almost got memorized."

"And the effect on your supranormalcy has been—?"

"Negligible."

"Then there seems to be little incentive to read them."

"There's a very strong incentive. The Seigneur wants you to do it," Mereth replied. "And perhaps you'll have better luck with them than I. In any case," she continued, "you won't spend all your time reading. You must practice your hand-exercises to increase flexibility and your mind-exercises to sharpen the inner vision. At the same time you'll work to perfect the Kronwido technique that permits focus and directing of supranormalcy in six dimensions by means of hand gestures in three dimensions—"

"Six dimensions?"

"The three you know, plus Time, Forn and Otherwards. But you don't need to worry about all that just yet, Master Kru. You'll find out more about it when you start reading. In the meantime, all you must know is that you can't even begin to work on your Kronwido until you've developed considerable hyperdigital dexterity, so you'll start at once with the hand-exercises. For example—do you think you can do this?" She pushed the long sleeves back off her wrists, lifted her elongated hands and wove the fingers into a knot of improbable complexity.

Relian examined the knot minutely. "I think so," he said, and approximated the position with fair success.

"Good, that's very good," Mereth told him. "Left ring finger over the thumb then back again. Good. This should be easy work for you, your hands are already so flexible. All right, can you do this one?" She placed a five-pyte piece on top of her right forearm, bent her right hand backward, arching the fingers bonelessly; grasped the coin between the extreme tips of index and middle fingers; brought the coin forward and deftly shuttled the silver back and forth, in and out among her fingers without use of her thumb to guide it. "Try." She flipped him the coin.

Relian managed to pluck the silver piece off his arm, but lost control of it thereafter and the coin dropped to the floor. He tried a couple more times and failed.

"You almost had it that time," Mereth encouraged. "You'll have better luck if you don't try to go so fast. Here, I'll show you again."

"These tricks are entertaining," said Relian, "but I find it hard to believe that they'll lead to anything significant."

"They haven't for me," Mereth confessed, "and I've practiced for years. But it may be different for you."

"Why should it be different? Because the Seigneur wills it so? Tell me, are you quite certain that Keprose has dealt honestly with you? Would he really want you to acquire powers equal to his own? Perhaps he might fear you as a rival?"

"There's little chance of that. The Seigneur is too confident of his powers to fear another supranormalist. Certainly he wishes me to develop my own abilities that I may lend him assistance in his projects, and possibly for other reasons." Her color rose inexplicably.

"What other reasons?"

She was silent.

"Do you want to assist him?"

"The question has little meaning. Do *you* want to assist him?"

"No, but I—"

"But you are here in this workroom, about to embark upon a course of study. Personal wishes are irrelevant in the face of the Seigneur's desires."

"But I wished to learn more of Keprose's abilities, I was about to say," Relian informed her. "Had I not been kidnapped, I'd have come here voluntarily."

"Are you a scholar, then? Or merely curious?"

"Neither. I sought to discover a sorcerer—although I hardly credited the existence of such beings. I wished to request his aid, or at least his advice. You see, throughout my entire life, I've been plagued with the most extraordinary—" Relian's explanation ended in a gasp of startled pain as Crekkid's little fangs pinched his neck.

"No more gossssip," the serpent commanded. "You work now. Work now. Work now. Work now. Work now."

Relian and Mereth obeyed. Hours passed and Relian learned the Basic Hyperdigital Flex, the Pautidish Knot, Forg's Tangle and the Moam Progression. Mereth demonstrated the various exercises with skill and ease. Her fingers were slightly shorter than Relian's and considerably thinner. She could twist and bend them with a seemingly unnatural facility that Relian, for all his flexibility, was unable to match. He felt clumsy, foolish and somewhat annoyed, as if he had been forced into a children's game at which he proved inept. Mereth, however, declared herself well pleased with his progress.

Around midday a servant entered bearing a tray. The Seigneur had provided a predictably modest lunch of bread, cold meat, fruit and faintly greenish wine. The two young people ate, drank and talked. Mereth proved to possess a sharp mind, good powers of observation, and an impressive store of knowledge culled from books combined with total lack of firsthand experience of the world outside the fortress. Her curiosity was boundless. She wanted information—all the information that Relian could provide concerning the lives, habits and thoughts of folk from Nidroon to Travorn. Relian answered as best he could, impressed by the strength of her thirst for the commonplace.

The conversation was enjoyable and would have been prolonged had it not been for Crekkid. The serpent grew restive, writhed and hissed, and presently issued commands in his nerve-jangling tin-whistle voice. Relian and Mereth returned to the hand-exercises. While Relian practiced, Mereth went to the shelves of introductory volumes, picked out Volume I, *Apprentice Supranormalist,* located and marked all references to hyperdigitation. Discourse the Third, *Prelude to Kronwido,* included an illustrated series of exercises and accompanying explanatory text. The explication of Moam's Progression was particularly enlightening, and Relian was soon performing the bizarre gestures with precision. Mereth was lavish of praise and Relian's annoyance began to abate. He had come close to resuming his usual state of controlled melancholia when the door swung wide and Keprose Gavyne swept into the workroom.

The Seigneur was arrayed in his customary black. His pinkish curls glistened. His plump cheeks bloomed with health and benignity. His hands, clasped and resting upon his stomach, were hidden within the folds of his loose sleeves. His feet were concealed beneath the skirt of his robe. Owing to the absence of visible appendages and the gliding smoothness of his gait, the Seigneur appeared to advance as if mounted on rollers. Amazing that so profoundly corporeal a lord could move in wraithlike silence. However, had it not been for the sound of the door opening, Relian would scarcely have noted the Seigneur's arrival. Not so Crekkid. The effect of his master's entrance upon the serpent was immediate. Crekkid reared his head in imitation of a cobra poised to strike. "Ssseigneur!" he hissed in metallic ecstasy. "Ssseigneur! Ssseigneur!"

"Good afternoon, my little friend," Keprose replied tolerantly. "Good afternoon my pretty Mereth. You are a pleasure to behold, as always." She did not reply. Her eyes were fixed on the wall in front of her. Keprose ignored the rudeness. "Good afternoon—what did you say your name is, young man?"

"Kru. Relian Kru."

"Of course. Hard at work, I see. Excellent. That is the proper attitude, young man. Study, study, and more study. It is the only means whereby the ill effects of a lifetime of intellectual sloth may be eradicated. Sad to say, prolonged and strenuous application has proved ineffective in the case of my Mereth, who displays not the slightest flicker of supranormal ability. It is to be hoped, sir, that you lack the young lady's mental disadvantages."

Without volition Relian glanced at Mereth. She sat very upright in her chair, regarding the wall with an expression of empty-eyed indifference. It seemed she looked at her mentor as little as possible. For the moment she appeared as dull-minded as Keprose deemed her.

"In all justice, Seigneur," Relian attempted, "I believe you underestimate your ward—"

"Possibly, but that is of no consequence at the moment.

We've matters of far greater import to discuss. Permit me to express my gratification, young man, at the wisdom you have displayed in choosing to accept the hospitality of Fortress Gavyne. I confess I was disappointed at the coolness of your initial response to my offer. A good night's rest, however, has put an end to your vacillations. Often thus does sleep warm the faintest heart with courage, strengthen the most timorous spirit, banish doubt from the weakest and most indecisive of minds. Wonderful, is it not?''

Stunned by the Seigneur's effrontery, Relian was briefly bereft of words. Not so Crekkid. "Do not trussst, Massster. No trussst," the serpent piped up. "Crekkid lisssten, alwaysss lisssten for Massster."

"My loyal little friend! And what has Crekkid overheard?''

"Much. Much. Lassst night, visssitor try to run away. Ssstupid. Crekkid ssstop him. Crekkid ssstop him for Massster. Crekkid did it alone."

"You shall bathe in oil, my Crekkid. But that was last night. We must assume that wise reflection has placed our young guest in a better frame of mind."

"Not ssso. Not ssso. Today he comesss to workroom, fightsss, breaksss glassss. Massster'sss glassss. Next, tellsss girl he will leave fortressss. Run away. Sssaysss girl can run away alssso. Crekkid hear all. Crekkid hear all for Massster. Tell all to Massster. Crekkid. Massster. Crekkid. Crekkid.''

Relian listened in disgust and Mereth stared blankly out the window. Keprose was not perturbed.

"I do not doubt the zeal and veracity of my most excellent little ally, for Crekkid is literally as true as steel." The Seigneur paused to savor his own wit. "However, our guest's comments anent departure were not meant to be taken seriously. They were idle pleasantries, a source of merriment, nothing more.''

"No, Massster—"

"But yes, I assure you. Our young visitor does not wish to deprive us of his company, my Crekkid. Attend. The world, as I have often explained to Mistress Mereth, is filled with every variety of peril. Without these walls existence is fraught with endless danger. But here within the confines of the fortress, all is peace and contentment. Where better than Fortress Gavyne shall a fugitive, a hunted man, find respite? Consider the case of a man prey to fear, misfortune, and all the thousand natural shocks that flesh is heir to—and then consider that same suffering mortal additionally subject to the persecution of his fellow men. For what reason should he be thus persecuted, you ask? Ah, does it really signify? Let us say that he is a criminal—a thief and murderer, if you will. Whether or not he is actually guilty of such crimes is unimportant. Guilty or innocent, the fact remains that he's hunted by representatives of institutionalized justice—representatives, for example, such as the man Scrivvulch, Accredited Agent of the Dhreve of Neraunce, who spent a goodly portion of the morning cooling his heels outside my gate.'' Relian stiffened and Keprose smiled benevolently upon him. "Master Scrivvulch was eventually persuaded to withdraw, but it is to be assumed that others of his ilk will follow. Such agents are dropped in litters and others will surely appear. That being the case, Fortress Gavyne becomes less a prison than a sanctuary. And that is why, my Crekkid, our young guest does not truly desire to leave us. He cannot be said to possess a first-rate mind, yet he is not altogether stupid.''

For a time there was silence as Relian strove to collect his thoughts. The news of Scrivvulch's arrival was unwelcome but not surprising. Scrivvulch had proved himself resourceful and hideously tenacious, qualities appropriate to a High Court Assassin. It was only to be expected that he would persevere. The references to the criminal charges, however, carried unsettling implications for which Relian had been unprepared. His first impulse was to deny the implied accusations. Keprose himself was obviously indifferent to questions of guilt or innocence, but Mereth watched with wondering eyes and Relian discovered that he desired her good opinion. If he explained the circumstances surrounding his flight from Neraunce, would she believe him? He was still pondering the matter when Keprose spoke again.

"No doubt you apprehend that I have not troubled to ascend to this chamber in order to discuss the aspirations of some trifling Neraunci bloodhound. I am here to observe the progress of my new protégé. I have placed most excellent facilities at your disposal, young man. You have access to my workroom, my equipment and my library. It is a rare concession and the only recompense my generosity requires is rigorous application on your part. I expect your best efforts. I demand them. You will provide frequent proof of increasing proficiency and you will begin today, instantly. Young man, you will now demonstrate what you have learned this morning." Keprose seated himself in a chair that creaked beneath his weight. "You have my full attention. I am waiting."

"I am not a performing ape—" Relian began, then broke off as Crekkid tightened ominously around his neck. Without further argument he performed the Basic Hyperdigital Flex, the Pautidish Knot, Forg's Tangle and the Moam Progression. By the time he had finished, his hands were limp with fatigue. As he completed the Progression, Relian shot a glance at Mereth. She was still seated, her body angled to maximize the distance between herself and the Seigneur. Her face remained blank, but as he caught her eye she smiled faintly. His performance had been perfect.

Keprose sat in thought for a time and then commanded, "Again."

Relian drew a deep breath and managed to control his temper. Without comment, he repeated the exercises—again flawlessly.

Keprose delivered judgment at last. "Acceptable," he conceded. "You exhibit more than adequate flexibility for a beginner. Your mechanical accuracy is unexceptionable, but unhappily devoid of the fire of inspiration. You are clearly no genius, but there is little reason to doubt that you will eventually prove capable of sound, pedestrian work. For the moment, I am satisfied." Keprose paused, awaiting reply. There was none, for Relian was still struggling with his indignation. "You will of course continue with your efforts. There will be a delay of indeterminate duration before the development of your supranormal abilities renders you fit to assist me. In the meantime there are other areas in which you may serve."

"Serve—you? Seigneur, you presume too far."

"Beware of ingratitude, young man. In exchange for the hospitality that shelters you from the vengeance of Neraunce, it behooves you to render me such slight services as lie within your power to perform."

"I haven't asked for your hospitality."

"True. It was not necessary. My generosity is often of a spontaneous nature."

"What slight services?" Relian demanded, white-faced with helpless fury.

"As for that, some explanation is required. I shall speak in the simplest possible terms, suitable to the limitations of my audience. You recall I have expressed my intention of putting an end to the career of Vanalisse the Unseen Hag, chatelaine of the Tyrant of Mists?''

"No easy matter, I suspect."

"Yet it will be accomplished, and soon. Behold the instrument of my triumph." The Seigneur's lordly gesture drew Relian's eyes to the three giant glass tubes. "You have examined the contents?"

Relian nodded, interested despite himself. "What are those lumps of jelly?''

"You have observed, but you have not comprehended. It is to be expected. Each of those 'lumps,' as you so gracelessly put it, is formed of living matter cultivated in layers around and upon a living seed. Each seed consists of a single fleck of the substance of my body, and within each seed is that which orders the totality. The seeds grow and change within their baths of nutrient solution. By means of my supranormal art I coax them to swift maturity. Thereafter, the possibilities are unlimited."

"Seigneur, your discourse is obscure. Do I understand you correctly? Are you suggesting that these white blobs will come to resemble men?"

"You do not begin to grasp the significance of this project. You appear to possess neither logic nor its occasional counterfeit, intuition. Did you not heed me when I explained that the seeds are derived from my own substance? Upon attaining maturity, each seed yields a body, mind and temperament identical to my own. They will share the Gavyne appearance, the Gavyne abilities, even the Gavyne thoughts and memories. They will be in all respects indistinguishable from their creator and prototype. Now do you begin to understand?"

Relian's eyes were glued to one of the translucent lumps that floated so unconsciously within its violet bath. "I understand, but I can't believe you."

"You did not believe that Crekkid lives, but experience soon changed your mind. This case will prove similar. Evidently you lack the imaginative power that permits ready acceptance of daring concepts, but no matter. Under my tutelage, your mind will enlarge."

"What point in quadruplicating yourself? Even if you succeed, the drawbacks are manifold. I don't understand your purpose."

"I did not hope to believe that you would. Use your mind, young man. Do you hear nothing, comprehend nothing? Re-

member the facts I have revealed to you. Firstly, that
supranormalcy is an inborn ability. Secondly, that the Seigneur Keprose Gavyne possesses extraordinary supranormal
powers. Thirdly, that supranormalcy at its most powerful is a
collective effort. Fourthly, that the Seigneur Keprose Gavyne
has a powerful enemy he wishes to destroy. Are the conclusions not obvious?''

"They are not." Relian's untruthful reply was designed to
elicit additional information.

"You are as stupid as Mereth and not nearly as pretty.
Young man, the alternate selves I create will share all my
thoughts, dreams and ambitions. In addition, they will share
my supranormal powers. The combined supranormal force of
the various Keproses will serve to destroy Vanalisse the
Unseen Hag. And there you have it.''

"And after she is dead?"

"We shall go on to greater things, my Selves and I.
Perhaps the nation may be peopled with Keproses. We shall
explore the exotic possibilities of multiplicity.''

"An ingenious scheme, Seigneur, but is it practical? In
view of the time element involved, the decades required to
bring these proposed artificial men to full maturity—''

"There is nothing artificial about them, young man. Understand that here and now. In terms of their embodiment of
all the characteristics that distinguish Man from the beasts,
they will possess a reality far more absolute than your own.
Decades will not be required to bring my Selves to maturity.
That feat may be accomplished within months, possibly weeks,
by means of supranormalcy. Essential to the completion of
my great project are certain elusive articles. In order to
acquire these items, I must rely upon the abilities of an
assistant possessed of agility, hardihood, and at least rudimentary intelligence. The lack of such an assistant has hin-
dered me too long. But now you have come and I am
convinced that you will suit my purposes adequately.''

"I'm surprised you've waited, Seigneur. Wouldn't one of
your nephews have served?''

"My sister's offspring possess two of the qualities I have
mentioned, but not the third. They are stupidly sly, and not to
be entrusted with any mission of importance. For my purposes, they are useless.'' A thought struck Keprose. ''But
no, that is perhaps not entirely true, for have they not unwittingly provided me with inspiration? Consider, young man.

For too many years I have beheld three faces, identically vacuous; three forms, identically coarse and vigorous; listened to three young voices, identically cacophonous; and I have wondered at the wholly unnecessary triplication of so inferior a being. If a man is to be replicated, should it not for the world's best benefit be a man of ability, of talent, even of genius? And so my course became clear. The world shall be graced with new Keproses. It is to my mind a thing remarkable that so exalted a concept should derive from so unpromising a source. But genius is the alchemical fire wherein lead transmutes to gold."

Keprose rose from his chair, advanced to the three great tubes, paused beside one to caress the glass. Relian took the opportunity to catch Mereth's eye. His look was questioning. The girl shrugged and shook her head as if to disclaim knowledge.

"Massster, visssitor and girl make sssignalsss," Crekkid warned. "Sssecret sssignalsss. Sssignalsss."

Keprose turned away from the tubes. "My friend, your vigilance on my behalf is heartwarming," he replied with an indulgent smile. "But I do not think our young visitor's actions give any cause for alarm at the moment."

"Quite true, Seigneur," Relian agreed. "As you've pointed out, Fortress Gavyne is less a prison than a sanctuary for me at this time. I'd not be so misguided as to attempt escape, hence there's no need to burden me with the steel serpent."

"Truth," Crekkid agreed surprisingly. "No need. Visssitor can't essscape, too ssstupid. Ssstupid. Ssstupid. Crekkid lonely, missssesss Massster."

"My sentimental serpent, I am touched yet saddened. Such devotion as yours deserves reward, and you shall have it. When I was informed earlier today of Mistress Mereth's attempted excursion, I realized at once what form this reward should take. I am delighted you have reminded me. Mereth attend, if you please. This concerns you as well."

Keprose glided across the room with his peculiarly noiseless gait and stopped directly behind Mereth's chair. She twisted in her seat to gaze up at him with eyes full of dread and defiance. In one swift motion Keprose reached down into his pocket, brought forth something long and silvery, which he adroitly looped around the girl's throat.

Mereth gasped and her eyes squeezed shut for a moment. She raised a hand to her neck and snatched it away with a cry of pain. Blood beaded on her fingers. A hissing sound was heard. Mereth's hands tightened on the arms of her chair and her jaw clenched spasmodically. Her eyes remained fixed on the face of her mentor.

Keprose met the shocked regard smilingly. "Thus is my pretty Mereth protected. No more shall she run the risk of inadvertently exposing herself to the dangers of the outside world. Behold my new friend Nurbo—a second steel serpent, a guardian to Mereth and companion to Crekkid. Mereth, are you content?"

Mereth did not attempt to reply. She seemed frozen, perhaps somewhat dazed. Relian watched with helpless pity. The snake was coiled closely around the girl's neck. It resembled Crekkid, but for its moonstone eyes.

"No answer at all? Well then, what of you, my Crekkid? Perhaps you have something to say?"

"Sssecond sssteel sssserpent? Another like Crekkid?" The metallic voice vibrated with emotion. "Another? Crekkid no longer ssspecial? Common, like other sssnakesss?"

"Crekkid can never be common, for he was created by Keprose. You do not understand, my friend. Nurbo is a companion just for Crekkid, created to make Crekkid happy. Nurbo is a female serpent, a mate for Crekkid."

"Sssssssssssssssssss." A protracted hiss, as Crekkid digested this information. "Female? Mate? Female mate?"

"For Crekkid. All for Crekkid."

"Ssshe isss Crekkid'sss alwaysss?"

"Always, my friend, for as long as you both shall live. She will give you sons. Crekkid is the patriarch of his race."

"Patriarch Crekkid?"

"Exactly so."

"Kind Massster. Kind Massster. Kind Massster." Crekkid eyed his new mate for a moment and then addressed her directly. "Crekkid greetsss Nurbo."

Nurbo slithered around until her head rested on Mereth's shoulder. Mereth shuddered, but made no sound. "Nurbo givesss thanksss." The voice was similar to Crekkid's, but pitched several tones higher. "Nurbo greetsss Crekkid."

"Nurbo'sss ssscalesss ssshine like sssilver. Her tongue isss like a double blade. Her voice isss like dropsss of rain falling on red-hot iron. Fair isss Nurbo."

Nurbo darted her tongue coquettishly. "The eyesss of Crekkid glint red asss coalsss at the heart of the fire. Hisss fangsss are daggersss of sssteel. Ssstrong and proud isss Crekkid.''

"Nurbo gleamsss like a necklace upon her human'sss throat.''

"The fangsss of Crekkid raissse red weltsss upon hisss human'sss throat.''

"Nurbo deliciousss asss oil.''

"Crekkid good asss blood.''

"Sssweet Nurbo.''

"Brave Crekkid.''

"Sssssssssssssssssssss.''

Keprose Gavyne rubbed his plump hands together in satisfaction. "A success,'' he opined. "Ah, love.''

      *   *   *

"Then you do not wish to see the three-armed baby? Twenty pytes hardly seems an excessive charge in view of the privilege.''

"That is quite true, Master Stipper. But duty first, despite all personal inclination, is a wholesome maxim. May I have an answer to my proposal?'' inquired Scrivvulch the Stick.

Scrivvulch sat in the parlor of Clym Stipper, Master Gatherer. He rested at ease in an upholstered armchair. A glass of Madeira stood untouched on the table before him. A sea-coal fire warmed the atmosphere. Through the large-paned front windows he could look out upon affluent Gavyne Square. The room, in fact the entire house, possessed an air of comfort, ease and wealth without elegance. So too did its owner. Master Gatherer Clym Stipper enjoyed the confidence and complacency of the self-made man. His sense of satisfaction with life and with himself was well deserved. Son of an impoverished Preserver, Stipper had begun work as a junior apprentice Bellowsman at the age of eight. From that lowly position he had by dint of application and dedication worked his way up by slow degrees, eventually attaining the eminence of Master Gatherer. In latter years Stipper seemed disposed to rest upon his laurels. Wise investments had long since assured his financial security. Moreover, his resources were further augmented by income deriving from exhibition of the popular three-armed baby. There was at this point little necessity for Clym Stipper to hazard life and lungs upon additional ventures into the Forest of Miasm. The dangerous search for Wingbane eggs could well be left in the hands of younger and hungrier Gatherers. Nonetheless, an expedition to a hitherto unexplored section of the Miasm—a laden nest discovered in a particularly inaccessible location; the rumor of a vicious Wingbane immune to the hypnotic influence of the Fist of Zhi talisman—such unusual challenges could still occasionally lure Master Gatherer Clym Stipper from the comforts of his home on Gavyne Square. Scrivvulch the Stick could respect such a man, with whom he felt he had much in common.

Clym Stipper swirled the Madeira in his glass and breathed its fragrance. A frown curdled his florid square face. "What do you think of this wine, sir?" he inquired. "Gaddo the wine merchant told me it's the very best; I always tell him to give me the best and I pay through the nose for it, I warrant you. But this swill tastes like sugar syrup to me. You seem a man of the world, Master Scrivvulch. Tell me, have I been rooked? If so, Gaddo will hear from me."

Scrivvulch sipped the Madeira with reluctance. It tasted like sugar syrup. "Excellent, quite excellent," he reassured his host serenely. "Now, Master Stipper, as to my proposal?"

"Oh, your proposal. So it's your suggestion that a band of townsmen under my leadership, accompanied by armed Guardsmen employed by the Guild of Gatherers, should ascend to Fortress Gavyne, parley with the Seigneur, and request or demand the surrender of the criminal you're after."

Scrivvulch nodded.

"The benefits of this scheme aren't clear to me."

"The benefits are manifold, Master Stipper. There is danger in your midst. I have already expounded at length upon the cunning, ferocity, lust and rapacity, cruelty and violence of Black Relian Kru. I have enumerated his thefts, his outrages, his slayings and assaults. I have related the heartrending tale of the Lady Mayoress of Rendendil. Surely it is clear that Black Relian represents a threat to the entire town? As long as he remains among you, not a citizen of Vale Jevaint is safe. Quite simply, I am offering to eliminate this danger. However, I require your assistance in order to do so. Surely you will not hesitate to serve both Justice and your community, sir?"

Stipper, evidently not a man of sentiment, remained unmoved. He considered the proposal briefly and replied in a businesslike manner, "Very good, but for one point. Let's say this Equalist Relian is every bit as bad as you claim. Still, he doesn't represent much danger to the townsfolk as long as he's shut up in the fortress. He might just as well be in prison for all the harm he's apt to do us. In which case, where's the sense or profit in dragging the townsmen away from their work, paying the extra wages those bloodsucking Guardsmen would certainly demand, and trekking all the way up to the top of the cliff to pester the Seigneur Keprose? And for what? For some foreign ruffian who's caused no problems here and isn't likely to? Look here, Master Scrivvulch, you're a man with a job to do and I can understand that. But you'll have to solve your own problems. It's no concern of ours.''

"Is it not your concern if the criminal chooses to prey upon the town? A blade hangs suspended above your throat, Master Stipper. At any time Black Relian may issue from his refuge, to the eternal sorrow of Vale Jevaint."

"If that should happen, then we'll do something about it."

"You prefer to wait until you have suffered damages? Think of the grief that may be averted if you take action now."

"The grief you speak of is theoretical," Stipper replied. "The inconvenience, expense and risk involved in approaching the fortress are not."

"There are larger issues at stake here than the safety of the town," Scrivvulch suggested. "There is the question of continuing cordiality between the states of Nidroon and Neraunce. I think I have already made it clear to you that his Dhreveship of Neraunce will regard it as a personal affront if the criminal Black Relian is not relinquished to my custody. His Dhreveship is of a passionate nature and his anger, once aroused, is not easily assuaged. Relations between Nidroon and Neraunce would inevitably degenerate."

"I should be heartily sorry for it." Stipper sniffed his wine critically.

"It is possible that your sorrow would have tangible cause. If I'm not mistaken, Nidroonish Wingbane eggs are transported across Neraunci territory on their way to the free Port of Trisque and the ships that bear them to foreign markets. Should the Dhreve's goodwill diminish, then Nidroonish access to trade routes might perhaps be curtailed."

"In which case, an alternate means of transport would be found." Stipper was undismayed. "Additional expenses would be offset by increasing the price of the eggs. Such prices would surely be paid, as all the world clamors for Wingbane eggs. But these matters are largely political and therefore the Seigneur's business. In fact, it seems to me that this entire affair is the Seigneur's business. Why don't you go directly to Keprose Gavyne, tell him everything you've told me, and ask him to hand over your man?''

"Alas, the Seigneur treasures his privacy and declines to grant me an audience.''

"You must make an appointment.''

"How?''

"I've no idea. Why not ask the Seigneur's porter?''

"I confess I am disappointed, Master Stipper.'' Scrivvulch shook his head in sad disillusionment. "I had hoped to encounter among the townsfolk a greater regard for the abstract concept of Justice.''

"Our Seigneur's concept of Justice isn't at all abstract, as those who have encountered his lightning bolts can attest.''

"Let us not niggle over insignificant points. I will speak of more substantial issues. You have cited as an objection to my proposal the additional expense involved in utilizing the Guardsmen employed by your guild.''

"That's right. It would be a waste of time anyway, Master Scrivvulch. You don't seriously imagine that a band of overfed civilian guards is going to frighten the Seigneur Keprose, do you?''

"That's difficult to judge in advance. In any case, it is not exactly my purpose to intimidate your Seigneur. It is only necessary to impress upon him the gravity of his subjects' objections to the presence of a notorious felon in their midst. Thus approached, the Seigneur will surely consent to admit the delegation, of which I shall be a member. Once inside the fortress, I shall trust to my own particular arts to accomplish my aim.''

"Well, I see you're a determined man and a bold one as well, for all your schoolmasterish air. But I tell you again—''

"Please hear me, Master Stipper. As I was about to say, I recognize the inconvenience that my plan imposes upon the Guild of Gatherers and will gladly provide indemnification.'' Scrivvulch withdrew a purse from his pocket and laid it on the table. "There is a sum much more than sufficient to compensate the Guardsmen for their labors. What is left over you may distribute entirely at your own discretion. You are Master Gatherer and stand at the top of your profession as I stand at the top of my own. I am content to place the matter in your more than capable hands.''

Clym Stipper glanced down at the purse and smiled. "A tempting offer, but you're a stranger here and there are certain things you don't know. First off, understand that I'm no coward. I've spent twenty-five years of my life gathering Wingbane eggs in the Forest of Miasm and let me tell you, it's dangerous work. I know what it feels like when the padded Gatherer's Suit gets torn and the fumes of the Miasm get in and start burning your flesh. I know what it's like when the Bellowsman takes sick or fumbles, and the air supply feeding into your helmet all of a sudden cuts off short and you don't know if it's ever going to start up again. I've felt how it is when your air hose springs a leak and you start breathing in Miasmic poison along with your air. I've been there when the Wingbane comes out of its trance, sees that its nest is being robbed and flies at your face with its great black wings battering your mask until you're sure the glass will shatter, and its wicked beak dripping venom as it stabs and tears at your suit. And I've seen it when my comrade's been struck with the Miasmic Madness, tears the air hose from his helmet and goes wandering off where no one can reach him or dares to try. I've seen a lot of good men die before my eyes and I haven't let any of it stop me from gathering. So you can't exactly call me a shrinking violet. But that doesn't mean to say that I'm reckless. A wise man knows when it's best to be prudent and prudence tells me it's an ill business to try the Seigneur Keprose's patience— at least, not for the sake of a foreign criminal and not for a purse of gold. If your man started robbing our coaches or hanging about our Egg House it might be a different story, but as it is— " Stipper shook his head. "So there you are, Master Scrivvulch. There's nothing more to say. You're on your own." The Master Gatherer held his Madeira up to the light and examined the color with an air of dissatisfaction. "Nauseous bilge," he observed. The interview was evidently concluded.

Scrivvulch smilingly replaced the purse in his pocket, rose to his feet and bowed. "I regret we have been unable to reach an agreement, Master Stipper," he remarked. "But you have provided me with information, and all information eventually proves useful. For in this dark, benighted world, 'tis Knowledge provides the flickering light that guides our footsteps."

"High-sounding philosophy, sir."

"But remarkably practical in its application, I have found. Master Stipper, I thank you and bid you farewell."

A servant conducted Scrivvulch from the Stipper residence. The Assassin found himself in the Gavyne Square, a neighborhood altogether too luxurious for his purposes. A perambulation along the cobbled streets brought him at length to a grubby enclave of poverty that yielded what he sought.

A beggar sat on the curb. His head was bowed and he radiated despondency. The fellow wore a purple kerchief around his neck. His right arm had been amputated at the shoulder. Apart from this mutilation, he appeared sound and hale. Scrivvulch approached and dropped a few coins into the beggar's cup.

The beggar raised his head. "Thank you, sir," he muttered in some surprise.

"What is your name, my unhappy friend?"

"Glench, sir."

"Well, Glench, you seem an honest fellow. Is there no work to be had, that you must beg for a living?"

The beggar must have felt that he was in no position to resent the inquisition for he answered readily, "I was a blacksmith, sir, until I lost my arm. It was the only trade I knew. The Seigneur Keprose, he—well, where's the sense in crying over it?"

"Ah, the world has treated you cruelly, but perhaps your luck is about to change. I've work for you."

"You, sir? But without my right arm—"

"That will not matter, as long as your eyes are good. Are you willing?"

"That I am, sir."

"Excellent." Scrivvulch dropped additional coins into the cup. "Your task is a simple one. You are to keep watch over the Fortress Gavyne from sunrise to sundown. I will pay you ten pytes a day. Is that satisfactory?"

"Aye, sir! What am I to watch for?"

"A gentleman of quality—around twenty years old, plainly attired, medium height or something over, thin build, black hair, black eyes, white complexion, long fingers. If the young gentleman emerges from the fortress, you will return to the Bearded Moon Tavern in town and inform me at once. If I am not there, leave a message for Master Scrivvulch. You will, I very much hope, be discreet. Should the Seigneur note your activities, he may well take offense."

"So much the better."

"Quite the contrary."

"Have no fear, sir. I'm your man."

"Agreed. You will begin this very day."

Scrivvulch departed. A few more minutes of reconnoitering led to a meeting with a brace of maimed beggars who were duly engaged to watch Fortress Gavyne in alternating shifts throughout the night. These matters concluded to his satisfaction, Scrivvulch directed his steps toward the Bearded Moon. As he walked, his mind continued active. He bestowed a lingering and very speculative glance in passing upon the guarded Egg House wherein reposed a priceless accumulation of Wingbane eggs awaiting export. At last he spoke aloud.

"Only as a last resort."

*   *   *

"Concentrate," Mereth directed. "Try to see *all* of it."

Relian heard her voice as if from a distance. He sat in the workroom of Keprose Gavyne. His eyes were shut. On the table before him rested a plain wooden box, painted gray. He could see the box in his mind almost as clearly as if he looked upon it with open eyes. The mental exercises he had been forced to practice so assiduously throughout the days of his captivity were showing results. His powers of concentration had waxed ferocious.

"Think of the texture of the wood, imagine the pores clogged with paint. Compare the reflection of light from the areas where the paint has sunk in with the areas where the paint has pooled on the surface. Visualize all the irregularities: the chip in the left corner, the split along the grainline on the right side, the raised flecks of grit that got caught in the paint before it dried. The shadows and highlights on those flecks. Can you see all of that?"

"Yes."

"Good. What else?"

"A circular spot on the front where the paint covers a knot. A splinter off the lower left edge, where the raw wood shows through. A vertical ridge on the back panel, where the paint dripped. A bulge in the paint at the bottom of the drip. Shadow beneath the bulge. I see it quite clearly."

"Good, Relian! You're doing wonderfully."

The warmth in her voice shook his concentration, but Relian exerted his will and maintained control.

"Can you see it so clearly that you all but feel the texture of the wood and paint?"

"Yes."

"Then we're ready to move on to the next step, which will involve simple Kronwido technique. Now, what you must do is use Moam's Progression to move your vision through Forn along the first Greej Pattern. It won't be easy, for you must continue to concentrate on the box at the same time you follow the convolutions of the pattern, which, as you recall, are intricate. But if you can do it—then your sight will penetrate the wooden box and you'll be able to tell me what's inside it. That would be your first experience of the Supranormal Vision. Are you ready?"

"Ready."

"Good luck!"

Relian's hands began to move. His tentacular fingers wove impossible patterns. He performed the gestures of Moam's Progression with accuracy and assurance, and his concentration did not falter. His mental vision cleared as if a veil of smoke had been blown away. Never before had his perceptions possessed such clarity. He repeated Moam's Progression and this time increased the tempo of his movements. The image of the box now glowed with colors visible to the mind but not to the eye. A mental tremor, a precarious floating sensation that he had never experienced before, signaled his first full consciousness of Forn.

Whether Relian possessed the power to guide his vision as instructed was not to be determined then and there. Hissing syllables impinged upon his consciousness.

"Sssweet Nurbo? Sssweet Nurbo? Sssweet Nurbo?"

Relian's concentration flagged disastrously. The image of the box faded from his mind and he strove in vain to recover it. His eyes opened reluctantly. He looked across the table at Mereth and saw the steel serpent writhe languorously upon her neck.

"Nurbo isss here," Nurbo responded. "What isss Crekkid'sss desssire?"

"Crekkid desssiresss Nurbo, loveliessst of ssserpentsss. The heart of Crekkid sssingsss at the sssound of her name. Nurbo. Nurbo. Nurbo. Nurbo."

"Listen, you two," Relian interrupted in some annoyance, "Mistress Mereth and I are trying to work here—"

The snakes ignored him.

"Nurbo drinksss the sssound of her lover'sss voice, drinksss it like blood. Ssshe longsss for hisss touch of sssteel."

"Crekkid burnsss to sssire the sssonsss of Nurbo. Crekkid and Nurbo, the parentsss of their race. Patriarch Crekkid."

"Matriarch Nurbo."

"Sssssssss."

"Please be quiet and let us work," Mereth appealed. "The Seigneur wants us to work."

The snakes appeared not to hear her.

"Cursssse the fate that partsss Crekkid from hisss Nurbo."

"Alasss. Alasss. Alasss. Alasss. The grief of Nurbo is molten. When ssshall ssshe entwine with her beloved?"

"The grief of Nurbo piercesss the heart of Crekkid. Ah, love, let usss hissss at Fate. Come near and let our coilsss mingle. We ssshed our grief like lassst year'sss ssskin."

"Ssshed ssskin?"

"Nurbo isss young. Ssshe will learn."

"Sssssssssssssssssss."

Without warning, Crekkid pinched Relian's earlobe. "Carry Crekkid to Nurbo," he ordered.

"Carry Nurbo to Crekkid," came the corresponding command from the female serpent. "Get up. Move. Now. Now. Now. Now." She dug her steel face persuasively into the hollow of Mereth's throat.

"Now. Now. Now. Now," Crekkid agreed.

"This isn't the time—" Relian began, and got no further. This time Crekkid's little fangs drew blood.

"Move. Move. Move. Move."

Mereth and Relian rose unwillingly from their chairs, approached one another from their respective sides of the table and met at the halfway point. The two stood face to face separated by no more than a couple of feet, but they were not close enough to suit Crekkid.

"Clossser," the serpent commanded. "Move clossser. Crekkid longsss for hisss Nurbo."

"Be reasonable—"

"Love isss stronger than reassson. Clossser."

Relian took another step forward. He stood near enough to Mereth to pick up her clean, fresh scent; near enough to see the reddish glints in her dark hair and the single anomalous thread of red-gold gleaming among her eyelashes. Mereth's eyes were lowered; impossible to judge whether she noted his scrutiny.

"Ssssweet Nurbo, thisss moment isss oursss." Crekkid stretched forward and Nurbo did likewise. Two forked tongues darted, clicked steel on steel. Rapturous hisses filled the air.

Crekkid had all but unwound himself from Relian's neck. In hope of exploiting his enemy's ecstatic distraction, Relian grabbed the serpent just below the bulge of the head, yanked and twisted with all his strength. A couple of bright scales dropped to the floor. A whistle of pain escaped Crekkid. The living shackle loosened and for a moment Relian imagined himself free.

Crekkid recovered quickly. "Traitor!" With a hiss of dire rage, he tightened his steel coils to the point of strangulation and buried his teeth in the thinnest flesh of his victim's throat.

Relian choked in agony. He could not breathe, but he was still capable of thought and it came to him that he had gone too far; this time, Crekkid would kill him. The intensity of the pressure on his windpipe informed him that the serpent was homicidal. There was room yet in his mind for astonishment. It was so shockingly abrupt, this transition from perfect health to moribundity. There had been no warning, no time to prepare. It was a random, pointless sort of death—fit conclusion to an existence replete with random and pointless misfortune. Burning lungs and dimming vision convinced Relian that the end was not far off. He struggled to speak, but produced no sound. He saw Mereth's contorted face, saw her lips move, but heard nothing coherent.

A shrill voice reached him. "Brave Crekkid! Ssstrong Crekkid! Fierce and ssstrong! Ssstrong! Ssstrongessssst!"

Mereth's cries surpassed Nurbo's. "Stop it, you're killing him!" Crekkid did not respond. Mereth turned and ran for the door. Probably she intended to summon help.

"Ssstay," Nurbo commanded. "Nurbo will not leave Crekkid. You Ssstay. Ssstay. Ssstay. Ssstay."

The tightening of Nurbo's coils around her neck stopped Mereth in her tracks. She gasped for air and took another few steps toward the door. The steel loop contracted, shutting off her breath.

"Ssstay," Nurbo advised. "Ssstay with Crekkid."

Mereth tore ineffectually at the serpent. She tottered and dropped to her knees.

Relian was barely conscious when the door opened and Keprose Gavyne strolled into the workroom. Keprose took in the situation at a glance. "Ah, naughty creatures," he chided.

It was not clear to which creatures he referred. Relian had no idea what the Seigneur did next. He heard and saw nothing for a time. Eventually he became aware that the strangling pressure had disappeared and that he could breathe again, albeit painfully. He opened his eyes and found himself lying on the workroom floor. He was drenched in cold sweat and spattered with blood. His throat ached fiercely. Mereth was nowhere in evidence. Keprose stood before the huge glass tubes, frowning into the violet depths. Relian sat up and spoke with difficulty. "Where is Mereth?"

Keprose turned to face him. "Ah, awake at last. I trust you have profited by this lesson, young man. Get up at once. You have wasted more than enough time for one day. I wish to speak to you."

Relian rose and collapsed into the nearest chair. "Where is Mereth?" A hoarse croak was all he could manage.

"Mereth? She is not required at the moment. She scarcely possesses the wit to comprehend the matter I wish to discuss."

"She's well?"

"Oh, quite well. She would have been in the way however, and therefore I dismissed her."

"With Nurbo," came the hateful voice from the region of Relian's shoulder. "Crekkid missssesss Nurbo. Nurbo. Nurbo. Nurbo."

Keprose smiled. "My amorous little friend! Take comfort, for you will soon be reunited with your love. But first, you must accompany this young man on his mission. A pity you have so depleted his resources," the Seigneur mused. "I fear you have lessened his already-limited effectiveness at an inopportune moment."

"Man ssstruck firsssst. Ssspoil ssscalesss of Crekkid," Crekkid justified himself. "Hisss fault, all hisss fault."

"No doubt. But I do not think he will repeat his error. Will you, young man?"

Relian did not answer the question directly. "You mentioned a mission?" he inquired. It hurt to speak. His voice was full of gravel.

"That is correct. Your memory is not of the most retentive, but perhaps you recall I have explained that certain elusive articles are essential to the completion of my great project?"

Relian nodded.

"I invite you to witness the progress of my Selves' development. Young man, you will approach the tubes and inspect the contents.''

Relian did so. Within their murky baths floated the three blobs, as repellently amorphous as ever.

''Look carefully. Do you note a tranformation in the aspect of these inchoate Keproses?''

Relian shook his head mutely, to spare his vocal cords.

''Observe closely. Surely you perceive a change?''

''No.''

''Correct. There is none.'' Keprose studied the tubes with an air of dissatisfaction. ''The days pass and my Selves remain as you see them. I tend them, I nourish them, I nurture them with supranormal devotion. Their needs are as my own, for they are I. Yet they do not progress, despite all my care. Something is lacking. An essence—a blood humor—a vital elixir—call it what you will. Suffice it to say that the substance I require enriches the blood of the Black Wingbane birds. It is hardly worth the trouble to describe the investigations that have led me to this conclusion. Such an explanation far exceeds the reach of your understanding. You need know only that I am dispatching you to the Forest of Miasm to secure me a living Wingbane. You will go today.''

Relian had braced himself for unpleasant news, but this was worse than anything he had imagined. His sore throat precluded prolonged reply, and he contented himself with a single terse observation. ''Infeasible.''

''Young man, you will spare me your feeble complaints, lamentations, arguments and pleas. I am not minded to listen and in any case, I have foreseen them all. Am I the Seigneur Keprose Gavyne for nothing? There is no contingency you can name for which I have not made provision. Attend.''

Keprose glided to the table on which lay several items that Relian had not seen there before. ''Doubtless you fear the poisonous character of the Miasm, as fear is the natural child of ignorance. It is not necessary to answer,'' the Seigneur forestalled his prisoner's rejoinder. ''I have already considered and mentally refuted all possible replies. Behold.'' The Seigneur displayed a pair of small flasks, one like a black pearl, the other opalescent. Beside the flasks stood a tiny stoppered vial. ''The dark flask contains a draught of my own devising, which will guard your internal parts against all poisonous vapors, corrosive liquids and noxious exhalations. The other contains an externally-applied balm that will similarly protect your outer skin. The vial contains eye drops which will theoretically preserve your vision. All three are brilliant in conception, flawless in execution, and as long as you carry them you need fear no poison. Alas that their efficacy is of a temporary and distinctly variable nature. But that need not concern you here and now. Say nothing,'' the Seigneur enjoined, as it appeared that Relian was about to speak.

Relian sighed and bent a gloomy stare upon the magical flasks.

"Here," Keprose continued, "is a large sack of durable construction. It will serve to contain and restrain a living, possibly demonstrative Wingbane. Yes, I am aware of the vicious nature of the adult Wingbane. You need hardly remind me, young man. Have the goodness to remain silent."

It was not easy, but Relian complied.

"Here are the means by which a bird may be lured and captured," Keprose went on. He displayed a mesh of silvery strands. "Observe if you will—a net of unusual properties, which by my reckoning should be fully resistant to the attack of Wingbane venom. It has never been tested, but I rarely miscalculate and never yet have erred beyond a single order of magnitude." The Seigneur dropped the net and picked up a small, greasy parcel. A disagreeable odor wafted to Relian's nostrils. "Here is the bait. It is well known that all Wingbanes share a fondness for decomposing meat. In view of that partiality, the discomfort involved in carrying the package is a minor price which you will cheerfully pay. And there you have it, young man—everything you could possible require to complete your task. As a master strategist, I have formulated a broad plan of attack. I leave the details of execution to you. But come, to work! Time is passing and you are doubtless eager to begin."

"A very dangerous mission," Relian replied. "What reason have I to perform it?"

"Perhaps Crekkid can answer that question more persuasively than I," Keprose suggested.

"No need. I'm already acquainted with Crekkid's eloquence. I'll do as you ask."

Keprose inclined his head in grave approval. "I am rejoiced."

"Shall I brave the Miasm alone, Seigneur?"

"Not at all. Crekkid accompanies you. You need not fear solitude!"

It was the answer Relian had hoped for. *None of the servants or nephews to watch me. This may be my chance,* he thought. *If I can only get back to town, then a blacksmith might be able to file or saw the snake off my neck. Once free of Crekkid and the Seigneur, I'll think of some way of getting Mereth out of here. Druveen's always desperate for money. I wonder if he could be bribed to help?*

Relians cogitations were interrupted by the mournful hisses of Crekkid. "Massster sssend Crekkid away? Away from Massster? Away from Nurbo?"

"Only temporarily," the Seigneur assured him. "You accompany our young guest here, you observe him on my behalf, you encourage him to diligence. At the successful conclusion of his venture, you return to Master, return to Nurbo."

"Kind Massster! Sssweet-ssshining Nurbo!"

"Correct, my devoted friend. And therefore you have every reason to speed our friend upon his journey."

"Yesss, Massster. Crekkid makesss him move very fassst. Fassst. Fassst. Come home sssoon."

Why is this necessary? Relian wondered. *Why send me into the Miasm, when he could so easily hire or else simply command the town Gatherers to bring him a live bird? Never mind, it gets me out of the fortress and after that—we'll see.*

His unvoiced questions were answered almost immediately. "The day is young," Keprose observed. "And your present procrastination is pointless. I suggest that you depart without further delay if you wish to reach the Miasm before noon. Do not travel by way of the Rising Road and do not approach Vale Jevaint. As you leave the fortress, turn sharply to your right and you will discover a path amongst the trees that will lead down the hills and across the fields by a circuitous route that skirts the town. Crekkid will provide guidance, should your sense of direction prove faulty. If you discover Bellowsmen on the fringes of the Miasm, take care they do not see you. Once within the forest, should you encounter any of the Gatherers, avoid their notice at any cost. In view of your activities, complete secrecy is desirable and extreme discretion essential."

"Why?" Relian inquired with a sense of foreboding.

"The townsfolk of Vale Jevaint are extraordinarily solicitous of the Black Wingbanes that are the source of all their prosperity. The birds are protected by the most stringent of laws. Captured poachers are blinded with Wingbane venom, stripped and shaven hairless, coated with pitch and black feathers, fitted with a false beak and crest. Thus adorned, they are exhibited in an iron cage for three days, at the end of which time they are torn apart with iron hooks. Upon decomposition, the fragmented corpse is fed to the Wingbanes. So zealous are the citizens in defense of their cherished birds that if you are caught, perhaps even I could not save you. To be frank, I should hesitate to intervene on your behalf.''

"And to think I used to be fond of birds," Relian croaked bleakly.

"And now you will wish to complete your preparations. The opalescent unguent should be applied lavishly over every inch of your body, including the scalp. I suggest that you withdraw to another room to do so. The unguent is efficacious but somewhat malodorous. I desire tranquillity at this time, and must not be troubled with offensive stimuli. Be certain you remove the other articles I have provided, particularly the package of rotting meat. Farewell, young man. I wish you the best of luck."

* * *

The morning sun was still low in the sky when the great gates parted to permit the departure of a solitary exile from Fortress Gavyne. A one-armed sentinel stationed discreetly among the pines perked up at the sight and his air of boredom vanished. Glench raised a spyglass to his eye and studied the emerging figure. He beheld a somewhat gaunt young man, pale of face and melancholy of aspect. The gentleman's attire was plain, but a silver band or collar glinted at his throat. He carried a cloth bundle of some kind. The hands were white and strikingly elongated, exactly as Scrivvulch had described. It was beyond question the man he sought. Glench turned and struck off at his best speed toward Vale Jevaint and the Bearded Moon Tavern. His step was light and he whistled as he went, for at last he felt that he was truly earning his ten pytes a day.

Relian heard the great portal crash shut behind him and instantly, with the instinct of an escaping prisoner, darted across the clearing toward the break in the stand of pines that marked the end of the Rising Road and the shortest route to

Vale Jevaint. He had taken no more than a few long paces
before the steel necklace tightened and the shrill voice hissed
in his ear.

"Wrong way. Ssstupid," Crekkid observed. "Ssseigneur
sssay turn right. Turn right. Right. Right. Right. Right."

Relian slowed to a halt. "The Seigneur doesn't care which
route I take as long as I reach the Miasm," he replied
reasonably.

Crekkid was not to be deceived. "You do what Ssseigneur
sssay. Ssseigneur sssay, turn right. Right. Now. Now. Now.
Now." Relian hesitated and predictably, the serpent nipped
him.

Argument with Crekkid was wasted effort. Suppressing his
frustration, Relian turned and located the path that Keprose
had described. It was a narrow, very infrequently used trail,
overgrown with weeds and half choked with brambles. The
slope was steep and the path was rocky but Relian, preoccupied with various dark concerns, scarcely noticed. His hopes
of reaching the town and there obtaining assistance had already been thwarted. Humiliating though it was to find himself at the mercy of so tiny and dull-witted a being as Crekkid,
there was no denying that such was his position. To be
controlled—derided—mastered by a creature at once trivial
and detestable was not to be borne. And yet—what help for
it? What defense against a moronic living collar capable of
choking the life out of him within seconds if it so desired?
Now the combined will of his incubus and its unspeakable
master forced him along a path that led to a poisoned forest
and a perilously illegal errand. If he failed in his mission, he
would probably not survive. If he succeeded, he might expect
more of the same, at the Seigneur's pleasure.

Slavery, pure and simple, Relian thought. *Keprose might
just as well have purchased me upon an auction block. If I
don't manage to escape, I may spend the rest of my natural
life in this condition. No—if it comes to that, I'll find a way of
killing Keprose. I'd die as well, of course, but it would be
worthwhile, if only to prevent him from enslaving anyone
else. And who knows—with Keprose gone, maybe the others
would let Mereth go. Go where, though?* And then the rational voice inside his head that so often preserved him from
major blunders spoke up. *Don't get carried away. There's
surely a way of freeing yourself and Mereth without losing
your life in the process. Keep thinking and it will come to you.*

So absorbing was Relian's introspection that he failed to note the large exposed root that snaked across the path in front of him. He stumbled and staggered several paces before regaining his balance.

"Ssstupid. Clumsssy. Clumsssy. Blind. Carelessss. You break leg and then how ssshall Crekkid return to Nurbo? Clumsssy. Ssstupid. Ssstupid. Ssstupid."

Relian paused on the trail. He had hiked some distance and his progress was marked by a new scent carried on the breeze. It was the distinctive, corrosive odor of the Forest of Miasm that smoldered in his nostrils and throat. His eyes watered and Relian started to rub the moisture away, then remembered that his hand was covered with the Seigneur's sticky unguent, as indeed was every inch of his body. His garments clung to his limbs and strands of hair had glued themselves to his forehead and the nape of his neck. The sensations were unpleasant, but presumably he was safe from the noxious Miasmic exhalations. And his eyes? Keprose placed great confidence in the efficacy of the drops he had provided—in which case, what accounted for the irritation and blurring? Loss of vision loomed as a hideous possibility. Relian recalled the effect of Bewbigo's Final Shadow—remembered his own fear and helplessness. Once again he pondered. Surely the Miasm might be avoided? If only Crekkid could be dislodged, or at least influenced—

"Move forward. Move forward." The serpent's shrill commands assaulted his victim's ears. "Lazy. Ssslow. Ssstupid. Move fassster. Fassster. Fassster. Fassster."

A bitter reply sprang to Relian's lips but he repressed it and resumed walking. His mind whirred. After a moment he spoke in reasonable tones. "See here, Crekkid—"

"Move. Move. Move. Move."

"You'd like me to complete my errand quickly, wouldn't you? Then you may return to Fortress Gavyne, to your kind master and your fair Nurbo."

"Yessss. Yessss. Kind Massster. Sssweet Nurbo. Sssteel-ssshining Nurbo. Nurbo. Nurbo. You move fassster."

Relian diplomatically complied. "But even when you are home again, you won't truly be united with your beloved," he pointed out.

"Crekkid sssee Nurbo. Crekkid ssspeak to Nurbo."

"Yes, but that's all. Crekkid will not truly *be* with Nurbo. Sad circumstances separate the two of you."

"Alasss. Sssad circumssstancesss. Sssad. Sssad. Sssad."

"And there's no reason for it," Relian suggested seductively. "No reason at all."

"The Ssseigneur willsss it and ssso it mussst be. For now. Alasss."

"No doubt the Seigneur is well intentioned, but he doesn't understand affairs of the heart. You shouldn't be parted from your beloved. It's not healthy for you or for Nurbo. She will pine for you. She will grow sick and die."

"Nurbo sssick? Nurbo die?"

"She will die for love if you remain apart. It has begun already. Her eyes have lost their luster and her tongue is flecked with rust."

"Russst? Fair Nurbo russst? Russst? Russst?"

"I assure you. She will die if you are not united, die of a broken heart. Female serpents are such fragile creatures."

"Sssssssssss! Nurbo!"

"There will be," Relian pointed out delicately, "no little ones. No sons."

"No Patriarch Crekkid?"

"None."

"Sssssssss!" Crekkid hissed and writhed in distress. "Nurbo mussst not die! Ssso young! Ssso beautiful!"

"A tragedy indeed, but not unavoidable. Crekkid and Nurbo must be united."

"Sssome day. Sssome day."

"You can't afford to wait. Nurbo needs you now, Crekkid. Without you she will die. It is up to you to rescue your beloved."

"Yesss. Yesss. Ssshe ssshall join Crekkid upon your neck."

"No, that isn't the way. Keprose will never agree. There's only one solution. Crekkid and Nurbo must flee the fortress together. In the depths of the forest, far from the sight of Man, Crekkid and Nurbo will live together in endless bliss."

"Blissss! Blissss! Blissss! Blisssssssssssssss!"

For a time Relian walked on in silence. Crekkid, apparently engaged in deep thought, hissed softly to himself. The trees were thinning out. Relian knew he would soon emerge from the woods to follow the trail down the sloping Miasmic Girdle, that desolate stretch of terrritory devoid of all but the hardiest of scrub vegetation that ringed the poisoned forest. Beyond it—the Miasm, possible blindness and death. "Well, shall your lady be rescued?" he inquired with false indifference.

"Quessstionsss. Quessstionsss. All isss unclear," replied Crekkid. "Ssshall Nurbo and Crekkid desssssert the kind Massster? Perhapsss you lie. Perhapsss Nurbo doesss not die."

"You'll see, but then it will be too late."

"Yesss. We ssshall sssee. Firssst you obey Ssseigneur'sss commandsss. Then return to fortresssss and we ssshall sssee."

"We must return now, and in secret."

"No. Foresssst firssst. Foresssst. You move. Go fasssst, return fasssst. Return to Nurbo. Fasssst. Fasssst. Fasssst."

"Don't you see, there's no time—"

"Move! You move! Now!" Crekkid, highly agitated, scored double puncture wounds in Relian's shoulder. The young man winced. "Go fasssst, return fasssst!" The serpent struck again and again.

Relian, his neck bloody, reluctantly quickened his pace and all too soon emerged from the shelter of the pines to find himself out upon the grim Miasmic Girdle. Here, amidst the stunted bushes with their glum brown leaves and the low, hardy weeds, the view was relatively unobstructed. Down below and off to one side, Relian could see the town of Vale Jevaint with its myriad domes and pennants. Straight ahead, at the foot of the cheerless slope rose the Forest of Miasm in all its menace. Beyond the forest loomed the ice-clad Bhorphins. It was Relian's first clear view of the Miasm, and the sight was not encouraging. The trees, tall and close-set, were covered with foliage that appeared black at a distance. Only a few of the topmost branches reflected red highlights. The dark tree trunks merged almost invisibly into dense shadow. Clots of brambles and groundcover appeared to block ingress. Above all hung the heavy, reddish cloud—the ghastly miasm that had lent the forest its name. A breeze fought free of the woods and Relian gagged on Miasmic exhalations. The stench was vile, suggestive of decay and corruption overlaid with chemical mordancy. A great midnight form sailed through the sanguinary mists overhead and he recognized the crest and hooked beak of a Wingbane. The creature's wingspan was huge, its aspect predatory and its ferocity legendary. As Relian watched, the bird vanished into the black heart of the Miasm.

"Go forward. Move. Move. Move. Move."

He hadn't realized that he had paused. A nip on the earlobe recalled him to his purpose. He advanced unwillingly.

"Good sssmell." Crekkid's wire tongue flickered appreciatively. "Good foressst. Good. Go forward. Fassst. Fassst."

Relian eyed the Miasm with extreme misgiving and his steps lagged. His gaze raked the Girdle in search of last-minute salvation, and as he watched, a small boat-shaped caravan emerged from the woods not far away. The distinctive shape and coloration signaled Turo ownership—for the wandering tribes of Turos that thieved and swindled their way across the face of every land claimed a seafaring origin, and the traditional boat-shape of their caravans was symbolic of an allegedly glorious past. This particular caravan was new and gaudy; brave with purple paint, rich in gilded curlicues, and drawn by a dappled cob. The figurehead was a carved dolphin from whose snout depended an iron cauldron. Blazoned along the side of the vehicle was a legend, HUNAK THE POT SURGEON. On the basis of the words and figurehead, it seemed safe to assume that Hunak was a tinker, doubtless come to ply his trade in Vale Jevaint. Tinkers always carried a variety of tools.

Relian ran to intercept the caravan.

"Wrong way," Crekkid complained, and his coils tightened fretfully.

Relian paid no heed. As he neared the caravan he spied the driver, a swarthy Turo possessed of a luxuriant moustache, oiled black curls and a gold-buttoned waistcoat the colors of a summer sunset. Evidently Hunak's trade prospered.

"Stop," Relian called and Hunak pulled up, his dark face a study in surprise. "Do you carry tools?"

"I never thought to meet a fellow mortal out upon the Girdle." Hunak's Turo accent lent his tones exotic flavor. "Not a Gatherer are you, young sir?"

"No. Have you any tools?" Relian repeated. At his throat the steel coils flexed restlessly.

If Hunak noted the other's discomfort he gave no sign. His expression was bland as he replied, "That I do, young sir. Have a pot that wants mending, do you?"

"Do you have pincers? A file or hacksaw?"

"I have them all."

A warning hiss escaped Crekkid.

"I need use of the tools and your assistance, Master Hunak."

"That's a fact?" The Turo's philanthropic instincts did not seem well developed.

"I'll pay you for them."

"Yes?"

"Wassste time. Wassste time. Wassste time," Crekkid accused.

Hunak eyed the snake with interest. "Talking automaton?" he inquired. "Best I've ever seen."

"Something like that. I'll pay you a Travornish ten-berverner piece for your help," Relian offered, and ended with a gasp as Crekkid pinched his earlobe.

"Something wrong with the automaton?" Hunak inquired.

"A little out of adjustment. Do you accept my offer?"

"Well now, this matter wants consideration, young sir."

"To foressst. Go. Go. Go. Go." Crekkid bit and a drop of blood appeared on Relian's jaw.

"Twenty berverners." Relian gritted his teeth. "But hurry."

"No sense in rushing into things, young sir."

"Move. Move. Move. Move." Crekkid squeezed significantly and Relian's face tightened.

Hunak did not bother to disguise his curiosity. "Having a problem with the automaton, young sir? Pity. You ought to have it mended, it's worth something. A fine piece of work like that would fetch a good price in Neraunce, where the Dhreve collects such novelties."

"I'll give him to you," Relian suggested, "if you can get him off my neck. Twenty berverners and the snake."

"A bargain, young sir. A bargain firm and sealed. One moment while I find my tools." Hunak disappeared into the back of the caravan.

"Sssssssssss! What do you do?"

"Nothing. Nothing at all."

"Why do we wassste time here? Go fassst, return fassst. Return to Massster, return to Nurbo. You go."

"Soon. Very soon."

"Now! Now! Now! Now!"

Hunak reappeared. Pincers and a file in hand, he jumped down from the caravan. "We'll set you to rights in a wink, young sir." He eyed the bloody marks upon his companion's throat. "But first, my twenty-five berverners. That's the twenty we agreed upon plus the special service fee for use of my new Zylstooth file."

There seemed nothing extraordinary about the file, but it was not the time to argue. Relian paid without comment.

"Enough time. No more talk." Crekkid struck and a grunt of pain escaped his victim.

"A *fine* piece of work," Hunak observed, and deftly clamped the pincers down on Crekkid's head.

Crekkid hissed in rage and agony. He thrashed and his coils clenched spasmodically. Relian choked and tottered.

"Easy, now." Hunak pried Crekkid's head and several inches of his slender length away from Relian's throat. The hissing increased in volume and bitterness. The coils tightened murderously, but unnatural extension had weakened the force of the serpent's grip.

"Stubborn little devil," Hunak observed admiringly. "I can hardly get it loose. Must be the best gears, the strongest springs. That's quality."

Deprived of speech, Relian could offer no advice, but Hunak seemed able to deal with the problem. The Turo tightened his grip on the pincers and applied the file. Zylsteeth bit into steel scales and Crekkid's contortions waxed hysterical. Hisses gave way to whistling woeful shrieks. Shining scales sprinkled the ground and a gash opened in Crekkid's neck. Thick, yellow fluid oozed out.

"That's a very odd sort of oil." The file slipped and steel scrapings flew. Hunak shook his head in regret. "A shame to mar the surface. Well, no matter. I'll shine it up as good as new before I present it to the quality."

Relian could feel the coils loosen. As Hunak continued to file, the serpent weakened. Air was finding its way into Relian's lungs and deliverance seemed but moments away. He was almost on the verge of permitting his spirits to rise when distant movement caught his eye. A figure on horseback approached from the direction of Vale Jevaint. As Relian watched, the rider caught sight of the caravan, clapped heels to his mount and came on at a gallop. There was something familiar about the figure with its gaunt, long limbs and awkward posture, suggestive of a scarecrow come to life. Recognition came all too quickly. It was the assassin Scrivvulch, and how he had discovered his quarry's whereabouts was not apparent. Relian automatically recoiled.

"Hold still, young sir," Hunak admonished. "This must be done with care if I'm to avoid destroying the little automaton."

"Destroy him by all means," Relian attempted to reply, but no words came out. Crekkid had been weakened but not conquered, and his resistance was apt to continue for some time to come. "Faster!" Relian implored, but produced only inarticulate mumbles.

"Softly now, softly," Hunak coaxed the serpent of his desires. "Come to me, my beauty, and you will adorn the palace of a Dhreve." Crekkid's answering hiss was vicious.

Scrivvulch sped on. The details of his costume were now discernible—brown suit, white cravat, ebony walking stick clasped in one hand and occasionally employed as a crop. Relian's recollections of the walking stick were vivid. He took a step backward but was brought up short by Hunak's grasp on Crekkid's head.

"Another moment," Hunak muttered and twisted the pincers sharply. Crekkid shrieked but retained his hold.

Relian's gestures conveyed desperation and Hunak finally took note of the approaching horseman. "An enemy? The law?" he inquired sharply.

Relian nodded and Hunak instantly released him. "Go, young sir," he advised. "I wish you good fortune. Come back to me when you're clear and we'll deal again. I've a mind to acquire the little automaton and will offer excellent terms."

Crekkid vented a hiss of pain and loathing, which the Turo ignored.

"Weapon," Relian requested painfully. "Pistol. Sword. Anything."

"Alas, young sir, I'm a simple, honest pot-surgeon, nothing more. It isn't for the likes of me to carry a weapon," Hunak responded unconvincingly. Evidently the traditional Turo sympathy for the outlaw was subject to limitation. "I've nothing to sell you, unless you can make use of a skillet—iron, of unusually good weight—which I am willing to sacrifice for the sum of thirty Travornish berverners."

Relian shook his head wordlessly, cast an alarmed glance at his rapidly-approaching enemy, and took to his heels.

"Good luck, young sir," Hunak called. "Guard the automaton. It will make our fortunes!"

"Ssstupid. Ssstupid," Crekkid hissed in low and deadly tones. "Ssstupid. Bad. Liar. Falsssse. Traitor. Sssneak. Cheat. Cheat. Cheat. If not for Massster, Crekkid kill you."

"If that man on horseback catches up with us, you won't need to kill me," Relian answered as he ran. "He'll do it for you."

"Good. Good. Ssserve you right."

Relian fled, wondering how an unarmed man on foot might evade a mounted pursuer. In open country, it couldn't be done. He needed cover, immediately. His eyes turned to the pinewoods from which he had lately emerged. The trees were spaced widely, offering scant refuge. Before him lay the poisoned forest, with its dense mists and inky shadows. There Scrivvulch could not follow and there lay the only hope of escape—provided the protective unguents of Keprose Gavyne proved trustworthy. Relian looked back. The distance between himself and Scrivvulch had narrowed. The Assassin galloped apace and now the mild, intelligent countenance, the downy hair waving in the wind, the silver tip of the ebony stick were all discernible. Relian lengthened his strides and behind him heard a voice uplifted in treacherous appeal.

"Do not flee, Master Kru. I mean you no harm!"

Barren earth and rock beneath his feet. This stretch of the Girdle was entirely devoid of life. But not far ahead sprouted clumps of low groundcover—virulent weeds bearing leaves of dull maroon marked with livid blotches. The vegetation was unmistakably poisonous, thus marking the extreme verge of the Miasm. Relian's instincts bade him halt, and his steps faltered a little. Behind him came the beat of galloping hooves and he glanced over his shoulder to behold Scrivvulch the Stick but a few short yards behind.

"You must stop, Master Kru," Scrivvulch called out amiably. "You have no choice. Flight into the Miasm is impossible."

Relian's pace picked up. He was in the midst of the motley maroon tufts and he crushed their leaves in passing. A vile stench arose. Tendrils of owl-colored vapor drifted from the ruined leaves to snatch at his flying ankles. There were grasses about him now, gunmetal spikes with veining pale as lightning, and green-brown shoots dewed with venom. A few paces ahead the wall of trees rose abrupt as a precipice, and toward that sinister shelter Relian directed his flight. Behind him sounded a frantic whinny and once again he chanced a backward glance. Terrified by the scent of the Miasm, Scrivvulch's horse had balked. Now the animal bucked and plunged wildly. Neither the blows nor the blandishments of its rider could induce it to advance another step. Relian wasted no more time, but turned his face to the Miasm, covered the last few yards of the Girdle in a few long paces and disappeared among the trees. He did not turn back again and did not note his pursuer's expression of undisguised amazement.

Scrivvulch sprang awkwardly to the ground, grasped his

horse's bridle and attempted to lead the animal forward. The horse laid its ears flat and reared, hooves pawing the air. Scrivvulch ducked, peered into the shadows that had swallowed his quarry, reluctantly loosed the reins and ran for the trees. He had not advanced a dozen yards before the noxious fumes forced him to a halt. The Assassin was seized with a fit of coughing. His eyes stung and watered profusely. He withdrew a handkerchief from his breast pocket, rubbed his eyes and applied the cambric protectively across his mouth and nose before resuming his advance. Burning vapors and acrid fumes impeded him. When his vision blurred and dizziness assailed him, Scrivvulch was forced to admit failure. He retreated, reclaimed the horse, and stood contemplating the poisoned forest until comprehension dawned and he spoke aloud to his trembling mount. "The Seigneur Keprose Gavyne has fortified him in some manner. The Seigneur's abilities have not been exaggerated. No matter, there are other ways."

Scrivvulch remounted and rode away from the forest. The horse trotted unsteadily, affected no less than its rider by the poisonous fumes. Scrivvulch guided the confused creature along the outer edge of the Girdle, over the crest of a small rise, down the slope and across the barren fields, always keeping as much distance as possible between himself and the Miasm. Soon he spied what he sought and kicked his horse to a wobbly canter. Scrivvulch was in a position to understand the animal's distress. His own flesh stung and itched. Glancing down at the hands that grasped the reins, he saw that they were red and slightly swollen. His face was heated as if with sunburn, and he could feel the swelling of tiny blisters around his lips and nostrils. He shook his head in bemusement.

Not far ahead, the ground dipped to a saucer-shaped depression whose sloping sides, built up with bulwarks of earth and stone, offered a modicum of protection from the punishing breath of the Miasm. It was here, where the roads from Vale Jevaint ended, that a group of Bellowsmen labored. There were ten or twelve of them assembled to operate a couple of the bellows used to supply air to the Gatherers at work in the forest. The huge contraptions pumped rhythmically, like immense leathern lungs. From the nozzle of each extended a number of long, flexible tubes of stout canvas coated with tar. The tubes ran along the ground over hillock and hollow, to vanish at last amongst the forest shadows. Each bellows was capable of supplying air simultaneously to several Gatherers; a sensible design, for Gatherers customarily foraged in groups, or at the very least in pairs. Despite all precautions, the mortality rate among them was high.

The Bellowsmen and their apprentices presented an odd spectacle. Unlike the Gatherers, they did not wear the cumbersome padded suit, so restrictive of movement; nor did they suffer the oppressive weight of the gilded steel helmet. The golden headgear, deplored by some as a mark of professional arrogance, was in fact valued for the sake of its unusual resistance to corrosive exhalations and its consequent longevity. A gilded helmet was ultimately the most economical, and it was paradoxically axiomatic among the Gatherers that gold was far cheaper than iron. The Bellowsmen, who did not actually venture into the Miasm itself, were attired in heavy suits of dust-gray canvas, leather boots and gauntlets. Flapped caps protected their heads and necks. Most of them wore canvas vizards with domed eyepieces of glass. The identical suits, concealed features and gleaming convex eyes lent the Bellowsmen an insectile air. Incessant industry strengthened the illusion. The bellows did not cease pumping as Scrivvulch brought his horse to the edge of the depression, stopped there and declared ringingly, "News, gentlemen! Urgent news!"

Blank glass eyes goggled up at him, but the Bellowsmen pumped on. So perfect was their discipline that the rhythm of activity did not fluctuate in the slightest, even as Scrivvulch announced, "Gentlemen, your Wingbanes are in mortal danger. A poacher stalks the Miasm and the Wingbane is his prey. I trust you will deal with him as the law dictates. Justice demands no less!"

*   *   *

The Miasm was appropriately dark. The trees were lofty and close-set. The light that managed to find its way through the branches was dulled and reddened by the ubiquitous mists. The forest floor was crowded with vegetation of the most spectacular and ominous description. Here a carnivorous shrub presented its hinged, fanged flowers tinted the pale beige of human flesh. A collection of transparent, veined wings scattered about the base of the bush—all that remained of a variety of blood-sucking insects—bore mute testimony to the power of the illusion. Here were tall stalks crowned with black-brown pods from which the pointed, hardened seeds occasionally shot with the speed and force of bullets. Here were silvery, liver-blotched vines sinking their vampiric tendrils into the stems of the neighboring succulents. Here were sulfur-yellow shoots alive and writhing with hundreds of voracious caterpillars, gathered there to imbibe the vitriolic sap. Here were low bushes with outlines softened and all but obscured by thick excretions of translucent jellied slime. And here was a garden of fungi. Everywhere the fungi throve—scores of different species, hundreds of shapes and colors. Most conspicuous were the earthen puffballs from which the spores drifted in corrosive black clouds; and the huge Deathshead toadstools, each the approximate size, shape and color of a bleached human skull. Most of the vegetation had never been named or catalogued. The Miasm would have represented a dream come true for any naturalist possessed of iron lungs and steel flesh, but for Relian it was a nightmare. Venomous plant life, no matter how exotic, held little appeal; and the stink was appalling. All very well to trust in the unguents of Keprose Gavyne. In the end, there had been little choice. But each draught of the vile atmosphere clawed at his lungs, and Relian sensed that only the flimsiest of barriers stood between himself and the terrors of the Miasm.

He looked back the way he had come. In this place, the feet of men had worn no trails. He had broken his own path as he walked, and his passage was marked by swaying branches, crushed blossoms and bruised fungi. The poison dripped like nectar from torn flowers. The stench of the toadstools was overpowering. Relian choked and wondered for the thousandth time how long his lungs could withstand the assault. There was no sign of pursuit. Scrivvulch the Stick had been foiled for the moment and all appeared deceptively calm. Then the poisoned tranquillity was broken by a sudden scream. A huge black form sailed through the mists overhead and Relian instinctively ducked. It was a Wingbane, whose presence recalled Crekkid to their purpose.

"Catch bird," the serpent commanded. "Why do you ssstand here? Lazy. Catch bird. Bird. Bird. Bird."

"As easily as that, eh? Did you see the size of that thing?"

"Coward, you fear bird?"

"With good reason. You should fear it too. If it spots us, that Wingbane could snap you up like a worm."

"Ssssssss! Never. Never. Crekkid sssteel ssserpent. Ssspecial. Ssspecial. Patriarch Crekkid."

"Perhaps." Relian noted with regret that Crekkid's spirit remained undampened, despite the recent battering at the hands of the Turo tinker. That the serpent had neither forgotten nor forgiven the incident, however, was unpleasantly apparent.

"Maybe you die here," Crekkid suggested with reptilian relish. "Poisssoned. Choked. Sssmothered. Finissshed. Dead. Dead. Dead. Dead."

"That's not what the Seigneur would want," Relian replied. "In any case, if I should die here, how will Crekkid return to Nurbo?"

"Crekkid go home. Ssserpent ssstrong, sssmart, ssswift. Sssteel ssserpent fearsss no poissson. Not like man, with sssoft, weak flesssh. Ssstupid. Weak flesssh. You die here, Crekkid laugh."

"I don't intend to die here."

"You die, the Ssseigneur laugh. Nurbo laugh alssso. Laugh. Laugh. Laugh!"

"Crekkid will not laugh if Relian gets hold of a file and pincers."

"You think?" Crekkid administered a warning squeeze. "Ssstupid. Ssstupid. Now you get bird. You get bird, maybe Massster needsss you no more. Massster sssay, 'Crekkid my friend, you do what you like.' And then what happensss? You guessss. Guessss. Guessss. Guesssssssssssssss."

Relian spoke no more and was silent for some time to come. Deeper and deeper into the Miasm he walked and as he went the red mists thickened, the light dimmed and the vegetation waxed in profusion and toxicity. The air was worse than ever—heavy and unbreathably foul. Relian's lungs ached with it. Despite the protection of Keprose's supranormal concoctions, he found himself prey to lassitude, pessimism and a certain odd confusion. He shook his head and his thoughts cleared, but unnatural fatigue still weighted his limbs. *Something's wrong.* The warning buzzed almost inaudibly in his mind. It occurred to him that the ground was uncommonly soft and inviting. A Deathshead toadstool would pillow his head in comfort. It would be good to rest, to recline and close his eyes, if only for a moment. He pushed such thoughts away, sternly. "Later."

"You sssay?"

He hadn't realized he had spoken aloud. "Nothing."

"Too slow. Move fassster. Fassster. Fassster."

For once Relian was in agreement. He nodded and quickened his pace. Deep into the forest now, past the noisome pools with their iridescent water-walkers and phosphorescent frogs; past the fallen trees encrusted with bracket fungi; along the bank of a red-tinged stream, domain of dark crustaceans armed with fighting claws and poison sacs; past communal nests where the needle-toothed, bright-scaled birds deposited their leathery eggs; and through a treacherous hollow where groundcover masked the patches of sucking mud.

On the far side of the hollow Relian thought he caught a wink of gold. He approached and discovered the gilded helmet of a Gatherer lying empty in the muck. He picked up the helmet and inspected it, wondering at its presence. What had become of the owner? The question was answered promptly. A few yards distant the Deathshead toadstools flourished. Among them lay the remains of a Gatherer. The man had rested there long enough for the corrosives of the Miasm to eat away most of his padded suit and all of his flesh. All that remained was a skeleton, with a skull almost indistinguishable from the surrounding fungi. He must have lost his companions, else his corpse would have been carried back to Vale Jevaint. Most likely he had fallen victim to the Miasmic Madness, under whose influence he had torn the air hose from his helmet and wandered aimlessly until overcome by the vapors. The Madness prompted men to varied acts of self-destruction. Relian considered his own impulse to rest, to sleep, and wondered.

The search continued amongst skeletal trees clothed in blue-green crystals. Relian saw no sign of a Wingbane colony and had no idea where to look. Time was passing and the power of Keprose's unguents was transitory. Already the Miasm exerted its baleful effects. He glanced down at his sleeve, now powdered with fine dust. He brushed the dust away and uncovered frayed spots that had not been there before. If the fabric was eaten away, what might be happening to his skin? He examined his bare hands. They were still safe beneath their greasy protective coating, but the unguent itself had changed color slightly. It was darker, as if it had absorbed poison from the surrounding atmosphere.

Where to go? His eyes searched the treetops, almost lost in the mists. No Wingbane in evidence. He paused to listen. For a time he heard nothing but the characteristic sounds of the Miasm: poisonous breezes sighing through venomous vegetation; the splash of lethal waters; a few birdcalls, the drone of insects, unidentifiable rustlings and scurryings. As he listened, the intolerable weariness stole over him again, his vision swam and he swayed on his feet. He knuckled his eyes. The lids seemed weighted and he could not hold them open.

He stood amidst exquisitely deadly ferns that would have gladdened the heart of Master Moon, and it came to him that ferns so sweetly scented would provide the loveliest of beds. His head was bowed and his eyes closed, but in his mind's eye he beheld himself at rest upon the perfumed greenery. The image was irresistibly alluring. Slowly his knees began to buckle. He might actually have lost consciousness then, had not a whiff of aromatic smoke jolted him back to alertness. Something was burning and it could scarcely be a campfire. Drowsiness fled and Relian was wide awake again. He tried to envision the consequences of a fire in the Miasm—the consumption of a vast tract of poisonous growths would release a cloud of toxic smoke that might render Vale Jevaint uninhabitable—might even rise as high as the towers of Fortress Gavyne itself.

Fire implied the presence of humanity. Relian recalled the fate of captured poachers and opted for discretion. Cautiously he stole through the forest, creeping with care from tree to tree. His search ended when he came upon a band of Gatherers. Relian stationed himself behind a slime-coated bole and settled down to watch.

There were four of them—outlandish figures in their padded suits, gilded helmets and trailing airhoses. They had paused at the foot of a tree in whose branches a ragged Wingbane nest was visible. A wooden-runged rope ladder had been affixed to one of the lower limbs and now a Gatherer was halfway up. His airhose dangled and one of his comrades performed the vital manipulations that held the line clear of ladder and branches.

A fire blazed on the ground at the foot of the tree. This fire, source of the smoke that had attracted Relian, was tended by the third Gatherer. The density, whiteness and pungency of the smoke implied an unusual fuel, but Relian paid little heed. His attention was focused on the bowl of boiling liquid that sat on a tripod above the flames. An object swam in the bowl. It was a dismembered hand and it appeared to be alive. As Relian watched in fascination, the hand splashed and cavorted. Its flesh and long nails were intact, and its hyperdigitation was very evident. Steam from the bowl, mixed with smoke from the fire ascended to bathe the branches in vapor. Upon a low branch perched a Black Wingbane, doubtless proprietress of the endangered nest. The bird sat motionless, her glazed golden eyes fixed on the swimming hand. She was larger than an eagle and her claws were like scimitars. She should have proved vicious in defense of her eggs, but seemed sunk in a torpor and entirely unconscious of the human raiders. The ascending Gatherer had reached the level of the Wingbane's perch and still the bird's eyes did not leave the hand.

The fourth and last member of the group carried a light fowling piece. The gun was trained steadily on the immobile Wingbane, as if to guard against the sudden lapse of the bird's passivity. Certainly the Gatherers would hesitate to destroy the potential source of countless eggs. Should the creature emerge from her trance, however, such destruction was often the sole preservation of men's lives.

The Gatherers worked efficiently, despite the clumsy suits. As Relian looked on the man in the tree reached the nest, removed the eggs, stowed them in his basket and descended. The fire was extinguished, the ladder taken down and coiled, the tripod folded. Once removed from its boiling bath, the hand continued to hop and wriggle. Finally it managed to leap from the grasp of its Gatherer-attendant. It landed on the ground, raised itself on fingers and thumb, and scuttled crablike for the underbrush. An agile Gatherer set his foot upon the fleeing wrist. The hand was recaptured and rubbed down with absorbent towels. As the moisture dried on its skin, the member gradually lost its vitality. The flesh shriveled, the fingers curled and the hand clenched itself into a fist, whereupon it was placed in a small iron-bound casket. This done, the four men departed in silence, leaving behind them a despoiled nest, a circle of scorched earth and a tranquilized Wingbane. The operation had been conducted with remarkable dispatch.

Relian gazed at the Wingbane where she hunched, motionless and apparently oblivious. He need only climb the tree, net and bag the helpless bird, then depart the perilous Miasm forever. Never again would so perfect an opportunity present itself. By the time the Wingbane regained consciousness, she would be halfway to Fortress Gavyne. Relian still carried the

sack supplied by Keprose Gavyne. Now he extracted the
metallic net, shook out its shining length and folded it over
his arm. The net was amazingly flexible in view of its substantiality. It resembled the lightest and tiniest of chain mail,
with a border of heavier rings and small lead weights at the
four corners. It should prove easy to manipulate but strong
enough to restrain a powerful captive. The parcel of decaying
meat intended for use as bait could be discarded, and Relian
thankfully did so. There would be no use for it now. He
advanced to the tree and began to climb. The trunk was of
moderate girth, affording no particular difficulty. The bird sat
among the lowest, most accessible branches. The task was
proving unexpectedly easy.

Relian ascended nimbly and his hopes did likewise. So
favorable did the situation appear that sudden misfortune for
once took him by surprise. The tree in which the Wingbane
roosted was of a shaggy, loose-barked species. The slightest
pressure upon the trunk served to dislodge a hedgehog's
arsenal of needle-sharp splinters. Relian's clothes were full of
them, which he had not yet noticed. Now he ran his hand up
the trunk at an unlucky angle and a long splinter drove like a
dagger into the fleshy part of his palm. He gasped and the
Wingbane stirred at the sound. Her eyes blinked. The great
black wings lifted, spread for an instant, furled again. Relian
froze, gazing up at his quarry. The bird had already relapsed
into her stupor, but still he remained motionless. He was
close enough now to observe details that had previously
escaped his notice: the drops of venom that hung like beads of
amber upon the terrible hooked beak; the bulges at the base
of the neck that marked the location of the poison glands; the
blue highlights on intensely black feathers. Observed at close
range, the Wingbane was daunting indeed. Relian raised his
hand to his mouth, absently licked and then bit the palm. He
became aware of his own actions, looked down and saw the
splinter embedded in his skin. The swollen, bright red flesh
itched furiously. So much for Keprose's guarantee of immu-
nity to Miasmic poison.

Relian resumed his ascent. Fearful of rousing the Wingbane,
he proceeded with extreme care, but his luck was characteris-
tically bad. A great curve of loose bark suddenly gave way
beneath him and Relian felt himself slipping. He tightened his
grip on the trunk, and hundreds of splinters stabbed his arms,
legs and chest. The startling pain loosened his hold and he

slid down another few feet before stopping himself. Friction drove the splinters deeper, and an involuntary exclamation escaped him.

The Wingbane's eyes blinked like signal-lanterns.

"Ssstupid," Crekkid observed. "Clumsssy. Fall out of tree. Ssstupid."

"Be quiet."

"Are you Massster, that you ssspeak thusss to Patriarch Crekkid? Clumsssy. Fall out of tree. Ssstupid. Ssstupid. Ssstupid. Ssstupid."

Relian did not reply, but his caution was pointless—the Wingbane was already awake. Her head twisted from side to side once or twice, her beak clacked and the midnight pinions fluttered.

"You wake bird," Crekkid accused brazenly.

The Wingbane eyed Relian and uttered a hoarse cry of warning. Her wings spread, she launched herself into the air and described an arc that lifted her to the despoiled nest. The next instant a shriek of avian agony tore through the Miasm. The Wingbane, eyes aflame and dripping beak extended, descended like a dark incarnation of misdirected maternal vengeance. Relian automatically threw up an arm to shield his eyes and the beak slashed through the fabric of his coat and into the flesh beneath, while the great wings battered his head. For a moment he was blinded and enveloped. His hold on the tree loosened and the next blow sent him plunging to the ground. He landed heavily on his back and the shock jarred every bone. The Wingbane followed. Relian jerked aside and she swept past, the wicked talons missing his face by a hair. He scrambled to his feet, breathing heavily. The bird screeched, circled high and swooped for him. He swung the weighted net and beat the furious creature aside. She was back again in a moment. He swung at her and missed. Then she was upon him and her beak tore a gash in his scalp. Relian fell back and the Wingbane flew at his face. His arms were raised to shield himself, and instantly the sleeves were in rags and the skin was laced with poisoned cuts. Her beak stabbed and ripped across his upraised wrist. Relian grabbed blindly and obtained an uncertain hold on her leg. The bird screamed furiously and slammed her wing against his temple, knocking him sideways. Her beak knifed at his throat and he heard a metallic click and a hiss as she encountered Crekkid. Another sledgehammer blow to the head sent him reeling. The

Wingbane wrenched herself free and mounted aloft. For a moment she soared screaming overhead, and Relian thought that he had lost his quarry but possibly saved his own life. Then she stooped, diving down through the air at him with the droplets of venom spraying off her beak in an amber cloud, black throat taut and a-quiver with shrieks of maniacal hatred. Relian lifted and spread the net before him. The Wingbane's talons hooked in the mesh, clutched and tore uselessly at the steel. She pulled back, found herself entangled and bated furiously. For a moment she fought in vain to free herself, then turned once more on Relian, wings beating and beak jabbing at the pale face she glimpsed behind the net.

Relian threw both arms around the Wingbane, enfolding her in the net as best he could. He could not envelop her entire body at once; her wingspread was too vast and her struggles too violent. By dint of exertion rather than skill he managed to fling the net across her back and over one wing. The Wingbane half fluttered, half fell to the ground and Relian threw himself upon her, pinning her beneath his entire weight. Even thus she was far from subdued. Her head and neck remained free of the net. The long neck twisted wildly from side to side and Relian felt the hooked beak tearing at his chest. The fabric of his coat and shirt, already weakened by the corrosive atmosphere of the forest, ripped like gauze. His jaw clenched as the beak sank into his flesh, three or four times within the space of a heartbeat. The blood welled and the wounds were strangely cold. He gripped the Wingbane around the neck with both hands and bore down with all his strength. She uttered a hoarse shriek of rage and her struggles increased in ferocity. Relian pressed harder, then recalled that he was not to kill the creature. Shifting his weight, he set one knee upon her breast, grabbed the trailing end of the net and tossed it over her head. After that the job became easier. Slowly and with infinite effort, Relian wrapped the bird in fold after fold of metal netting until he had produced a silvery cocoon through which a pair of golden eyes gleamed balefully. The Wingbane was helpless, incapable of anything more than a feeble flutter, but her glittering eyes and the hoarse rasp of her voice bespoke defiance.

The empty sack lay nearby. Relian retrieved the bag, thrust the netted Wingbane into the canvas depths and knotted the drawstrings firmly. This done, he collapsed full length upon the ground and lay there gasping. It was a long time before he could catch his breath and even then, respiration seemed unnaturally difficult. His clothing was in tatters and gouts of blood stained his chest and arms. Blood still welled from the cut in his scalp, and a thin stream trickled down his face. His arms and shoulders ached, probably bruised purple by the blows of the bird's powerful wings. His face was sore and he suspected that one or both eyes had been blackened. His wounds alternately burned and froze. The frigid sensation was puzzling and he wondered vaguely if it had anything to do with the various poisons he had absorbed during the course of his Miasmic sojourn. But somehow it didn't seem to matter much. He lay staring vacantly at the low weeds that thrust their spikes out of the soil a few inches from his eyes. A jewel-bright beetle crawled along one of the spikes and it seemed to Relian that nothing in the world could match the significance of that slow coleopterous progress. He could watch it, if need be, forever. And as he watched, with the venom of flora and fauna coursing through his system and the exhalations of the forest savaging his lungs, the lassitude returned full force. It was only with an effort that he held his swollen eyelids open to observe the beetle's movements. Presently the eyelids drooped.

"Get up now," Crekkid advised. "Lazy. Get up. Now. Now. Now."

Relian took no notice. The beetle crawled off among the dusky grasses and disappeared from view. Relian's eyes closed and his labored breathing slowed.

"Get up now. Get up now. Get up now."

There was no response. Relian lay as if dead. He was unaware that the canvas sack on the ground beside him had started to twitch. The Wingbane within had not abandoned her struggles and was now slowly working her way free of the binding net. But Relian did not note the ominous signs.

Crekkid hissed impatiently. "Lazy. Lazy. Lazy. Lazy."

Relian did not stir. He might have lain there until the flesh dropped from his bones, had he not been roused by the blast of a shotgun. A spattering of lead pellets zipped by his head. He sat up to confront three suited and helmeted figures. They could not have been Gatherers, for they carried no baskets or climbing equipment. Two of the men bore fowling pieces and the third was armed with a flintlock musket. One of them was reloading. The other two guns were aimed at Relian's chest. Wide awake now and completely at a loss, Relian stared.

What did they want of him? The man with the musket jerked
the barrel of his weapon commandingly. The heavy, glass-
fronted helmets precluded audible conversation, but the meaning of the gesture was obvious—Relian was to approach.
Presumably they meant to place him under arrest of some
kind, but for what? Trespassing? Then he remembered that he
was a poacher subject to the stringent ordinances of Vale
Jevaint. His reaction was instinctive. Heedless of the firearms
trained upon his heart, he seized the canvas sack, jumped to
his feet and ran. The three townsmen, taken by surprise,
hesitated an instant before firing. The guns roared and lead
flew. A couple of pellets grazed his upper arm, the musket
ball sang by his ear, and then he was running through the
underbrush with the townsmen lumbering in surprisingly swift
pursuit. It should have been easy to evade them in the mists
of the Miasm. But the sack was heavy; exhaustion, venom,
and a profusion of superficial wounds were taking their toll.
Relian's pace was slackening. His movements were as heavy
as those of the men encumbered with padded suits. His heart
hammered, there was a stitch in his side and already he
panted for breath. The crashing footsteps of his pursuers had
not fallen any further behind. He could not outdistance them,
and a hiding-place was essential. Not far away, a clump of
shrubbery the color of old bloodstains seemed to offer refuge.
He headed for the thicket, but as he drew near, a brace of
helmeted men stepped from the shadows and moved to bar his
path. Both men bore muskets. Relian instantly changed direction, cutting through the undergrowth at an angle that carried
him away from both sets of pursuers. Someone fired, but the
shot went wide. Fresh alarm lent Relian momentary fleetness.
As he ran, he wondered: How had they managed to find him?
Had it been pure chance? Was this new calamity simply the
latest manifestation of his customary bad luck, or was there
anything more to it? Then he remembered the scarecrow-on-
horseback that had pursued him to the edge of the Miasm;
recalled the resourcefulness of Scrivvulch the Stick, and
wondered no more.

His brief burst of strength was fading fast. His legs were
rubbery and the hands that clutched the canvas sack were
sore. He glanced down at his hands and beheld new misfortune. His flesh was marked with oily black stripes; all that
was left of Keprose's unguent. The balm, originally colorless,
had darkened as it absorbed Miasmic poison, eventually as-

suming the hue of charcoal. Its absorbency now exhausted, the unguent streaked and ran. The bare flesh between the rivulets was cushioned with big yellowish blisters. Similar blisters oozed upon his arms, their moisture splotching the remains of his sleeves.

The sack shivered in his grasp and as Relian watched in dismay, the tip of a hooked beak poked through the canvas. At the same time, the trio of townsmen hove into view, spotted him, lifted their weapons and fired. Pellets from one of the fowling pieces whizzed by like hornets. Relian turned to flee and tripped over a rock he should have seen. His vision was dim and curiously gray. His eyes burned, and the flow of tears increased the pain. The proximity of his enemies forced him on his way. He stumbled through fog, while panic gnawed at the base of his mind. Such panic was a more dangerous enemy than the Miasm itself. At the first opportunity Relian paused, closed his eyes, took a deep, calming breath of the foul air. When he opened his eyes again, the world was in sharper focus. He could see the phosphorescent lily pads alight upon the black surface of a forest pool. He could see the swollen weeds that choked the bank—weeds that swayed ceaselessly, although the air was still. And he could see a tangle of brambles, the sticky branches laden with the corpses of countless small insects. Relian tottered forward, sank to his knees and then to the ground; crawled in under the bushes, dragging the sack behind him, until he reached the thorny shadows at the heart of the thicket, where he huddled in wretched silence.

They were only a couple of minutes behind him. The five of them arrived together and paused not twenty feet from the thicket. The townsmen appeared confused. For a time they conferred by means of hand-gestures, the traditional Miasmic Voice known only to members of the Guild. Relian held his breath. With any luck, they would soon depart to continue their search elsewhere. *Luck? You know what that means.* As if in sympathy to unvoiced pessimism, the sack vibrated. The hooked beak rent the canvas and a fierce, crested head emerged. Golden eyes blazed hatred as the captive Wingbane strained against the cloth. Relian extended a hand and she struck at it like a snake. Her beak gouged one of his blisters open, and clear fluid spurted. He bit his lip, blotted the moisture on his cravat and tried again. This time he obtained a good hold on the back of her neck, whereupon the thwarted bird raised her

voice in cries so shrill and piercing as to penetrate the headgear of the townsmen. The five men studied the thicket
attentively.

Relian managed to stuff the bird's head back inside the
sack, but in doing so he jostled a branch. The bushes trembled. The watching townsmen conversed in silence, then
advanced. As Relian watched despairingly, they spread out to
surround the thicket. In his heart the fugitive cursed recalci-
trant Fate. Fate's riposte was instantaneous. The Wingbane
thrust her screeching head forth. The rent in the canvas
widened and the upper portion of her body appeared. Relian
pushed the creature back and reluctantly reached in through
the tear to grope for the loosened net. He encountered a
heaving feathered breast and at the unaccustomed touch the
Wingbane stabbed viciously. Her beak raked his fingers twice
before he found the free end of the net, in which he enfolded
her head and neck. Relian withdrew his bleeding hand and his
attention returned to his pursuers. The men stood ranged
about the bushes. One of them approached cautiously and
squatted, peering wide-eyed into the shadows. Soon he signaled his cohorts, who raised their weapons; and Relian knew
he had been discovered. Desperation made him reckless.
Ignoring the brambles that tore at his face and limbs, he burst
from his refuge to charge the squatting man. The townsman,
evidently no hunter, froze momentarily then hastily yanked
the trigger. Surprise and imbalance spoiled whatever aim he
might have possessed. He missed, despite the point-blank
range, and then his quarry was upon him. The others, unwilling to risk their companion's blood, held their fire.

Relian's arms were folded firmly about the sack, but his
feet were free and he used them to good advantage. A well-
aimed kick caught the townsman full in the padded chest. The
attack was unexpectedly effective. The suited man, balanced
precariously on the balls of his feet, was knocked backward.
His helmet banged against a rock so violently that the bright
metal was dinted. For a moment he lay still, his airhose
tangled beneath him. As he groggily raised himself to a
sitting position, the hose tore loose and with it went the
unfortunate's supply of breathable air. The features behind
the glass face-plate twisted in fear and astonishment. The
gloved hands clamped down on the opening at the back of the
helmet. Relian paused, almost inclined to aid his stricken
enemy. But the four remaining townsmen lumbering near

were doubtless better qualified than he to deal with the situation. Relian took to his heels amidst a hail of lead pellets. Only once did he look back to see two of the townsmen refastening the airhose to the helmet of their comrade. A third was reloading and the last was taking aim. Relian ducked behind a tree. He heard a sharp report and a slap as the ball flattened itself against the trunk. Hesitating no longer, he turned and fled. He did not pause until pursuit had been left far behind.

*   *   *

Relian rested beneath a tree whiskered with bone-white moss. Movement was difficult, for his wounds had stiffened. His rags were heavy with caked blood. His eyes were blurred and no amount of rubbing would quite clear them. He was weary, sick, and nearly devoid of hope. Willingly would he have lingered there on the ground, risking capture or slow suffocation, but Crekkid would not have it so.

"Lazy," the serpent observed. "No more ressst. Get up now. Go home. Home. Home. Home. Home."

"Soon."

"Now," Crekkid insisted. "Home to Massster. Home to Nurbo. Now. Now. Now. Now."

There was no response and the serpent administered a disciplinary nip.

Relian opened his eyes reluctantly. Blurred vision notwithstanding, he perceived that the mists had thickened. A dank chill in the air presaged sunset. The prospect of wandering the Miasm by night was grim enough to hail him to his feet. He squinted through the trees and mists to glimpse a ruddy brightness that pointed the way west. Fortress Gavyne rose atop its cliff to the southeast of the forest, and there he turned his lagging steps. As he went the forest darkened. The sun had set or else he was going blind. He shuddered at the thought and the sack jerked responsively. At last he arrived at the edge of the woods. Before him stretched the twilit expanse of the Miasmic Girdle and beyond that rose the unpolluted pines. Relian paused to survey the landscape and saw no sign of Scrivvulch the Stick. A breeze swept the Girdle and he drank in air comparatively free of Miasmic malignancy.

"Go home now. Home. Home. Home. Home."

Indignation lent Relian the energy to reply. "You might

never have gone home had those townsmen shot me, but you didn't warn me that they were near," he accused.

"Maybe you wisssh to ssspeak with them," Crekkid suggested maliciously. "Maybe they have filesss. Or pincersss."

Relian lapsed into disgusted silence. Without another word he abandoned the cover of the trees, quickly crossed the fringe of venomous weeds and so passed from the Miasm.

It was a long hike back to Fortress Gavyne and most of it was uphill. Many a time he was tempted to drop the canvas sack, to stretch himself upon the ground and sleep his exhaustion away. He knew better than to try it—the bite of steel fangs would punish such self-indulgence. He trudged on, wholly preoccupied with pain and fatigue. Only dimly did he note the darkening sky, the emergence of stars and moon. He was aware that the steep path before him was difficult to navigate. He knew that the air was breathable, that the Wingbane was momentarily under control and that there was no pursuit. Little else concerned him. Thus sunk in semi-somnambulism he would have proceeded, had not the crash of an explosion overhead rocked the ground on which he walked.

Relian looked up to behold a spear of scarlet lightning winging across the heavens. He recognized it as an artificial thunderbolt designed by Keprose Gavyne to wreak havoc upon the house of his enemy Vanalisse. As he watched, the lightning vanished into the fog that shrouded the Tyrant of Mists. Booming thunder, and then there was silence so complete and protracted as to suggest the success of Keprose's attack. Relian halted, his eyes raised to the cliffs. The silence continued for another moment and then Vanalisse struck back. Mind-rattling explosions shook the hills and out of the mists shot six blue lightning bolts in rapid succession. For the space of several seconds the radiant missiles were simultaneously airborne. The sky was lit with a blue glare that illuminated the countryside for miles around. Wood, field, and the town below were bathed in icy light. Relian shut his smarting eyes, dazzled by the unnatural brilliance. The bolts arced overhead, then descended upon their target. The world darkened again.

Fortress Gavyne was blocked from view by trees and crags. Relian wondered whether the ancient building could withstand such a merciless hammering. He might return to find the place in ruins, the inhabitants trapped, crushed or incinerated. He thought of Mereth and quickened his pace.

The sky was briefly shot with red as lightning issued from Fortress Gavyne. Keprose's response to his enemy's attack was halfhearted at best. The single bolt of energy was short, dull in color and so weak that it failed to clear the valley. The scarlet streak lobbed in a slow, high curve, seemed to hang suspended for a moment at the zenith of its arc, then descended far short of its target to fall upon Vale Jevaint. A far-off explosion was audible and fire bloomed near the center of town. Doubtless the citizens would know how to deal with such matters; their experience was extensive.

No sign of life from the Tyrant of Mists. Vanalisse the Unseen disdained to reply.

Relian completed his journey as quickly as exhaustion and nightfall would permit. Fortunately it was a clear and moonlit evening. Pallid gleams illumined his path and by that fitful light he picked his way up the hill. After about forty minutes of walking, the towers of Fortress Gavyne became visible, and then the way was easier. The windows were alight—a surprising expenditure in view of the Seigneur's habitual frugality. It was unlikely that lantern and chandelier had been lit in order to guide the wanderer back. The blaze of light suggested Seigneurial perturbation. As Relian drew near the fortress, the cause of that distress became apparent. At least one of Vanalisse's missiles had done its work well. A chunk of roof and wall had been neatly bitten from the northeastern tower.

Relian reached the gate at last and found to his relief that the porter had been left instructions to admit him. He did not waste time attempting to question the man, whose conversation was limited, but went directly across the courtyard—now littered with the remains of the lost turret—into the cavernous entryway and thence to the Great Hall, where he found the entire household assembled. It was clear that the recent attack had wrought confusion.

Lady Fribanni appeared distraught. Her face was red and contorted—teeth bared, puffy eyes screwed shut, flesh soaked with sweat and tears. Sobs and wails of terror shook her, and the floor at her feet was strewn with sodden handkerchiefs. The disheveled triplets clustered protectively about their mother. She did not hear their words of sympathy, for her clenched hands were clapped tightly over her ears.

Keprose Gavyne ignored the transports of his sister. The Seigneur's vast, black-clad form was slumped in the chair atop the dais. His chin rested on his hand and his expression reflected brooding dissatisfaction.

Mereth stood at the shuttered window, gazing out through the chinks at the moonlit courtyard. She stood very still and straight. Her expression was not visible, for her back was deliberately turned on her companions.

At the sight of his loved ones Crekkid cried out in joy. "Massster! Massster! Sssweet Nurbo! Patriarch Crekkid hasss returned!"

The hisses were audible over Fribanni's whimpers. Mereth started at the sound and spun around. Her eyes widened and Relian realized that he presented a horrible spectacle. He was filthy with blood and nearly every inch of his exposed flesh bulged with oozing blisters.

The others stared at him wordlessly. Fribanni's keening intensified.

Silver glinted at Mereth's throat as Nurbo's wiry tongue darted. "Brave Crekkid! Sssafe! Sssafe! Sssafe! Sssafe!"

"Sssweet Nurbo, fair as food! Kind Massster, great and wissse! Massster! Massster! Massster! Massster!"

Internal turbulence stirred the Seigneur's black robes. Keprose lifted his head and spoke bleakly. "Welcome home, my Crekkid. Much has transpired during your absence. Once again we have suffered the unprovoked aggression of Vanalisse the Unseen Hag. Her vile, unheralded attack wreaks havoc upon my house."

Fribanni caught the last remarks and a piercing howl of grief escaped her.

"Silence," Keprose enjoined his sister sternly, and her sobs cut off at once. "In view of the provocation, vengeance becomes no less obligation than recreation." He turned to Relian. "Young man, your excursion has been inordinately prolonged. Such inefficiency in pursuit of a well-defined objective reveals a lack of self-discipline. Your debilitated state suggests leisurely ramblings in the Forest of Miasm. Clearly you fail to recognize the value of time. This is a serious defect. Nonetheless, I am by nature disposed to generosity and I am prepared to overlook your failings at this time if you have successfully completed your mission. The bulging sack you carry gives me cause to hope that you have done so. Am I correct?"

Relian nodded.

"I am content. The sack, if you please."

Relian approached and willingly relinquished his burden. "The bird is strong and savage. I would caution you—"

Without an instant's hesitation, Keprose loosed the draw-strings. The Wingbane had succeeded in working her way partially free of the net. As the mouth of the sack gaped, she wrenched herself completely clear of the entangling folds and with a scream of triumph, exploded from her canvas prison. Relian flinched in expectation of the terrible, stabbing beak. But the Wingbane mounted, swept the length of the hall on outstretched wings, then circled shrieking below the vaulted ceiling.

Fribanni cowered and the triplets shouted. Druveen rummaged in his pocket and brought forth a slingshot. Mereth bestowed a single pitying glance upon the captive bird, and then her attention returned to Relian. He felt the anxious scrutiny, caught her eye and smiled reassuringly. It hurt his face to do so.

"It is as I had hoped." Keprose Gavyne beamed ineffable approval. "Sister, pray instruct your son to relinquish that weapon ere I am moved to bond his hands permanently to his buttocks."

Druveen hastily returned the slingshot to its resting place.

"Yes, it is as I had hoped," the Seigneur repeated. "The sacrifice of this bird will mark a milestone along my road to multiplicity. I grow. I prosper. Vanalisse the Unseen Hag is doomed. And my name shall be Legion."

*   *   *

For two days following his return from the Forest of Miasm Relian stayed in bed, asleep most of the time. During that period his blisters subsided and his cuts started to heal. Perhaps the protective unguents were more effective than he had guessed, for recovery was remarkably swift.

He was left strictly alone. There were no visitors and no messages. He suspected that Keprose had ordained his isolation in order to discourage prolonged malingering. The only human being he saw was an uncommunicative servant who brought meals and supranormally-devised restoratives twice a day.

By the evening of the second day, Crekkid was chafing both figuratively and literally at the enforced inaction. "Lazy," the serpent opined contemptuously. "Good-for-nothing. Lazy. Lazy. Lazy."

Crekkid's impatience was shared by his master. On the morning of the third day, Relian woke to discover a note on the floor by the door. He rose from bed, found himself tolerably steady, picked up the note and read:

Young Man—
This is to notify you that delivery of meals to your chamber is hereby terminated. As this service is performed by the staff at the expense of far more significant household duties, I cannot countenance its wholly unnecessary continuation. You are strongly encouraged at this time to return to work. Your progress toward supranormalcy has not been so impressive as to justify prolonged self-indulgence. To imagine otherwise argues most unbecoming complacency on your part.

—Keprose Gavyne

"Pompous ass," Relian muttered and tossed the paper aside.

"Pompousss? Assss? Pompousss Assss?"

"Not you."

Relian washed and shaved. While he slept, his clothing had been cleaned and very neatly mended. Some of it, presumably unsalvageable, had been replaced. He had been given a linen shirt, slightly frayed at the wrists, and a coat of brown frieze—plain, serviceable garments similar to those worn by Keprose's servants.

He dressed cautiously, for his cuts were still painful and a few of the worst blisters had not completely drained. He was a little weak, but glad to be back on his feet.

Relian ascended to the tower workroom, taking the stairs in easy stages. He entered and headed straight for the great glass tubes as if yanked on an invisible leash. Keprose Gavyne had made good use of the Wingbane. So much was obvious at a single glance.

The blobs within the tubes had changed beyond recognition. They had grown with supranormal speed and now lacked but a couple of inches of the height of their prototype. Moreover, they had assumed recognizably human form. Within each tube floated the parody of a man, with hairless, faceless, misshapen head; disproportionately long arms trailing off into sprays of tentacles where the hands would one day be; short, sturdy legs and amorphous feet. Along with their height had increased their girth. Their bellies pressed against the glass as if seeking escape. Even at this early stage of development, the resemblance was striking enough to justify Keprose's descriptive term ''Selves.''

Relian watched, fascinated. The plentiful flesh of the Selves remained pure white and slightly translucent. The surrounding nutrient baths lent them a slightly violet cast. Beneath the flesh the tracery of veining was visible. The arms of the Selves flexed gently. The tentacular fingers stirred like seaweed in the pastel currents. Relian stared at the faceless head of the nearest Self. The blank white expanse, awaiting the development of features, was turned in his direction. So were the non-faces of the other two Selves. Despite the absence of sensory organs, he could almost have sworn that the uncanny creatures were somehow aware of his presence. He shivered and turned away from the tubes.

The workroom door opened and Mereth stepped in. He realized then that she had hovered around the edges of his awareness throughout his Miasmic sortie and that she had occupied the greater part of his conscious thoughts since his return.

She was dressed in her usual dark garb, the plainness relieved only by the silvery glint of Nurbo at her neck. She was pale and her expression was somber as Relian's own. When she saw him, her face brightened wonderfully. Her color rose and for a moment she resembled the carefree young girl she ought to have been. ''Relian, it's good to see you! You're looking fine. You're all better, then?''

''Nearly. I—''

A rapturous hiss drowned his reply. ''Sssweet Nurbo! Sssweet Nurbo! At lassst!''

Nurbo responded with equal ardor. ''Brave Crekkid, hero of the Miasssm! Crekkid, Conqueror of black birdssss!''

''Matriarch Nurbo!''

''Patriarch Crekkid! At lassst! At lassst!''

Nurbo writhed in ecstasy. Crekkid did likewise.

''Mereth, I'm all right.'' Relian raised his voice to be heard over the reptilian hisses. ''I've missed you. What's happened during the last three days? I've spoken to no one.''

''Throughout the endlessss daysss of ssseparation, Nurbo longsss for her valiant Crekkid!''

''Crekkid droopsss. Crekkid pinesss. Crekkid sssighsss.''

"You've spoken to no one because Keprose wouldn't allow anyone near you," Mereth replied. "He gave orders that you weren't to be disturbed under any circumstances. He said that distractions would impede your recovery, but personally I believe he did it out of spite. After I'd mended your clothes, he wouldn't even let me return them to you, but had one of the servants do it."

"You were the one to mend them, Mereth? That was good of you."

The color in her cheeks deepened. "I wanted to. I felt—"

"The heart of Crekkid isss full of russst. Even now, he isss far from hisss Nurbo," Crekkid complained.

"I can tell you in a few words what's happened during the last three days," Mereth offered. "Shortly after sunset on the day that you were gone, Keprose launched an attack on the Tyrant of Mists. He hurled his bolts of force across the valley and Vanalisse responded in kind, as she always does. Ordinarily such exchanges are inconclusive, but this one was different."

"It ssshould not be ssso," Nurbo fretted. "Nurbo ssshould be with Crekkid. Nurbo. Crekkid. Nurbo. Crekkid."

"Vanalisse's missiles are deflected by means of the supranormal shield with which Keprose encloses the fortress during the attack," Mereth continued. "The shield is impervious to many natural forces, including fire and lightning. Magnets do not work across it, but light passes through freely. So do material objects and living creatures, curiously enough. As you've seen, Keprose's lightning passes from the fortress and I can only infer that a gap exists in the shield. Presumably a similar gap exists in Vanalisse's shields, and this is the target at which Keprose fires blindly. I can't be certain of that—when I've asked Keprose about it, he's replied that an explanation would surpass my limited powers of comprehension."

"I suspect he's wrong," said Relian.

"Wrong. Wrong. Wrong. Wrong," Crekkid brooded. "It isss wrong to ssseparate two loving heartsss. Wrong. Wrong."

"Vanalisse replied to the attack with a very heavy barrage of her own," Mereth went on. "And this time, something happened. For the first time, one of the blue bolts penetrated Keprose's shield. I don't mean that it came through a gap—No, it just beat its way straight through by sheer force. I'll never forget the way it sounded. There was a crackling, sizzling sort of sound, a terrific flash of light outside—for a moment it looked like noon—and then a rush and an explosion as the energy passed on and struck the northeastern tower. The turret gave way; I could hear rocks clattering and the building literally shook. There was a peculiar scorched odor—at first I thought that a fire had started, but I was wrong. Something had happened to the air itself and for a few minutes, while that smell lingered, it was hard to breathe.''

"Hard. Hard. Hard to be apart,'' Nurbo mused. "Mussst loversss sssuffer thusss?''

"Do you know whether Vanalisse's powers would inform her that her blow struck home?'' asked Relian.

"I think probably yes, but I'm not certain,'' Mereth replied. "Anyway, the tower fell and I don't know how it happened. Either Keprose is getting weaker, or Vanalisse is growing stronger, or perhaps it was pure chance. In any case, Keprose descended from his workroom shortly thereafter, looking black. Lady Fribanni became hysterical, fainted and was revived twice. You returned and took to your chamber. And the triplets departed, for the tavern in Vale Jevaint, I believe.''

"Duty keepsss Nurbo from Crekkid. Alwaysss Duty. What of love?'' Nurbo, prey to conflicting passions, seized a strand of Mereth's long hair and pulled hard.

Mereth absently disengaged the strand and continued without pause, "The next day, things were very quiet. The triplets were gone, you and Lady Fribanni remained within your respective chambers, and Keprose didn't emerge from his workroom. All through the day and far into the night he labored, intent upon his Selves. The day after that—yesterday— was the same. By that time I was getting worried about you and decided I'd visit you whether Keprose liked it or not. Late in the evening, when I judged that everyone was asleep, I headed for your room. I'd only gone as far as the Great Hall when Nurbo complained. She thought I was trying to leave the fortress. I explained that we were going to see Crekkid—''

"Brave Crekkid. Crekkid. Crekkid. Crekkid,'' Nurbo sang.

"By that time our conversation had attracted the attention of the triplets, who were just getting back from the tavern. All three of them were drunk. They made themselves so troublesome that I was obliged to return to my room and lock myself inside. They sat by my door for hours,'' Mereth continued, "alternately pounding, pleading, threatening and singing. It was the singing that was hardest to bear."

"Lonelinessss isss hardesssst to bear," Crekkid observed gloomily.

"I didn't dare come out of my room for the rest of the night. If you hadn't turned up here this morning though, I'd have found some way of seeing you or at least sending a message."

"I wouldn't have wanted you to run any risks," Relian replied, concerned for her safety but absurdly pleased by her interest. "The Seigneur—"

"Risssksss. Risssksss. Love isss worth risssk," Nurbo declared.

"The Seigneur—" Relian persisted.

"The Ssseigneur doesss not undersssstand," Crekkid interrupted. "Patriarch Crekkid and Matriarch Nurbo mussst be asss one. Crekkid risssk all for love and count the world well losssst!"

"Brave Crekkid! Ssstrong Crekkid!"

"Fair Nurbo, let usss ssseize the moment. Time fliesss."

"Fliesss! Fliesss!"

Relian could feel the excited vibrations shake Crekkid's slender coils. "I hope you're not thinking of—"

"Thisss insssstant isss oursss. Bear Crekkid to Nurbo," Crekkid commanded regally. "Now. Now. Now. Now."

Relian did not bother arguing. He advanced and positioned himself before Mereth, so close that his breath stirred her hair. Nurbo lifted her silvery length and Crekkid bent to meet her. The steel coils intertwined, scale clicked on scale and the wire tongues flickered too fast for the eye to follow.

Relian looked down at Mereth. Her eyes were lowered, as they had been once before under similar circumstances. Without deliberation, he gently tilted her chin up and kissed her. For a moment she seemed frozen with surprise, and then she returned the kiss. The effect of this behavior upon the snakes was startling.

Amidst much writhing, flurried activity, the serpents disentangled. Whistling hisses, shrill with consternation, issued from two metallic throats.

"Ssstop! Ssstop now! Now!" Crekkid's coils contracted torturously.

Relian choked and quickly drew back from the girl. The

pressure eased, but Crekkid continued to whistle like a boiling kettle.

"You kissss! Ssslut! Ssslut! Ssslut!" Nurbo denounced the red-faced Mereth. "Kissss! Ssslut!"

"What's the matter with you two?" Relian demanded, indignation overcoming caution. He felt Crekkid's fangs in his earlobe and cursed. "What concern is it of yours?"

"You cheat Massster! Sssneak! Cheat!" Crekkid accused.

"Cheat Massster, great Massster, kind Massster," Nurbo chimed in.

"What are you talking about?" Relian noticed that Mereth, although distressed, seemed neither confused nor even particularly surprised. "What has this to do with Keprose?"

"Ssshe isss for Ssseigneur. For Ssseigneur, not you. Ssseigneur," Crekkid announced.

"Your tiny mental gears are jammed," Relian replied, and Crekkid hissed angrily. "What nonsense is this?"

"Nonssssenssse? Not ssso. Ssstupid. Ssshe isss for Ssseigneur," Crekkid repeated, evidently incapable of providing detailed information. "When ssshe isss worthy. If ever."

"Worthy? Mereth, what is all this?" Relian inquired.

Mereth studied her elongated fingertips with care. "From time to time the Seigneur has mentioned the possibility of, as he puts it, 'elevating' me," she explained. "This has been suggested as a reward for successful development of my supposed latent supranormal abilities. I think he intends it as an incentive to study. The Seigneur has never explained exactly what is meant by 'elevation,' and I've never been able to bring myself to inquire. I merely assert that I am unworthy of such honor, and to date he has always agreed."

"He can't be planning to force you—"

"Production of heirs is one of the basic obligations of Seigneurship," Mereth replied unhappily. "The House of Gavyne must continue, and I don't think that Keprose would be willing to entrust the responsibility to his nephews. Without doubt he'll take a wife one day. It's my belief that he intends the wife to be supranormal."

"And if you exhibit signs of supranormalcy—"

"I shall be elevated."

"You sssee?" Crekkid interjected. "Ssshe isss for Ssseigneur. If he wantsss her."

"But ssshe kissss another. Ungrateful ssstrumpet. Ssslut.

Ssslut. Ssslut.'' Nurbo sank her fangs into Mereth's neck and the girl's face twitched.

"There's the reason that your supranormalcy has never manifested itself. You haven't wanted it," Relian observed.

"I've studied very hard," Mereth replied defensively.

"How could you, when success would bring elevation? You've told me, and the books confirm it, that exercise of supranormal power involves absolute concentration and focus of the will. How can you focus your will on what you have reason to dread?''

"As far as I know, I've done my best. Perhaps the ability just isn't there.''

"Perhaps. But I think you should keep trying. In fact, you should try harder than ever before. There's a reason for it.''

"What reassson?" Nurbo inquired.

"Massster'sss favor," Crekkid explained.

Relian hesitated a moment, then walked to the table, took a sheet of paper and one of the many sharpened quills that lay there, dipped the quill and scribbled:

> Develop Supranormal Tactility. Use on snakes. Weaken or stupefy. Remove snakes, escape fortress together.

Mereth scanned the note with interest, took up the quill and replied:

> Very dangerous. One attempt fail, Keprose know all. Reprisals.

Relian wrote:

> Try?

She nodded vigorously.

"What do you do?" Crekkid inquired. "Why make marksss on paper? Marksss?''

"It's nothing," Relian assured him. "A game."

"Game? Crekkid knowsss your gamesss. Gamesss with pincersss. Gamesss with filesss.''

"You shouldn't brood on past misunderstandings," Relian advised easily. "It will upset your digestion, and we wouldn't want that.''

"You think? Ssstupid. Nothing upssset Crekkid'sss digessstion. Crekkid digessst your blood one day. No trouble. Jussst wait.''

Relian was wisely silent.

"Lazy. Trifler. You are here to work. Work. Work. Work.''

"You're right,'' Relian agreed meekly. He carefully shredded the paper into microscopic particles, walked to the open window and scattered confetti upon the breeze. "You see? No more games.''

"No more gamesss. Work. No more gamesss.''

"And no more gamesss with *her*.'' Nurbo tightened spitefully. "Ssstrumpet.''

Relian and Mereth resumed work. Once again Mereth placed the gray box on the table and Relian attempted to slide his mental vision through the wooden walls by way of Forn. He concentrated strenuously. A score of random thoughts, observations and impressions clamored for attention, but he disregarded them all. Weeks of intensive application had bought him mastery of Uy's Mindwall, which blocked intrusive thoughts. He constructed it now and the Mindwall held strong. The world receded. Relian's fingers began to undulate through the gestures of Moam's Progression. Once, twice, and again—he picked up tempo as he repeated the Progression. Otherworldly colors; almost painful clarity of internal vision; a floating sensation he had experienced once before; and then he caught the sense and direction of his movement through Forn, of which he had hitherto been unconscious. Uy's Mindwall held astonishment, trepidation, confusion and disorientation dungeoned below the level of awareness. The image of the wooden box remained clear and bright in his mind. He saw the solid gray walls, but also saw for the first time that a view of the interior might be attainable through Forn, provided he could bypass the intervening Blindnesses. The First Greej Pattern marked a path among the blank areas, along which he now guided his sight until his view was unobstructed and he beheld a fist-sized cluster of colorless crystal lying on a square of quilted cotton.

"Quartz,'' said Relian. "Three long crystals and five or six small ones.'' He opened his eyes. The flash of Vision faded and the world returned to normalcy. Uy's Mindwall fell and there was room in his mind for wonder.

It seemed almost superfluous to open the box but Mereth did so, lifting the lid to display the crystalline contents. Her smile bright with genuine pleasure, she took a spontaneous

step toward him and stopped as Nurbo hissed a warning. But
the smile still shone as she exclaimed, "Relian, you have
definitely got it!"

*   *   *

It was evening and the common room of the Bearded Moon
was crowded. Scrivvulch the Stick sat at his customary table.
Over the course of his tenancy, the table had come to be
regarded by owner and patrons as his alone. The remains of
his dinner had been pushed aside. A book lay open before
him and his downy head was bowed studiously over the
pages. From time to time he refreshed himself with a sip of
herbal tea. Presently a shadow fell athwart the print and he
looked up to find Master Moon standing at his side. Master
Moon carried the thick notebook containing *Ode to a Venomous Fern*, and Scrivvulch suppressed a sigh. He knew what
the notebook portended and he feared there was no escape.

"Glad tidings, Master Scrivvulch!" Moon beamed radi-
antly. "I have completed yet another canto of one hundred
verses. As you are a man of culture as well as an honored
patron, you must be the first to hear."

"Really, Master Moon, you flatter me but I am hardly—"

"I esteem your learning, Master Scrivvulch, and treasure
your regard for the art poetical. Listen carefully." Moon
opened the notebook and began to read:

"Canto the Twenty-fourth

I.

In olden days green was not counted fair,
And Beauty did not dye her cheek that hue.
But thou lend'st green a loveliness so rare
That Beauty learns to paint her face anew.

II.

She stains her lip, her eyes and hair with green.
She tints her limbs, her fingers, knees and toes.
Bright Beauty's choice enthrones thee as a Queen.
Thy diadem in poison'd splendor glows.

III.

The green-fac'd goddess grants thee royalty.
Thy fronds reflect triumphant battle-light.
The vassals of the Sun shift loyalty,
And thou hast made the Moon thy satellite.''

Moon paused for breath and Scrivvulch seized the opportunity. ''Excuse me, Master Moon,'' he interrupted, ''but who is that gentleman just coming in?'' The Assassin indicated a sedately-dressed citizen of middle years whose face was marked with recent, bitter lines.

''Him, sir? Well may you ask. That's Councilman Gyf Fynok, and he's been kind of a local celebrity ever since the Seigneur blasted his mansion to rubble a few weeks ago.''

''Oh, my. Oh, my. And why did the Seigneur do that?''

''Couldn't say, sir. No doubt the Seigneur had his reasons, in this case as in all the others. It may have had something to do with Fynok's opposition to the new tax increase. The thing about Fynok is, after his house burned he still didn't resign from the City Council, and he serves on it to this day. He and his family are living in a shack on the outskirts of town, but whenever there's a Council meeting, Fynok spruces himself up, comes in and takes his seat. He's a game one.''

''So it would seem.'' Scrivvulch regarded the oppressed Councilman with interest. Fynok, now seated beside the fireplace, stared broodingly into the flames. ''Master Moon, I must speak with him.''

''Well, I fear you won't find him jolly company, sir. Wouldn't you rather stay and listen to my twenty-fourth canto? It contains an extended poetic conceit wherein my fern engages in heroic battle with the sun for sovereignty over all the planets and the moon—you perceive the witty play on words, sir? 'Tis very poetical and very symbolical—''

''I shall look forward to hearing it. Alas that duty claims my attention at this time. Sir, my compliments.'' And Scrivvulch fled.

Councilman Gyf Fynok did not relish company. He looked up from the fire as Scrivvulch took possession of the neighboring chair and his expression was forbidding.

Scrivvulch refused to be discouraged. ''Councilman, 'tis said you are a man of courage as well as a patriot,'' he announced without preamble.

Fynok's brows lowered like stormclouds. "Said by whom?"

"By all the world, sir. It is to that courage and patriotism that I now address myself. Permit me to introduce myself—"

"I already know who you are, Master Scrivvulch."

"Indeed? Then I may assume you know why I am here?"

"Yes, I've heard about the Equalist holed up in Fortress Gavyne. So has everyone else in town by now." Fynok drew a clay pipe from his breast pocket and fiddled with it moodily.

"I trust you share my concern?"

"I've much to concern me, sir."

"Ah, I have heard of your misfortune." Scrivvulch permitted himself a sympathetic smile. "I applaud your courage, sir, in maintaining your position on the City Council in the face of all adversity."

"And so I shall continue to maintain it, come what may. Come fire, flood, whirlwind or lightning, I will hold fast," Fynok announced grimly. "I speak what I believe and no man hinders me. Gavyne was wrong about the surtax on Neraunci canvas and I say so to this day. As for my seat on the Council, it is mine and nothing short of death shall deprive me of it. I stand firm, sir. I do not waver."

"No more do I, Councilman," Scrivvulch returned lightly. "Well, as you are aware of my mission, my request for your assistance can hardly come as a surprise."

"What assistance do you ask?"

"I've been informed that I require the invitation or sponsorship of a member in order to address the City Council. I must address the Council, and I desire your sponsorship. No doubt you will lend your support to so vital an undertaking."

"Vital to you alone, Master Scrivvulch."

"More than that, Councilman. Is not the presence of a poacher in the Forest of Miasm—a despoiler of nests, a slayer of Black Wingbanes—is this not a matter of concern to all the town?"

For the first time since the conversation began, Gyf Fynok exhibited signs of interest. He tapped the bowl of his pipe ruminatively a few times and asked, "Is it your belief that the poacher recently spotted and pursued in the Miasm was—"

"Black Relian Kru. Yes, Councilman. Your poacher and my Equalist are one."

"It was reported that you were the man to alert Bellowsman Dedon and the others of the intruder's presence."

"That is correct. I pursued Black Relian to the very edge

of the Miasm, where I was halted by noxious fumes. Knowing the malignant character of the fugitive, I could not but surmise that his presence constituted a danger to your noble birds, hence it was incumbent upon me to warn the townsfolk.'' It would have come as a surprise to Scrivvulch the Stick to know that his suppositions concerning Black Relian's poaching activities were in fact accurate. "And now," Scrivvulch continued, "duty and conscience demand that I warn the Council itself of the danger threatening the town. Grown weary of his recent slothful ease, Black Relian has emerged from the fortress. The depredations have begun."

"Perhaps." Fynok sucked the stem of his pipe with a thoughtful scowl. "And what do you expect the Council to do about it, Master Scrivvulch?"

"That I leave to your wisdom to decide," Scrivvulch returned modestly. "However, if I may be so bold, it is my recommendation that a delegation of Councilmen, Guardsmen and concerned citizens present the Seigneur with the town's absolute demand—namely, the immediate surrender of Black Relian Kru."

"Such a demand might well prove offensive to the Seigneur."

"Quite possibly. Your Seigneur Keprose has chosen to shelter a criminal, for reasons best known to himself. No doubt your Bellowsmen reported to you," Scrivvulch observed, "that Black Relian was able to walk the Miasm without benefit of protection. No airhose, no suit, no helmet— nothing. He breathed vapors that might have shriveled the lungs of a normal man, yet they did not harm him. Now what does that suggest?"

Fynok's scowl darkened. "Take care, Master Scrivvulch."

"I see you understand me. Black Relian was fortified in some manner, and who but the Seigneur could be responsible? I am a simple man and I cannot pretend to guess at your Seigneur's intentions. That his actions are hostile to the interests of the townsfolk is scarcely open to question. What remains to be seen is the citizens' response to tyranny. Will they defend themselves, or will they submit in silence to the loss of livelihood, as some have already submitted to the loss of property?"

"We will hold our rights, in the Miasm and elsewhere," Fynok replied doggedly. "If the man the Seigneur shelters is truly a poacher, then it must be ended. It is a question of self-defense."

"I applaud your resolution, sir."

"Nothing has been proven."

"Granted. That is why I desire an opportunity to address the Council. I shall present my proofs at that time," Scrivvulch promised.

"If the Seigneur harbors a poacher, then he's overstepped the bounds of his rightful authority and he must be stopped at any cost," Fynok mused heavily. "He is our hereditary Seigneur and a wizard to boot, and therefore we've endured much at his hands. But there are limits."

"Indeed there are."

"I own that we of Vale Jevaint fear Gavyne. His lightning is a terrible thing, and too many of us have felt the power of it. Should it prove necessary to move against him, we'd be obliged to seek reinforcements—perhaps send to the King of Nidroon, to whom Keprose Gavyne technically owes allegiance, although he doesn't pay it."

"I have considered that problem," Scrivvulch murmured, much encouraged by his apparent progress. "It occurs to me that in the event of an emergency, the town might apply for assistance to the supranormal Lady Vanalisse the Unseen."

"She is unknown to us." Fynok appeared nonplussed.

"That condition can be rectified. But I speak only in anticipation of dire necessity that may never arise. In the meantime, I think it best to proceed with restraint," Scrivvulch opined. "Best to obtain our objective with as little fuss and pother as possible, is it not? That much a long and not uneventful career has taught me. For in this bustling, strife-ridden world, 'tis economy of effort that purchases the jewel-precious moments of respite," Scrivvulch intoned.

"Steadiness. Determination. Steadfastness. Those are what see a man through," Fynok replied.

"No doubt. Then let us proceed one steady foot before the other, like sensible men. You'll permit me to address the City Council, whose members will be urged to draft a letter of petition demanding the surrender of Relian Kru. With any luck, that will be all we need."

"You are an optimist, sir."

"Always. Always. I enjoy excellent digestion, and intend to continue so. Are we agreed?"

"I will think it over. Such a grave matter requires thought."

"Certainly. And when may I expect an answer?"

"When I have finished thinking. At that time you will hear

my decision which, once formulated, will be inalterable. I bid you good evening, sir.'' Fynok rose and left the Bearded Moon, without ever once having lighted his pipe.

Scrivvulch remained where he was, much heartened by the results of the conversation. A benignant smile signaled his satisfaction. Contentment dulled his perceptions. He became aware too late of Master Moon's approach. Master Moon carried his notebook and radiated a determination fully equal to that of Councilman Gyf Fynok.

*   *   *

It was the dead of night and the inhabitants of Fortress Gavyne slept. Moonlight pouring through the windows of the tower workroom played upon flask and vial, retort and stoppered bottle, jar and beaker; gleamed on the three great glass tubes wherein reposed the hopes of Keprose Gavyne. Light swam through nameless nutrient solution to illumine the white, unconscious forms within. The moon was full and its light uncommonly brilliant. The pale beams seemed to waken the instincts of the unfinished Selves. Within their tubes the bodies stirred. The movements of all three were identical and simultaneous—a rippling of tentacle-fingers, a shifting of weight, a quivering of mountainous paunches. Identical currents and eddies swirled through the three tubes.

For at least the space of three hours, the synchronized agitation continued. Then at last when the moon had dipped and hovered sluggishly over the Miasm as if stupefied by the vapors, a change took place. The movements of the Selves grew more precise and purposeful, as if the night had seen the birth of self-will.

The three of them bobbed gently, and the rise and descent of the huge bodies sent violet solution sloshing rhythmically against the walls of glass. The solution was of a buoyant character, and the Selves bounded high. Presently three pallid arms caught like puffy grappling hooks on the rims of the tubes. Three bald and featureless heads broke surface. Three vast white bodies slowly lifted themselves; caught at stomach level upon the rims of their respective tubes; hung there, balanced precariously between floor and ceiling; and then, with a great, heaving effort, pulled themselves over and tumbled headlong to the workroom floor. For a time they floundered and flopped like stricken whales, while the fluid streamed from their limbs to collect in puddles beneath them. At last a common impulse moved them to rise. They did not yet possess full mastery of their bodies. It was only following repeated false starts and with much straining, wasted effort that they finally managed to drag themselves to their feet and take their first faltering steps.

The purpose or essential instinct that had hitherto driven the Selves now seemed to dissipate. The three dripping figures tottered aimlessly around the workroom until they blundered very heavily against the table, which fell with a tremendous clatter. Scores of books, dishes, documents and instruments hit the floor. The Selves could not have heard the noise, for they owned no ears. Nonetheless, the sound attracted them; perhaps they felt the vibrations through the soles of their shapeless feet. Back and forth they stumbled across the wreckage, unconscious of the menace of broken glass. Jagged shards embedded themselves in the pallid flesh, but the Selves took no notice.

Presently they overturned a glass-fronted cabinet, and with the cabinet went hundreds of glass jars and bottles, the spilled contents of which began to eat into the stone floor. Choking vapor arose, but it did not dismay the Selves, whose means of respiration was obscure.

The mindless moonlit rampage continued. Two more cabinets and all their fragile contents went down amidst great destruction. Chairs skidded and a bookcase crashed to the floor. Eventually one of the Selves lurched against the workroom door. The portal was insecurely latched and it gave way before the inadvertent assault. The door opened into blackness. The Self stumbled out of the room and his two alter egos soon followed.

Blindly they advanced to the head of the stairs. Another step pitched them over the brink and sent them rolling down through the darkness to land in a heap at the bottom. The mishap failed to extinguish their stubborn vitality, and after a moment they moved to extricate themselves. The task was beyond their power. The damp pile of flesh jiggled and jerked in vain. The Selves lay in a writhing tangle of limbs throughout the night.

*   *   *

Keprose Gavyne found them in the morning. The Seigneur,

having arisen early to check the progress of his beloved doppelgangers, discovered the three battered figures prostrate and squirming at the bottom of the stairs. His first response was to place them all in a deep sleep—a minor accomplishment in view of their primitive level of consciousness. His next action was to check the condition of the workroom. The carnage he encountered there did not improve his mood.

Keprose instantly mustered the servants, among whom he numbered Relian and Mereth. The three nephews were exempt from service, having wisely elected to spend the night carousing at the Jewel Inn in Vale Jeviant.

The first order of business was the restoration of the workroom, a project of several hours' duration. The broken glass and debris on the floor were cleared away, the fallen furniture set to rights. Then pulleys were attached to the ceiling rafters. Following the installation of the pulleys, Keprose commanded the recovery of his Selves.

Relian assisted in the portage. It was prolonged and difficult work. Each of the three unconscious figures was in turn carried up the steep stairs; disposed upon the workroom floor; enmeshed in a network of ropes attached to the pulleys; hoisted into the air and carefully deposited feet first in its glass tube.

It took hours to replace all the Selves. At the end of that time, the three pallid figures once again floated peacefully in their nutrient baths. Each showed signs of considerable wear— cuts and dark blotches disfigured the formerly perfect whiteness of flesh. One of them had lost a tentacle. A cloud of murky liquid hung about the wound.

Keprose Gavyne inspected the damage with a frown of dissatisfaction. "It is—insufficient. Something more is needed. I shall consider the possibilities," he decided, and turned to study Relian with a speculative air that the latter found disquieting.

*   *   *

Two days later Relian was commanded to demonstrate his supranormal accomplishments. Under the critical regard of Keprose Gavyne he performed a number of arcane hand-gestures, including the difficult Fenn's Multi-Dimensional Transfer; spoke intelligently on the subject of Kronwido; and finally exercised his supranormal Vision to identify a variety of objects concealed in the gray wooden box. His Vision failed, however, when he was separated from the box by a distance greater than five feet; when the hidden contents were liquid or gaseous, rather than solid; and when a solid barrier of any kind was interposed between himself and the box.

"Rudimentary, but well enough as far as it goes," Keprose conceded at the conclusion of the demonstration. "I had hoped to see you attain a higher level of proficiency by this time and you have failed to meet my expectations, which should hardly surprise me. Nonetheless, there are more or less unmistakable signs of progress here and therefore I shall continue tolerant."

Relian and Keprose faced one another across the workroom table, the surface of which was once again littered with books, instruments and dirty dishes. The room had been restored to normalcy. Only the comparative dearth of glass bottles, flasks and jars bore testimony to the recent attack of the Selves. The Selves floated motionless and mindless within their respective tubes. Keprose had effected minor repairs—the cuts and punctures had healed and the bruises had faded. Otherwise, the three creatures had not changed since the night of their illicit excursion. The shock of that experience had put a halt to their supranormally swift evolution. Despite their lack of facial features, hair and color, the Selves were noticeably similar to their creator in general conformation. Relian found himself glancing covertly from tubes to Seigneur and back again. The bulge of the three bellies—the curvature of vast buttocks—the sagging lines of the throat—all belonged to Keprose. The process of replication was fascinating if unsettling to behold.

"Kindly pay attention, young man." Keprose rapped sharply on the tabletop and Relian jumped. "Do you hold my discourse so cheap that you can afford to ignore it?"

"Not at all, Seigneur."

"Very well." Keprose appeared mollified. "I am in an open, warm and genial frame of mind this morning. Take care you do nothing to alter it. Weigh every word with care before speaking, for I must not be troubled or grieved. As it is, however, you will reap the benefit of my present golden tranquillity. I will so far unbend as to confess my absolute confidence in the ultimate development of your supranormalcy. Yes—I will say it—assuming intensive effort on your part and continuing patience on mine in the face of your incessant early blundering. I do not doubt your eventual success."

To hear his master reward Relian with even the faintest of praise was more than Crekkid could stand. The serpent shifted his coils irritably and hissed, "Ssseigneur! Ssseigneur! Lisssten to Crekkid, Ssseigneur! Lisssten!"

"Yes, my little friend?"

"Lisssten! Newsss! Treachery! Betrayal! Sssneaking!" Keprose's brows rose inquiringly and Crekkid declared, "He kisssss girl. He kisssss girl. Crekkid ssseesss it. Kissss on lipsss. Lipsss, Massster, lipsss! Punisssh, Massster? Punisssh?"

Relian felt his face redden.

"Is this true, young man?" Keprose demanded. "Am I to understand that you have forced your attentions upon my Mereth?"

"He kisssss her, Massster! Crekkid sssee!"

"*Your* Mereth?" Relian inquired. Anger caused his customary self-control to slip and he was momentarily careless of consequences. "In what way is she yours, beyond the fact that you are her gaoler? Or do you regard her as your property?"

"Ownership is a somewhat nebulous concept," Keprose returned. "It may be defined in legal, moral, sentimental or practical terms as the occasion warrants. In a perfectly real sense the girl may be regarded as my property. I enjoy absolute power over her, as I do over you, young man. Please—" Keprose held up a hand, "do not trouble me with arguments and recriminations. I state the simple facts. Your approval is not required and I am not minded to endure the tedium of a discourse upon ethics. However, as I am by no means devoid of sentiments at once ardent and elevated, I will consent to reassure you that my intentions toward the girl are honorable—indeed, almost foolishly generous, should she prove worthy. If all falls out as I intend, she shall be honored with the title of Lady Gavyne. Perhaps I condescend too far. But what care I for the world's opinion? Such is my intention."

"I see." Relian drummed his fingers nervously on the tabletop. His worst suspicions had been confirmed. "Has Mistress Mereth anything to say about this?"

"What should she have to say beyond the conventional expressions of gratitude? In any event, her conversation fails to engage me."

"But what of her preferences, her fancy, her inclination? What, in fact, if she should turn you down?"

"I should be forced to question her sanity. However, she can scarcely turn down what has not been offered. I shall make no offer until I am satisfied that the girl fulfills my requirements. She shows no sign of doing so and at times I am tempted to conclude that she is nothing more than the sullen lackwit she appears."

"I presume you speak of supranormalcy, Seigneur."

"I do. It is for obvious reasons desirable—even essential—that Keprose Gavyne take unto himself a supranormal bride. The offspring of such a union will surely enjoy enormous supranormalcy, and their burgeoning powers will enhance my own. The present belongs to my Selves; the future, to my children."

"Quite. And what if Mistress Mereth's supranormal abilities never manifest themselves at all?"

"In that case, her situation remains unchanged. The Seigneur is merciful. I would not turn the girl out to starve in the streets. She will remain at Fortress Gavyne, where any number of uses may be found for her."

"No doubt your nephews can think of several."

"Come, come, young man. You are in no position to criticize my wretched nephews. If Crekkid is to be trusted, your own conduct is hardly above reproach."

"He isss guilty, Massster," Crekkid affirmed and added hopefully, "Punisssh? Punisssh? Punisssh?"

"Unnecessary and undignified, my Crekkid. Punishment implies significant offense, and our young friend's minor impertinences are scarcely worthy of such attention. He has been made aware of the girl's position in this household and will no doubt conduct himself accordingly in the future."

"Or elssse," Crekkid concluded.

"Mistress Mereth may prove less amenable than you expect," Relian suggested mildly. "She strikes me as a lady of some character."

"Indeed?" Keprose inquired indifferently. "I have seen little evidence of it beyond a certain morose intractability similar to that of a mule. But that is irrelevant. It is her supranormalcy that concerns me, and in that respect I have been thwarted since the day I acquired her."

"How did you acquire her, Seigneur? Where does she come from?"

"You need not occupy your mind with such trifles. We've matters of infinitely greater interest and significance to discuss."

Relian eyed him warily. "Which include—?"

"My Selves. Look at them, young man." Keprose's gesture encompassed his sleeping doppelgangers. "It is obvious to the meanest intelligence that their development has ceased. They languish. They stagnate. Premature activity has damped their spirits, and their plight touches me to the heart. I must rekindle their courage and fire their hearts with fresh confidence. This incendiary operation requires the use of a Mercenary's Heartstone, which at the moment I lack. You will obtain such a stone for me."

"I am not going back to that forest." Relian folded his arms. "There is no threat you can offer that will induce me to go."

"That is a very debatable point, young man. Fortunately for all concerned, we need not put it to the test. I am not sending you back to the Miasm. The Mercenary's Heartstones lie elsewhere."

"Where?"

"At the base of the outer wall of the Tyrant of Mists."

"That's little improvement. I'm not going there either."

"Take care, young man. I cannot brook contradiction. I was not made to bear it."

"Nor was I made to bear a condition of involuntary servitude," Relian replied coldly.

"Servitude? You regard the opportunity I have offered you as servitude? Ah, how swiftly is the bright sun of just gratitude obscured by filthy clouds of personal cowardice! Fortunately for your conscience, these defects of character shall not be permitted to govern your actions. You will be rescued from your own baser impulses."

"Crekkid sssee to that, Massster." The serpent did not even trouble to tighten his coils.

"You wouldn't allow your metal creature to kill me," Relian observed. "Not while you believe you've a use for me."

"Quite true, I would not encourage my Crekkid to kill you," Keprose returned equably. "But he can make your life so miserable that you will long for death."

"Punisssh, Massster? Punisssh? Punisssh?"

Relian was silent. There was little to say.

"And now," Keprose continued, his good humor intact, "you will note that the hour is early and the weather is fine. No doubt you are impatient to be off, and I will not stand in your way."

"What do you expect me to do?"

"Is additional explanation really required?" Keprose sighed.

"I see that it is. When shall I learn that others cannot keep pace with an intellect such as mine? Alas, I create my own disappointments. Well then, I shall state the matter as simply as possible. You are to visit the Tyrant of Mists and secure a Mercenary's Heartstone, which you will deliver to me. Does that clarify matters?"

"Not entirely. What dangers shall I encounter at the Tyrant of Mists, and how may I best prepare myself?"

"The nature of the Tyrant of Mists is unknown. There is no reason to assume that you will face danger of any kind."

"Perhaps I may consult some townsman who's actually visited the fortress. Do you know of any?"

"I know of many, but you cannot consult any of them."

"They're dead?" Relian guessed bleakly.

"Missing. All missing. They approached the fortress of Vanalisse the Unseen Hag, entered the region of mists and never emerged. That is all."

"Were there no inquiries? No search parties?"

"There were both. The Unseen Hag did not deign to reply to inquiries. As for the search parties, they too vanished. This situation is open to any number of interpretations. It reveals a mean-spirited pessimism on your part to assume the worst."

"One of my many failings, yet so often justified by events. Is it safe to assume that the Lady Vanalisse keeps close watch over her doubtlessly valuable Heartstones?"

"Again you parade your ignorance, young man. In the first place, the Mercenary's Heartstones are not valuable. As I understand it, hundreds of them lie scattered about the grounds outside the fortress wall. They are of no commercial value. It is only the unique nature of my own project that dictates my current need. In the second place, the Heartstones lie without the property of the Unseen Hag and therefore she possesses no legitimate title to them. Should she dare to claim ownership, the presumptuous female does so wrongfully."

"From my point of view, the technical legitimacy of her claim is not of paramount concern," Relian pointed out dryly. "I am no naturalist. How shall I recognize a Mercenary's Heartstone?"

"They are unmistakable, as they exactly resemble human hearts."

"Is there a reason for that?"

"There is. Generations ago, my ancestor Chiss Gavyne engaged a sizable troop of mercenaries to send against the

Tyrant of Mists. The soldiers encountered no resistance as they approached the fortress. But when they stood at the very base of the outer wall, the chatelaine demonstrated her disapproval. A great light flashed from the fortress and the hearts of two thousand men turned to stone within their bosoms. The corpses rotted there at the wall. The air was foul for weeks and the breezes carried the stench to Vale Jevaint, where pestilence raged. Eventually the bodies turned to earth. All that remained were the stone hearts and they lie there to this day—that is, those that have not been carried away to be sold to the vulgar as souvenirs. But that is a distasteful topic,'' Keprose concluded fastidiously.

"Seigneur, considerable time and effort have been expended on my training. Not five minutes ago, you expressed your complete confidence in my eventual success. That being the case, is it reasonable at this point to risk squandering all that effort by exposing me to unknown dangers and possible death by cardiac petrifaction?"

"Your heart is quite safe, young man. Vanalisse the Unseen Hag has never been known to resort to such tactics. As for the possible waste of the attention that has been lavished upon you, pure altruism guides me. In short, I will sacrifice all in the interests of my Selves. And now—"

"Ssseigneur? Ssseigneur?" Crekkid interjected.

"My friend?"

"Patriarch Crekkid longsss for Nurbo. When ssshall their coilsss mingle?"

"Soon, my ardent little ally. Very soon. We shall speak of it when you return from the Tyrant of Mists. Thus you have good cause to hasten our friend along upon his journey, have you not?"

"Sssssssssssssssssssss!"

Twenty minutes later, the fortress gate groaned shut behind Relian Kru. Relian's request for a weapon had been denied by the Seigneur. The young man had considered asking Mereth to secure him a pistol, but was forestalled by the thought that all such transactions would be carried out under the eyes of two very vocal steel serpents. Mereth's complicity would be reported, and she would probably suffer for it. He had therefore returned briefly to his chamber to collect the only weapon available to him—his straight-edged razor. Armed with the razor, he set out to confront the Tyrant of Mists.

Relian's emergence was observed by the one-armed senti-

nel Glench, who immediately departed to carry the news to
Master Scrivvulch. At the Bearded Moon Tavern, Glench
conferred briefly with his employer; informed Scrivvulch of
the direction taken by his quarry; and finally imparted a
warning most familiar to all denizens of Vale Jevaint—that
the fog hanging eternally about the Tyrant of Mists was
fraught with extreme, albeit mysterious, danger.

                    *   *   *

The Rising Road took Relian down to the foot of the cliffs.
At that point the road swung sharply to the right toward Vale
Jevaint. Gladly would he have followed that route, but the
way was barred to the poacher of the Miasm. Thus Relian
crossed the valley by a circuitous route that skirted Vale
Jevaint on the side farthest from the Miasm. In doing so he
unwittingly eluded the vigilance of the half-dozen Guardsmen
selected by Master Gatherer Clym Stipper to watch for the
Equalist Captain Kru.
    The sun had attained its zenith by the time he reached the
base of the cliff. Here was no Rising Road counterpart to
bring him to the Tyrant of Mists. No well-delineated thoroughfare connected the domain of Vanalisse the Unseen to
the town of Vale Jevaint. Ascension was obviously discouraged. The difficulty of ingress seemed to define the relation-
ship of chatelaine to townsfolk, and indeed to all the world.
    Relian studied the wooded hills. The way was steep and
clogged with underbrush. About halfway up the slopes the
celebrated mists thickened abruptly, increasing in density as
they increased in altitude. The summit of the cliff was entirely hidden from view. There the mists sprawled in massive
clouds that never lifted. Nothing hinted at the presence of the
fortress.
    Relian methodically surveyed the terrain and at last discov-
ered a narrow, overgrown, almost invisible trail angling up
through the trees. He began to climb, picking his way over
fallen branches, exposed roots and loose rocks. Half a dozen
times he stumbled, and only his youthfully quick reactions
preserved him from bruises and sprains. At length he came
upon an open space where the grass was studded with black
flowers, and on the far side of the clearing the mists began.
They rose in a seemingly solid wall, and Relian paused to
stare. Those mists were a blindfold. He would creep sightless

to the house of Vanalisse. His every instinct urged retreat, and he might have heeded the primal promptings but for the determination of his companion.

"Go forward," Crekkid commanded pitilessly. "Go. Go. Go. Go."

He moved forward at once and was instantly ashamed of his unthinking acquiescence. *Another few weeks of this and I'll be the perfect slave, as obedient as Keprose desires. Obedient to such a creature as Crekkid!*

"Go fassster. Fassster. Fassster. Fassster."

Relian deliberately slowed his pace and fangs sank petulantly into the back of his neck. Despite the lagging footsteps he soon found himself enveloped in fog. The world dimmed and grayed around him. With sight all but obliterated, he strained his ears to catch each fleeting sound, but they were few: rustling leaves, the distinctive giggle of a native bird, and little else. Or did he hear a footstep close at hand? He stopped and listened intently. No footsteps. Nothing. A suggestive flexing of the steel loop at his throat sent him on his way.

He pushed on and the mists thickened perceptibly as he went. He could not see the surrounding trees, nor could he discern the narrow path before him. The world shrank inexorably. He could not see the ground, and his legs from the knees down were ghostly. Something clutched at his ankles, snagged his stockings and breeches. He kicked wildly at the invisible assailant, felt the lash of resilient branches, felt his stockings rip. Relian found that he had wandered into a tangle of thorny bushes. He disentangled his garments with difficulty, cast about and discovered brambles on all sides. He had wandered from the path, and finding it again would be well-nigh impossible. Persistent ascent would eventually lead to the top of the cliff and the fortress he sought, but now he would have to struggle every inch of the way over fog-haunted trackless terrain. The hike would take all day or longer.

"You climb," Crekkid urged. "Lazy. Ssslow. Climb. Climb. Climb."

Relian gingerly forced a passage through the brambles, sustaining many a scratch in the process. Soon he encountered bushes so tough and wicked of thorn that his progress was effectively barred and he was forced to return to his starting point.

"Lazy. Ssstupid. Ssstupid." Crekkid complained.

Relian rubbed his chin thoughtfully. Was it possible, he wondered, to use his fledgling supranormal Vision to pierce the fog and show him the path? It was worth a try. He spoke aloud to his incubus. "We are lost."

"Lossst? Lossst? Your fault. Ssstupid. Ssstupid. Ssstu—"

"I'm going to try something," Relian interrupted. "If it works, it will set us back on the right path, thus shortening the term of your separation from Nurbo. However, I need your cooperation. Don't distract me for a few minutes."

Surprisingly Crekkid did not argue, but remained silent and motionless for a time, during which Relian stood staring into fog as opaque as gray milk. Eventually impatience overcame the serpent, who hissed and accused, "Wassste time. Lazy."

The reproaches passed unnoticed, for Relian had succeeded in constructing Uy's Mindwall, which excluded extraneous stimuli from its architect's consciousness. Admonitory nips drew no response and Crekkid lapsed into sullen quiescence.

Moam's Progression now came easily. Relian performed the gestures effortlessly and soon experienced Forn. It was much easier, he found, to see through fog than to see through the walls of the wooden box on which he had so often practiced. Most of the landscape sprang into sharp focus, as if the mists had been burned off by the sun. He saw the surrounding bushes clearly and easily located the path, which lay only a few yards distant. At the top of the hill he glimpsed the Tyrant of Mists, with its tremendous outer wall and its gaunt keep. So impervious were the mists swathing the ancient structure that even a supranormal Visional image was faint. Certain Blindnesses impeded his sight and he did not as yet know a Greej Pattern to provide guidance. He dimly perceived a number of shadowy figures scattered about the area. The figures were upright like men. Most were motionless, but a few were ambulatory. Their movements seemed aimlessly random. Were they human? If so, who were they? Uy's Mindwall blocked out surprise and curiosity. Relian merely observed and mechanically filed observations for future reference, as he had been trained.

A narrow break in the ranks of brambles was now visible. It was through this gap that he must have entered the thicket, and it was the only way whereby he might leave. He took a couple of steps toward the gap. It was the first time he had ever attempted movement other than hand-gestures during the exercise of the supranormal Vision, and the effect on his perceptions was profound. He felt the impact of his feet upon the soil and that impact violently toppled Uy's Mindwall. Sensory impressions stormed his mind. With them came a rush of thought and feeling. All that had been dammed from awareness now came flooding in. The Vision was instantly extinguished. Fog smothered the world. The sudden crash of the Mindwall, the resulting blindness and torrent of conflicting thoughts left Relian prey to confusion. Instinctively he rubbed his eyes as if to restore his lost Vision. Sound, smell, taste and tactile sensations battered at him. For a moment he forgot where he was, and stood blinking in bewilderment.

Gradually the mental tumult subsided and he was able to sort through his impressions, among which was included the sound of footsteps. Relian's brows rose. "Did you hear anything?" he inquired.

"Ssstepsss," Crekkid replied. "Clossse. Lisssten."

This time there could be no doubt. The thud of footsteps and the crackling of twigs underfoot were clearly audible. The unseen presence seemed to make no particular effort to conceal his or her whereabouts. Relian's pulse quickened. His hand slid into the pocket of his coat to touch the handle of the straight-edged razor. Minimally reassured, he crept noiselessly through the gap in the brambles, then paused to listen again. A twig snapped. Relian edged toward the sound and soon discerned a human figure drifting through the mists like a lost specter. The figure appeared misshapen and for a moment Relian thought he saw a hunchback. Closer inspection revealed that the stranger, a sturdily-formed man of middle years, was bowed beneath the weight of a large pack. His neck was laden with ornamental chains, ribbons, loops and skeins of yarn. Around his waist he wore a belt from which depended a variety of small, useful articles: eyeglasses, pocketknives, scissors and mousetraps. He was quite obviously a peddler—or had been. His movements were slow and erratic, his expression vague. The round eyes were so heavily glazed that Relian suspected idiocy. The stranger, unaware of another's existence, was on the verge of drifting by without acknowledgment until Relian spoke. "A moment, sir, if you please."

The peddler halted obediently. The glassy eyes turned in the appropriate direction, but seemed to perceive nothing.

"Have you come from the Tyrant of Mists?" asked Relian.

Response was delayed while the peddler considered. "I don't know," he replied at last in tones slow and hoarse.

"You don't remember?"

"No."

"What is your name?"

The peddler thought about it, then lost interest in the matter. His empty gaze reflected fog. He took a dragging step backward."

"Wait. Where are you going?"

"—Going?"

"Are you lost?"

Silence. Glazed incomprehension.

"How long have you been wandering about in this fog?" Relian noted with misgiving that the man's hair and beard were unshorn, his garments ripped and soiled, his fingernails long.

"I don't know."

"Are you hurt? Have you been in an accident?"

The peddler's jaw hung slack. Silently he turned and shuffled away.

"Wait!" Relian appealed, but the retreating figure did not pause, and soon vanished into the fog.

Relian made his way back to the path without difficulty. The memory of his supranormal Vision was still clear in his mind. He recalled that the way was unobstructed for the next several hundred yards, then blocked by a fallen tree trunk. Beyond the trunk, the path twisted up the slope to the gate of the Tyrant of Mists. He remembered the stark outline of the keep, and felt a thrill of pride that he had succeeded, if only briefly, in penetrating the mists of Vanalisse the Unseen.

The fog seemed less unnerving now, for he knew his Vision could pierce it at will. This sense of mastery was a pleasant novelty. His spirits rose and his recollections of a past life of persistent misfortune receded. His memories were curiously insubstantial, as faded as last week's dreams. Contentment stole along his veins like a drug, lulling his vigilance. His attention wandered. A moment later he tripped and fell over something lumpy and yielding.

Crekkid contented himself with a single, wordless hiss of contempt.

Something squirmed feebly beneath him. Relian found that he had tripped over a human being, a plump and puppy-featured adolescent attired in the gray canvas suit of an apprentice Bellowsman. The young fellow had evidently been sitting or squatting motionless in the middle of the path, and the collision had knocked him over. Now he made ineffectual efforts to raise himself. His movements were slow and uncoordinated, his expression confused. Relian extended a helping hand, which the apprentice either ignored or did not see.

"I'm sorry, I didn't see you. Are you all right?"

No answer. The apprentice gazed up at him with glazed spaniel eyes.

"Are you hurt? Are you lost? Can you understand me?"

"Yes." An uncertain tenor voice.

"Which question are you answering?"

"Yes."

Relian studied the youth, who was pale and sluggish but otherwise healthy enough. "Why are you sitting here in the fog?"

Silence.

"Perhaps you'd like to come with me? I must visit the Tyrant of Mists. After that I return to the house of an unpleasant but undeniably clever man who may be able to help you. I think you'd better come along."

Relian stood up and pulled encouragingly on the young man's arm, which remained bonelessly limp within his grasp. A look of faint perturbation tightened the apprentice's features. His muscles relaxed and he flopped over on his side.

"Please get up. I'm trying to help you—"

"Delaysss. Delaysss. Lazy. You climb," Crekkid commanded.

Relian ignored the serpent. "You can't just stay here. You'll starve or sicken. Do you understand me?"

The apprentice lay motionless, eyes wide but blind. His lips moved, but no sound emerged.

"Go. Climb. Now. Now. Now. Now." Crekkid squeezed impatiently and Relian gasped.

"Listen, you metal-minded little monster, this lad needs help— "

"Not yoursss. Not now. Not important. You climb now."

"Not yet. First I'm going to—"

"Ssstupid. He doesss not want your help. Sssee."

As Relian watched, the apprentice crawled off into the mists and vanished quickly from sight.

"Now you wassste no more time. Climb. Climb. Climb."

He hesitated another moment. But the apprentice was gone,

time was passing and Crekkid's fangs were sharp. Relian reluctantly resumed his journey. Another half hour of walking brought him to the fallen tree revealed by supranormal Vision. He skirted the obstacle without mishap and hiked on. Twenty minutes past the tree trunk he glimpsed a ragged human figure loitering under a pine. He called out, but the stranger drifted off unheeding. A little further along the way, a shriveled ancient lay squarely across the path. The old man's long white hair and beard spread on the ground like patches of dirty snow. Only a few scraps of clothing covered an emaciated frame marked all over with cuts and bruises. The yellowing fingernails were unpleasantly reminiscent of Wingbane talons. The old man lay supine, his dull eyes fixed on nothingness. Only the slow rise and fall of his chest gave evidence of life. He was unaware of events around him and no amount of pleading or prodding elicited a response. Relian eventually gave up trying. There was little assistance he could offer. Moreover, he found himself curiously unconcerned. In the past he would not have been so indifferent, he was certain—and yet the past seemed immensely distant and unaccountably difficult to recall.

It might have been his imagination, but it seemed that the fog was lightening. Earlier in the day the promise of a clear sky would have quickened his blood with hope, but not so now. He had grown accustomed to the mist and now it was less a blindfold than a protective cocoon. He would feel uncomfortably exposed without it.

There could be little doubt, however—the mists and the trees were both thinning. Relian passed one more silent, bedraggled human figure squatting stilly atop a flat rock, then emerged into a quiet clearing. Before him the ground sloped up sharply, and at the top of the rise towered the outer wall of the Tyrant of Mists. He recognized the structure he had viewed supranormally—how long ago?—but he could see it far more clearly now, and was awed by the colossal size and scale of the place. It was vaster than he had dreamed, built as if to house a giantess. He saw for the first time that the wall was unbroken by gate or aperture of any kind. The fortress presented a solid expanse of masonry to the world. Truth or illusion? Did Vanalisse the Unseen remain eternally immured within her fortress? Or was there indeed a portal that was hidden from his sight? The latter was a distinct possibility, for the entire area—fortress and its environs—nearly sang with supranormalcy. The air itself was subtly charged with force, as if a thunderstorm were imminent. In the days before he had studied supranormalcy, Relian would have been unconscious of this force; but he was intensely aware of it now, and he knew that he saw only what Vanalisse chose to permit. The sense of his own powerlessness abashed him. *Why did I come to this place? What am I doing here?* It was with some surprise that he realized that he remembered neither his purpose in coming nor any of the circumstances surrounding his journey. He was fairly certain he had been sent upon an errand of some kind, but he could not recall its objective. Recognition of this mental lapse provoked puzzlement and some uneasiness, but no genuine alarm. His mind was blanketed in fog.

He stood staring up at the Tyrant of Mists until Crekkid grew restive.

"You wassste time. Get ssstone. Ssstone. Ssstone. Ssstone."

The Mercenary's Heartstone. That was what he had come to find at the behest of Keprose Gavyne. He remembered it all quite clearly now—the cessation of the Selves' development, Keprose's commands, the journey from Fortress Gavyne. How could he have forgotten, even for a moment? Relian shook his head and cast another wary glance up at the silent fortress. Was the Unseen aware of his presence? Did she watch him even now? No guard or sentry paced the ramparts. All appeared deserted, but appearance meant nothing. He wondered whether his Vision might penetrate the granite keep, and decided to make the effort. He performed the supranormal preliminaries without unusual difficulty; experienced Forn; but found his sight irrevocably halted at the fortress wall. There was no hint of a path through the granite by way of Forn or by any other method he had studied. The entire wall constituted one huge, unified Blindness impossible to avoid or to pierce. Relian expelled his breath in a sigh and disassembled the Mindwall. The world pressed in on him.

"—pid. Ssstupid. Get ssstone now."

He took a deep breath and forced himself forward to the base of the wall. The skin between his shoulder blades itched in anticipation of the stab of Vanalisse's lightning bolts. But there came no sign of hostility or even of life from the Tyrant of Mists. All remained silent and tranquil. Relian's palms were sweating and he wiped them brusquely. *No time for nerves. Find the stone and leave.*

The ground was strewn with hundreds of rocks. They lay everywhere. *How long will it take to find what I'm looking for in the midst of all this? Keprose claimed that two thousand hearts turned to stone, but that was generations ago. How many remain? Of those remaining, how many are still above ground? And what if the entire tale's a hoax to begin with?* But doubts and questions were equally pointless. Relian stooped and began to paw through piles of rock. Much of it was granite, gray flecked with pink and white, similar to that used in the fortress wall. Most of it was unidentifiable gravel. *What if time and friction have eroded the contours of the Heartstones to the point of unrecognizability? The search could take days.*

Crekkid spoke as if in answer to his thought. "Find ssstone. Fasssst. Fassst. Fassst. Fassst."

Could I use the Vision? Relian wondered. *I might slide my sight through these piles of rock faster than I can sort them by hand.* He attempted it, focusing his attention on the largest pile. The stones on the ground were not imbued with resistance to supranormal scrutiny, and offered no obstacle comparable to that presented by the fortress wall. Nonetheless, Relian's fledgling Vision penetrated only the topmost layer. Beyond that point, he was blind. He saw no Heartstone. Another approach was needed.

"Why do you jussst sssit? Lazy." Crekkid's complaints went unnoticed.

Next time, Relian directed his Vision at a patch of bare ground and obtained encouraging results. It was comparatively easy to see through dirt. His Vision dove at least a foot underground before it lost its power. The topsoil was riddled with rocks which he perceived imperfectly in hazy outline. He searched among them swiftly, then drew his Vision back to the surface and directed it at another patch of clear soil. Down he plunged. And there, some six inches below the surface, he encountered a fist-sized rock with a roughly triangular shape and a twisted crown of truncated veins and arteries. Relian abandoned Forn, and the solid objects surrounding him regained their visual imperviousness. He drew the razor from his pocket, and with its handle dug away the soil. Six inches down he found the stone.

He pried it carefully from its resting place, brushed the clinging dirt from the surface and examined his discovery with interest. The Heartstone was deep red in color and

covered with traceries of a darker shade that perfectly preserved the pattern of the original blood vessels. It looked
most lifelike, but was cold, still and very heavy. Obviously
the petrified organ retained qualities transcending those of the
marble that now composed it, else Keprose Gavyne would
have no use for it. But what those qualities might be Relian
could not guess and Keprose would probably decline to reveal. The answer might be found in Wefkrone's great reference work, *Essential Essences*; and Relian, thoroughly intrigued,
determined to investigate the matter upon his return to Fortress Gavyne. An alternative source of information might
be—what was the set of volumés on the bottom shelf of the
central bookcase in Keprose's workroom? He could not remember. It was ridiculous; he had used those books dozens of
times. They took up half the shelf, the rest of which was
occupied by—what? Again, he could not recall. Relian frowned
vaguely. Something was quite wrong. He had grown completely familiar with the contents of Keprose's bookcases
since he had come to Fortress Gavyne from—where was it he
had come from?

As Relian sat pondering the matter, a voice spoke within
his mind.

You are supranormal.

It was a woman's voice, unlike any he had ever heard
before—passionless, unimaginably old, remote as the stars.
Human and something more. Relian froze, hands clenched on
the Heartstone. Shock ripped the cobwebs from his memory.

You are afraid.

He found his own voice at last. "Are you Vanalisse?"

I was.

"I do not understand."

Silence. No reply, but Relian felt the freezing tentacles of an
alien supranormalcy invade his mind, and shuddered at the sensation. Never during the course of his unwilling association with
Keprose Gavyne had he experienced anything akin to it. In desperation, if only to put a halt to the intolerable mental exploration,
he spoke again. "Do I trespass upon your property, Madam?"

My property? A pause. *I recall the concept. The question
has little meaning.*

"Is my presence acceptable?"

*Your supranormalcy is barely realized. Its frustrated exis-
tence blights your life.*

The abrupt change of topic threw him off balance, but he

collected his thoughts quickly. "How do you know that, Lady Vanalisse? Do you read all my thoughts and memories?"

Thoughts and memories are the thin outer layer. Clarity lies deeper. You are slave to a tyrant.

The subject was painful, but he answered steadily, "Keprose Gavyne imposes his will upon me and will continue to do so until I am strong enough to win free. And I grow stronger every day."

Keprose is irrelevant. You are slave to your own supranormalcy, which consumes like an ungoverned blaze and rules where it should serve. You are ignorant and a slave to misfortune. Grow wise.

"Madam, I've known much misfortune throughout my life. I am hopeful that mastery of supranormalcy will change all that."

Supranormalcy unmastered and unrecognized is the source of your misery. The talent unused will fester, poisoning all of life.

"I wish to continue my studies, but not to serve the purposes of Keprose Gavyne."

All action on behalf of Keprose is futile. You do not serve him for you cannot.

"I do not pretend to understand you. Do you know why I've come?"

You have come a distance in search of an object, for you have not yet grasped the principal of universal fungibility, a supranormal truth not immediately apparent. You may take what you desire.

"I thank you, Madam. But I think it only fair to warn you of Keprose Gavyne's intent. He has sent me to secure a Mercenary's Heartstone that will further the development of his three self-replications, whose combined supranormal powers will be directed against you."

"You ssspeak to yoursssself. Ssstupid. No one here. Ssstupid." Evidently Crekkid was unaware of Vanalisse the Unseen.

A dire prospect, were I flesh. As it is, Keprose may at worst inflict damage upon my house, an expendable structure.

"Are you not flesh?"

Occasionally. All substances are fungible. It is your flesh that is now at risk of undesirable transformation, for successful completion of the Selves of Keprose Gavyne terminates your indispensability. Your enemies grow restive and Keprose will choose to pacify them for his own ease. But I see you have already considered this.

"I have considered it, yes. The Selves of Keprose are far from completion. There is some time left for me to find means of delivering myself." Relian hesitated. "Might I ask your assistance, Madam? Keprose Gavyne is your hereditary enemy. In helping me escape his power, you help yourself."

"Ssstupid. Ssstupid. No one here. No help. Ssstupid." Crekkid's hiss carried sneering overtones.

Silence from the fortress and then the voice rang in his mind. *Enemy. I recall. Such terms have lost their immediacy.*

"Keprose would not agree."

These matters fail to engage my attention. My concerns lie elsewhere.

"Then in simple charity if nothing more, will you not help me?"

Your request is not specific.

"I will make it so. I beg you to remove the steel serpent from my neck."

"Sssssssssss! Ssstupid. Mad. You talk to the air. Mad," Crekkid opined.

I will not divert your lifestream. The consequences might not meet your expectations.

Relian clenched his jaw as he saw hope slipping away, but when he spoke, his voice was even. "May I not be the judge of that?"

Can you trust your judgment? Is it now unclouded?

On the point of emphatic affirmation, Relian paused to recall the recent caprices of his memory. "Have you a reason for asking, Lady Vanalisse?"

You have wandered at length amidst mists that kill the past and future.

"You speak in riddles, Madam."

All your past life is yours no more. The flying hours are gone. Without the past, there is little future. Such is the nature of the mists that veil this granite shell.

"I'll leave this place with all speed. But before I go—I ask you once more. Grant me one favor—free me of the serpent."

A favor may be less than it seems. Grow wise. Farewell.

Abruptly the huge alien intelligence departed his mind, leaving him confused and disoriented. "Lady Vanalisse—?" he appealed, but received no answer. She was gone, leaving him alone upon the ground at the foot of the fortress wall. Alone?

"Wassste time. Ssstupid. Lazy. Mad. Talk to air. You have ssstone, we go home now. Home. Home. Home. Home."

"Yes." Relian spoke dully. "I suppose we must." He looked down at the Heartstone for a moment, then dropped it in his coat pocket. "We have what we came for, there's nothing to hold us now."

His stomach rumbled and it occured to him that he was hungry. He did not think he had eaten since earliest morning, but it was difficult to remember. What time was it now, and how long until evening? Fog hid the face of the sun and it was impossible to judge the hour. Relian rose to his feet and struck off wearily along the path. He faced a long hike back to Fortress Gavyne and already he was hungry, dejected and fatigued.

For a time he stumbled along, his mind almost blank. The trail was downhill, and gravity aided his progress. He heard nothing, felt little save hunger, and his eyes were filled with fog. At length he paused to look back the way he had come, and found that the Tyrant of Mists was no longer visible. Its disappearance bewildered him. Had he truly visited the fortress or had he dreamed it? Was there a fortress there at all? Reality consisted of mist, dimly-realized trees and moist soil underfoot. Was there anything more? The images in his mind—the faces, the places—were they true memories, pure fancy, or something in between? Relian unconsciously passed a hand across his face, but his eyes remained misted and his confusion deepened.

Where was he going? A fortress, wasn't it? Or had he just come from a fortress? There was no point in going on until he had settled the question, so he stopped to think. Twenty minutes later he was still standing there, motionless in the middle of the trail. His face was ashen, his jaw hung slack, and his staring eyes were heavily glazed.

Another five minutes passed and Crekkid grew impatient. "Ssstupid. Wassste time. We go home now."

Relian emerged from his trance. "Home?" he repeated blankly.

"Home to Massster. Home to Nurbo. Home. Home. Home. Home."

"Yes. Then there is truly a fortress?"

"Sssssssssssss! You asssk? Ssstupid. Mad. Ssstupid. Brain sssoft. Weak."

"Where is the fortress?" Relian inquired. He had the vague impression that the answer might be significant, but couldn't bring himself to care much. His emotions were numb as his intellect.

"You forget? Or you play trick?" Crekkid paused for reply, but there was none. The serpent flexed irritably. "Move forward along path. Move. Move. Move. Move."

Relian obeyed, for there seemed no reason to refuse. Only once as he passed through a patch of palpably dense fog did his footsteps falter. A nip of steel fangs urged him on his way, and thereafter he marched along at a good pace. He did not pause to accost any of the empty-faced compatriots he spied drifting among the mists, for his curiosity slumbered. In any event, Crekkid brooked no delay.

He had forgotten where the serpent was directing him and why. He had forgotten his past and its attendant woes. He had forgotten everything, and the fog was all his world. Somewhere just below the level of consciousness lurked the knowledge of danger, of ineffable wrongness, an unquiet sense that things should be somehow other than they were. But such sensations were weak and sporadic. For the most part he was contented enough, and all that really disturbed his tranquillity was an occasional pang of hunger. The hunger was curiously easy to ignore and presently ceased to trouble him at all.

"Sssssssssssss! You walk off path! Blind!" Crekkid squeezed angrily and pain briefly jolted Relian from his daze.

"Path?"

"Ssstupid! Blind! Blind!"

They had come to a point where the trail took a sharp bend to skirt a stand of thornbushes. Relian had continued a straight course and now wandered amidst thick undergrowth. The serpent was hissing furiously at him. He did not know why and did not greatly care; but the creature's torments could not quite be ignored.

"Turn around. Go back to path. Turn. Turn. Turn. Turn."

"Path?"

"Ssssssssssss! Brain sssoft! Sssoft!" Crekkid plunged vicious fangs into the back of his victim's neck. Relian's response was sluggish and the serpent whistled in frustration. "Brain sssoft. Weak. Mad. No good! Weak flesssh, brain rot inssside head! Rot! Not like ssstrong ssssteel brain of Crekkid. Now go back. Go. Go. Go. Go."

Relian obediently turned and slogged his way back to the path. Thereafter, his incubus maintained strict vigilance and no additional deviations from course occurred. The fog lay heavier than ever upon Relian's mind. He advanced mechanically at the will of the serpent, but lost all sense of his own movement and imagined himself floating weightlessly, at one with the mists.

He had walked for miles and eaten nothing for many hours. He should have been tired and ravenous, but felt nothing. He was unaware of his own progress and did not note the thinning of the mists. The outlines of the trees were sharpening as the range of visibility steadily increased. He had descended about halfway down the hill and was now emerging from the region of Vanalisse's foggy veils. Before him the ground sloped away, and the dips and hollows were free of all but the thinnest rags of pale vapor. The sky opened up and its monotone cast was only the ordinary gray of a cloudy afternoon.

Relian gazed expressionlessly down at the valley below, then turned his back on the light and made for the comforting shelter of the fog. A squeeze from Crekkid halted him in mid-stride. He paused, frowning faintly.

"Turn," Crekkid commanded. "Go down hill. Go. Go. Go. Go."

Relian hesitated and the serpent's fangs drew blood. "Home now. Home to Massster. Home to Nurbo."

Relian's reluctance could not express itself in words. "The fog," he managed to reply, his brow furrowed with effort. "The fog?"

"Home. Move. Move. Move. Move."

Relian cast a last longing glance back over his shoulder before resuming his descent. Had his mental processes not been slowed to the verge of extinction, he would have been astonished at Crekkid's next command.

"Ssstop. Ssstop. Ssstop. Ssstop."

Relian wordlessly halted. Only his eyes still roamed in search of fog.

"Man waiting," Crekkid observed. "Ssskinny old man. You do not notice? Ssstupid."

Relian stood among the trees that edged a long, steeply-inclined clearing. The clearing and all the land below it were free of mist. At the far end of the flower-starred expanse waited a downy-haired gentleman neatly attired in brown. The gentleman sat with his back propped against a boulder, his spindling legs extended before him. His head was bent over a book. An ebony cane lay on the ground at his side. From time to time he raised his head and briefly surveyed the landscape. His vantage point afforded a clear view of the trail and much of the valley below. Relian looked on without comprehension. Once again he experienced that remote, uneasy sense of wrongness, but could not identify the cause. After a moment's indifferent inspection he lost interest and his eyes slid away from Scrivvulch the Stick.

"You sssee man?"

"Yes," Relian replied tonelessly.

"Enemy. Chassse you before. You run."

"Enemy?"

"Sssssssssssss! You forget? Ssstupid. You are dead if Crekkid doesss not think for you."

It took extraordinary effort and concentration, but Relian succeeded in framing a question. "Why?"

"Why enemy? Who knowsss? Maybe man doesss not like you. Crekkid does not like you either. But Crekkid sssave you for Massster. Thisss time. Now turn left. Quiet. Left. Left. Left. Left."

Relian obeyed. The serpent's insistent advice steered him off the trail and around the clearing in a wide curve that bypassed the Assassin by a safe margin. Progress was slow. The undergrowth was riddled with thorns and Crekkid insisted on absolute silence. The cloudy sky was darkening and the chill of dusk was in the air when Relian finally made it to the bottom of the hill where the trees ended. The valley floor spread out before him. Not far away, the lanterns of Vale Jevaint were starting to flicker to life. High up on a cliff across the valley, Fortress Gavyne loomed as a black silhouette against the iron sky.

"Ssstop. Ssstop. Ssstop. Ssstop."

Relian halted, his empty gaze fixed on the golden lights of the town.

"We wait for darknessss. If man ssseesss you, you die. You cannot fight or run—too weak, too ssslow, too ssstupid. We wait for darknessss."

They waited. It was a fairly lengthy delay, but it did not occur to Relian to sit down. He stood like a mannequin under the pines. When a gegrim lighted upon his hand and began to suck his blood, he made no motion to slap the insect away. There was no visible sunset, for the sun was already obscured by clouds. The sky darkened slowly from gray to black, and the breezes of night stirred the treetops.

"We go home now," Crekkid announced. "Go. Go. Go. Go." Relian did not move and Crekkid employed his teeth. "Move. Now."

Relian advanced mechanically. The night was dark and the ground uneven. It took him at least three hours to work his way across the open fields to the opposite side of the valley and the Rising Road. When he finally arrived, his knees were covered with scrapes and scratches, the result of numerous falls. He was exhausted and his movements were snail-slow. Nor could Crekkid's persuasions induce greater speed.

To climb the steep Rising Road without benefit of a lantern on a moonless night would have been difficult at the best of times. Under the present circumstances it was impossible. Crekkid grudgingly permitted his victim respite, and Relian spent the night sleeping under a bush at the side of the road.

He woke at dawn. His cuts and bruises had stiffened during the night and he ached all over. His perceptions remained dulled, however, and he was scarcely conscious of the pain.

"Get up now. Get up now. Now. Now. Now. Now," Crekkid shrilled, and Relian obeyed.

A series of nips and squeezes goaded him on his way. Relian commenced climbing and arrived at Fortress Gavyne well before noon. There he delivered up the Heartstone. Keprose Gavyne professed himself well pleased with the stone, but not with the mental condition of its bearer. Relian was ordered confined to his chamber until such time as he recovered his wits—a matter, as it turned out, of some ten days.

*   *   *

Once again the moon was full over Fortress Gavyne. Once again the white beams slanted in through the windows of the abandoned workroom to play upon the great glass tubes. Within their respective tubes the sleeping figures bobbed in unison.

The addition of Heartstone essence to the nutrient solution wherein reposed the Selves had wrought many changes. The solution itself had changed color slightly, darkening from violet to a murky maroon. This alteration was visible even in the deceptive moonlight. More apparent yet was the transformation of the Selves. Each of the three rotund bodies was now complete, from hyperdigital fingers tipped with translucent maroon nails, to sagging paunch, to dimpled knees and bandy calfs, down to the archless feet with their weirdly elongated toes that echoed the overdevelopment of the fingers. Fine maroon hair feathered the bodies. The formerly bald skulls were now covered with pinkish curls. Each face now comprised the broad cheeks, receding multiple chins, broad nostrils and cupid's bow lips of its prototype. Each Self was in fact a perfect physical replica of Keprose Gavyne. Three Keproses floated within their tubes, each indistinguishable in appearance from the original and from one another. They remained unconscious. The eyes were closed and the faces were blank.

And yet the moonlight seemed to stir deep instincts. As the white beams bathed their bodies, the Selves simultaneously turned within their tubes, slowly—very slowly—spinning like immense baroque pearls pendant upon invisible chains. The pallid bulges reflected shifting highlights. Nude buttocks and bellies flattened against the glass as the doppelgangers hitched themselves around to face the bone-white moon. At last, when all three bodies were properly oriented and all three faces were lifted to the light, a final change occurred. Three sets of pink-lashed lids slowly lifted. Three sets of identical blue eyes gazed out through walls of glass. In terms of size, shape and color, they were the eyes of Keprose Gavyne. But where the eyes of Keprose were filled with complacent intelligence, the eyes of the doppelgangers were empty. Vacuous, blue and totally expressionless, they gazed upon the world without comprehension. Eyes so blank might have stared blindly from the faces of drowned corpses at rest beneath a maroon ocean. Only the occasional tremor of a heavy lid gave evidence of life.

*   *   *

"Ready to give it another try, Relian?"

"I suppose so." Relian sighed as he regarded the materials spread out before him on the workroom table. There were books, folios and pamphlets piled on it, with pertinent passages marked for easy reference. A space had been cleared among the books and in this space rested a small drift of gray goose down, the object of his concentrated attention. In the days that had passed since his recovery from the effects of Vanalisse's mists, Relian had been studying the rudiments of the supranormal Tactility. While his progress with the Vision was more than satisfactory, he had achieved no similar success with the Tactility. The project assigned to him by Mereth involved the use of Tactility to pull a feather from the pile. It should have been a relatively simple exercise, as no levitation was required, but Relian found unusual difficulty in focusing his attention. Perhaps it had something to do with the presence of the Selves. The resemblance of the three Keproses asleep in the tubes to their prototype was disagreeably exact and almost impossible to ignore. It was as if Keprose himself were eternally present in triplicate, and the effect was distracting as a mental itch. The Selves were motionless, their heads bowed and their eyes shut. They were unconscious, or else not alive at all. But somehow, he could not have said why, Relian knew they were very much alive. Possibly the recent development of his latent supranormalcy was responsible, but intuition informed him that the Selves were not only alive, but changing. Asleep they might be, but they possessed primitive identity and perhaps more awareness than their apparent somnolence suggested. His eyes turned involuntarily to the corpulent figures. They were motionless as ever, or nearly so. Small eddies stirred the pinkish curls. Had the three white bodies quietly shifted to face him, or had they been positioned thus ever since he entered the room? Relian stared narrowly. No movement at all. They were still as idols. He shrugged and turned away.

"I think you might have better luck if you use the Vision to build supranormal momentum, then slide from Moam's Progression directly to the Invisible Hand," Mereth suggested. She spoke casually, but her normally pale cheeks were becomingly flushed. "You already know how to create the Hand, and now it's only a question of learning to control it. Once you achieve that, you can start adding more Fingers."

Relian examined her, noting the elongated hands, the intelligence in the wide gray eyes, the facial mobility reflecting acute sensitivity to varied stimuli—the essential attributes of the successful supranormalist. He wondered aloud for the hundredth time, "Mereth, I don't understand why you can't perform these exercises yourself. You certainly have the learning."

"I've tried many times. All the learning in the world won't help if the basic ability isn't there."

"You don't know that it isn't there, and if you could only learn to use it, we—" He caught the eager silvery flash of movement at her throat and deliberately stopped himself.

She met his eyes and nodded slightly. All of her movements and gestures were restrained, as if she wore invisible chains. Her infrequent laughter was similarly subdued. The constraint, together with her air of melancholy, evoked sympathy despite all her stoicism. Relian wondered what it would be like to see her move freely, to run, jump or even dance. Had she ever had the chance to learn how? "If I succeed this time, will you give it another try?" he asked.

Mereth smiled. "Agreed. In fact I'll try it even if you don't succeed, for that is the desire of the Seigneur."

"Ssseigneur. Wissse Ssseigneur. Great Ssseigneur," echoed Nurbo, who had evidently missed the note of sarcasm in her bearer's last remark.

"But don't expect too much," Mereth concluded.

"You may surprise yourself one day. All right, I'll go first and I'll take your suggestion about starting off with Moam's Progression and the Vision," said Relian.

"Good. Then use it to read what's written here." Mereth produced a folded scrap of paper and laid it on the table.

"What's that?"

"Practice."

Had it been anyone other than Mereth he would have suspected a practical joke. As it was, he took her at her word.

The achievement of Forn had grown almost effortless. The task of reading a folded message was a simple one and Relian, confident of his power of concentration, did not bother with Uy's Mindwall.

It was far easier to see through paper than to see through wood or earth. The Blindnesses that blocked his Vision were small and few. The First Greej Pattern could have guided him had he chosen to employ it, but his store of knowledge was increasing and now he realized that in this particular case, the Third Greej Pattern would provide a shorter path and greater clarity. Sliding his Vision lithely in and out amongst the Blindnesses, Relian penetrated the folded paper and read the message:

I love you.

Instantly the paper regained its opacity. The unfamiliar happiness that crashed upon his unprepared mind broke his concentration and blinded his Vision. He saw a blank, folded paper. Raising his eyes to Mereth's face, he needed no supranormalcy to read her suspense. Apparently his expression allayed her fears, for her face relaxed and her rare smile shone.

"And I love you." Relian spoke without thought of consequences and promptly had cause to regret his incaution.

"You sssay?" Crekkid inquired. "What do you sssay?"

"Nothing," Relian assured him. "Nothing that concerns you," he amended and looked to Mereth. Her expression reflected a mingling of exhilaration and alarm such as he had glimpsed only once before in his life—on the face of Squire Vorpiu's second daughter when the horse she was riding had bolted.

"He ssspeaksss of love," Nurbo explained. "Love. Love. Love. Love."

"Why doesss he ssspeak thusss? Why do you ssspeak of love?" Crekkid punctuated the question with an irritable squeeze. "Why?"

"Just an idle expression," Relian answered when he could catch his breath.

"Idle? Idle? Yesss, lazy. You are here to work," the serpent observed. "Dare you ssspeak of love when Matriarch Nurbo and Patriarch Crekkid mussst sssigh in vain? You work, and no more talk of love. Work. Or elssse."

"Brave Crekkid! Ssstrong Crekkid!" Nurbo admired, and Crekkid flexed complacently.

"They're right, I suppose," Mereth remarked. "We must get back to it. But first let me congratulate you on your progress. What you have demonstrated this morning pleases me beyond expression."

"I'm equally pleased," Relian responded with a cautious glance at Mereth's snake, "and intend to further my progress at the earliest opportunity. I can only hope that I shall not tread this path unaccompanied."

"You may rely upon my continuing assistance. I'll exert my best efforts on your behalf," Mereth returned helpfully.

"You sssay?" Crekkid's inquisitive hiss bit into the oblique conversation. "Ssspeak plain!"

"We were saying that we'll combine our supranormal efforts," Relian explained smoothly. "Remember, the Seigneur teaches us that supranormalcy at its most powerful is a collective endeavor."

It was doubtful that Crekkid caught the full sense of this explanation, but he managed to grasp the essential point. "Ssseigneur sssay! Ssseigneur! Ssseigneur!"

"Just so. Mereth, shall we try for Tactility?" Relian asked. She nodded and they went on to work.

Relian immediately set about constructing Uy's Mindwall. Without the protection of the Mindwall, his mental turmoil would have precluded all chance of success. Construction proved difficult, but eventually the wall rose to shield his consciousness. That accomplished, Relian achieved Forn with relative ease, and for a moment gave himself over to the floating sensation that signaled progress through the first of the various obscure dimensions. His eyes were closed, but the image of the folded message was clear and sharp in his mind. The Third Greej Pattern guided him among the Blindnesses, and a focusing of will increased his speed. Relian's Vision cut through the paper like a blade, and once again he scanned the message: I love you. He read the words unmoved, for the Mindwall blocked pain and pleasure alike. Slight tremors shook the foundation, but he concentrated powerfully and the barrier held. His supranormal perceptions retained their clarity. But the emotions barred from his consciousness seemed to possess a force that must find outlet; a force that lent him the power to generate the Invisible Hand and to control it as never before.

The Hand was ghostly—dim, transparent, insubstantial and indistinct. Its strength and flexibility were minimal. At this point it might better have been called a claw than a hand, for it consisted of nothing more than thumb and index finger. Only time and practice would teach Relian to generate a supranormal member possessed of substantiality, power and multiple fingers. Nonetheless, this apprentice Hand owned acute sensitivity, and Relian could feel the air currents passing over the supranormal skin.

Now came the hard part. He would have to open his eyes and it was here that all of his previous efforts had failed. In every case, the attempted use of ordinary eyesight had resulted in the instant evaporation of the imperfectly-realized flesh and bone.

Relian's lids lifted slowly. He beheld the Hand floating in midair, but connected to his wrist by an attenuated strand of cloudy matter. As he watched, the insubstantial flesh lightened and the outline swam briefly. He held his breath and exerted his will. Today he possessed unwonted power. The flickering ceased and the Hand remained. Faint it was, and barely discernible. It would not be visible at all to ordinary eyes, but it was undoubtedly there. He released his breath slowly. The Mindwall excluded relief, surprise, satisfaction, nervous tension.

He could now afford to look around him. Mereth sat on the opposite side of the table. Her eyes were closed, her face

white and still. A faint vertical crease marking her smooth
brow was the only sign of intense mental effort. Were her
efforts successful? An accomplished supranormalist would
have known at a glance, but Relian found it impossible to
judge. Was that a smudge of mist floating before her, or did
he imagine it? It was not the time to wonder, and he turned
his attention to the heap of gray down on the table in front of
him. Should he prove capable of pulling one of the feathers
from the pile, it would mark the beginning of his mastery of
the Tactility.

Moving the Hand was even more difficult than he had
expected; it was like trying to blow smoke upwind. Progress
was agonizing but perceptible. Slowly the Hand swam through
air that seemed thick and heavy as yesterday's porridge. At
last it was poised above the goose down and Relian paused to
rest briefly. He was already tired and the worst was yet to
come.

He took a deep breath and exerted mental force. The Hand
descended, settled like fog upon the feathers. The finger and
thumb felt like stuffed bolsters. Relian bore down with all the
force of his mind and found that he could bend them. Slowly
the digits curved to encompass the empty air. He had missed
his target entirely. The next two attempts were equally unsuccessful. He assessed the situation quickly, made an estimate,
shifted the Hand a couple of inches to the left and tried again.
This time the fingers closed on the chosen feather. When he
tugged at the fluff, it did not move. Relian pulled harder. He
thought he felt the feather stir slightly, but it was hard to be
certain—a random breeze could have been responsible. Another effort, and this time he pulled with all the pitiable
strength of his Hand.

The feather moved. It took every ounce of his power and
determination to drag it from the pile. And he had moved it
no more than half an inch or so before the Hand was seized
with cramps that even Uy's Mindwall could not altogether
exclude.

Relian's concentration was broken once and for all by the
pressure of an insistent hand upon his shoulder. Mereth stood
at his side and she was shaking him. He looked up at her
dazedly. The Hand disappeared. The Mindwall crashed and
the world swam back into normal focus. Only the lone gray
feather lying half an inch from the pile gave evidence that the
Hand had ever existed and functioned.

"Relian!" She was yelling for his attention. Mereth, who rarely raised her voice, was yelling.

"*Relian*!" She pulled at a lock of his hair, pinched his earlobe and shook him again. "Come back!"

"I'm back. What is it?"

She pointed mutely. Relian turned to behold the Selves of Keprose Gavyne bobbing energetically within the tubes. Their blue eyes were wide open, their arms upraised and their motions perfectly synchronized. Up and down—each leap brought them nearer the freedom they sought. Already the maroon nutrient solution was sloshing over the tops of the tubes to rain upon the workroom floor.

"When did they start?"

"Only just now, while you were closed off behind your Mindwall."

"What set them off?"

"I don't know—perhaps the supranormal activity. They're going to get out if we don't do someth—"

Before Mereth had finished speaking, three dripping arms hooked on three glass rims. With surprising adroitness the doppelgangers hauled themselves up and out of the tubes. The three nude bodies struck the floor simultaneously. The Selves arose and stood gazing about the workroom with their empty eyes. They were now the perfect triple image of Keprose, save for a faint translucency about the elongated fingers. Their senses were fully developed—they could see, hear, touch, taste and smell, which had not been the case upon the occasion of their previous excursion. But no trace of human intelligence lurked in the china blue eyes. The minds remained dormant, unable to decipher the coded messages of the senses.

A tiny, ecstatic whistling arose. "Three Ssseigneursss!" Crekkid was entranced. "Three! Ssseigneursss! Three!"

The noise attracted the attention of the Selves, who waddled toward the source. Relian retreated hastily, and the Selves followed. One of them brushed against a cabinet in passing, and the contents rattled. Caught by the sound, the creature paused to give the cabinet a shake.

Relian instinctively stepped forward to lay a restraining hand upon the Self's arm. The creature, imbued with all the natural arrogance of its creator, jerked itself free and swung its arm in a wide arc. The open-handed buffet took Relian under the ear. It was unexpected, and delivered without ves-

tige of restraint. Relian staggered and fell. Crekkid's hiss
mocked his bruises. The victorious Self watched vacantly,
then turned and headed for the open door. Its alter egos
shambled in its wake.

"Quick, Mereth—run to the door and lock it."

She attempted to do so, but it was already too late. The
Selves did not brook interference. A sweep of a huge arm
easily scooped the girl out of the way. Mereth landed lightly
on her feet, scowled in frustration, and went to Relian's side.
"Are you all right?"

"Yes." Relian stood. "We'd better find some way of
stopping those creatures. There's no telling what they'll do."

"We can't stop them by ourselves. We'd best go find
Keprose." Mereth pronounced the name distastefully.

But they did not move, for the Selves blocked the only
exit. The doppelgangers crowded the landing at the head of
the steep stairway. Then all three of them, impelled by identical unknowable impulses, moved to descend. The stairway was
too narrow to permit the bulbous Selves to walk abreast.
Thus, following an initial bout of jostling, Nature's abhor-
rence of equality dictated an order of precedence.

They moved in a single file. It was a jerky, halting progress, for they had not yet learned to bend their knees. The
Selves descended stiff-legged. Each step jarred the mountainous
bodies to set jowls and bellies a-quiver. Near the bottom of
the stairs, the first Self stumbled. The creature's arms flailed
wildly. It grabbed at the walls, teetered a perilous instant,
then tumbled the remaining few steps. The other two Selves
followed to stumble and fall at precisely the same point. The
three bodies sprawled at the foot of the stairs. For a moment
they lay there, limbs entwined, occasional tremors rippling
the plentiful flesh. Six blue eyes regarded the floor, walls and
ceiling with equal indifference. Then, as if acting upon an
unheard signal, the Selves simultaneously raised themselves
to sitting positions and from thence to their feet. Their heads
drooped and their bodies swayed as they shifted weight from
foot to foot, each striving to build the energy to overcome
massive inertia. The moment arrived and progress resumed.
The Selves lurched forward and the corridor resounded to the
rhythm of their synchronized footsteps.

Relian and Mereth watched from the landing. Relian spoke
in perplexity. "Where are they going? What do they want?

Mereth, you've read everything in Keprose's library. Do you understand this?''

She shook her head. ''There's nothing written about the creation of Selves. I don't think it's ever been done before. Keprose must have taken extensive notes on his experiments, but you may be certain I've never been permitted to see them. At to where the Selves are going and what they want, I don't think they're driven by any particular purpose. Considered in light of their prototype's character, it seems more likely that they're simply motivated by disinclination to tolerate restraint.''

''Then you don't think they're really dangerous?''

''Probably not—as long as no one gets in their way. Actually, I don't know.''

Together they descended the stairs and went in search of Keprose Gavyne.

*   *   *

The fortress was large, its corridors seemingly endless. The Selves wandered, devoid of knowledge and purpose. Along the echoing galleries they lurched, through empty chambers and down the great central stairway with its carved stone balustrade that could have provided invaluable support had they but known how to use it. As it was, they wobbled and tottered dangerously upon the treads, and at the same instant all three sat down hard. They rose with comparative ease— despite their dormant intellects, their physical self-control was undoubtedly increasing—and resumed the aimless trek.

They had now reached the ground level. The chambers they traversed were no longer uniformly deserted. Here and there they encountered liveried servants who gaped in superstitious awe as the damp triple image of their naked Seigneur shuffled past. Some of the menials fled for the safety of the servant's quarters. Others, more courageously inclined, remained to watch. The Selves took no notice. On they went, under an archway and into a hall whose wall was pierced at regular intervals by tall windows, shutters thrown back to admit the morning sun. The bright streams of light attracted the attention of the Selves. The three of them clustered at a window, gazing out at the garden with all its greenery, not yet conquered by the chill breath of autumn; at the clouds trudging across a picture-perfect blue sky; and above all at the sun, which utterly confounded their unpracticed eyes. For the

first time, sound escaped them—low, uncomprehending grunts
arising from the depths of their bellies. They pressed closer to
the window, each pushing aggressively for the best vantage
point. It seemed that the sight of the sun had aroused the first
glimmerings both of curiosity and of competitiveness. One of
the Selves shoved clumsily at the back of an alter ego block-
ing its vision. The Self thus provoked drove a pudgy elbow
backward into the protruding abdomen of its attacker. The
grunting among the Selves waxed in volume and urgency.
The intensity of effort increased. Presently one of the Selves
fell over the ledge and slid through the window to land face
down in the moist garden soil. The texture of loam was
unfamiliar. The Self raked its fingers back and forth while its
two alter egos looked on. Soon the other two, impelled by
newly-awakened inquisitiveness, crawled awkwardly through
the window and dropped to the ground to experience the dirt.
After a time they rose to wander through the shrubbery. From
the fortress windows a battery of servants watched without
daring to intervene. A question arose from assorted throats:
"Which is the Seigneur?" And the answers collided: "None
of them." "All of them."

The Selves waddled on until, moved by common impulse,
they paused to inhale deeply. The scents of fresh air, soil,
vegetation and fish frying in the distant kitchen were wafted
to their nostrils. They snuffled vigorously for a time before
continuing along the garden path.

*   *   *

In the garden grew a maze of boxwood hedges, fruit of the
Lady Fribanni's romantic fancies. The paths were few and
their pattern simple, but it was a maze nonetheless, and thus
fulfilled the desires of its creator. In a small grassy clearing at
the center of the maze stood a gazebo, all marble fretwork
and gilded rafters. Eight twisted white columns supported an
onion dome of copper weathered to the color of a Miasmic
fern. It was to this pastoral retreat that the Lady Fribanni
often withdrew to peruse her prized volumes of perfervid verse.
She was there now, seated on one of the benches with a book
spread open on her lap. At her feet lounged her three sons,
to whom she read aloud. *Cold Hemlock*, the work of Master
M—, an anonymous local bard, failed to arouse the admiration
of the triplets, who sat nearly comatose with boredom.

Lady Fribanni concluded Canto the Twentieth and paused to take a breath before continuing. Her son Druveen perceived and seized the opportunity.

"Should we really be listening to any more of this, Mum?" Druveen inquired with an air of concern.

"Indeed you should, my lamb," Fribanni replied. "I want my darling boys to experience the elevated sentiments inspired by great art. I want them to become men of culture, refinement, moral sensibility—"

"That's just what I mean, Mum," Druveen interrupted. "This poetry, it's so—what'd you call it—elevated, that we can only take a little bit of it at a time."

"A little bit," Pruke concurred.

"Otherwise," Druveen continued, "it's—it's too much for us. It's too strong. Like rays of light in our minds."

"Or an explosion in our hearts, breaking us up inside," Pruke suggested.

"Or kind of like being out back in the alley with one of the wenches from the Jewel Inn—" Vazm interjected, but threatening glares from his brothers swiftly quelled him.

"Why, I'd no idea that my precious lads have such feeling for poetry!" Fribanni's narrow face was rosy with pleasure.

"Oh we have, Mum," Pruke assured her. "We most certainly have."

"Yes we do, Mum. Why, today I feel like I've reached a sort of new spiritual level," Druveen announced. "I can't go any higher right now or something inside me will just pop. You know how it is."

"That's why we can't listen to any more," Pruke concluded. "We don't dare. There's nothing for it but to ride on down to town and stay there until we've calmed down."

"Maybe it will take two or three days," Vazm guessed.

"Dearest children, are you quite certain—"

The conversation was cut short by the tramp of approaching footsteps. Fribanni and the triplets swiveled to face the sound. Into the clearing through a break in the hedges stepped the figure of Keprose Gavyne. Fribanni's eyes widened and the triples gaped.

"Dear Brother—" Fribanni ventured to break the silence. She spoke with some delicacy. "Dear Brother, you are . . . unclothed."

"Naked as a plucked capon, Uncle," Druveen observed.

The newcomer was silent. His blank blue eyes contained no spark of recognition or understanding.

"Been swimming, Uncle?" Druveen inquired. Behind him, Pruke and Vazm snickered uncontrollably.

"*Children!*" Fribanni hissed. She turned back to the silent, rotund figure and gazed into the eyes of an imbecile. "Dearest Keprose, are you quite *well*?"

There was no response.

"I don't think he hears you, Mum," Druveen whispered loudly. "Maybe the old boy's lost his hearing."

"Or his wits," Pruke speculated.

"Or else he's drunk," Vazm suggested. "Eh, Uncle—the brandy-wine too much for you this morning?"

"*Hush*, you naughty boy! You know your Uncle's habits are temperate!"

"Are they? What about the bonbons, then?"

"Bonbons do not affect your Uncle's mind!"

"Then what's wrong with him, Mum? Why's he staring like that? He's giving me the cold shivers," Pruke complained.

"I don't know what's wrong, my darling. But I'm sure it's nothing serious—"

No sooner had Fribanni spoken than the other two Selves entered the clearing and ranged themselves beside the first. Fribanni waited two or three seconds before she began to scream. Jumping to her feet she took a backward step, tripped over the bench and fell to the mosaic floor. Her wild shrieks increased in volume.

The triplets rose and stared for a wordless moment. Three identical sets of youthful blue eyes met three pairs of equally identical and similarly blue middle-aged orbs. Or apparently middle-aged, for no one observing the network of fine wrinkles, the shadows and sagging pockets of flesh that surrounded the eyes of the Selves could have guessed that the three Keproses were newly-formed. Triplets stared at triplets in silence, until an irrepressible exclamation burst from Druveen. "I'll be kicked—the old boy's *split* himself!"

Lady Fribanni lay on her stomach. Her face was buried in the crook of her arm. Her shoulders shook and her frizzled curls vibrated. She still screamed, but the noise was muffled. Pruke and Vazm grasped their mother under the arms and hauled her to her feet. Fribanni's legs would not support her and she clung desperately to her sons.

"It's all *right*, Mum," Vazm promised.

"Uncle is a clever man. He's sure to find some way of putting himself back together," Pruke opined.

It was doubtful that she heard them. Her eyes were glazed, her face the color of cheese, and her hands jerked spastically. Glancing back over her shoulder she beheld the motionless simulacra and found the sight insupportable. Her screams, which had subsided somewhat, rose like trumpet fanfares. Shriek after shriek clawed the cool air of morning and at last the noise attracted the attention of the Selves. All three advanced upon the source.

Lady Fribanni's voice was beginning to fail. Her screams subsided to whimpers and she gasped for breath. The Selves drew nigh. They mounted the low steps and entered the gazebo. Fribanni took refuge behind her three sons. "Boys!" she appealed weakly.

The triplets exchanged glances. After a moment, Druveen reluctantly stepped forward to address the Selves. "Uncle, is something wrong?"

No answer.

"Uncle," Druveen pointed out, "I don't know what you're about, but you're upsetting Mum."

The implied reproach produced no effect.

"You might at least answer, Uncle. Is this supposed to be some kind of a joke, or what?" The Selves simply stared, and Druveen began to lose his nerve. "No offense intended, Uncle Keprose."

The Selves, their empty eyes still fixed upon the whimpering Fribanni, took a step forward. Three fleshy arms reached out, three hands pawed the air. Fribanni cowered and Druveen knocked the foremost hand aside. Its owner's uncomprehending gaze shifted from Fribanni to hand and back again. Quiet grunts escaped the Selves.

"Whatever he's done to himself has turned his brain," Druveen observed. "He's loony, all three of him."

"Don't talk that way about your Uncle!" Fribanni admonished. "He is a great genius. Keprose? Dear Keprose, do you not know your own sister?"

Once again the feminine soprano drew the attention of the Selves, who grunted and resumed their march. Fribanni squealed and, prompted by his mother's terror, Druveen unwisely attempted to halt the advance. Placing both hands on the chest of the nearest uncle, he gave a forceful shove. The Self tottered backward a few paces, its arms flapping like wings.

The effort to maintain balance failed and the Self went down, its huge buttocks plopping on the tile floor. It sat still for a moment, then carefully rose and lurched forward. Its face remained eerily expressionless. Its grunts had given way to a low-pitched gobbling sound, the significance of which was unclear. The sight was alarming, but Druveen stood his ground.

"Here now, Druveen, maybe we'd better get out of here," Pruke suggested nervously.

"I'm not going anywhere. Are you two rabbit-minded cowards going to help me or not?" Druveen snarled. After a brief pause, his two siblings stepped unwillingly to his side to form a living wall between their mother and their quasi-uncles.

The Selves, although primitive, were not unable to profit by experience. Without awaiting additional provocation, they lumbered forward to the attack.

Three great arms swung powerfully. The triplets, taken unawares, neither dodged nor parried, and each of the young men received a tremendous blow. Druveen hit the floor hard, skidded and crashed into a bench. Vazm reeled, clutched one of the twisted columns, and so saved himself from falling. Pruke sailed across the floor, struck the low railing, toppled over and clear out of the gazebo. He rose from the grass cradling his jaw.

"Boys!" Fribanni's cries soared. "Druveen!"

But Druveen, dazed and aching, could not answer.

"My dearest!" Fribanni attempted to rush to the side of her battered son, but three Selves blocked her path. "Let me by! Keprose, let me go to my boy!"

The Selves regarded her blankly. One of them reached out to poke a pudgy finger into her disheveled frizz of hair.

"My baby needs me!" Fribanni beat her fists on the chest of the nearest Self and then, growing frantic, rammed her shoulder into its abdomen. A squirrel might just as well have attacked a mountain. The Self glanced down incuriously—perhaps studying the woman, perhaps examining the decorative floor.

"Druveen! Mother's coming!" Fribanni, incensed to the verge of hysteria, lifted her skirt to deliver a vicious kick. The pointed toe of her high-heeled slipper slammed into the Self's kneecap. The Self gobbled and its blue eyes narrowed. Fribanni paid no heed. Finding her way still blocked, she stamped down on the Self's foot, grinding her sharp heel into its instep with all her strength. The Self attempted without success to withdraw its foot. "Mother's coming!"

The Self shifted its vast bulk, studied the rabid human squirrel for a moment, then hoisted its arm and struck. The blow caught Fribanni in the throat and lifted her clear off her feet. Her body arched backward through the air and she hit the floor head first. Her limbs twitched briefly and then she lay still, eyes and mouth wide open. The Selves approached and nudged her gently with their bare feet, but she did not stir again. Soon they lost interest and wandered away.

As soon as the Selves withdrew, the triplets sped to the side of their prostrate dam. A single glance served to inform them of her death. The unnatural angle of her neck and the staring, sightless eyes spoke volumes. A whispered conversation ensued.

"She's dead. Uncle's killed her!"

"He's murdered Mum!"

"What'll we do? We can't complain to the authorities—it's a family matter and no one else's business."

"Besides, Uncle *is* the authority."

"Which one did it?" The speaker cast a sidelong glance at the bloated figures loitering on the opposite side of the gazebo. "Which one of him bashed Mum?"

"The one on the left, next to the column."

"I think it was the one in the middle."

"Wrong, Mole-Eyes."

"I'll put money on it. Three hundred pytes on the Uncle in the middle. He'll be the one with the bruise on his foot."

"What bruise?"

"Mum stomped him before he got her."

"Good old Mum!"

"Does it matter which one of them actually killed her?" Druveen interrupted impatiently. "They're all the same, so what difference does it make?"

"Well I think that's pretty unfeeling of you, Dru—"

"I'll tell you what does matter, though," Druveen continued. "When it gets out that Mum's dead, if we don't look sharp, folk will think *we* did it."

"*Us*—kill our own Mum? You've a mind like a dung heap. Why would anyone think we'd do a thing like that? What for?"

"Get hold of her jewelry and sell it," Druveen explained shortly. "Everyone down in that kennel of a town knows the affairs of their betters. Everyone knows we need money."

"Sell her jewelry. I never thought of that." Pruke's eyes

rested with new interest upon the ring-laden fingers of his dead mother.

Vazm's brow was beginning to shine with sweat. "It's not fair!" he burst out in tones of suppressed panic. "We tried to help her and it's not *our* fault she's dead! And it's not *our* fault that Uncle split himself in three and lost his wits!"

"That doesn't matter either," Druveen informed him. "The question is, what are we going to do now?"

"We could head for the Neraunci border."

"Then everyone would be *sure* we did it, Turnip-Head."

"We could hide Mum's body. No one would know she was dead at all."

"We could say she fell down the stairs by accident and broke her neck."

"We could send word to the King. We could turn Uncle in. With his mind gone, Uncle wouldn't be using his powers to defend himself."

"And we're his heirs, aren't we?"

As if they somehow understood the last remarks, the three Selves wheeled and lurched toward the triplets. Vazm, Pruke and Druveen jumped to their feet.

"He heard that—his wits aren't completely gone!"

"We can't talk here. We can't think here."

"Let's go. The Bearded Moon's the place. We'll have a pint and decide what to do."

"And leave Mum lying here?"

"You want to carry her?"

The triplets backed hastily away from their mother's corpse as the Selves closed in. With one accord they turned tail, vaulted the gazebo railing and sprinted for the gap in the hedges at the edge of the clearing. The Selves watched unblinkingly, but did not attempt to follow.

Vazm, Pruke and Druveen raced through the green corridors of the maze. Their faces were white behind the freckles, their eyes wide and staring. But color suddenly flooded the pallid cheeks as the triplets turned a corner and found themselves face to face with Keprose Gavyne. Beside Keprose stood Relian and Mereth. The young men stopped in their tracks.

"Another of him!" Druveen exclaimed. "Is there no end?"

"At least this one is dressed," Pruke observed.

Keprose was attired in his customary loose black gown. His pink curls were neatly pomaded, his pink moustache perfectly waxed, his cheeks rosy with good health and ill temper. His expression, as he addressed his sister's sons, reflected fastidious distaste. "Nephews, your obvious alarm, your confusion, and the extreme inanity of your discourse give me cause to hope that the object of my search is close at hand."

"This one talks," said Vazm.

"Nephews, I will endeavor to avoid overtaxing your powers of understanding. You need only inform me whether you have lately encountered three beings who bear a more or less marked resemblance to myself. You appear more than ordinarily befuddled. A simple yes or no will suffice. If you are incapable of coherent speech, you may nod or shake your heads, as appropriate."

"You're very cool, Uncle," observed Druveen, "considering what you just did to Mum."

"Your own sister," Pruke accused.

"You should be ashamed," Vazm concluded with great daring.

"You will be so good as to explain these callow impertinences," Keprose commanded.

"I don't know what you're about, Uncle," Druveen replied sullenly, "but I say it's an ill business. A very ill business indeed. Come on, brothers—Since Uncle's recovered his wits, we'll let him deal with his own handiwork."

So saying, Druveen and his brothers hurried away. Keprose watched them go with a faint frown, then shrugged dismissively. Turning to Relian he observed, "I believe the quarry is near. My nephews' aspect of mixed fear and belligerence suggests misfortune. It is my suspicion that the Selves, unable to tolerate the officious impudence of fools, are roused to noble wrath. If such is the case, there may be danger at hand. Therefore, young man, you will precede me through the maze, as my life is too valuable to place at risk."

Relian nodded and stepped to the fore.

"I'll go with him," Mereth offered.

"By no means. You would undoubtedly blunder. Remain at my side," Keprose commanded.

A few more yards, a couple more turns and they entered the clearing to behold Fribanni's body stretched on the gazebo floor. On the far side of the clearing, the Selves sought exit. Having failed to discover the way out, the creatures now tore clumsily at the hedges.

"My Selves, alive and well!" Keprose exclaimed. "Their misadventure has not harmed them!"

"But I don't think the same can be said for your sister," said Relian. He and Mereth hurried to the fallen woman's side. Keprose followed at a leisurely pace.

Relian shut Fribanni's eyes. "She is dead, Seigneur. I am sorry."

"As indeed you should be, young man," Keprose returned, "in view of the fact that your careless indifference permitted the escape of my Selves in the first place."

"Carelessss. Carelessss. Carelessss," Crekkid sang.

"They escaped the workroom under your very eyes," Keprose continued. "And you did not lift a finger to restrain them. Who knows what harm might have befallen them? Who knows what mental anguish they have already endured as a result of your stupidity?"

"Ssstupidity. Ssstupidity. Ssstupidity."

"We both tried to stop them—" Mereth began.

"Silence, girl—your excuses are superfluous. I do not hold you responsible in any way, for I recognize the matter far exceeds your mental competence."

"Seigneur—" Relian held his temper with difficulty, "have you no concern for your sister?"

"She is dead, and thus beyond my concern or anyone else's. Nor will I stoop to the hypocrisy of sentimental display. I leave such histrionics to thespians and to women, whose rightful province they are," Keprose replied. "At the moment my concern is not for the dead, but rather for my living Selves, who require their author's assistance."

"Are you certain it's the Selves who require assistance?" Mereth asked.

It was not an idle question. The arrival of the little party had aroused the curiosity of the doppelgangers. All three of them had quietly abandoned the hedge, returned to the gazebo, and were now waddling toward the knot of newcomers. Their few experiences had already influenced their behavior. As they approached, their great arms swung vigorously.

Having felt the weight of those arms, Relian and Mereth quickly retreated. But Keprose Gavyne was not perturbed. "Incomplete as they are, already they demonstrate the valor and proud spirit of their creator," he murmured in admiration, then jerked his head back as a plump fist whizzed by a whisper short of his nose. Another fist flew and Keprose dodged with surprising adroitness. The blow just barely grazed his temple. "Softly, my dear ones, softly," he soothed. "You are too valiant for this sorry world." He spoke quietly to himself. A blankness settled over his features and his white fingers twisted themselves into boneless knots. Before Relian had time to guess the nature of the supranormal exercise, the result had been achieved. The idiot eyes of the Selves turned up until nothing but white showed beneath the drooping lids. Three jowly jaws dropped, three bulbous bodies swayed and simultaneously slumped to the floor. They lay motionless a few feet from the corpse of their victim. Their lips were parted and gobbling snores emerged.

"They sleep." Keprose eyed his creatures fondly. "For the moment, they are free of pain and care."

As I might be if I could learn that trick, thought Relian. *If I could put Crekkid and Nurbo to sleep, the rest would be easy. Mereth and I could be clear of the fortress in minutes.* And for the first time the thought arose, *Yes, but then you'd learn no more of supranormalcy.*

Would you care? came the cold voice of the eternal internal interlocutor. *Do you want to learn more? Think.*

He did not need to think. He realized that he very much wanted to learn more of supranormalcy. He stole a glance at Mereth. Her head was bowed and the large eyes fixed upon the corpse of Lady Fribanni were stormy with conflicting emotions.

I must get her away from Keprose Gavyne. That is what matters most.

The voice of Keprose intruded upon his thoughts.

"Why do you stand witlessly agape, young man? There is much to be done. First and foremost, my Selves must be returned to the workroom. Then the interment of my unfortunate sister must be arranged, and in both projects your assistance is required. And after that—we shall see what additional service you may render." The Seigneur grew thoughtful. "My Selves near completion. In terms of their physical development, nothing is wanting—they have achieved perfection. Alas that the same cannot be said of their intellects. The magnificent potential of their minds has yet to be realized."

"And what do you intend to do about it?" Relian inquired uneasily. He suspected he did not want to know.

"I am not yet certain. When I have reached a decision, you will be informed. The great venture goes forward and you may rest assured that you will play your part. Have no fear, young man—you shall not be neglected!''

* * *

The Lady Fribanni, her hands quite denuded of rings, was laid to rest in the crypt of the Gavynes and suitably mourned by her sons. Her brother's strength of character was such that personal grief was not permitted to hinder his experiments for so much as a single day.

In the end, Keprose changed his mind about returning the Selves to the workroom. Their physical development was now complete, and additional immersion within the bath of nutrient solution would serve no practical purpose. The doppelgangers were accordingly installed in a large second-story chamber, luxuriously furnished by the standards of Fortress Gavyne. There were three vast beds of dark wood; three clothespresses, each stocked with voluminous black robes; three identical washstands, each equipped with shaving implements, hair pomade and moustache wax; and a constantly-replenished supply of bonbons. Save for the last item, these offerings went untouched. If it was Keprose's intention to educate his alter egos by surrounding them with the trappings of civilization, his efforts were doomed to failure. The animal innocence of the Selves remained proof against all encroachments of human artifice. The gifts of clothing and grooming implements were equally despised. Naked they roamed their locked apartment. Their hair and beards sprouted in pink profusion. Their fingernails curved into talons, further extending the length of tentacular digits. Periodically they slept, curled up together upon the floor, their plump limbs intertwined. At first they lay in contact with the cold stones. Later on, when they had accumulated the wherewithal, they reclined upon piles of bonbon wrappers, the crackling consistency of which was reminiscent of dry leaves. Use of the washbasin and the chamber pot were alien to the Selves, and presently their apartment, and later the corridor outside it, acquired a cloacal stench. The household servants, emboldened by revulsion and fear, unanimously refused to enter the locked chamber. Neither the threats nor the blandishments of their master could shake their resolve. Fortunately, the doppelgangers themselves seemed undismayed by the state of their abode. Their health was excellent, their appetites unfail-

ingly voracious, and together they throve like hogs in a
wallow.

Keprose ordered the construction of a peephole and when
the work was completed, he devoted himself to the observation of his unconscious creatures. Every day for hours on end
he would stand with eye glued to the hole. The feeding,
sleeping and excretory activities of the Selves were endlessly
fascinating. If he hoped for a sign of nascent intelligence,
however, Keprose was disappointed. Not a single flicker of
awareness animated the dull blue eyes of the Selves.

Only once did he venture into their chamber, and the
experiment was not a success. Keprose walked in, a bowl of
bonbons in hand. His lips were curved in a sentimental smile.
His eyes were moist and beaming with Self-love. He clucked
and crooned paternally, but the Selves were not reassured.
They advanced en masse, grunting and swinging their fists.
Keprose extended the bowl, which was snatched from his
grasp. The contents were rapidly consumed and the bowl
discarded. Acceptance of the gift did not signify similiar
acceptance of the donor, in whom the Selves utterly failed to
recognize a fourth member of their fraternity. The aggressive
character of their grunts intensified, and a new accomplishment now manifested itself—they had learned to gnash their
teeth. Keprose prudently retired. Thereafter, in view of the
servants' recalcitrance, the task of feeding the Selves de-
volved upon Relian. Owing to his caution and fleetness,
Relian successfully avoided injury.

The Seigneur's intense Self-absorption at this time afforded
Relian the opportunity to perform vital research of his own
into the nature of the supranormal technique employed to
deprive the Selves of consciousness on the day of Fribanni's
death. It did not take much searching to discover the necessary information, for the feat was comparatively commonplace. The best description was found in Nygorn's *Principles
of Mind-Mastery*. Relian learned that recourse to both the
supranormal Vision and Tactility was required. The Vision
was employed to locate the various centers of awareness
within the mind of the subject; the Tactility, to exert equal
and simultaneous pressure on all such centers. The technique
demanded considerable expertise when practiced upon creatures of human complexity. It was a fairly easy matter, however,
to subdue lower animals possessed of simple minds.

Relian's Vision informed him that Crekkid's rudimentary

brain possessed but two centers of awareness. The knowledge
was of little practical use, for the young man's supranormal
touch could not penetrate steel scales and bone to wander the
tiny labyrinth of Crekkid's mind. Relian lacked the power.
His two-fingered spectral Hand clawed in vain at the serpent's
skull. Crekkid remained oblivious of the ghostly assault.

Relian practiced fanatically and his Tactility strengthened.
Upon the day he first sensed that success was drawing near,
his efforts were interrupted by a summons from Keprose
Gavyne. He was ordered to Keprose's study, a sanctum wherein
he had never before ventured. The room was furnished simply, with a writing desk and a single huge, overstuffed armchair. The walls were lined with bookshelves, the contents of
which were guarded by triple-locked iron-barred gates. Evidently these shelves housed the most precious volumes of the
Seigneur's collection. The surface of the desk was piled with
dirty dishes, fruit peels and gnawed bones whose presence
suggested that the study had lately replaced the workroom as
the Seigneur's favorite retreat.

Keprose himself occupied the great armchair. On the far
side of the room stood Mereth, with Nurbo gleaming at her
throat. Upon catching sight of one another, Crekkid and
Nurbo hissed ecstatically. Mereth's arms were folded and a
look of apprehension shadowed her features. Relian wondered briefly at her presence but had no time to speculate, for
the Seigneur was speaking.

"Young man, I will be brief. I will not waste time in
useless verbal ornamentation, for I loathe superfluity and I
hate pointless elaboration. I despise repetition, reiteration and
redundancy as the eagle soaring beneath the azure vault of
heaven must hate the smoke that rises from Man's hovels to
obscure the face of the sun. Therefore know that I have
reached my decision. You are to secure the Fist of Zhi for
me. You will do so tonight. Do I make myself clear?"

"Not very," Relian admitted.

Keprose sighed. "I feared as much. Shall I never learn to
recognize the limitations of my associates? Very well, young
man. What points require clarification?"

"What is the Fist of Zhi?" asked Relian. "Where would I
find it? It's not in the Miasm, is it? How shall I recognize it
and how do I obtain it? What do you want it for? Is there
danger? If so, what precautions shall I take? How does—"

"Enough, young man. I will enlighten you as best I may.

The Fist of Zhi is all that remains of the greatest of Strellian supranormalists—or necromancers, as the Strellians will express it in their barbarous fashion. Zhi was renowned in his day for his extraordinary dominion over the minds of men and beasts. He has been dead these two millennia, but the power of his right hand endures. Through a series of circumstances that I will not trouble to explain, the Fist came into the possession of the Guild of Gatherers of Vale Jevaint. The Gatherers, having little understanding of the potency of their acquisition, make use of the member to stupefy the Black Wingbanes of the Miasm, thus facilitating the collection of Wingbane eggs.''

Relian's mind returned to the clearing in the poisoned forest where the Gatherers toiled and where he had seen a live, dismembered hand frisk in a bowl of boiling liquid. Beyond doubt, that hand was the Fist of Zhi.

"The Fist reposes in a locked chamber in the Egg House in Vale Jevaint," Keprose continued, "and it is there that you will go tonight to find it. The Egg House is heavily guarded and fortified—understandably so, for it contains the townsfolk's chiefest treasures. You appear troubled, but there is no need. I do not think so highly of you that I imagine you capable of completing this mission unaided. My orphaned nephews, who spend their days carousing at the Jewel Inn, have received instructions. At midnight they are to create a diversion that will draw the sentries from their posts—''

"What kind of diversion?"

"That does not concern you. Enough to say that the sentries will depart, thus allowing you access to the Egg House. The back door, which opens onto Footpad Alley, will of course be locked. However, a few drops of the liquid contained herein—'' Keprose produced a small flask and laid it on the desk, "judiciously applied, will serve to destroy the strongest of locks. That done, the rest of your task is simplicity itself. Why do you continue to frown, young man? I believe I have effectively resolved all possible difficulties.''

"One remains," Relian informed him. "This Fist of Zhi is a treasure that guarantees the livelihood of its possessors, and hence of all the town. What becomes of the citizens if it is stolen?''

"They will shift, no doubt," Keprose shrugged. "What, after all, did they do before they acquired the Fist?''

"Died by the hundreds in the Miasm, most likely. I'm not

familiar with the history of the town, so I can't answer with any certainty. I can only state that I do not wish to commit a theft likely to inflict hardship upon so many people—who have already suffered enough at your hands. For the sake of my own conscience, I don't wish to commit any theft at all.'' Relian's gaze was directed steadily at the Seigneur, but out of the corner of his eye he noted Mereth's nervous start. She did not speak, and once again he wondered at her presence.

Keprose drummed his white fingers upon the desk. His face was tight with impatient disapproval. ''It is probable that you have failed to grasp the significance of my purpose—''

''I'd hazard a guess that you intend to use the power of this Fist to stimulate the mental development of your Selves,'' said Relian.

''That is correct. Inasmuch as you are capable of comprehending my intentions, you will also appreciate the necessity—''

''I understand quite well, Seigneur, but it alters nothing.''

''You are extraordinarily impudent, young man.''

''Impudent. Impudent. Impudent,'' Crekkid echoed. ''Punisssh, Massster? Punisssh? Punisssh?''

''It will not be necessary, my loyal Crekkid.'' Keprose considered briefly before addressing Relian again. ''Young man, you are obviously unaware that my position as hereditary Seigneur of Vale Jevaint lends me full authority to commandeer lawfully such items as I deem needful to my household.''

''Then why do you not do so, Seigneur?''

''Prolonged debate with the Guild of Gatherers, during the course of which the Fist might well vanish, suits neither my convenience nor my temper. Moreover, should I openly appropriate the Fist, the resulting demonstrations of civic discontent could necessitate forceful disciplinary action. In order to uphold my rights, I might find myself obliged to incinerate the entire town, to the disadvantge of all.''

''I sympathize, Seigneur. In that case, would it not be possible to obtain the Fist on loan, with the consent of the Gatherers? Or perhaps mutually satisfactory terms of rental might be arranged?''

''Rental? That is an interesting idea,'' Keprose admitted. ''But I've no inclination to negotiate at length with tradesmen— or with you, for that matter. We shall proceed with the plan I've outlined, and you will visit Vale Jevaint tonight.''

''I decline.'' Relian spoke with apparent coolness, but

privately wondered what form the Seigneur's vengeance would take.

"Ssssssssssss. Impudent. Impudent. Impudent. Crekkid make him obey, Massster," the serpent offered eagerly.

"You have heard, young man. Shall I grant my Crekkid his desire?" Keprose inquired.

"As you please, Seigneur. It will make no difference."

"You might be astonished. But we shall not put it to the test, for there is one here whose persuasive power exceeds even Crekkid's." Keprose turned to face Mereth, but it was not to the pale girl that he spoke. "Nurbo? Attend, if you please."

"Yesss, Ssseigneur?" the female serpent responded. "Yesss? Yesss? Yesss?"

"I am displeased with your human, Nurbo. She is in need of chastisement. See to it at once."

"Yesss! Ssseigneur, yesss!" Nurbo instantly and joyfully drove her fangs into the side of Mereth's neck. An involuntary shriek escaped the girl. The cry was choked off as the steel coils tightened cruelly. Nurbo struck twice more, and blood spattered the collar of Mereth's dress. The girl, gasping desperately for breath, sank to her knees.

"Stop it!" Relian did not realize that he spoke aloud. Rushing to Mereth's side, he strove frantically but uselessly to dislodge the homicidal serpent.

"Ssstupid. Ssstupid. Weak. Ssstupid," Crekkid observed with disdain. Nurbo, much occupied, offered no comment.

Mereth was suffocating. Her face was purple and her eyes screamed. One side of her neck ran wet with blood.

"Stop it!" Relian wheeled to face the Seigneur.

Keprose shrugged and spread his hands eloquently. Mereth toppled to the floor. Her struggles were already weakening.

"You're killing her!"

"Alas, that is a possibility. I should much regret the pretty creature's death, particularly as I still perhaps foolishly cherish some faint hope of her supranormalcy. But in view of your obstinacy, young man—"

Mereth lay on her back, still struggling feebly. Her tongue protruded and her eyes bulged horribly. Her face was almost unrecognizable.

"I'll do anything you want."

"Then I may rely upon your assistance in Vale Jevaint tonight?" Keprose inquired.

Relian nodded.

"You have relieved my apprehensions. Nurbo," Keprose
commanded, "desist, if you please."

Nurbo plunged her fangs into the flesh of her victim one
last time, then reluctantly loosened her hold. Mereth lay
breathing in shallow gasps. Her eyes were closed. Her dress
was foul with blood and her neck pocked with puncture
wounds. A broad red welt marked the skin chafed by Nurbo's
coils. Relian knelt beside her, but she did not open her eyes.

"Excellent, Nurbo," Keprose commended his creature.

"Excellent, Nurbo. Excellent. Nurbo. Nurbo. Nurbo. Sssweet
Nurbo."

Nurbo hissed in acknowledgment of the compliments.

"All is well," Keprose reassured Relian. "Pretty Mereth
has not been seriously injured and will no doubt recover
quickly. You have been persuaded to undertake your new
responsibilities. No lasting harm has been done, and all has
turned out for the good, as it generally does in this best of all
possible worlds. I regret that our happy accord could not be
reached without recourse to some unpleasantness, but I am
hopeful that this exchange obviates the necessity of future
demonstrations of a similar nature. If so, it has served a
worthy purpose."

Relian's hands itched to close on Keprose Gavyne's throat.
He glanced down and saw that the hands were shaking. There
was a curious hollow feeling in his chest, and for a moment
he was almost light-headed. He did not trust himself to speak.
A torrent of hatred sought outlet, but he sternly dammed the
flood. *Some day, somehow, I'll kill that swine—*

Why wait? There's a razor in your room. Use it.

I'm not thinking straight. Calm down. Calm. Deliberately
he unclenched his jaw and took a couple of deep breaths.
Calm.

"I take your silence for assent. It pleases me that you
appear to harbor no animosity," Keprose remarked. "Well
then, as Mistress Mereth seems disinclined to rise, I will
summon a servant to assist her to her chamber. No—don't
you do it." He forestalled Relian's move to lift the girl.
"You would be well advised to conserve your strength in
anticipation of the evening's activities. I want you at your
best, young man. Your best is scarcely adequate, but this
time it must serve. We shall fortify you as much as we can,
and hope for incompetent guards at the Egg House door."

Stay calm.
I want to kill him—
Calm. Calm. Calm.

*   *   *

The moon shone bright on Footpad Alley, illuminating piles
of refuse, mounds of ordure, stagnant puddles and loosened
cobbles. Relian lurked in the shadow of a deeply-recessed
doorway. A few yards distant stood the Egg House—an
imposing foursquare structure with the stone walls of a fortress; barred windows set well above ground level; and a
domed roof surmounted by a small bell tower. Before a heavy
door flanked by lanterns lounged the sentry. The fellow was
dull-eyed, slovenly, and yawningly bored. He wore no uni-
form, but the white cockade on his hat marked him as a
member of the civilian Guardsmen employed by the Guild of
Gatherers. He appeared neither alert nor athletic; but he bore
a musket, and a stout cudgel was thrust through his belt.

Relian had been waiting over an hour, each separate minute
of which seemed to limp by on crutches. The wait had not
been pleasant. The stench of Footpad Alley was disturbing;
the turbulence of his emotions infinitely more so. Each time
he thought of Keprose Gavyne, his pulse jumped. Each time
the image of the fleshy, smug countenance scorched his
imagination, he went queasy with helpless rage. Again and
again he thought of Mereth as he had last seen her—prostrate,
bleeding, bound in living steel. He thought of his own steel
tormentor and of his prolonged servitude. He contemplated
his impending descent from servitude to thievery, and was
forced to consider the consequences of his burglary. Pangs of
anticipatory guilt added to his misery.

Relian peered forth from the shadows for the thousandth
time. The sentry, quite unconscious of observation, performed
the leisurely ritual of filling and lighting a clay pipe. Relian's
nerves tightened.

Was it not yet midnight? Keprose had promised that Vazm,
Pruke and Druveen would create a diversion to draw the
attention of the guard upon the stroke of midnight. Relian had
believed him perforce. But time was passing and nothing
happened. Surely midnight had come and gone. Where were
the triplets? Had accident befallen them, had their plans gone
awry? Had they any plans at all? Was it not more likely they

had simply forgotten their uncle's injunction and were now lying comatose—drunk under the table at the Jewel Inn? The more he thought about it, the less likely it became that the triplets would prove capable of carrying out an effective plan of action. They would inevitably bungle the job.

But what if they didn't? What if they actually succeeded in luring the guard from his post? In that event, the path to the Fist would still be blocked by a massive portal reinforced with steel and triply locked. Keprose's fluid was supposed to destroy locks—but would it work? Relian fingered the small flask in his pocket and breathed an inaudible sigh. Earlier that evening, his first act upon his emergence from the fortress had been to unstopper the flask and apply a liberal dollop of the contents to Crekkid's head. The results of the experiment were disappointing. Crekkid had hissed and complained of a tickling sensation. If the serpent's thin steel scales were resistant to the fluid, then surely the heavy locks on the Egg House door would prove altogether impervious?

And then he heard it—not far away, chimes sounded the hour of midnight. The last chime rang out, hung in the air for a moment and died. There was silence and Relian held his breath. The silence lengthened. Nothing happened. That was it, then. The triplets had failed. They were drunk, they were forgetful, they were moronic incompetents—and perhaps it was just as well. He could leave now. He could—

The ground shook slightly and the crash of a terrific explosion thundered through the streets and alleys of Vale Jevaint. A huge orange tongue of flame leaped for the moon and a sudden rain of burning debris descended on Footpad Alley. Although shielded by the overhang, Relian instinctively shrank to the rear of the recess. The Egg House sentry, less fortunate, was pelted with smoking fragments that left his coat a mass of blackened holes. Shouts and cries were carried on the wind.

Relian ventured a glance from his refuge. The great tongue of flame had subsided, but an ominous orange glow lit the sky. The smell of smoke was already perceptible. Somewhere nearby a tremendous fire was raging and Relian wondered whose property had been selected by the triplets for sacrifice. Had they chosen an enemy of their own or of their uncle's? Or more likely, had they struck at random, as mindlessly destructive as a force of nature? *Did Keprose know that those*

*three murderous fools would choose such a method? Have
they managed to kill anyone?*

The shower of fire ended, but smoldering debris lay everywhere, and the alley was filling with smoke. The sentry
removed his hat and fanned himself. He coughed, and Relian
was seized with an almost irresistible urge to do likewise. The
sentry's head was cocked, his expression dubious as he listened to the shouting. He eyed the glowing sky, took a few
steps toward the mouth of the alley, hesitated and returned to
his post, where he stood fidgeting.

The sentry's dilemma was resolved by the hurried arrival of
a brother Guardsman, who announced, "Explosion on Tallow
Street—warehouse on fire. We're ordered over there to help
put it out before it spreads all over town."

"What about the Egg House?"

"Locked up tight and safe for now. The fire's more important. Step lively."

The two men exited the alley. The Egg House door was left
unguarded, but there was no telling how long it would remain
so. Relian threw a cautious glance up the street. There was not
a soul in sight, but the babble of excited human voices was very
audible. A large crowd must have collected at the site of the fire.
Hesitating no longer, he abandoned his hiding-place and darted
across the street to confront the locked portal, with its keyhole
set in a plate of iron and its two big padlocks. He withdrew
the flask from his pocket, pulled the stopper and, with a
certain sense of fatalism, anointed the three keyholes.

Keprose's fluid worked promptly and perfectly. A sweet
fragrance filled the air, a scent of honeysuckle or devenderia.
The locks responded like sailors seduced by the lure of sirens.
They snapped open in quick succession. The flowery perfume
grew sweeter, stronger. There was a hint of jasmine about it
now. The two padlocks jiggled off their staples and thudded
to the ground, where they lay clicking orgasmically.

Relian pushed on the door, which yielded easily. Blackness
met his straining vision. He reached up, seized one of the
lighted lanterns from its wall bracket and entered the Egg
House, carefully shutting the door behind him.

*   *   *

"Canto the Twenty-Fifth, Verse VI," announced Master Moon.
Scrivvulch the Stick sighed and wished himself a thousand

miles away. His martyred gaze swept the common room of
the Bearded Moon, which was still fairly well-populated,
despite the lateness of the hour. Not far away, Master Gatherer Clym Stipper hoisted a tankard, his last of the evening.
Beside the fire brooded Councilman Gyf Fynok, who appeared gloomily unaware of the passage of time. Scrivvulch
would gladly have accosted either gentleman, particularly
Fynok. But he was captive to his host's loquacious Muse,
helpless as a fiend chained upon a lake of fire.

"My progress is excellent, is it not?" inquired Moon, and
without awaiting confirmation, commenced reading:

VI

"Thy killing beauty robs my heart of rest.
  My mind is darkened and my soul benighted.
  Corrosive torment ravages my breast,
  For I suspect my love is unrequited.

VII

Alas, 'tis so. My flame melts not thine ice.
  Green chastity is cold as it is artless.
  Or am I gull'd? Is cruelty thy vice?
  Art thou less innocent than wanton-heartless?

VIII

Doth thy resplendence batten on my groans?
  Drinks't thou my tears that deck thy fronds like dew?
  Dost thou hear music in thy lovers' moans,
  And dost thou feed on hearts replete with rue?

IX

Doth thy pride swell upon thy lovers' pain?
  Ah, thou know'st not the sting of Love's fell arrow.
  Never hast thou breath'd thy sighs in vain,
  And never bled thy heart beneath the harrow.

X

Thou knowest not the promptings of the blood,
Art ignorant of Passion's thunderclap.
'Tis meet thou scorn'st the Senses' heated flood—
Thy veins are grac'd with coolest virgin sap.''

Moon paused for breath and Scrivvulch cast his eyes about
in hopeless search of rescue. Fate favored the Assassin. The
door opened and a man entered the common room. Scrivvulch
leaned forward in his chair for a better look and brightened in
recognition. The newcomer was one Neelo, a thumbless for-
mer tailor hired to keep watch on Fortress Gavyne during the
first night shift. Neelo surveyed the room, spotted his employer and approached.

"A moment, Master Moon," Scrivvulch interrupted the
innkeeper's flow of poesy. "I believe this good fellow here
has a message for me. Am I correct, my friend?"

"Aye, sir," replied Neelo. "Your young gentleman quit-
ted Fortress Gavyne several hours ago. I shadowed him and
soon saw he was heading for town."

"For town?" Master Moon interrupted. "Is this the wicked
scoundrel Black Relian Kru that we're talking about?"

"The same, Master Moon," Scrivvulch replied, noting
with satisfaction the innkeeper's expression of alarm. "Say
on, good Neelo. What next?"

"Well, sir, I trailed him all the way down the hillside into
town, and as far as Footpad Alley. He went into the alley and
didn't come out again. I waited, but he didn't show his face,
so I thought I'd best come and report to you."

"You have done well, my friend, and you deserve reward," Scrivvulch assured his minion. "The reward will be
doubled if I succeed in persuading you to accompany me to
Footpad Alley to assist in the apprehension of the criminal.
Are you willing?"

"Yes, sir," replied Neelo. "It's to be the two of us against
the Equalist, then?"

"Certainly not, my friend. We can do better than that. I do
not doubt that any number of concerned citizens will consent
to lend their aid, provided the matter is presented in the
proper manner."

"What's the proper manner, sir?"

"The simplest, good Neelo. For in this complex, overpowering world, simplicity is the natural spring whereat the travel-weary spirit drinks and is truly refreshed. I will demonstrate.'' Scrivvulch untangled his long shanks, rose from his chair, and spoke in a carrying voice. "Master Stipper! Councilman Fynok! Your attention, at once!"

The designated citizens glanced up, startled by the Assassin's imperative tone.

"Gentlemen, I have just received news of the gravest significance,'' proclaimed Scrivvulch. "The town of Vale Jevaint is threatened and you, her leading citizens, are hereby called upon to aid in her defense.''

"What's all this?'' demanded Clym Stipper.

"I have warned you all of danger and now it has come to pass,'' Scrivvulch informed his audience. "The notorious criminal Black Relian Kru has been seen roaming the streets of the town. I am told that he has gone to ground in Footpad Alley—an appropriately-christened refuge, to be sure. Correct me if I am mistaken, but I seem to recall that Footpad Alley is the site of one of the entrances to your Egg House.''

"What do you suggest, sir?'' asked Gyf Fynok.

"You think your man's got designs on the eggs?'' Stipper inquired. The other customers present listened in tense silence.

"Gentlemen, you may depend upon it,'' Scrivvulch assured them. "I know my man, and you may be certain he is a desperate character who will stop at nothing to gain his ends. Do not count upon the guards at the Egg House door to protect your property—they cannot know with whom they deal. Black Relian is abroad, and your treasure is at risk. If you would preserve what's yours, then make haste to the Egg House—there is not a moment to be lost!''

"Just one moment, Master Scrivvulch.'' Gatherer Stipper's enthusiasms were not easily inflamed. "We've only your word for this, and 'tis known you've a personal interest in the matter.''

"Sir, what have I to gain by deceiving you, beyond universal opprobrium?'' Scrivvulch inquired reasonably.

Scrivvulch's hireling now spoke up. "Master Stipper, Councilman Fynok, and all the rest of you. I'm Neelo the Tailor, and I've lived in this town all my life. Most of you know me and know I don't lie. And I'm telling you it's true. The young gentleman—Equalist or whatever—is hanging around Footpad Alley outside the Egg House door. I don't know what he's doing, but he is—or was—certainly there.

His listeners believed him.

"Mercy! Will you call the Guardsmen, gentlemen?" inquired a flustered Moon.

"There's no time for that," Clym Stipper replied. "We'd best get over there ourselves."

"Weapons," observed Fynok. "Kru's dangerous. We need weapons." He raised his voice to address Moon's patrons. "Every man among you carrying a weapon—firearms, sword, even a cudgel—you're needed now. Who's with us?"

Shouts of accord arose. Most of the customers were carrying weapons of some sort, and most were willing to join. Under the leadership of Stipper and Fynok, the party of vigilantes was quickly organized.

"Your townsmen are keen on the scent, Councilman," observed Scrivvulch.

"We will defend what's ours," Gyf Fynok replied heavily.

"Thus Justice and the community are served—admirable. Admirable," approved Scrivvulch. "May I ask, Councilman, that you and Master Stipper encourage your followers to take Black Relian alive, if possible? It is my duty to return the young scoundrel to the dungeons of Neraunce. Perhaps I am overly scrupulous, but I shall not feel that satisfaction which is the truest reward of my profession until I have personally dealt with young Kru."

"As to that, we'll see what comes," Fynok replied indifferently; and Scrivvulch was forced to content himself with this.

Within minutes the armed party was out on the streets of Vale Jevaint. Clym Stipper, Gyf Fynok and Scrivvulch the Stick walked at the fore. There were plenty of torches and lanterns to light the way and the men proceeded at a good pace. Even so, it was a long walk from the Bearded Moon to Footpad Alley. They were still some distance from their destination when the stroke of midnight sounded. A moment later a tremendous explosion roared. A jet of orange flame shot into the air and the men paused to stare in consternation.

"That looks to have come from Tallow Street," observed Clym Stipper. "If there's a fire, they'll need all the help they can get."

"First things first, gentlemen," replied Scrivvulch. "If Black Relian pillages your Egg House, 'twill do more harm than a dozen such fires. In all conscience, I cannot bear to see it happen." Without awaiting reply, he resumed walking.

After the briefest of hesitations, the others followed.

*   *   *

The flickering light of the lantern illuminated a wilderness of wooden packing crates. There were hundreds, perhaps thousands of them, side by side, stacked up to form high walls that divided the cavernous interior of the Egg House into a maze of passages. Relian wandered the endless lanes in some confusion, now turning left, now right, in his quest for the Fist of Zhi. The search promised to be prolonged. So vast was the chamber that the walls and ceiling were lost in shadow. His own shadow loomed large in his wake, and echoes magnified the sound of his stealthy footsteps. He saw nothing but boxes—so many that he was astounded. How many generations' worth of Gatherers' labor did this collection represent? On impulse he stooped to lift the lid from the nearest crate, and found it filled with soft cotton batting. He stripped away layers of the flimsy stuff to uncover a single lividly-splotched Wingbane egg. Each crate apparently contained but one egg—but there were still thousands of them, probably held off the market for years on end in order to maintain elevated prices. The Gatherers of Vale Jevaint were undoubtedly canny folk. A distressing thought struck Relian. Perhaps the Fist of Zhi was hidden in one of these anonymous crates? If so, he might search for hours without finding it—and he did not have hours. Sooner or later the guards would return to the Egg House door and his intrusion would be discovered. He straightened up, thoughtfully studied the ranks of boxes, and shook his head. Unlikely that it was there. The Fist, a particularly prized artifact, was probably maintained in unusual state. In any case, hadn't Keprose mentioned a locked chamber?

He resumed his search, traversing indistinguishable avenues, wandering among identical crates. But not absolutely identical—the boxes were marked with stamps of various colors, perhaps indicative of the age, size or quality of the contents. Such information was of limited interest to him, however.

Relian came to a wall, probably the one opposite the alley entrance. Owing to the erratic course of his wanderings, it was difficult to be certain. A few feet off to the right was a door whose height, ornate lintel and elaborate hinges marked it as the main entrance opening onto the Guild Square. Relian followed the wall. When he came to a corner, he turned. It was his intention to complete a circuit of the entire chamber, but long before he had done so he came upon a pair of sturdy oak doors set in an alcove. He tried the doors and found that both were locked—a promising sign.

Keprose's fluid made quick work of both locks. Relian opened the first door and thrust his lantern into the small room beyond. The weak yellow light played on shelves of oversized leather-bound ledgers. There was a writing desk, a couple of chairs and an open coffer filled with unbound correspondence. Relian entered, plucked a ledger from a shelf and opened it at random. He saw columns of figures, calculations, entries and notations in a neat, fussy hand. He had stumbled upon the financial records of the Guild of Gatherers. A tax collector in the employ of Keprose Gavyne might have found the contents enlightening, but Relian did not. He replaced the ledger and went on to the next room.

Upon opening the door, he beheld the object of Keprose's desire. In the middle of a windowless stone room lined with stacked crates stood a low platform of black marble supporting a square glass-walled tank. The tank was fitted with a domed lid of glass and filled with a faintly blue liquid whose motion as it rolled against the transparent walls was not that of water. Within the tank swam the Fist of Zhi, graceful and tranquil as a fish.

Relian approached for a closer look. It was certainly the same dismembered hand that he had glimpsed in the Forest of Miasm. There were the same hyperdigital fingers, the same long talons, the same protuberant knuckles and juiceless flesh. A rapid clenching and unclenching motion propelled the hand through its liquid environment. Relian stared, fascinated. Despite his experiences of recent weeks, his sense of curiosity remained undiminished.

The Fist, which evidently possessed obscure powers of perception, swam to the side of the tank, where it paused, palm pressed flat to the glass. Its stationary position was maintained by a slight vibration of the severed wrist. Relian had the sense that he was being observed. He placed his own palm against the glass in deliberate imitation. The tank was unexpectedly warm. After a moment, the Fist began drumming its fingers against the barrier. The rhythm tapped out by the long nails was staccato but repetitive. Was a message intended, or was this but a memory of the nervous impulses of the long-dead Zhi?

Relian tapped his fingers against the glass in response. It was a mistake. The Fist clenched spasmodically at the sound, then shot with astonishing speed to the far side of the tank, where it cowered trembling in a corner. Its fingers dug nervously into the silt that lay at the bottom.

It seemed to be trying to bury itself.

The liquid—oil, plasm, whatever it was—was not unduly deep. Relian stepped up onto the platform, removed the lid of the tank and set it aside. He bent over, plunged his arm shoulder-deep into the blue depths and made a grab. The Fist darted agilely out of reach. When he approached again, it eluded him with ease, pushing off against the side of the tank to send itself gliding across the silt-covered bottom. Relian made two more attempts and missed both times. His arm and the entire front of his coat were soaked. At the center of the tank the Fist hung vertically, its thumb and two fingers stiffly extended in an archaic Strellian gesture of insult.

Another approach was called for. How did the Gatherers handle this problem? Relian cast his eyes about the chamber and found the answer at once. Propped against the wall in the corner was a serviceably long-handled net. Relian fetched the implement and returned to his work. With some difficulty he chivvied the Fist into a corner. Following several unsuccessful passes, he managed to net his quarry. Carefully he lifted it from the tank.

The Fist's struggles were violent. Hysterically it clawed and tore at the imprisoning net, twisted and flung itself from side to side. Relian unthinkingly reached down into the net to withdraw his catch. The Fist of Zhi pounced on him, digging its wicked talons deep into his flesh. Relian yanked back his hand, to which the Fist still clung like an angry cat. Once clear of the net, the maddened member loosed its hold and dropped to the floor, where it lifted itself on fingers and thumb and scuttled for the shadows. Relian slammed down the net—too late. He missed, and the hand disappeared into the crevice between two stacks of crates.

Relian knelt and shone his lantern into the narrow space. He could see the hand clearly where it huddled against the wall. He thrust his arm into the opening as far as it would go, but could not reach the fugitive Fist. Sensing this, the Fist scurried forward, raked its assailant's palm, and swiftly retreated again.

Relian pulled his arm back. For a moment he crouched,

watching his quarry. The Fist lay on its side, fingers snapping in obvious agitation. In order to reach it, he might move an entire stack of crates—a cumbersome procedure. Or else he might—

Relian reversed the net and thrust the long wooden pole of a handle into the crevice. It was easily long enough to reach the wall. The blunt tip touched the Fist, prodded gently. The hand backed away and the questing pole followed. It was Relian's plan to flip the Fist neatly from its refuge, but the opportunity did not arise. The Fist charged, scampering back along the narrow passage straight toward its enemy. The net was unusable. Relian dropped it, snatched at the speeding Fist with his bare hands and missed. The Fist whisked neatly between his legs, emerged behind him and sprinted for the corner, where a rope dangled from the ceiling. Relian sprang to his feet and gave chase, but the Fist had a good lead. It reached the corner, grasped the rope, rapidly climbed a couple of feet; loosened its grip and slid down; then very abruptly arrested its own descent an inch or two from the floor. The bell to which the rope was attached was cunningly balanced to toll at the slightest touch. Now the tocsin pealed from the tower atop the Egg House dome. Only a single stroke sounded before the Fist abandoned its efforts, but how many citizens had heard it? How much time did he have left now?

As Relian drew near, the Fist released the bell-rope and dashed for the nearest stack of crates. Relian jumped to intercept it and the Fist swerved, heading for the open door. The huge outer chamber, with its maze of passageways and its towers of crates offered countless hiding-places. If the racing hand reached that haven, it would escape once and for all. Relian might search all night and never find it.

Desperation lent him fresh speed. He launched himself into a flat dive and as he came down, his outstretched hands encountered the Fist. He clamped down on it with all his strength, and the Fist was crushed to the floor. It struggled bravely, bucking like an unbroken horse and raking the floor with its long nails. But its palm was pressed firmly to the flags and escape was impossible. The hyperdigital fingers curved backward to claw their captor's flesh, but inflicted little damage.

Without relaxing his grip, Relian rose to a kneeling position. He placed one knee atop the Fist and gingerly withdrew his hands. Talons scrabbled desperately on stone, but the Fist remained captive. Relian produced a linen handkerchief in which he deftly enshrouded his prisoner. He knotted the corners tightly and deposited the squirming bundle in his coat pocket. Done.

There remained only the return trip to Fortress Gavyne, which he hoped would prove uneventful.

Lantern in hand, Relian returned to the outer chamber. Eager now to be away, to be done forever with the entire abhorrent mission, he made his way back along the perimeter of the room to the Footpad Alley exit.

I must never let him force me to do anything like this again.

He opened the door a crack and peered out. Seeing no one, he cautiously poked his head out, glanced hurriedly right and left. All appeared deserted. The guards were still busy with the fire on Tallow Street.

I wonder if anyone was hurt in the fire? Or killed? If so, I am partially to blame. How many more will suffer before Keprose is done?

He took a deep breath and slipped out into the alley.

Relian had taken but a few steps before he found his escape route cut off. A group of armed men materialized at the mouth of Footpad Alley. Many of them bore lanterns or links, and he could see their faces clearly. Among those grim, purposeful countenances, one in the forefront stood out by reason of its mild and amiable expression. With a thrill of alarm, Relian recognized Scrivvulch the Stick.

Scrivvulch saw Relian at the same moment and his smile beamed with pleasure. "Master Kru—" he began.

Shouts drowned out the voice of the Assassin.

"It's him—Black Relian!"

"The famous Equalist—"

"—Himself!"

Famous Equalist? Relian met the smiling eyes of Scrivvulch and knew the source of the description. Could he persuade the townsmen of his innocence?

What innocence? You broke into their repository and stole their property.

Attempting neither denial nor explanation, he let fall the lantern and turned to flee.

Footpad Alley was a short cul-de-sac that ended in a blank stone wall. The open end was blocked by the townsmen. The only possible way to go was straight through the Egg House and out the front door to Guild Square. The front door might or might not be guarded. He would find out when he got there. Relian bounded back to the Egg House, flung wide the unlocked door and ducked inside.

Fresh shouts of wrath arose and the townsmen surged in after him. Relian could hear their pursuing footsteps echo through the cavernous chamber. Their lanterns lit the interior with a feeble orange glow. Their shadows, grotesquely elongated, leaped along the walls like avenging spirits. Relian ran lightly, making as little sound as possible. He could hear many of their comments.

A strong voice that he did not recognize commanded, "You three stay by the door in case he tries to double back. Keep your pistols ready."

A slower, very deliberate voice directed, "Spread out in pairs through this entire room. If anyone spots the Equalist, give a yell."

"Don't forget the Records Chamber and the Tank Room. Vormer's got a key."

"Gentlemen, there is another door, is there not?" It was the voice of Scrivvulch. "It had best be guarded, and quickly."

"Correct, sir." The first voice again. "Three of you—*you three*—do as he said. Look sharp!"

And then the voices died away to murmurs as the vigilantes warmed to the hunt.

Relian quickened his pace. If he failed to reach the front door ahead of the armed townsmen, he would be captured or killed outright. If he was captured, they would either hang him or else hand him over to Scrivvulch. And even as he considered the prospect, the voice of his nemesis rang through the vaulted chamber.

"Master Kru." The echoes transformed Scrivvulch's pleasant voice into a brazen gong. "Young Kru, listen to me. We have all been the victims of a misunderstanding here, but now is the time to set things right. Show yourself. Talk to us, and all difficulties will be smoothed. You have my word there is nothing to fear. You will not be harmed. Show yourself."

So persuasively did he speak, with such gently reasonable conviction, that for one mad moment Relian was tempted to confront his pursuers. He recognized it for what it was— something akin to the hypnotic lure of a river rushing to the edge of the falls; one longed to jump in to know how it would feel. Deliberately he recalled Bewbigo's Final Shadow. The recollection raised gooseflesh along his arms.

This section of the Egg House was dark. Relian felt his way along the wall and presently encountered the door. The pressure at his forehead and temples relaxed somewhat, thus notifying him of its existence. His hand fell on the latch. The door was locked. Relian drew the flask from his pocket and found the bottle perilously light. If only he hadn't wasted so much of the precious contents upon Crekkid's unyielding scales! Quickly he felt for the keyhole, located it and shook out the last reluctant drops of Keprose's fluid. The familiar perfume caressed his nostrils. The click of the suddenly-released lock sounded to Relian loud as a pistol shot and he wondered that every one of his pursuers did not hear it. Perhaps some of them did. The gleam of an approaching lantern threw the edge of a nearby tower of crates into sharp relief. Mumbling voices could be heard, and footsteps clunked on stone. Relian wrestled blindly with the door.

And then two tremendous cries rang out in quick succession.

"Master Stipper—the Fist is gone! He's got the Fist of Zhi!"

"THERE HE IS! WE'VE GOT HIM!"

Lantern dazzled Relian's vision as the three citizens assigned to guard the front door rounded the tower of crates. Voices babbled in excitement from every corner of the room.

"Stand fast or you're a dead man." The townsman's pistol was leveled at Relian's heart.

Relian pushed open the door and ducked through. The townsman fired a moment too late, and the bullet buried itself in the wooden portal. The blast of the gun echoed beneath the vaulted ceiling, disguising the origin of the shot. Cries of urgent confusion added to the uproar. The townsman with the pistol bellowed helpfully, "He's out on the Guild Square!" and dashed off in pursuit, followed by a straggling procession of his cohorts.

An instant later, Scrivvulch the Stick arrived at the Egg House door. With him came Master Gatherer Clym Stipper, Councilman Gyf Fynok and a sizable band of citizens. Scrivvulch noted the speed and agility of his escaping prey. "Oh, my. Oh my, what a famous runner the lad is," he admired, shrugged lightly and turned aside. His upraised hand halted the advance of his companions. "Master Stipper, Councilman Fynok—a word, if you please."

"Not now," wheezed Stipper, his broad face crimson with unaccustomed exertion. "No time!"

"There is little point in pursuing him through the streets," Scrivvulch observed calmly. "Alas that Black Relian's life of desperate enterprise has endowed him with considerable fleetness of foot. Quite simply, we are not young men, and we've little chance of catching him. Ah, look—the lad has already reached the far side of the square."

"We'll not give up searching until he's found," replied Fynok. "No matter how long it takes. Now out of the way, Master Scrivvulch!"

Scrivvulch remained unruffled. "Gentlemen, I've a simpler and more efficient plan. This town affords a thousand hiding-places, but one thing is certain. Before the break of dawn, Black Relian will return to Fortress Gavyne, where he is assured of safe refuge."

"Well, if he makes it back to the fortress, he's foxed us," said Stipper.

"Exactly. Hence he must not make it back. We need only intercept him along the road," Scrivvulch informed his dawningly appreciative audience. "We require horses—quickly, my friends, quickly. Where may they be obtained?"

Anonymous voices spoke up:

"Mine's still over at the Bearded Moon."

"And mine, with a gig."

"Master Moon'll lend us some. Particularly if he don't know about it."

"We could hire some at Noio's—"

"—Or the posting-house."

"Which is closest?" asked Scrivvulch. "The posting-house, is it not?"

"Closed now, sir."

"They will no doubt open to assist us at this moment of civic crisis," returned Scrivvulch. "Very well, gentlemen. We shall equip ourselves with horses and divide into two parties. One, under the command of Councilman Fynok, will patrol the Rising Road just outside the town limits. I, together with Master Stipper and sundry others, will haste to the fortress. And now," he concluded zestfully, "to the posting-house, then ho! for hare-and-hounds."

*   *   *

With the mummified Fist still bouncing in his pocket, Relian sprinted at top speed across the broad, open expanse of the Guild Square. Behind him he heard the baying of his pursuers, and then a fresh cry went up:

"STOP, THIEF!"

There was nobody to heed the appeal. The Square was deserted. What few citizens might conceivably have been found there at that time of the night were gone. Probably they were off in Tallow Street, along with the Egg House guards and half the adult population of Vale Jevaint, all gathered there to fight the fire that had flared so mysteriously upon the stroke of midnight. Relian glanced off to his left. The domed and pinnacled roofs of the municipal buildings that fronted on the Guild Square showed in black silhouette against an orange sky. The fire still raged. Vazm, Pruke and Druveen had done their work all too well.

On the far side of the Square, a row of townhouses served by tiny individual alleys seemed to offer refuge, and there Relian directed his steps. He dashed on, fleet and as yet untired. The cries that followed were growing fainter, and he risked a look back over his shoulder. His pursuers had fallen far behind. Unlikely that they would catch him, provided he did not manage to trap himself in some unlooked-for dead end. Given the customary nature of his fortunes, such a possibility was not to be overlooked.

Relian reached the houses that edged the Guild Square, plunged into the nearest alleyway, took the first turning and ran for a hundred yards along a dark passageway so narrow that he fancied himself caught in the jaws of a monstrous press. At the end of the passage his way was blocked by a wooden gate, which he nimbly scaled. He dropped down on the other side into somebody's private garden, where bare branches and barren earth proclaimed early winter's reign. He stood still a moment, head upraised to catch any sound borne on the sharp-edged breeze. There was no sign of his pursuers. Relian skirted the edge of a tall stone dwelling, every window of which was dark; climbed another fence and came down in the street. It was a broad, quiet avenue lined with pillared mansions—evidently a fashionable section of town. Fairly certain now that he had evaded pursuit, he set off along the street at a fairly leisurely pace, and as he went his eyes rose to the cliff overlooking the town, where the lights of Fortress Gavyne shone like beacons in the night. Odd that the words of Keprose should prove true; at this moment, the fortress seemed less a prison than a sanctuary.

Relian turned a corner and came upon a quartet of link-bearing townsmen. They saw him and the cry went up, "There he is!"

He turned and ran. Along the streets he fled, through a small park, through a warren of alleyways—but this time he did not succeed in throwing them off his track. They were not so swift as he, but they knew the town well. Turn and twist and double as he might, he could not entirely lose them.

Relian was growing winded. He needed to leave Vale Jevaint as quickly as possible. Once clear of the town, he might easily lose himself in the woods that blanketed the surrounding hills. A brisk hike in any direction would soon carry him beyond the town limits. He had barely begun to walk before the familiar quartet reappeared behind him. He ran, and felt that his pace was flagging. There was a stitch in his side. His forehead and neck were clammy with sweat, despite the chill of winter. The scene began to assume that nightmarish quality with which he was too familiar.

Relian cut across a square dominated by a statue whose curly locks and receding chin marked the subject as a Gavyne. The hum of human voices reached him, growing louder as he left square and statue behind. The air seemed to lose a little of its chill as he proceeded, and the breeze carried a throat-grabbing scent of smoke. The sunset glow in the sky intensified. The vocal hum resolved itself to shouts and cries underscored by the roar of the conflagration. When he rounded the corner of a building whose doors had been left wide open in evidence of the tenants' haste to depart, he beheld the handiwork of Vazm, Pruke and Druveen.

They'd had the sense to choose a fairly isolated building—probably more for the sake of their own safety than any other reason. Only four small wooden houses stood in the immediate vicinity of the sacrificial warehouse and all of them were lost to the flames. The warehouse itself had blazed for nearly an hour, despite the best efforts of a bucket brigade that stretched in two great human chains: from the fire site in Tallow street to the well and pump in Menders' Row to the east; from Tallow Street to the well behind the Jewel Inn to the south. The flames could not be quelled. The warehouse roof was gone. The northeastern wall was also down, destroyed in the initial blast of the explosion. Three walls remained standing, but they were cloaked in fire and clearly doomed. Even as Relian watched, a section of the northwestern wall collapsed amidst a shower of shooting sparks. The flames leapt and smoke billowed chokingly over Tallow Street. Several of the fire fighters paused to wipe their stinging eyes. Orange light played upon a crowd of sweat-drenched, soot-blackened faces. Waves of intense heat smote the volunteers. One man in the forefront of the brigade, overcome by heat and smoke, dropped his bucket and slumped to the ground. Spilled water trickled uselessly over the cobbles. The stricken man was carried off to the side of the road and deposited among a number of others similarly afflicted. Buckets continued their journey from hand to hand, and the fight went on without a break.

Relian skulked on the outskirts of the crowd. The fire fighters paid him no heed. It was almost like being invisible. He savored the momentary sense of security, but knew it for a delusion. His pursuers would soon arrive, and he could not lose himself in the crowd for very long. Even as he urged haste and caution upon himself, five townsmen emerged from a side alley to stand blinking in the glare of the fire. He recognized four of them. The indefatigable quartet had somehow acquired a new member.

He attempted to slide from their line of vision. His furtive lateral movement immediately caught the attention of one of the men, who raised a cry of alarm. Relian dashed through Tallow Street, with the townsmen howling behind him. Their cries, lost in the shouts of the crowd and the roar of the fire, attracted little attention. No one attempted to halt the fugitive; not when he jostled a bucket-bearing Gatherer and knocked two pails of water to the ground; not when he elbowed a harmless apprentice and sent the young fellow sprawling. Indignant exclamations arose in his wake, but no one laid a hand upon him. He quickly widened the distance between himself and his hunters, but found himself wondering: Were the men of Vale Jevaint part bloodhound? Was there no losing them? Then, when his breath was coming in gasps and his heart was pounding, he spied salvation in the form of a saddle horse left tethered to a post at a safe distance from the blazing warehouse. It was but the work of a moment to unhitch the animal, mount and clap heels to its sides. He urged the horse to a gallop and sped down Tallow Street, leaving fire, crowd and screaming pursuers far behind. Tallow Street fed into a wide, clear thoroughfare. He looked right and left in search of a familiar landmark. On his right stood the Bearded Moon, its windows still alight. He was on the Rising Road and he need only follow the avenue straight out of town, across the field and up the hill to Fortress Gavyne. Relian did not permit the stolen horse's pace to slacken. Although he believed himself past danger, he would not feel truly safe until he was clear of Vale Jevaint.

A few minutes of hard riding took him to the edge of town. He pressed the horse to its best speed. Before him stretched the moonlit fields and beyond them, the wooded hills. Relian was halfway across the meadow when he became aware of the horsemen behind him. He looked back to behold a posse of eight galloping hot on his trail. Several lengths ahead of the others rode a familiar spindling figure. Scrivvulch the Stick rode hunched over his horse's neck, his knees and elbows protruding at odd angles. His technique, however graceless, was effective; or perhaps he had been wise in his selection of a mount. Whatever the reason, he was rapidly drawing farther ahead of his companions.

Relian dug his heels sharply into the horse's flanks but found the animal incapable of additional speed. Just ahead the Rising Road, now narrowing to a mere path, climbed sharply. The way darkened as it snaked under the trees. Relian sped up the hillside at a dangerous pace. Should his horse stumble and fall, the game of hare-and-hounds would draw to a swift finish.

I wish you hadn't thought of that. If it's bad luck and it can happen, then it will happen.

But it did not.

The path was almost lost in shadow. Only the occasional faint moonbeams slanting down through a break in the pines served to light the way. He reined the horse to a walk. He dared not career blindly through the darkness; moreover, the horse was heavily lathered and nearing exhaustion. Relian straightened in the saddle and strained his ears for the sound of pursuing hoofbeats. He heard nothing. For the moment, his enemies had fallen behind.

The zigzagging ascent seemed interminable. But it ended at last and he emerged from the forest to confront the great outer wall of Fortress Gavyne. Relian completed the last few yards of his journey at a canter. Dismounting before the horse had come to a full stop, he ran to the gate and rapped imperatively. For a moment there was no response and in that moment he heard the thud of horses' hooves. He pounded furiously. The panel opened, a gleam of candlelight escaped the interior and the porter's sleep-sodden face appeared. The porter, having received instructions from the Seigneur earlier in the evening, admitted Relian without demur. The gate opened. Relian cast one last look behind him as he slid through. The beat of hooves grew louder. A gangling rider broke from the cover of the trees.

"Close it," Relian commanded tersely.

The porter was not gifted with quick responses. Scrivvulch the Stick was but a few feet distant when the gate banged shut in his face.

*   *   *

Councilman Gyf Fynok and his mounted companions had patrolled the Rising Road through half the night, but the Equalist they sought was absent or else invisible. Now Fynok was growing restless. It appeared that the man Scrivvulch had been mistaken. That was only natural—what kind of sober good sense could be expected of a feckless Neraunci? Not an ounce of steadiness in those Nerauncis, any of them. Scrivvulch, Clym Stipper (ordinarily a man of sound judgment, but now misguided) and about half the original party from the Bearded Moon had gone pelting up the road toward Fortress Gavyne hours earlier, and they had not yet returned. Fynok wished them joy of *that* journey. A wild goose chase it was, a waste of men and horses, and likely to offend the Seigneur as well. The Equalist, Fynok firmly believed, had gone to ground somewhere in Vale Jevaint. A methodical, building-to-building search would soon flush the fugitive. Any other approach to the problem was certainly useless.

Fynok frowned. He wasted time loitering here, and time had become precious in view of the problems besetting Vale Jevaint. Affairs of the town had come to a sorry pass indeed. In the first place, there was the matter of the Seigneur's Jovian assaults upon the property of individual citizens. Ever since the destruction of his own mansion, this subject had occupied much of Fynok's attention. Now the Fist of Zhi, which had safeguarded the lives of generations of Gatherers, was gone—snatched by an Equalist enjoying the protection of the Seigneur. And on the very same night, a mysterious explosion had destroyed a warehouse and its neighboring buildings. It occurred to Councilman Fynok to wonder whether the theft and the fire might not be connected. His cogitations were interrupted by the arrival of a mounted messenger from the town.

"Councilman Fynok?" The messenger spoke in discreetly low tones. "I've been sent to fetch you, sir. You're wanted at the Council Hall."

"At this time of the night? Why?" Fynok inquired.

"There's matter brewing, sir. About the great fire in Tallow Street—" The messenger's voice sank lower yet, and Fynok had to lean forward to hear him. " 'Twas suspected by all that it was no accident. So the Guardsmen went sniffing about and soon proved beyond doubt that the business was very arsonical."

"What's that you say?" asked Fynok.

"Arson, sir. The Guardsmen, being well advised, hastened to the Jewel Inn, where the culprits were surprised and apprehended. Being somewhat the worse for drink, 'twas easy to take 'em."

"They're in custody, then?"

"Aye—held under guard at the Council Hall. Three of 'em, sir."

"Why, all's well, then. They'll be turned over to the Seigneur for judgment in the morning, and they'll find that the Seigneur's not one to be trifled with."

"Well—there's the matter I spoke of, sir." The messenger looked uncomfortable. "And a delicate business it is, that wants men of good sense to deal with it."

"I'm for plain speaking. What hinders us from handing the three bloody-minded rogues over to Keprose Gavyne in the morning?" Fynok demanded.

" 'Tis best you come and see for yourself, Councilman."

Gyf Fynok took leave of his companions and accompanied the messenger back through the streets of the town as far as the Council Hall, which stood diagonally opposite the despoiled Egg House on the Guild Square. He proceeded quickly to the main Council Chamber, where he found a number of his fellow Councilmen, a bevy of Guardsmen, and three identically pink-haired, blue-eyed, sullen-faced prisoners in manacles. Fynok recognized the young arsonists and comprehended the messenger's embarrassment.

Druveen lifted his head and addressed his captors with

scowling defiance. "You peasants must be mad or stupid if
you think Seigneur Keprose Gavyne is going to stand by
while you lay hands on his kin. You people will regret this."

"Just wait," Pruke suggested, taking the cue from his
brother.

"If you think you can keep us locked up, you don't know
our Uncle," proclaimed Vazm.

"That fire at the warehouse is nothing compared to what
Uncle will do when he finds out you've put chains on his
favorite nephews," Druveen promised. "Uncle will blast
every building from one end of this town to the other."

"He can do it, too."

"Uncle's got a way with lightning. You'll see."

Councilmen and guards exchanged uneasy glances.

Druveen observed their discomfort and smiled. "So you'd
better learn how to treat gentlemen," he advised. "Turn us
loose and just be grateful that we're kindhearted and bear no
grudges. Let us go—"

"Or else you'll be hearing from Uncle. Uncle won't be
pleased."

"Uncle won't like it at all."

*   *   *

In the morning, an emergency meeting of the Council con-
vened. As a gesture of courtesy, Scrivvulch the Stick was
permitted to attend. Scrivvulch had not slept the previous
night, but nonetheless appeared fresh and impeccable as he
stood to address the governing body of Vale Jevaint. His
manner was affable and moderate as ever, his voice pleasantly modulated as he urged the townsmen to march on
Fortress Gavyne. The Seigneur Keprose, he argued, would
surely consent to a peaceful parley with a delegation of his
loyal subjects. In token of good faith, Scrivvulch himself was
willing to accompany the delegates.

Response to this suggestion was unenthusiastic. With the
example of Gyf Fynok ever before them, the Councilmen
displayed little willingness to confront the Seigneur face to
face. An alternate plan was proposed, wherein the Seigneur
Keprose would be offered the freedom of his three incendiary
nephews in exchange for the Fist of Zhi. It took all the
eloquence of which Scrivvulch was master to persuade the
Councilmen to add the surrender of the Equalist Black Relian

Kru to the list of their demands. In the end he succeeded, but the victory was too insignificant to afford satisfaction. For the first time since he had come to Vale Jevaint, a shadow of care darkened the brow of the High Court Assassin.

*   *   *

Following Relian's return with the Fist of Zhi, Keprose Gavyne vanished, and for some days was seen by no one. At first it was thought by the servants that the Seigneur had departed the fortress, as he did from time to time. Not long after, however, the cook noted that food was disappearing from the pantry. Suspicious of larceny on the part of his subordinates, the cook mounted surveillance from a place of concealment just outside the pantry door. In the dead of night the thief appeared. By the light of a single candle, the distinctive form of Keprose Gavyne was recognizable. Keprose bore a sack in which he placed four cold roast fowls, a smoked ham, a cylinder of ripe blue cheese, four loaves of bread, a crock of truffled pâté, eight bottles of claret and two of port, and several boxes of bonbons. That done, he took his leave. The fascinated cook silently shadowed his master up to the second story and saw Keprose vanish into the chamber occupied by the mysteriously malodorous entities.

Thereafter the servants kept close watch on the second floor room. None presumed to enter, but throughout the ensuing days, a footman or kitchen boy could usually be found with an ear pressed to the door. Inexplicable noises emerged—grunts, gobbles, thumps, urgent scufflings—and above all, the sound of Keprose Gavyne's voice. For three days running, Keprose spoke ceaselessly. His voice rose and fell in a droning, rhythmic chant indicative of supranormal activity. The voice grew tired and slow, but the hours passed and it neither paused nor faltered. The servants, oppressed with a sense of nameless dread, went quietly about their tasks. Periodic reports issued from the sentinels. The Seigneur was still speaking—his voice was hoarse but he spoke yet—a fight had broken out in the chamber and the sound of glass breaking could be heard, but the Seigneur still spoke—spoke yet—words unintelligible—groaning—whispers—the Seigneur's voice slowing—and then, silence. Absolute silence.

The tentative knocking of the servants drew no response. Silence reigned for three days and three nights, and it was suspected the Seigneur was dead. But no one dared venture into the chamber to verify the rumor, not even when a messenger from the town arrived bearing a parchment sealed and stamped with the insignia of the Governing Council of the City of Vale Jevaint. It was obviously a document of significance, but it languished unread for days. Eventually, for lack of a better plan, the senior footman thrust the parchment under the door of his master's retreat. Whether the townsmen's communication found a sentient audience or not was anyone's guess.

At last, when the domestics had begun to speak cautiously among themselves of breaking down the door—at about the time they had agreed that the opinion of the young Travornish gentleman, who seemed to have a head on his shoulders, ought to be solicited—it was at this time that the voice within the chamber resumed.

Keprose's soliloquy was curious. He no longer chanted and droned. Rather, it was as if the Seigneur carried on a conversation with himself; or perhaps performed a play wherein he took every role. His actual words were muffled by the chamber door, but his inflections conveyed much. He lectured, he reasoned, he coaxed, he scolded. He asked himself questions and answered them at length. At times he seemed to quarrel with himself, his voice sharply acerbic. Occasionally he produced witticisms and responded to his own sallies with bursts of appreciative laughter. This laughter—a rich, snuffling chuckle, uniquely Keprose's—seemed to arise simultaneously from every corner of the room; an auditory effect that caused the perplexed servants to wonder whether their lord possessed hitherto undisclosed mastery of ventriloquism.

At this time, another change occurred. The scrape of moving furniture was heard. The Seigneur's heaving grunts bespoke untoward exertion. Shortly thereafter, an avalanche of detestable effluvia burst from the window of the locked room to descend upon the courtyard. The splash of water was heard within and the stench that had polluted the corridor for so long began to lift.

The servants' speculations were feverish but inconclusive, and the matter remained a mystery. No one was as yet aware of the Seigneur's triumph. No one shared in the sensations he had experienced upon gazing into the awakening blue eyes of the first of his doppelgangers and hearing it declare in a voice indistinguishable from his own, "I am Keprose Gavyne."

*   *   *

"Ssstupid. Ssstupid. Ssstupid," Nurbo hissed derisively. "Inept. Ssstupid."

"I'm afraid she's right, Relian," Mereth admitted. "I can't do it."

The little pile of gray goose down lay intact on the workroom table before her. Mereth's brow was damp with effort, but her Tactility did not serve to stir a single feather.

Relian sighed. During the period of Keprose's self-imposed isolation, he had studied and practiced strenuously. His own Tactility, while weak, nonetheless showed signs of improvement. The same could not be said of Mereth, whose efforts bore no fruit. Now her lips were curved in a sneer of self-contempt that he hated to see. Words of comfort and encouragement hovered on the tip of his tongue, but he dared not speak them. The least sign of excessive warmth, much less affection, between himself and Mereth would be swiftly punished by the snakes.

"Well, don't give up on it yet, Mereth. Perhaps if there were a change in surroundings—maybe if you practiced this exercise in another room—it might make a difference." There was far more expression in his eyes than in his words or voice. Relian silently prayed that she recognized the falsity of his nonchalance and understood all that he could not express before a steel-scaled audience. He met her eyes and saw there a flash of comprehension. The set of her mouth relaxed somewhat.

Mereth shrugged with assumed indifference. "Perhaps," she replied and added almost unconsciously, "And even then, we'd both still be here, as always."

"Alwaysss. Alwaysss. Alwaysss," Nurbo agreed. "Lucky humansss have home here alwaysss. Great isss the charity of the Ssseigneur."

"But when ssshall the charity of the Ssseigneur permit Patriarch Crekkid and Matriarch Nurbo to join?" inquired Crekkid. "Crekkid heatsss for Nurbo like sssteel in fire. He glowsss. He meltsss. He waitsss. Waitsss. Waitsss. He asssksss when thisss joining ssshall be. When?"

Relian, whose own problem was not dissimilar, could almost sympathize with the amorous serpent.

"Sssoon. Sssoon. Sssoon. Sssoon," Nurbo reassured her intended. "Ssseigneur hasss great concernsss now. He caresss little for humansss we ride. They work, they do not work—thessse daysss, Ssseigneur doesss not care. He asssksss not, doesss not care."

With some surprise, Relian recognized the truth of Nurbo's observation. Preoccupied with his supranormal studies, he had scarcely noticed the waning interest of Keprose Gavyne.

"Sssun up, sssun down, Ssseigneur comesss not," Nurbo continued. "Sssoon he no longer needsss humansss, no longer wantsss. Then we kill them, drink blood. Crekkid and Nurbo together at lassst. Forever."

"The voice of Nurbo lovely asss musssic. Ssshe isss wissse asss ssshe isss fair."

"Brave Crekkid!"

"Ssssweet Nurbo!"

"Forever!"

Relian stirred uncomfortably. He noted that the color had fled Mereth's cheeks. The girl rose abruptly from her chair, walked to the window and stood gazing out across the valley at the fog shrouding the Tyrant of Mists. The view was unobstructed since the removal of the three glass tubes that had once contained the Selves. Relian stared at the back of her head for a while, then hit upon something almost certain to cheer her. "Still no sign of Vazm, Pruke and Druveen?" he inquired.

She turned away from the window, her expression noticeably brighter. "Why, no. Nobody's seen or heard from them since the night they went down to the town. Sometimes they've stayed away for several days at a time, but never as long as this. It's been like a holiday."

"Yes, hasn't it? I wonder if anything's happened to them."

"But you said that Lady Fribanni's stories about the giant carnivorous plants choking the path down to Vale Jevaint were lies."

"Carnivorous plants aren't quite what I had in mind. Has anyone made inquiries among the townsfolk?"

"Not that I know of. Keprose doesn't seem to have noticed—"

"No more!" The conversation had gone on too long to suit

Crekkid, and the serpent tightened petulantly. "No more gossssip. You work now."

"Why?" Relian asked. "As you've already noticed, Seigneur Keprose no longer seems to care."

"No matter. You are here, you work. Work. Work. Work. Work. Crekkid sssee to that. Crekkid the Ssscourge of the Ssseigneur!"

"Ssstrong Crekkid!" Nurbo could not contain her admiration, and Crekkid flexed exultantly at the sound of her languishing hisses. "Kingly Crekkid! Crekkid, Ssscourge of Ssseigneur!"

To avoid giving Crekkid an excuse to demonstrate his zeal, Relian returned to work. His power of supranormal Tactility was growing. He could now, while sitting motionless in his chair, easily whisk the goose down across the tabletop. He was arranging the feathers in a neat pattern of concentric circles when a messenger entered the workroom. The breeze from the doorway sent the feathers flying. Relian noted the entrance of the servant and deliberately permitted Uy's Mindwall to crash. His supranormal Hand floated an instant longer, then ceased to exist. He accepted the message, unfolded and read:

> Young Man—
> Your presence is required in the chamber of the Selves. You may bring Mistress Mereth or not, as you choose. Come at once.
>
> —Keprose Gavyne

Relian frowned. During the period of Keprose's withdrawal he had been spared the ordeal of contact with the mindlessly violent Selves, and had hoped he need never approach them again. Now it appeared that the respite was ending. "Did the Seigneur give you this?" he asked the servant.

"No, sir. It was found lying in the corridor just outside that room on the second floor. The Seigneur must have slipped it under the door. We reckoned 'twas meant for you, sir."

"I see. Thank-you."

The messenger departed and Relian extended the note to Mereth, who read it at a glance. "What do you make of that?" he asked uneasily.

"He must need you for something," she replied. "Perhaps those creatures of his are out of control and he wants assistance. Let's go find out."

"I don't think you should come," Relian told her. "For two reasons. One is that Keprose could hurt you. Remember what happened the last time he wanted me to do something and you were in the room?"

Mereth's hand rose to her throat, which still bore the marks of Nurbo's attack. She flinched at the memory, but answered with spirit, "That won't happen today. If Keprose had anything like that in mind, he wouldn't simply consent to my presence. He'd have *ordered* me to go, as he did the other time. What's your other reason?"

"It's the creatures themselves. You know what they did to Lady Fribanni. They're dangerous. They also happen to be disgusting—gross, unspeakably filthy, and in every sense obscene—but that's a relatively minor point. The fact is that it's unsafe to go into their room. The only reason Keprose has had me do it is that he regards my life as expendable."

"He's been shut up with them for days now, so he must be able to deal with them," Mereth pointed out. "In any case, I want to see for myself."

"That's just what you said to Fribanni about the carnivorous plants."

Relian had no choice but to accept her decision. Together the two of them descended from the tower and made their way to the chamber lately barred to all visitors. As they drew near, Relian warned, "Brace yourself, Mereth. The stench of the Selves and their apartment is vile. The air in the corridor outside the chamber is foul beyond expression, and once you get inside, it's nearly unbreathable. The room itself is a shambles, strewn with broken furniture, glass, excrement and decaying food, so take care where you set your feet. Don't go anywhere near the Selves—they're very free with their fists, and monstrously strong. I'm not trying to frighten you, but you should be prepared."

She nodded and took a deep breath. As they came to the door they sought, she released the air from her lungs and observed, "I don't notice any stench. Well—there *is* the trace of an unpleasant odor, but it's weak."

Relian sniffed the inoffensive atmosphere. "It certainly is. If you could have smelled this corridor a few days ago—! I wonder if Keprose used supranormalcy to clear the air? Now, stay well behind me. The Selves may be waiting beside the door. They sometimes do that when they hear me coming in, and it's one of their more unpleasant tricks. The only thing that will hold them off at a time like that is food, and I'm not carrying any.''

He rapped on the door and the voice of Keprose Gavyne answered, ''Come.''

The door was unbarred. Relian opened it and paused staring on the threshold. His back blocked Mereth's view. She craned her neck to see around him, and what she saw made her catch her breath. Shrieking whistles escaped Crekkid and Nurbo. The chamber, miraculously transformed since Relian's last visit, was now tolerably habitable. The floor was free of filth, debris, and bonbon wrappers. The furniture was ranged symmetrically against the walls, and broken pieces had been discarded. All the windows were wide open, despite the wintry weather. The atmosphere, while hardly fragrant, no longer rivaled the exhalations of the Forest of Miasm. On the floor in one corner lay a flat white object. It was a folded parchment, and the wax seal had been broken.

But it was not the transformation of the room that froze Relian on the threshold. Before him he beheld the Seigneur Keprose Gavyne in quadruplicate. The four massive figures, lined up neatly in a row, were identical down to the last dapper detail of pomaded pink curl and waxed moustache. They were clothed in identical black robes. Their neatly-manicured hands were clasped upon their respective bellies. The four curly heads were cocked at precisely the same angle. Four pairs of rosy brows were lifted in polite inquiry. Four sets of Cupid's bow lips were bent in identically complacent smiles. Four pairs of blue eyes beamed amused condescension.

Relian looked upon the Selves of Keprose Gavyne and, despite his heartfelt hatred of their creator, was moved to admiration of superlative supranormalcy. ''Seigneur,'' he confessed, ''I congratulate you.''

Four pink heads dipped in acknowledgment of the tribute.

Relian examined the Selves minutely. Try as he would, he could discover no difference among them and finally admitted defeat by asking, ''Where is the Seigneur Keprose?''

Four voices answered as one, ''Here.''

The four exchanged glances of identical annoyance. After a moment, all spoke with increased emphasis. ''*Here.*''

''No, Beloveds.'' The denial came from the Keprose at the left end of the line. ''You are my alter egos, my doppelgangers, my other Selves and I love you as I love myself. That is, you are I. I love you for your beauty of mind and spirit, for your wit, strength, prowess and distinction. But *I* am your creator, your prototype, and in a sense, your father. I am the true and original Keprose Gavyne.''

''You are the Prototype,'' admitted a Self. ''So you have informed me, and—''

''—So I must believe,'' another Keprose finished. ''But does a chronological accident make you—''

''—Any the more Keprose than I?'' concluded the third Self.

Relian realized that their very thoughts were identical and simultaneous, to the point that they completed one another's sentences.

''Do your powers of mind or body—''

''—Exceed my own? Do you—''

''—Surpass me in virtue, in prowess, or in—''

''—Any manner of natural excellence?''

''Clearly, you do not and therefore I—''

''—No less than you, possess the right to regard myself—''

''—As the true Keprose—''

''—Gavyne.''

''Not so, Beloveds.'' The Keprose grudgingly acknowledged by the others as the ''Prototype'' was evidently the real Seigneur. ''I possess the preeminent claim, for I occurred in nature. I was born of fleshly parents, and over the course of decades I ripened to manhood. Upon attaining maturity, I was desirous of reproducing the mental and supranormal perfection that I embody—hence, I cultivated my Selves. And I may assure you that my Selves are my finest creation. But that creation, Beloveds, is very recent.''

''Perhaps it is so,'' a Self conceded with a touch of sadness. ''For I do recall dimly as a fleeting dream, the moonlight shining into my eyes—''

''—Through the glass wall of the great tube,'' another took up the thought. ''Perhaps this body is newly-formed, but I possess the memories of—''

''—A lifetime, from my precocious childhood and the—''

''—Early manifestation of my supranormalcy, to the wondering admiration of those around me—''

''—To the remarkable accomplishments of my adolescence, to—''

''—My emergence as the foremost supranormalist of my time—perhaps of all time.''

''Subjectively, I have existed for decades, and there is

within me the certainty of unique identity,'' asserted one of them defiantly.

''It is not acceptable to my sense of pride, of—''

''—Self-worth, of—''

''—Self-respect, to believe that I am one of many, turned out in batches like—''

''—Pastries upon a baker's sheet. *I am Keprose*—''

''—*Gavyne!*''

''I am not willing to share my individuality—''

''—My essence, my—''

''—Very being. I look about me and I behold a triple image of—''

''—My own face. So much cannot be denied. I will acknowledge our outward similarity, our—''

''—Brotherhood, but that is the limit of acceptance. These others are not as I—''

''—For there is but one Seigneur and—''

''—I am he!'' The perfectly-synchronized triple affirmation resounded.

The man on the left, the true Keprose, sighed and answered sympathetically. ''Beloveds, I recognize and understand your indignation. Loss of individuality is insupportable to the noble spirit. Let me hasten to reassure you. There is indeed a difference among you, by virtue of the simple fact that you occupy three separate volumes of space. Because of this separation, the sights that meet your eyes; the sounds and scents that you experience—in short, the impressions of all your senses—differ from one Self to another. These differing impressions result in subtly dissimilar memories imprinted upon your respective minds, which will in turn lead at last to variations in thought. The divergencies are infinitesimal as yet, but they will increase over the course of time. And therein lies your true individuality; it is the inevitable end result of the physical separation of your bodies. Therefore, dear ones, let your hearts be consoled.'' Leaving his Selves to ponder this, Keprose turned to Relian and Mereth, still spellbound in the doorway, and remarked, ''No doubt you are wondering why I summoned you here today.''

''To marvel at your accomplishment, Seigneur?'' Relian suggested diplomatically.

''Partially correct, young man. It is true that the soul of an artist nourishes itself upon the adulation of the multitudes. It argues a shallowness of mind on your part, however, to suppose that such gratification fulfills my entire purpose. You will be so good as to enter the chamber."

"Your nervous hesitation upon the threshold is reminiscent of the rabbit frozen with terror at sight of the hunter," remarked a Self.

"It is gauche as it is absurd," observed another.

"Well said, Beloveds," said Keprose. "I could not have stated the matter more aptly myself."

Relian and Mereth entered. For a moment there was silence broken only by the soft, ecstatic hisses of Crekkid and Nurbo.

"Your presence is required as a means of testing the knowledge of my Selves, young man," Keprose explained. "And it does not displease me that you have seen fit to bring Mistress Mereth as well, as she too may perhaps prove useful."

"Her utility is open to question," opined a Self. "Beauty serves many functions—"

"—But none suited to our present needs—" another added.

"—When unaccompanied by intelligence," the third concluded.

Mereth flushed and Relian's jaw hardened. "Exact replication," he observed.

"It was not long ago," Keprose continued, "I informed you that my completed Selves should share in my knowledge and recollections. No doubt you have failed to retain that information and therefore I remind you."

"I remember," Relian replied evenly.

"Ah. Excellent. I am now engaged in testing the memories of my Selves—specifically, their power of recognition." Keprose turned back to the Selves. "Beloveds," he suggested, "Indulge your creator. Please examine these young people and tell me who they are, if you will be so kind."

Three sets of blue eyes fastened on Relian and Mereth. Fascinated despite his animosity, Relian awaited the verdict, which came promptly.

"The young man—whose name I can never recall—is a Travornish gentleman possessed of youth, hardihood, sound intelligence and considerable impudence."

"He possesses native supranormal ability, hitherto ignored and undeveloped."

"His talents may serve to augment my own, provided—"

"—That he is well curbed. The girl Mereth is physically

appealing and probably capable of producing supranormal offspring, but—''

''—She is hostile and insolent. Therefore—''

''—I take a certain pleasure in baiting her.''

''The steel serpents, Crekkid and Nurbo, are my own creations. They are—''

''—Beautiful, useful, affectionate and—''

''—Intensely loyal. I shall fill the fortress with such serpents.''

''Ssseigneursss!'' The snakes vibrated like tuning forks. ''Ssseigneursss! Many Ssseigneursss! Many ssserpentsss! Many!''

Having completed their analysis, the Selves fell silent.

''Thank-you, Beloveds. You have done well, as I knew you would. Well, young man,'' Keprose inquired, ''What do you think of this demonstration?''

''It is extraordinary, Seigneur,'' Relian replied. ''I take it you did not provide the Selves with this information in advance?''

''Young man, your question is offensive as it is jejune,'' replied a Self, its nostrils flared disdainfully.

''Your narrowness of vision never fails to sadden me—''

''—Although I should—''

''—Be accustomed to it by now,'' the Selves concluded in unison.

Mereth was startled into speech. ''Impossible. This is the first time you've encountered Relian or me since your . . . awakening.''

Identical tolerant smiles beamed upon her and identical overlapping voices replied, ''My pretty Mereth should not meddle—''

''—In matters that far exceed—''

''—Her powers of understanding.''

''How could I fail to recall the many pleasant hours—''

''—I have spent in the company of—''

''—My Mereth? How could I forget the time that I have squandered in my fruitless efforts to develop her supranor-malcy?''

Mereth addressed the Selves collectively. ''That wasn't you. It wasn't any of you. It was that man yonder.'' She indicated Keprose.

''The memories are mine—''

''The mind and thoughts are mine—''

"The face is mine—"

"Mind and body are the man. Thus by all reasonable standards of judgment—"

"—My Mereth's longtime patron, her protector, her benefactor— "

"—Is I," announced the three Selves.

"Gentlemen, your argument is specious—" Mereth began.

"Listen to them!" Keprose interrupted. "Listen to their wit and eloquence! Young man, do you yet doubt my triumph? My Selves are complete and perfect!"

"Perfect?" inquired Relian, somewhat incautiously. "Are you certain of that? Isn't it spreading an identity rather thin to distribute it among four bodies?"

"It is not *distributed*—your analogy is entirely inappropriate," Keprose replied. "The personality has been replicated, and the process may justly be compared to the minting of identical gold coins."

"The Selves exist as counterfeit Keproses—yes, I understand your comparison, Seigneur."

"Your sophomoric effrontery is unworthy of my anger. Imagine, if you are able, a mind possessed of four bodies to perform its bidding. Think of it—eight eyes, eight hands, eight legs, all under the dominion of a single mind. The ability to be in four places at once, to perform four disparate tasks, to behold four individual scenes in one moment. That is what it means to possess four bodies, and that gift I have bestowed upon myself."

"But have you? What of the impending divergencies you mentioned not five minutes ago? Are you so certain of the continuing complaisance of your Selves?"

"Certainly," Keprose snapped. Relian's query appeared unwelcome. "How could their desires and intentions deviate from my own? Divergence of thought will be the veneer that masks the underlying unity of mind-matter. We are as one, my Selves and I. And when it comes to the exercise of supranormalcy, our combined power will prove incalculable."

The Selves' concurrence overlapped.

"The Prototype is correct. The powers of these others—"

"—Will greatly enhance my own—"

"—Supranormalcy, as Vanalisse the Unseen Hag—"

"—Shall soon discover to her cost."

"Valiant spirits!" Keprose applauded.

"Do they actually possess supranormal power?" Relian asked.

Three multi-tiered chins lifted haughtily.

"My supranormal powers are unequaled—"

"—Now as always."

"Moreover, I take it very ill, young man—"

"—That you persist in directing your remarks to the Prototype alone, as if—"

"—I were bereft of understanding."

"You will modify your behavior at once."

The Selves exchanged simultaneous scowls of annoyance.

"And *I* take it very ill," one of them addressed the others, "that you facsimiles persist in completing my sentences."

"*Your* sentences? Alas, we must share them."

"Multiple existence is a rare privilege, but—"

"—Burdensome in some respects."

"See them, listen to them!" Keprose exulted. "They are perfect! In every thought, in every word and gesture—they are Keprose Gavyne!"

Relian and Mereth were bleakly silent.

Not so Crekkid. "Ssseigneursss! Massstersss! Many Ssseigneursss!" Excitement sharpened the tiny voice. "Now that you are many, no more need for human that Crekkid ridesss. Throw him away, no matter. Ssshall Crekkid now be free to join Nurbo?"

Keprose shrugged irritably. "I must not be vexed with such questions at this time. Weighty matters occupy my mind, yet all the world persists in plaguing me. I have not yet decided what, if anything, will be done about the human that Crekkid rides. The townsmen clamor for his blood." Keprose's impatient regard shifted for a moment to the parchment on the floor. "They have gone so far as to present me with a written demand for the surrender of the young man, together with the Fist of Zhi, in exchange for the lives of my wretched nephews. I should perhaps be willing to agree, did I not apprehend that compliance affronts my dignity. Do townsmen dictate to the Seigneur? Perhaps their presumption should be punished. Moreover, it is possible that the Fist, and even the young man, may prove useful at some future date. If that is the case, I will not relinquish either of them. In any event, I cannot spare time to ponder these questions now. I cannot bear distraction! At this time, my thoughts and hopes anchor upon my Selves. I will work with them and we shall strive to combine our forces, a feat I have never attempted before. Beloveds, we shall learn together. The prospect is exquisite.'' For a moment the beaming Seigneur and his beaming Selves seemed lost in a happy reverie, and then Keprose recollected Relian's existence. ''Young man, you have served your purpose here and your presence is no longer necessary or desirable. I would be alone with my dear ones. You are dismissed.''

*   *   *

In the days that followed, little was seen of Keprose. The Seigneur remained closeted with his Selves. The arrival of a second sealed parchment from the Council was ignored. The babble of identical voices could be heard at all hours inside the locked chamber on the second floor. The nature of the prolonged communion was not disclosed. But at last the Keproses emerged and the astonished household servants faced a quartet of indistinguishable masters.

The four of them were inseparable. They ate together, slept together, perused the library volumes together, walked the gardens together. Those of the servants overhearing scraps of conversation noted that the confusing discourse seemed to center upon supranormalcy. The Keprose addressed by his companions as ''Prototype'' forever exhorted the others to increased effort. They practiced continually. Their tentacular fingers wove bizarre patterns in the air, and droning syllables dropped from their lips. The results of these exercises were sometimes startling. On one occasion, four miniature clouds materialized to shed snow at the four corners of the fortress courtyard—but the Prototype appeared dissatisfied. The servants did not know why. The Seigneur's purpose was unknown to the observers, who wisely refrained from inquiry.

Keprose seemed to have forgotten about Relian. His interest in the state of his protégé's supranormalcy had lapsed completely. Keprose no longer demanded proofs of industry, and Relian might easily have dispensed with his studies altogether, had he wished. However, the opposite was true. Relian studied harder than ever before, studied all day, every day, working like a man whose days are numbered, which was what he sensed himself to be. For it seemed only too likely that Keprose would ultimately find it expedient to hand him over to the townsfolk of Vale Jevaint. And whether the townsmen elected to hang him out of hand, or whether they chose to deliver him intact to Scrivvulch the Stick was a question of minor significance, amounting to a choice between rope and blade. Therefore Relian forfeited his rest and drove himself without mercy until the normal pallor of his complexion intensified to a corpselike hue, and black shadows ringed his eyes—for in supranormalcy lay his only hope of escape. Beyond question, his power increased. His Vision sharpened and he learned to add a second finger to his supranormal Hand, but practice did not lend him strength to lift the living collar of slavery from his throat. And Mereth, who often studied beside him, achieved no discernible results at all.

During this period Relian rarely glimpsed the Selves, and knew little of their progress. Only once, while roaming the wintry garden during one of his rare study breaks, did he come upon Keprose and the doppelgangers. They were occupied and did not note his presence. Relian slipped behind a tree trunk and paused to watch. As always, he marveled at the perfection of Keprose Gavyne's self-replication. He saw before him four black-clad figures, identical in gait, gesture, vocal inflection and facial expression. Impossible to judge which was the original Seigneur. The question was resolved when one of the men spoke.

"Beloveds, we must try again," declared Keprose Gavyne. "We must think and act as one. Only then will our forces truly unite. Now, then—to the target. Again."

The "target" was a pole sunk in the ground some distance from the Seigneurs. The pole was composed of a dull black substance and crowned with branching antlers. The four Keproses spoke in low tones. Their fingers writhed. There was a crackling sound and the air before them glowed hotly. The glow brightened and coalesced. Swirling smoke materialized and out of the smoke sprang four tiny, separate bolts of scarlet lightning. Keprose Gavyne's radiant missile struck the pole, and sparks arced among the points of the antlers. The other three bolts plunged to the ground short of their mark, flared and extinguished themselves. The Selves muttered in discontent.

"It is not your fault, Beloveds," Keprose consoled them. "Additional practice is required, that is all. You must have faith in yourselves and in your creator. Soon our powers will merge and increase a thousandfold. Upon that happy day, all the cosmos reveals itself to us, and our knowledge shall exceed even our power. So strive, my beloved ones, strive! The goal is almost within reach! Now, once more—together!'' Eight white hands were set in motion.

Relian did not stay to view the outcome. A sense of impending personal disaster oppressed him and he alleviated it in the only way he knew. Returning to the tower work-room, he took up his studies with renewed fervor. His progress was perceptible but too slow, and he suspected he did not have much time left.

*   *   *

"Canto the Twenty-Fifth, Verse LI,'' announced Master Moon.

Something snapped in the mind of Scrivvulch the Stick. His benign expression did not alter. Not a muscle in his face moved, but in that instant he knew he could stand no more.

Weeks had passed since the capture of Keprose Gavyne's nephews, but the demands of the Council had gone unanswered. An outright refusal could not have conveyed the contempt of the Seigneur so clearly as this silence. The Fist of Zhi remained immured within Fortress Gavyne, and all gathering activity accordingly ceased. The Gatherers and Bellowsmen, bored and depressed, spent their days drinking at the Bearded Moon. In the meantime, the three hostages languished in fairly comfortable captivity. Vazm, Pruke and Druveen were held in an unused storeroom in the Council House. They were destructive, demanding, expensive to feed, and wont to terrorize their guards with threats of Seigneurial retaliation. No one knew what to do about them. In view of the refusal of Keprose to hand over the Fist and its thief, it behooved the townsfolk to punish the prisoners according to their deserts. The crime of arson was a hanging offense. Ordinarily the culprits would have been submitted to the judgment of the Seigneur, but that course was impractical in the present case. The solution to the dilemma was obvious, but nobody dared to act upon it. Keprose Gavyne might demonstrate little concern for the welfare of his delinquent nephews, but that indifference could alter should Gavyne blood actually be shed. The citizens of Vale Jevaint, only too familiar with the wrath of their lord, were disinclined to provoke it. Thus the matter stood, and promised to continue so indefinitely.

A torrent of poesy gushed from the lips of Master Moon.

Scrivvulch dammed his ears as best he could and gazed about the common room in search of rescue or at least diversion. The scene that met his eyes had remained unchanged for weeks. There were all the regular patrons of the Bearded Moon. Scattered among them were the unemployed Gatherers. There was Councilman Gyf Fynok in his usual seat by the fire, and there at a table in the corner sat Master Gatherer Clym Stipper. The same, every evening exactly the same. These hopelessly passive townsfolk needed to be taken in hand. Effective leadership was required and Scrivvulch, who did not number indecisiveness among his failings, resolved in that moment to provide it. The extended period of inactivity preyed on his spirits. Famous for his swift efficiency, he did not ordinarily countenance delays. Scrivvulch was tired of Vale Jevaint, tired of its insular inhabitants, tired of the Bearded Moon, and above all, tired to death of his host's poetic effusions. If left to their own devices, the citizens would never move. A flick of the crop was needed, a touch of the spur. He would furnish them willingly. Now that he perceived the time for action had definitely arrived, Scrivvulch's course lay very clear before him. The imminence of change soothed his spirit like a balm. For the moment, he could afford tolerance. He sat back comfortably in his chair and regarded Master Moon with renewed kindliness.

At the conclusion of Verse LXXX, Moon raised his eyes from the notebook and was struck by the uncommon warmth of his guest's expression. Only one explanation suggested itself. "Enjoying the poem, are you, sir? The airy flights of fancy, the sparkling wit, the felicity of phrasing—?"

"Indeed yes, Master Moon. I recognize and share your joy in artistic expression, as I consider myself something of an artist in my own right. For in this tawdry, much-bedizened world, 'tis the tangible products of Man's quest for sublimity that gleam with the luster of true gold," Scrivvulch intoned.

"That's just exactly the way I see it. Exactly. Permit me to say, sir, that you seem to be in a jolly mood this evening."

"That is correct, my friend. I am filled with optimism and a sense of happy anticipation."

"Anticipation of what, sir?"

"Success, Master Moon. Success at last."

*   *   *

Hours later, Scrivvulch the Stick lurked in Footpad Alley. Before him rose the fortified Egg House, almost—but not quite—as Relian Kru had beheld it. In the aftermath of the intrusion, the Egg House defenses had been strengthened. Two armed sentries paced before the building. New, extra-heavy locks secured the doors. Scrivvulch observed the sentries from concealment. He occupied, although he did not know it, the same shadowed alcove that had once sheltered Relian Kru. Presently the moon dipped below the skyline and Scrivvulch acted. Lifting his ebony stick, he took careful aim and activated the hidden mechanism. The triangular blade shot from the end of the cane, flew through the air and found its resting place in one of the sentries' throats. The man fell without a cry. His throat was dark with blood.

The second sentry spun around to behold his companion prone upon the cobbles. Without thought, he rushed to the fallen man's side. Scrivvulch removed the lower portion of his cane to uncover the steel spike. He stepped quietly from his refuge and sank the spike into the second sentry's back. His eye and aim were unerring.

The victim straightened, his eyes wide with near-comic incomprehension. A gurgling sound escaped him. He fell face forward across the body of his comrade and quickly died.

Scrivvulch's spike was freed as the dying man fell. He wiped the steel and replaced it in its sheath. He retrieved the blade from the first sentry's throat, dried it and returned it to the cane. This done, he stepped to the door, removed a slender instrument from his pocket and expertly picked the three locks. The door swung open. Scrivvulch lifted one of the lanterns from its wall bracket and entered the Egg House.

His eye roamed the huge chamber with its stacks of wooden crates. He paused a moment to collect his bearings, then made his way swiftly and silently to the Tank Room, whose location he had ascertained during his previous visit. He picked the brand-new lock on the oaken door and walked into the chamber, where his eye fell on the glass tank, formerly the home of the Fist of Zhi. The tank was empty now, its liquid contents siphoned off in the absence of the tenant. This was a matter of little interest to Scrivvulch. His attention was fixed on the wooden crates that lined the walls. It was here, in this stronghold-within-a-stronghold, that he might reasonably expect to discover the finest, the rarest, the most treasured specimens in all the vast collection of Wingbane eggs.

Most of the crates were marked with circular red stamps. A few dozen bore raised golden seals. Scrivvulch set his lantern on the floor, opened a red-stamped crate and removed layers of cotton batting to uncover an egg of extraordinary size, easily as large as a rutabaga. The shell was purple-brown, marked with blotches and veins of violent, almost incandescent green. A second crate yielded another egg of similar size and coloration. A third crate, bearing a gold seal, was found to contain an egg that dwarfed the first two—a monstrous specimen whose polished black surface was rough with mulberry warts. The price of such an extraordinary egg might have purchased a mansion in the most fashionable section of Vale Jevaint. There was no telling how long the egg had lain in its crate. No doubt the canny Guild would reserve such a prize for sale to the most exalted of customers—quite probably to foreign royalty.

Scrivvulch laid his cane on the floor beside the lantern. He needed two hands to lift the huge egg out of its box. His thoughtful gaze wandered the small chamber and came to rest on the glass tank. Tucking the egg under one arm, he crossed to the tank, removed the lid and set it aside. He paused a moment, shrugged in whimsical regret, then struck the egg smartly on the rim of the tank. The shell cracked down the middle and a foul odor was released. Scrivvulch separated the two halves, allowing the semi-gelatinous contents to drip into the tank in a sluggish stream. When the halves were empty, he tossed them to the floor. He returned to the crates, collected two more eggs, cracked and emptied them into the tank. Following several repetitions of this operation, the bottom of the tank was thick with bile-green slime, and the atmosphere of the room was loathsome. Scrivvulch went on with his work. Crate after crate he methodically rifled, and the slime in the tank increased to a depth of several inches.

A rustle, a footstep, and a shifting of shadows informed the Assassin that he was not alone. He spun on his heel to behold a white-cockaded, fresh-faced young guard framed in the doorway. Following the Fist's disappearance, the Guild of Gatherers had stationed a roving watchman inside the Egg House. In his left hand the watchman carried a lantern. In his right, he held a leveled pistol.

The appearance of the watchman came as a complete surprise to Scrivvulch, but surprise in no way impaired his reactions. His walking stick lay on the floor, several feet distant. There was no immediate possibility of reaching it. Scrivvulch unobtrusively pressed his right elbow to his side. The movement released the catch that held a broad-bladed knife strapped to his right forearm, allowing the weapon to slide down his sleeve and into his hand. The hand was blocked from view by the skirt of his coat. Scrivvulch smiled mildly, and the guard appeared nonplussed. "My friend, I trust you would not kill an unarmed old man. Be at ease. I am quite harmless, and my presence here, while somewhat irregular, can readily be explained. No doubt these circumstances appear peculiar, but I would urge you to withhold judgment until you have learned of my extraordinary—nay, call it miraculous—discovery. I first became aware of the phenomenon when I took the liberty of examining the contents of that crate over there—" An expansive gesture of the left hand caught the watchman's eye. At the same moment, Scrivvulch's right hand came up and he threw the knife. The knife flew straight and true to the watchman's chest. The young man uttered a cry and his finger tightened convulsively on the trigger. The shot blasted far wide of its mark. The watchman dropped the pistol and fell, hands pressed to his wound. Scrivvulch stepped forward without haste. A kick sent the pistol skidding out of reach. The Assassin bent over his victim to note the welling blood, the labored breathing. "Ah, barbarous—the light has thrown my aim off. Still—touched a lung, I warrant, and the poor wretch is not long for this world." He met the shocked eyes of the watchman briefly as he stooped to retrieve his knife. Blood gushed as the steel was withdrawn, and the wounded man groaned.

"Softly, my poor friend, softly," Scrivvulch advised. "You overtax your strength." He eyed the watchman speculatively, then nodded to himself as he arrived at a decision. "Yes. This unfortunate mischance may yet be turned to good account."

So saying, he grasped his victim by the ankles and dragged him across the floor to the foot of the great glass tank. The shock of movement tore another groan from the wounded man's lips. Upon reaching his destination, Scrivvulch dropped the ankles and stepped around to kneel at the watchman's side. Sliding one arm around the other's shoulders and one under the knees, Scrivvulch managed to lift the watchman off the floor and over the wall of the tank. The watchman, conscious of his fate but incapable of resistance, moaned and plucked futilely at his killer's cravat.

"I truly regret this necessity," Scrivvulch murmured, his breath a little shortened by exertion. "But my needs are pressing. I do not undertake such action lightly, my friend. Never think it." He tumbled his victim into the tank.

The watchman landed face down, and gelatinous egg meat spattered the glass walls. Scrivvulch leaned over the side, pulled his cuff back and pressed his victim's face firmly into the muck. The watchman's struggles were brief and few. A little thrashing, a couple of final spasms and it was over. The body floated, buoyed up by the dense egg substance. The sight was ghastly, but Scrivvulch was not altogether satisfied. The Assassin returned to his interrupted labors. He broke and emptied scores of additional eggs before achieving the effect he desired.

At last, when the tank was about three-quarters full, and the corpse of the watchman was thickly coated with green slime, Scrivvulch desisted. The majority of crates in the Tank Room had been pillaged. The minutes were passing and eventually the dead sentries in Footpad Alley would be discovered. It was time to leave. The Assassin surveyed his handiwork critically. After a moment he returned and bent to grasp the watchman's arm, which he draped carefully over the edge of the tank. This arrangement conveyed the impression that the corpse strove to drag itself from the putrescent ooze in which it lay. The finished composition was not only horrific, but possessed a grotesquerie calculated to startle and outrage the sensibilities of even the most phlegmatic citizens.

Scrivvulch wiped the egg meat from his hands. The stuff was sticky as it was fetid. Curious to imagine that matter so repulsive possessed curative properties. For a moment the Assassin pondered the paradox, pondered the nature of Wingbane eggs in general. What effect, he wondered, might be produced upon the eggs in the tank were they subjected to the heat of a fire? Would they thicken to a foul custard, or would they simply scramble? More to the point, was such a gesture likely to intensify the townsmen's sense of outrage? The experiment was easy to perform, but arguably exceeded the limits of good taste, and therefore Scrivvulch the Stick held back. "For in this world of surfeit and excess, moderation is the hallmark of the well-governed intellect," he observed aloud.

There was nothing more to be accomplished here. Scrivvulch bestowed a last look upon the bizarre tableau, picked up his lantern and stick, and silently took his leave.

All was quiet on Footpad Alley. The two dead sentries lay undiscovered and undisturbed. Scrivvulch left the Egg House door insolently agape behind him. He exited the alley and made his way through the streets of the town without conspicuous haste. Within the hour, he was safely ensconced in his chamber at the Bearded Moon. Although fatigued, he did not permit himself the luxury of immediate rest. There was more to be accomplished before he might retire in good conscience.

Paper, ink and quills lay on the table beside the window. By the light of a single candle, Scrivvulch sat up scribbling far into the night.

*　　*　　*

The murders and devastating vandalism were discovered at dawn by the change of guard. The Guardsmen carried the information to their superiors, who in turn informed the officials of the Guild of Gatherers. By way of the Guild the story came to the ears of the Councilmen, and by early evening the news had spread all over town. Dissemination of information was expedited by means of certain broadsides, freshly printed and nailed up in every street and square. The broadside—upon whose composition Scrivvulch the Stick had lavished considerable care—bore the title, *Egg House Atrocity*, and in smaller print below, *Bloodthirsty Equalist Preys Upon the Town*. The text went on to reveal the vicious destruction of human life and property as the work of the notorious Equalist, Black Relian Kru. Black Relian, positively identified as the thief of the Fist of Zhi, currently enjoyed the protection of the Seigneur Keprose at Fortress Gavyne. The concluding plea for justice was couched in terms of passionate grief and anger.

The citizens were further enlightened by means of a song, hawked in the streets and taverns for a pyte a copy. "The Ballad of Black Relian at the Egg House," in which the murder of the watchman was described in detail, was of a gruesome character that ensured immediate popularity. Stories of the incident spread and were embroidered in the retelling. Civic outrage waxed apace, attaining a dangerous level at the time of the martyred guards' funeral services, which were attended by nearly the entire population. The obsequies were prolonged. An oration at once affecting and inflammatory was delivered by Master Moon of the Bearded Moon Tavern. As Moon was renowned as a poet of talent, few dreamed that the speech had been composed by the Neraunci gentleman, Master Scrivvulch. Following the oration, spontaneous demonstrations of rage and sorrow broke forth among the mourners.

The pressure of public opinion soon forced a meeting of the City Council—an unusual meeting in that the Council Chamber was open to all. There were many speakers, many conflicting points of view, and the resulting debate often verged on acrimony. What emerged clearly, despite the confusion, was the existence of widespread public anger—against the murderous Equalist, and against the Seigneur who sheltered him. Many were the ferocious denunciations of Black Relian; but in the case of Keprose Gavyne, the outcries dwindled to sullen mutters. Few cared to risk open defiance of the Seigneur; few cared to brave the lash of the Seigneur's lightning. What was called for was a plan of action that combined daring and caution. The citizens were eager to listen to all suggestions, and thus it was that Scrivvulch the Stick received permission to address the assemblage. Scrivvulch's brief speech was a masterpiece of civilized eloquence, wherein he urged upon the townsfolk the same scheme he had once proposed to Councilman Gyf Fynok in the common room of the Bearded Moon. A peaceful delegation of citizens would ascend to the fortress and meet face-to-face with the Seigneur to request the surrender of the Equalist and the Fist. Once apprised of the civic suffering attendant upon the crimes of Black Relian, then the Seigneur, as a reasonable lord, would surely take pity upon his loving subjects.

This plan was much applauded for its wise moderation, and when volunteer delegates were called for, a hundred men offered themselves on the spot. This show of spirit much heartened the audience, and there were yet more volunteers. The burgeoning solidarity produced a curious change in the attitude of the delegates. As their numbers increased, their courage mounted and with it their belligerence. They remembered the countless injuries suffered at the hands of the Seigneur Keprose, and their resentment sharpened. Presently their projected requests were transmuted to demands. With a force so numerous as theirs had now become, they were

confident of commanding the attention of the Seigneur. Never
before had they dared unite against him, and the novel accord
fostered an almost intoxicating sense of optimism. Whether
this newfound assurance was in any way justified remained to
be seen. They would put it to the proof when they marched
on Fortress Gavyne in the morning.

*   *   *

When Relian was forbidden the tower workroom, he knew
that Keprose Gavyne's great moment was drawing nigh. Seigneur and Selves required the workroom for their own purposes. Relian and Mereth were instructed to conduct their
studies elsewhere and accordingly withdrew to the Great Hall,
where they were assured of comparative privacy. With them
they brought armloads of Keprose's reference works. The
books were deposited upon a makeshift table set up beside the
empty fireplace. There, wrapped in rugs and blankets to ward
off the frigid drafts that swept the huge old room, they
practiced supranormalcy and plotted escape. The written notes
they exchanged were invariably destroyed.

In the meantime the door to the workroom remained firmly
shut and no one, from footman down to potboy, knew what
transpired within. The rhythmic drone of four identical voices
could often be heard, and the aura of supranormalcy was
almost tangible. The fortress residents sensed impending cata-
clysm, the exact nature of which remained mercifully obscure. Days passed, and the doomful atmosphere intensified.
It was generally agreed that events of historical significance
were in the offing. Premonitions of such events killed all
mundane tranquillity, and the servants walked in fear. Their
apprehension sharpened upon the prematurely dark, unquiet
winter's eve that the Seigneur commanded an enormous dinner to be prepared and left on trays outside the workroom
door. The meal, enough to satisfy a dozen ordinary appetites,
consisted of heavy dishes intended, as the Seigneur described
it, to "fortify myselves against the coming vigil." The sense
of this remark was unclear, but certain facts were noted by
the uneasy servants: The trays of food promptly disappeared;
and voices rose and fell within the workroom all through the
night.

The morning dawned gray and dangerous as a starving
wolf. Relian awoke with more than his usual sense of misgiv-

ing. Cold dim light washed his chamber. The air was dank and still. Silence reigned. Relian threw the covers aside and rose to face the icy morning. He walked to the window and stared up at a sky that threatened snowfall. The clouds were dense and featureless. The world was wrapped in the magical silence that so often accompanies snow. He watched the sky for a few moments, and saw the first few flakes drift down to touch the courtyard. Others followed, and soon the air was dancing. Ordinarily Relian would have enjoyed watching the first snow of the season, but now he shrugged and turned away, his thoughts leaden.

He crossed to the washstand, stood staring bleakly at the unshaven face mirrored in the glass. Crekkid's burnished scales winked in the gloomy light. *The face of a slave*, Relian reflected bitterly. *Forever, unless you do something about it.* He reached for the pitcher and froze, arm extended, as an explosion rocked the fortress. The floor quivered and the implements cluttering the washstand jumped. The noise was overwhelming, louder than the roar of a battery of cannons, and he instinctively clapped defensive hands to his ears. Crekkid hissed and tightened in sudden fear. The reverberations died away and the serpent relaxed. Relian could breathe again. Even in the midst of his surprise and alarm, he was conscious of familiarity. He had heard that noise in the past, though never before so loud. He recalled the night he had first approached the town of Vale Jevaint, remembered the explosions thundering over the hills and the lightning that flew between Fortress Gavyne and the Tyrant of Mists. He had witnessed a similar exchange upon the night of his return from the Forest of Miasm. Now the same explosions were repeated and the inference was obvious. Keprose Gavyne, at last fully confident of the power of his Selves, had launched his great attack on Vanalisse the Unseen.

Relian ran to the window but found the view from his ground floor chamber limited. As a second explosion sounded overhead, he left the room, raced along the corridors to the foot of the Cloudmaster stairway and climbed until he reached the first narrow window, halfway up the tower. From this vantage point he could see the countryside spread out below, and he could glimpse the cliffs that walled the far side of the valley. He did not think to turn his eyes down to the town. In any case, trees and crags blocked the view. Even had he looked, he would not have seen the crowd of men, nearly two hundred strong, marching along the Rising Road toward Fortress Gavyne.

He leaned out the window, turning his head to gaze up at the Cloudmaster summit. As he watched, the fortress trembled, the deafening thunder was felt rather than heard, and a bolt of scarlet lightning flashed from the workroom window. Relian drew in his breath sharply. He had seen the lightning more than once, and he now knew that the phenomenon was produced by means of the exacting, exhausting Whuuru's Swift Substitution—a technique far beyond the range of all but the most accomplished supranormalists. With knowledge and familiarity had come the inevitable lessening of wonder. But Relian's sense of awe was reawakened now, for the lightning he beheld exceeded all previous manifestations as the crossbow quarrel exceeds the dart of a blowgun. The bolt passed directly over his head and seemed so near that he automatically ducked. It was huge as a flying serpent of legend, so vast and long that the head was halfway across the valley before the tail was free of the Cloudmaster. The color was deeper, stronger, and more brilliant than any he had ever seen. This then was the power that Keprose Gavyne had dreamed of—the combined supranormal strength of multiple adepts, augmented and raised to unparalleled heights. With power such as this, Keprose and his Selves would make themselves known in the world beyond Vale Jevaint. The knowledge was likely to prove unpalatable to humanity. And afterwards—would there be more Selves to come? Would the world truly be peopled with Keproses? The possibilities, as the Seigneur was wont to observe, were almost limitless.

Lightning cleft the snowy skies, winging its way high over the town to pierce the mists of Vanalisse like a sword of fire. So intense was the brilliance that for one brief moment the fog that sheathed the opposing peak seemed to waver a little, to flicker as if wounded by the light. For an instant, Relian thought he glimpsed the twisted towers of a fortress remote and unknown as the heart of a witch. The moment passed and the mists resumed their opacity, so quickly as to leave room for doubt that they had ever lightened at all.

Keprose allowed his opponent no respite. Before the bolt had vanished into the fog he launched another. Perhaps the Selves were just now hitting their stride, for this latest missile was the largest yet. The lightning sped from the tower window and the air sizzled in its wake. High over the valley it curved, superb in its unconscious power. The fog gave way before it. No material or supranormal barrier could stand before it. The lightning sundered the mists, passed through and struck at the fortress of Vanalisse. Far away, fire leaped and sparks flew as a slender tower collapsed. For an instant, the scene was clearly visible—the gaunt old fortress, the stricken tower, the sudden gout of flame. Then the fog closed again, the Tyrant of Mists vanished and the view was obscured by the whirling snow.

Won't she fight back? Relian found himself hoping for a force to counter the newfound might of Keprose Gavyne and the Selves. *Is she able to defend herself?*

She would certainly try. A rumble of thunder, and the blue lightning of Vanalisse winged over the valley. Relian watched analytically. The force of the Unseen was unexpectedly small and weak, or perhaps seemed so by comparison. The azure bolt struck far short of its mark. A second bolt shot from the mists, streaked to its target and passed harmlessly overhead.

Keprose's response was crushing. A great jagged bolt leapt from the Cloudmaster, and then three more flew in quick succession. The glowing volley shot over the town and plunged into the heart of the mists, inflicting significant damage. The fog thinned, flickered, lightened to the point of translucency. For the first time in human memory, the shadowy outlines of the Tyrant of Mists stood revealed to the world. Relian saw a huge, gaunt old pile, similar in design to Fortress Gavyne, but distinguished by its eccentric, twisted towers, several of which showed signs of mutilation. Two were completely destroyed. So much was discernible, even through the snow and remaining fog. Somehow it seemed impertinent, an invasion of privacy, to look upon the Tyrant unveiled. Perhaps Vanalisse agreed, for she sent a great whip of blue energy slashing viciously through space. Relian experienced the momentary delusion that the lightning was aimed straight at his head. His hands tightened on the window ledge as he stood and watched it come for him.

Vanalisse's missile never made it through Keprose's supranormal defenses. Some distance from the fortress itself, the bolt collided in midair with an invisible barrier, and spent its force in one tremendous, searing blue burst of light and heat. Relian involuntarily flinched and shut his eyes against the flash. A scorching odor assailed his nostrils and he remembered Mereth's description of Vanalisse's last attack, during which the blue lightning had battered its way straight through the barrier. As it had happened that day, so it might occur again. The thought of Mereth brought renewed fear and Relian's overwhelming impulse was to find her and protect her if he could.

Protect her? the interior voice sneered. *When you can't even manage to get her or yourself out of this fortress?*

Can't I? Not even when Keprose's attention is entirely diverted? We'll see. With that thought came recognition of his own supranormal development. He had striven for weeks to achieve the power to free himself and Mereth. He wasn't sure that he was ready yet. But another such opportunity was unlikely to present itself. It was the best chance he'd ever have.

She might have been anywhere about the fortress; either watching the battle from a tower window, or—more prudently— hidden away in the deepest subterranean chamber. But instinct sent him to the Great Hall.

He reached the Hall just as Mereth entered under another archway. She looked calm, but her face was wax-white and her jaw was set hard. When she saw Relian whole and sound she stopped, and the pale, frozen face seemed to crack in places. An explosion roared like a beast overhead, the floor quivered perceptibly, and a few bits of masonry dropped from the ceiling. Mereth took a couple of uncertain steps toward him and Relian ran to meet her. An instant later they stood clasped together, and for once the serpents did not object.

The two tiny silver heads went questing. The lithe forms intertwined. Steel tongue clicked on tongue and fervent hisses arose.

"Sssweet Nurbo!"

"Brave Crekkid!"

"United in the midssst of danger!"

"Ah, danger lendsss ssspice to love!"

"Sssssssssssssssss!"

Another explosion above, and Relian felt Mereth's nervous start. Fresh masonry rained from the ceiling.

"Isss the hour of doom upon usss?" Nurbo inquired. "Ssshall Nurbo be one with Crekkid in death?"

"Not ssso," Crekkid assured his beloved. "For the Ssseigneur ssshall prevail."

"In life and in death, Nurbo isss true to Patriarch Crekkid."

Relian took advantage of the serpents' ecstatic preoccupation to whisper hurriedly, "I'm going to try it, Mereth." Her eyes, only inches from his own, widened. She shook her head in doubt. "Keprose is busy, distracted. Now's the time. I think I'm ready. I believe I can do it."

Quiet though her comment was, it did not escape the attention of Crekkid, who writhed suspiciously and inquired, "You sssay? You sssay?"

"Nothing."

"You ssspeak of Ssseigneur. Crekkid hearsss you. You sssay?"

"He sssaysss?" Nurbo demanded with an authoritative squeeze. Mereth gasped and jerked back. Relian, linked to her neck, was pulled off balance. While the serpents were interlaced, his plans could not go forward.

"I only said," Relian remarked blandly, "that the Seigneur no longer troubles to concern himself with the activities of his apprentices. He doesn't care what we do, hence will not discourage my attentions to Mistress Mereth." He bent and kissed Mereth on the lips. The kiss was warmly received. The effect on the snakes was all that he desired.

"Ssstop! Now! Ssstop! Now!" Crekkid whistled in outrage. "Now. Now. Now. Now."

"Ssslut! Ssslut! Ssslut! Ssslut!"

"Ssshe isss for Ssseigneur. If he wantsss her."

"You let him touch you, ssslut!"

"You move away from her. Move! Move! Move! Move!"

"I can't," Relian pointed out reasonably.

The two serpents immediately disengaged, breaking the knot that bound Relian to Mereth. "Ssseparate! Now! Now! Lussstful humansss."

"Ssslut! Ssslut!"

Relian took a couple of steps backward. He allowed his eyes to meet Mereth's. She watched him anxiously, and he smiled with spurious confidence. There was a crackling of force and a flash of blue light outside as another of Vanalisse's missiles smashed itself against Keprose's barrier. The scorching smell filled the air again, and distant shrieks mewed faint as lost kittens. The Seigneur's servants, huddled together in the kitchen, were unable to contain their fears, and their cries were pitiable. It would not be simple to achieve the level of concentration that the supranormal feat before him demanded, but never before had the incentive been so great.

Mereth's eyes were fixed upon his face, and she silently mouthed, *Good luck*.

He nodded acknowledgment, turned his back on the window, took a deep breath and closed his eyes.

"What do you do?" Crekkid demanded, but received no reply. "Clossse eyesss, sssee nothing. Ssstupid."

Still no reply.

Another explosion rattled the fortress, another scarlet bolt streaked above the valley. Relian's attention was caught for a moment, and his partially-constructed Mindwall collapsed. His eyes turned to Mereth, who stood still and silent, as unobtrusive as humanly possible. Patiently he cleared his mind and started again. Today Uy's Mindwall presented unusual difficulties, but Relian completed construction at last. The varied physical and emotional distractions were blocked, leaving him free to direct his supranormal Vision through bone and steel scale by way of Forn, deep into the mind of Crekkid. The simple little mind was familiar territory. He had examined it more than once, he knew the twists and turns as he knew the corridors of Keprose's garden maze. He located the two centers of awareness easily and kept his Vision fixed there while he generated his three-fingered supranormal Hand. So far events had proceeded smoothly enough, but it was at this point that he might expect problems. The Mindwall blocked out trepidation, uncertainty and all else that might have seriously shaken his concentration. Nonetheless, Relian experienced a certain suspense as he extended his Hand to probe the mind of the serpent. For the first time, his power of Tactility was sufficient to reach through bodily barriers down into the brain itself. His fingers sank through layers of steel, bone and spongy mind-stuff until they rested upon the nodes that contained the two centers he sought. He touched the knobby little protrusions, noted the squashy consistency. In order to deprive Crekkid of consciousness, he must press down upon both nodes simultaneously. Relian attempted to do so and discovered that the substance that seemed so soft and yielding easily defied the strength of his Hand. He pressed once—pressed again. Nothing happened. Crekkid's mind was as unimpressionable as granite. Relian's muscles were stiff with tension and his brow was damp. He became aware of his own nervousness and in that instant felt Uy's Mindwall totter. He paused briefly to fortify the Mindwall before trying again. This time, he was determined it should be his best effort. He flexed the invisible Hand, shifted the fingers a trifle, focused his attention and concentrated powerfully. He pressed and felt one—not both—of the nodes give way under the pressure.

"Crekkid feel ssstrange." The tiny hiss seemed to come from far away.

"Crekkid sssick?" Nurbo inquired solicitously. "Need blood? Oil?"

"Not sssick. Not hungry. Not thirsssty."

"Crekkid ssshedding ssskin?"

"Don't know."

"Nurbo longsss to comfort Crekkid."

Crekkid's responsive hiss conveyed somnolent gratitude.

Relian bent his will upon the remaining node. It did not yield, and the effort was beginning to tire him. He did not yet possess the stamina to continue at this level indefinitely. If he did not achieve success within the next few moments, he would surely fail. The thought sank spurs into his mind. He redoubled his efforts, but desperation now undermined the foundation of Uy's Mindwall. Aware of the danger, he strove to arrest the erosion. He had barely achieved a precarious stasis before the floor underfoot shook again. High above the valley, a red lightning bolt encountered a blue bolt, and the two crossed like swords in midair. They were instantly consumed in a spectacular burst of purple light. The heavens resounded, the air sizzled, and purple fire rained down upon the town. Crekkid, roused from his sluggishness, tightened restlessly and Relian choked. Uy's Mindwall crashed, a flood of impulses swamped his consciousness, and the supranormal Hand ceased to exist.

Relian glanced out the window. Purple sparks and snowflakes rode the winds above Vale Jevaint. On the far side of the valley, the Tyrant of Mists stood denuded of all save a few pathetic clinging wisps of fog. The twisted towers were battered and broken. The great outer wall was half in ruins. The central keep stood unscathed, but surely could not continue so. Keprose's lightning reddened the skies like early sunset. Successive bolts hammered the Tyrant relentlessly, and it could not be long before Vanalisse's last defenses would crumble.

Relian turned away and caught Mereth's wide gray gaze. He shrugged and shook his head. "Couldn't do it. Not enough power."

"You sssay? Power for what?" Crekkid inquired.

"*Almost* enough," Relian continued bitterly. "*Almost* had it."

"Had what?" asked Crekkid. "What? What? What? What?"

"So close. Just a little bit more strength would have done it."

"Try it again," Mereth urged. "If you came that close, another attempt might do it."

"I don't think so. That was my best, that was all I had, and it wasn't enough. I can't do it alone, not yet. Mereth, you must help."

She looked startled. "Help you with the Tactility? But I can't. You know that."

"Ssshe cannot help," Nurbo agreed. "Too ssstupid."

"Help with what?" asked Crekkid. "What do you do? Anssswer."

"I think you could do it if you really wanted to," Relian encouraged.

"I do want to, especially now. But I can't, it's impossible. We'll have to wait for another time."

"Now is the time. It may be the last chance we'll have."

"I don't see why you say that. There's no reason to assume—"

"Listen, Mereth. Keprose has succeeded with his Selves. You need only see what's happening to the Tyrant of Mists to know that. With his Selves to aid him, he has no need of apprentices. That being the case, he'll certainly want to make his peace with the townsfolk, and therefore he'll decide, sooner or later, to deliver me into their hands. If I'm lucky, the townsfolk will hang me out of hand—"

"Relian, stop this—"

"—And if I'm not lucky, they'll inflict the poacher's punishment upon me. If you don't know what that punishment is, it's just as well. Enough to say it's protracted and inventive. As for you," Relian continued, "the Seigneur in his charity will permit you to remain here all the rest of your days. In fact, he'll insist on it. If you demonstrate your supranormalcy to his satisfaction, you'll have proved yourself a worthy broodmare. You'll be elevated and you will bear innumerable little Gavynes, each no doubt a replica of its sire. If you do not prove yourself thus worthy, you'll live out your life as a kitchen slavey or concubine, depending on the Seigneur's whim. If Keprose tires, Druveen is certainly interested. When

Druveen's finished, Pruke and Vazm will be standing in line—''

"*Shut up!* Do you think you're telling me anything I haven't already thought of?''

"I imagine you have. I'm not trying to be cruel, I only want to prove how important it is that we do this thing *now*—''

"What thing?'' asked Crekkid. "What?''

"You've made your point,'' Mereth assured him. "I'll do my best, for the sake of both our lives. I'll try as I've never tried before.''

"Then you'll succeed.''

"Sssucceed at what?'' Crekkid demanded, and sank his fangs irritably into Relian's earlobe. "What? Tell. Ssspeak. Now. Or elssse.''

"Or elssse,'' Nurbo echoed faithfully.

"We'll do better than that,'' Relian told them. "We'll show you. Ready, Mereth?''

She nodded, her expression tranquil. No telling what that calm mask concealed. She came and stood very near him, as proximity to the object of supranormalcy would minimize the difficulty of her task. The serpents hissed yearningly at one another.

Once again Relian built the Mindwall. Outside, lightning still struck from fortress to fortress. He was tired now, and the pyrotechnics nearly broke his concentration. Construction was harder than ever before. Finally it was done, freeing his Vision to move along Forn to the sites of Crekkid's awareness.

He opened his eyes and risked a glance at Mereth. She stood but inches away. Her long fingers wove expertly in and out, more flexible than Relian's. Her eyes were lowered, her expression unreadable. The slightly furrowed brow suggested mental effort, but there was no gauging the result of that effort.

Relian guided his Hand to Crekkid's skull, sank fingers into the brain as far as the vital nodes. He pressed ineffectually, and knew that useless pessimism loomed up like a black cloud directly behind the Mindwall. He pressed again, with little expectation of success. Crekkid's mind proved resistant as ever. Relian paused to marshal his faculties for a final attempt. He thought for a moment that he felt a very slight alien pressure glide along the back of his Hand, but dismissed the sensation as illusory. Discouragement leaned heavily on

the Mindwall. He pressed the nodes with all his supranormal
force and found that power insufficient. But as he strove, he
felt small, light supranormal fingers descend upon his own.
The two sets of fingers easily melded to combine strength.
Astonishment battered at the Mindwall, but the barrier held
and Relian continued to function. He glanced at Mereth's still
face. Not a flicker of expression indicated surprise or elation
at her first manifestation of supranormalcy. It was to be
assumed that her own Mindwall blocked distracting emotions.
Mereth's rudimentary Hand—a thumb and one finger—was
tiny, clumsy and childishly weak. Alone, it would not have
served to lift a feather. But as the near-impotent fingers
bonded with his, Relian experienced a disproportionate surge
of strength, and recognized it as the phenomenon once described by Keprose Gavyne. Combined supranormal power,
Keprose had confided, is far greater than the sum of its
individual parts.

Together Relian and Mereth bore down upon Crekkid's
brain. The nodes yielded. A single, puzzled whistle escaped
Crekkid before the serpent lost consciousness.

Relian felt the sudden relaxation of the steel coil that bound
his throat. Crekkid slept, draped loosely over his victim's
shoulders. As if in a dream, Relian reached up, grasped the
steely length and dragged it from his neck. He ignored Nurbo's
horrified hiss. Crekkid lay limp in his hand. Relian examined
the conquered incubus. The Mindwall momentarily blocked
joy, disbelief and triumph, but he knew he would soon experience them all. The barrier was quivering under the assault of
intense emotion. Relian took a moment to strengthen the
wall. He allowed himself to meet Mereth's eyes. She was
impassive, mouth tight with determination as she struggled to
maintain her own Mindwall.

Relian opened his hand and Crekkid dropped to the floor.
The steel body clinked on stone and lay still.

"Crekkid! Patriarch! Ssstruck down!" Nurbo's grief stabbed
eardrums. "Ssso young! Ssso brave! Ssso ssstrong! Ssso
handsssome! Alasss!"

The amalgamated Hand still existed, floating in midair and
doubly tethered by strands of nebulous matter extending to
both its creators. Now Relian guided the Hand to Nurbo,
swiftly explored the brain and located the vital centers. Mereth
and Relian clamped down simultaneously, and Nurbo's plaints
were stilled. Mereth tore the serpent from her neck and

dashed the silver body to the floor. Emotion too strong to be denied toppled Uy's Mindwall. Her concentration failed and her supranormal fingers ceased to exist. Relian felt the weakening of the Hand. He saw the joy and hope light Mereth's eyes. His own control slackened, his Mindwall crashed, and the Hand was gone.

"Mereth, you did it!"

"I know—I can hardly believe it! Relian, I could *feel* with that Hand, and it felt so—I don't know how to describe it—well, you already know what it's like!" Her cheeks were flushed with excitement, and her gestures animated. She looked more free, more alive and younger than he had ever seen her.

"Could you see anything? Inside Crekkid's mind, I mean."

"No, I was blind. I just groped around the snake's head until I felt your Hand, and followed it on in. I came to a barrier—Crekkid's skull, I guess it was—and wouldn't have been able to get past it alone. But I felt my way along the back of your Hand and that got me through, and I just kept going until I found your fingers. Oh, it must be wonderful to be able to *see* as well as feel!"

"It is," he assured her. "But you'll find that out for yourself very soon."

"You really think so?"

"I know it. Mereth, you managed to create a Hand—that's much more difficult than use of the Vision. If you've got the Tactility, then the Vision will be easy for you."

"Oh, I hope so, I really hope so!" She laughed, and he stared at her in pleasant wonder. He had never heard her laugh so freely, never seen her habitual melancholic stoicism so transformed. "It's so hard to believe I can do these things, and at the same time it feels so natural, so right—"

"I know, it's—"

A crash overhead cut the conversation short. Stone pelted the courtyard, and the entire fortress seemed to cringe in pain. Relian felt the shock of a violent impact transmitted along the floor. The scorching odor permeated the atmosphere. Evidently one of Vanalisse's bolts had breached the barriers and found its mark.

"We must go," said Relian. "Now, while we can."

"Just leave? Right now?"

"Right now. Is there anything you need to take with you?"

"From this place?" Mereth half smiled. "No. Nothing." The smile faded.

"What's wrong?" asked Relian. "Worried?"

"Yes—afraid," she replied. "Where will we go? What shall we do?"

"We'll go to Travorn," he told her. "With any luck, we'll find Trince there. You'll like Trince. When we get there, we can decide what we want to do. There's no time to think about it now."

She nodded and linked hands with him. Hand in hand they fled the Great Hall.

*   *   *

Intermittent flashes of lightning struck glinting lights off the two small bodies stretched on the floor. At last Crekkid stirred and woke. The darting forked tongue tasted the air. The ruby eyes wandered the hall and came to rest upon the still form of Nurbo. Crekkid's dire hiss approximated a human shriek of horror. "Sssweet Nurbo—dead!" In an instant he was at her side, his wiry tongue flicking her face, his voice an octave higher than usual as he called her name. "Nurbo, sssweet sssilver-ssshining Nurbo, do not die! Return to your Patriarch! Wake. Wake. Wake. Wake."

Her moonstone eyes brightened as consciousness returned. Slowly Nurbo coiled her silvery length and lifted her head. "Brave Crekkid—alive!" She was still somewhat dazed. The motion of her tongue was sluggish. "Patriarch Crekkid bessside hisss Nurbo! Doesss Nurbo sssee true?"

"True, sssweet Nurbo. True asss sssteel. Crekkid and Nurbo together at lassst!"

"At lassst and forever!"

Their tongues touched. As the lightning flared, their bodies lanced forward, met and intertwined to form a shining knot of awesome complexity. The faint rasp of scale upon scale was lost amidst the crash of supranormal explosions overhead, but piercing whistles bore testimony to the rapture of their long-delayed union.

It was only when ardor was spent that Nurbo thought to inquire, "How can thisss be?"

"Sssweet Nurbo, it wasss meant to be. Now Crekkid'sss life isss complete."

"Humansss gone," Nurbo pointed out. "Disssappeared. How? When? Why? Where? Where? Where? Where?"

Crekkid mulled it over. "Crekkid doesss not know," he admitted. "Nurbo and Crekkid sssleep, humansss go."

"Go where?"

"Sssssssssss!" Crekkid concentrated, but reached no satisfactory conclusion. "Crekkid and Nurbo sssearch," he decided. "Find humansss and punisssh. Punisssh. Punisssh. Punisssh."

"Sssearch where? Humansss here, there—anywhere. Maybe they run away," Nurbo suggested.

"Run? Run?" Crekkid writhed in dismay. "They belong to Ssseigneur, and they mussst ssstay. Do they not undersssstand? Ssstupid humansss!"

"Ssstupid. Ssstupid," Nurbo agreed. "We mussst find Ssseigneur. Ssseigneur knowsss what to do."

"Great Massster. Wissse Massster," Crekkid sang.

"But where isss Ssseigneur?"

"In tower. When lightning comesss and goesss, Ssseigneur in tower. Alwaysss. Come, sssweet Nurbo. Patriarch Crekkid will lead the way."

Together the serpents slithered from the Great Hall. It was with some difficulty that they navigated the many steps leading to the summit of the Cloudmaster. But their determination was limitless, and at last they reached the workroom. The door was shut, but the gap between portal and floor admitted the passage of the two slim bodies. Once inside, Crekkid and Nurbo halted, dazzled by the sight that met their eyes. Before them stood the four identical Keproses, each a lord of lightning, each enveloped in a glowing crimson nimbus. From the sanguinary clouds issued lashes of force that merged to form the vast scarlet bolts that vaulted through space to strike with killing power at the Tyrant of Mists.

For a moment the serpents were struck dumb. With such divinity was their master hedged that they hardly dared approach, much less address him. Their forked tongues were paralyzed, and they pressed their tiny heads to the floor in mute adoration. Remembrance of duty eventually broke the trance. Crekkid and Nurbo approached their replicated lord, hissing timidly, worshipfully for attention. Their presence went unnoticed and the hissing became more insistent. But it was no easy matter to capture the regard of a supranormalist intent upon his work of destruction. The serpents halted some distance from the Seigneur and Selves, for the luminous scarlet cloud daunted their courage. Their plaintive hisses increased in volume, to no avail.

"Ssseigneursss fight," Crekkid explained. "Who can ssstand againssst Ssseigneur? All the world ssshall be hisss lair."

"Great Massster. Wissse Massster. Patriarch Crekkid and Matriarch Nurbo alwaysss at hisss ssside."

The cloud brightened, lightning flew, and the resulting crash rocked the tower.

"Massster conquersss," Crekkid observed. "We attend hisss victory. Humbly the Matriarch and Patriarch await hisss notice. We wait."

They did so, but took advantage of the opportunity once more to seek each other's coils.

*　　*　　*

Relian and Mereth raced down the broad central staircase, through the vaulted entryway and out the door. The cold air smote them, for they wore no cloaks. The snow still fell and was just beginning to stick. A few patches whitened the ground. It flashed through Relian's mind that the footprints they left would mark their trail should Keprose choose to initiate pursuit, but he quickly dismissed the thought. The footprints would be obscured within minutes. In any event, Keprose was otherwise occupied and would probably continue so for some time. As if in confirmation of the thought, a blue bolt flared in a gorgeous death-agony as it collided with the invisible shield.

The shield!

Struck at once by the same thought, the fugitives exchanged alarmed glances.

"Mereth—do you know if we can pass through the barrier?"

"Stray dogs and cats have sometimes done it," she replied. "And birds have flown through more than once. But I don't know if it's ever been crossed by a human being."

"We can wait," he offered. "We can hide ourselves until the battle's over and we know the shield's down."

"And Keprose will have discovered our escape by then," she replied. "No more waiting, please. No more."

The courtyard was behind them. They had reached the outer wall. The archway piercing the immense thickness of the wall formed a tunnel, closed off at each end by massive, iron-bound oaken doors. The inner gate gaped open. The other was heavily barred. Between the two gates, enclosed within the thickness of the wall itself stood the porter's lodge. Its square windows opened onto the courtyard. The shutters of one window were open, and Relian peered in. The lodge was deserted. No doubt terrified by the exchange of lightning, the porter had fled, probably to take refuge with his companions in the fortress kitchen.

Relian and Mereth entered the tunnel. The gate at the far end was secured by a great bar of iron as long as a sapling, heavy and stout enough to withstand the assault of an army. The bar was linked by steel chain to a system of pulleys and counterweights that allowed it to be raised by the lone porter. Relian scanned the mechanism quickly, located the appropriate lever and depressed it. The bar lifted smoothly. He grasped the iron ring set in the oak and pulled with all his strength. The gate creaked partway open. Pale light streamed in and a breeze whooshed through the tunnel. He heard Mereth draw in her breath, and remembered that she had never set foot beyond the wall before. He extended his hand. She took it and held on tightly. Together they slipped through the opening and out of the fortress.

The snow-powdered clearing stretched before them, and it was not empty. Out of the surrounding woods poured a stream of men—scores of them; perhaps hundreds of them—advancing in quiet, well-ordered ranks. Their quadricorner hats marked them as townsmen. Their expressions were formidably grim. From time to time many cast uneasy glances skyward, where the lightning played over the valley. Their faces were unknown to Relian, with one exception. At the forefront of the party shambled a familiar scarecrow figure. Relian's gaze was magnetized, and he found himself staring into the mild, intelligent eyes of Scrivvulch the Stick. The sight froze him in his tracks.

"Young Master Kru!" Scrivvulch's lips curled whimsically. His stride lengthened. "I must confess, I did not expect you to greet me at the door. Needless to say, I am more than pleased—"

The Assassin's pleasant voice was drowned out by the shouts of his companions.

" 'Tis the Equalist there—Black Relian himself!"

"Bold as you please!"

"Murderer—thief—scum!"

Someone picked up a rock and threw it. The stone missed Relian, but grazed Mereth's arm. An exclamation escaped her and she turned to Relian, her eyes wide. *"Who are they?"*

There was no time to answer. The townsmen broke their orderly ranks and surged forward. Fresh shouts arose.

"Hang 'im here and now!"

"Too easy for a murdering poacher!"

"He's for the cage and hooks!"

Relian seized Mereth, ducked back through the open gate and closed the oaken door. Howls of fury pursued him. He turned to the wall and yanked the lever that raised the iron bar. Nothing happened. Apparently another lever was employed to lower it. He cast his eyes desperately over the elaborate system of pulleys and weights, followed the steel chains across the arched ceiling and down the opposite wall to a protruding steel shaft. He jumped for the shaft and his hand closed upon it a moment too late.

The door began to open. For a moment Relian and Mereth strove to hold it shut. Their combined strength was no match for the mob outside, and they were forced inexorably backward as the gate swung toward them.

The downy head of Scrivvulch thrust itself through the opening. "Master Kru, if I might beg your indulgence—" The pressure of humanity behind him propelled Scrivvulch into the tunnel.

As the door opened, Relian and Mereth turned and sprinted for the fortress. Scrivvulch observed his fleeing prey, lifted his cane and aimed carefully. Before he had launched his blade, the townsmen were in the tunnel, milling in droves between Assassin and target. Scrivvulch suppressed a sigh, lowered his stick and followed his enraged cohorts across the courtyard.

*   *   *

Mereth looked back over her shoulder as she ran. "They're coming in after us—I never thought they'd dare!"

"I knew Scrivvulch would."

They bounded up the three low stone stairs with their pursuers but a few yards behind. Attaining the sanctuary they sought, they entered, slammed the door and threw the bolt. A moment later, the door began to shake under the blows of many angry fists.

"That should hold them," Mereth opined.

"Don't be too sure," Relian advised. "They might decide to break the door down."

"Never. They'd never dare to risk Keprose's anger. They know what he can do. His lightning—"

"Don't depend on it. They've dared a great deal already. What's to prevent them from taking the next step? They've obviously never been this angry before."

They stood in the entrance hall. The place was deserted; the servants had all fled or hidden themselves. Explosions still roared above—so frequently that the listeners had become somewhat inured to the sound. But the suppressed terrors of the townsmen served to intensify their wrath. When the demise of one of Vanalisse's greatest bolts sent a glare of blue light stabbing through the narrow windows cut just below the arch of the ceiling, the cries outside waxed in bitterness.

Relian pressed his ear to the door. "I can hear them muttering out there, but I can't make out what they're saying. They're planning something, I think."

Mereth shrugged. "There's little they can do. Keprose has terrorized them for years, and they've never presumed to cross him. They've been afraid, and with good reason. It won't be any different now. Within minutes they'll recognize their own folly and run for home. How could it be otherwise?"

"My poor fair and learned friend, you've been shut up in this place all your life. You've read widely, but seen little of living men. They aren't always so—"

Relian's reply was interrupted by the hollow thud of iron on wood. Mereth stared wordlessly. The door shook under the impact and the old bolt rattled. There was a brief pause and an excited exchange of opinions or instructions outside. After that, the blows descended steadily and rhythmically. No need to wonder what battering ram was in use. The townsmen had lifted the iron bar from the Seigneur's outer gate.

"They'll be through that door in seconds." Mereth spoke wonderingly. "Have they forgotten the Seigneur's power? What's possessed them?"

"Outrage, it seems. I can't altogether blame them."

The door quivered. As they watched helplessly, a fissure opened along the grain of one of the great planks. They shrank from the portal.

"Relian, we must go to Keprose. He's your only protection."

"Don't hope for much from the Seigneur. He's got little enough reason to exert himself on my behalf now."

"One strong reason—his arrogance. In any case, that mob out there means to kill you, there's nowhere to hide, and Keprose is your only hope."

He nodded. They crossed the hall and mounted the great staircase. They were halfway up when the door gave way before the makeshift battering ram. A splintering crash of ruined timber announced the townsmen's success. The door burst open and for the first time in human memory, citizens of Vale Jevaint forced their way into the stronghold of the Seigneur.

The cry went up at once. "Black Relian—there on the stairs!"

The fugitives broke into a run, and the crowd came thundering after. Up the ancient stairs sped the men of Vale Jevaint and leading them all came Scrivvulch the Stick, who displayed considerable agility, the clumsiness of his conformation notwithstanding. His spidery legs carried him up three steps at a time, and soon he drew ahead of his companions.

Relian and Mereth ran for the Cloudmaster. As they went, Relian heard the footfall of his nemesis behind him and cursed the unthinking impulse that had sent him from his chamber without a weapon. He had not thought to take the razor, to pick up a table knife or even so much as a stout stick. Once again Scrivvulch had surprised him unarmed, and this time would probably be the last. Mereth was fleet and light of foot. He did not need to slacken his pace on her account. They came to the end of the hallway and the Cloudmaster entrance. And then they were on the endless stairs that went spiraling up to the summit of the tallest tower of Fortress Gavyne.

Cut into the outer face of the tower at regular intervals were observation slits. Relian glanced through one in passing and caught a quick glimpse of the Tyrant of Mists, bereft of its protective veiling and nearly in ruins now. For a moment pity touched him, but even as he watched, a bolt of force launched itself from the Tyrant's one remaining tower. Vanalisse the Unseen was not finished yet.

Footsteps pounded on the stairs and below him Relian spied the top of a downy head. Several panting townsmen climbed in Scrivvulch's wake. The Assassin himself continued to ascend three steps at a time. Evidently his energy was far from depleted.

Before they reached the landing they could see that the workroom door was closed. Relian silently prayed that it was not locked. They came to the top of the stairs, and he found that his ill luck had lapsed. The door yielded to pressure.

Relian and Mereth paused in the doorway, struck by the same spectacle that had awakened awe in the hearts of the steel serpents. The lucent crimson nimbus still enshrouded Seigneur and Selves. The clouds had assumed a deeper, richer tint, as the four Keproses achieved ever-strengthening unity. The robed figures gestured identically, and short, brilliant arcs of force leapt and crisscrossed in midair to form fleeting patterns elaborate as fiery lace. It was the necessary preliminary to the generation of the huge, killing bolts. The sight had served to convince the serpents of their master's divinity, but apprentice supranormalists were somewhat less impressionable.

"Strimba's Aura Incarnadine," Relian observed.

Mereth nodded judiciously. "He—they—he performs it magnificently, doesn't he?"

Approaching footsteps recalled them to the danger at hand. So far, the Keproses had taken no notice of the newcomers. If they were aware of the intrusion, they gave no sign.

"Seigneur!" Relian raised his voice authoritatively as he and Mereth advanced to the verge of the Aura. "Seigneur Keprose!"

Four heads swiveled at the sound. Four pairs of eyes gazed incuriously out of the red mist, then turned away. The Keproses showed no sign of surprise, curiosity, or irritation at the interruption. Presumably Uy's Mindwall—or a more powerful and advanced variation thereon—blocked distraction.

"Seigneur, listen to me. The townsmen—hundreds of them— have invaded your fortress. In a moment they will be here—"

Once more the brief, incurious flick of identical eyes. Strimba's Aura Incarnadine may have dimmed minutely. It was difficult to be certain.

"Seigneur, they are angry. Be warned—"

Slight frowns marked four brows. The attention of Seigneur and Selves had been captured, and not a moment too soon. As Keproses turned slowly from the window, Scrivvulch and the most determined of the delegates reached the head of the stairs. At the appearance of the invaders, the Aura pulsed.

As the vanguard of the townsmen caught sight of their quadrupled lord, cries of fearful amazement arose. More and more men arrived, and the shouting grew frenetic. Soon the pressure of those behind them on stairs and landing forced the leaders through the doorway and into the workroom. They went unwillingly. The citizens, already in awe of the Seigneur, were thoroughly demoralized at the sight of four of him. Gladly would they have abandoned their mission then and there, without another thought to the Fist of Zhi or to the Equalist Black Relian who now faced them—composed, white-faced and cornered at last. But their compatriots streamed up the narrow staircase, and retreat was impossible.

Strimba's Aura Incarnadine flickered. Perturbation quivered the jowls of the Seigneur and Selves. As more and more yelling citizens crowded the workroom, synchronous concentration weakened and supranormal unity inevitably deteriorated. The Aura lightened to a rosy cloud, and the bolts that arced within lost much of their brilliancy.

Although startled, Scrivvulch the Stick did not lose his composure. Detaching himself from the crowd, he advanced, cane in hand. After a moment, Master Gatherer Clym Stipper and Councilman Gyf Fynok joined him. When he saw the eyes of the Seigneurs fixed upon him, Scrivvulch spoke. "Gentlemen, all—I request the privilege of addressing the Seigneur Keprose Gavyne."

"I am he." The four replies were simultaneous. "You intrude."

"Which gentleman is the Seigneur, may I ask?"

"*Here.*" The four voices rang out as one.

Stipper and Fynok were ashen, but Scrivvulch's courteous smile did not falter. "I see. Permit me to introduce myself. I am Scrivvulch, Accredited Agent of the Dhreve of Neraunce. Acting in my official capacity, I do request—"

"I know who you are, sir, as I recall ordering you from my property not long ago. I repeat that order now. Go. Your presence within my fortress is unwelcome. Your invasion of my workroom is intolerable. Go at once, and be thankful that I do not stoop to punish your presumption. All of you—go." It was the Seigneur nearest Scrivvulch who spoke, and probably the original Keprose, although all questions of authenticity seemed academic at that moment. As Keprose spoke, Strimba's Aura Incarnadine faded. Evidently surprise and anger could break the concentration of even so accomplished a supranormalist as the Seigneur.

"If I may be permitted to explain my purpose—" Scrivvulch attempted.

"I am already aware of your purpose, sir." This time the Keprose beside the window answered. "You and these unruly subjects of mine desire the blood of this young man—" All four of them indicated Relian.

"—As well as the Fist of Zhi," concluded the Keprose at the left of the group. "I cannot be troubled with such trifles at this time. I must not be vexed! I've matters of infinitely greater significance to concern me. Come back to see me another day, fellow. And make an appointment."

"Seigneur—" Scrivvulch's smile vanished and he assumed an admonitory tone. "This is a matter of grave importance, most worthy of your Lordship's closest attention. May I remind you that I represent his Dhreveship of Neraunce? Moreover, I have been moved in this instance to act on behalf of these good townsfolk here—"

"The Dhreve of Neraunce, your peevish master, owns no authority here. If you imagine otherwise, then your impertinence is exceeded only by your ignorance of geography," observed the fourth Keprose. "As for the 'good townsfolk' here, they fail disgracefully in the duty they owe the Seigneur who protects them from the depredations of Vanalisse the Unseen Hag."

At mention of the name, Relian's eyes automatically jumped to the window. What he saw added to his already-profound discomfort. On the peaks across the valley, the fog was beginning to thicken around the Tyrant of Mists. The fortress was still visible, but the outlines were blurring. Evidently Vanalisse the Unseen was taking advantage of the respite to repair some of the damage inflicted by Keprose's missiles.

"Seigneur Keprose." Clym Stipper stepped forward and spoke for the first time. His manner was respectful, but not as subservient as Keprose might have desired. "You know me. I'm Stipper, Master Gatherer of the Guild."

"Be brief." The Keproses folded their arms and lifted their chins. The crimson Aura had dimmed out of existence. "The Hag is clearly vanquished and all but helpless. So confident am I of victory that I consent to hear you. But be brief indeed."

"Seigneur Keprose, this Neraunci fellow here has the right

of it. We've come here today to ask you—most respectfully, sir—to give us back the Fist of Zhi, without which we Gatherers can't get on with our work. No gathering means no eggs, and no eggs means no income for the town and no taxes for you. So as I see it, it's to your benefit as well as ours to return the Fist, if you've gotten what you want from it. That is what we're asking for, Seigneur. We await your reply.''

Keprose considered. "Very well," he decided at last. "Your demands are objectionable and your intrusion unpardonable, but never let it be said—"

"—That Keprose Gavyne—" chimed in a Self.

"—Is anything less than—" continued another.

"—The most moderate and equitable of Seigneurs," concluded the last.

"I will permit you the Fist. I believe it is on that table. You may take it if you can find it."

Clym Stipper eagerly rummaged through the gnawed chicken bones, empty bottles, bonbon wrappers and parchment scrolls that cluttered the table. Presently he came upon the desiccated member lying forgotten and neglected beneath a soiled napkin. Stipper plucked the Fist from the welter, wrapped it in a clean handkerchief and dropped the bundle in his coat pocket. "Thank-you, Seigneur." His relief was palpable. "We are grateful."

"And now, Master Gatherer, if that contents you—"

"A very good beginning, Seigneur, but there is more," interrupted Scrivvulch the Stick.

Relian felt Mereth's fingernails dig into his palm.

"Yes," Gyf Fynok agreed bluntly. "There's the Equalist. The thief. The poacher. The murderer. We want him."

All eyes turned to Relian. Relian stared steadily at Scrivvulch the Stick, who met the regard benevolently.

"We will talk of it another time," Keprose promised, his voice sharp with irritation. "Already I have been more than patient. Do not give me cause to regret my generosity, my forbearance. You will go now."

"Black Relian has broken the laws," Gyf Fynok insisted doggedly. "Those who break the laws must pay."

"I'm not minded to surrender my apprentice," snapped Keprose. "He is an agile, hardy sort, and who knows what further use I may find for him? You have already deprived me the use of my nephews, is that not sufficient? Do townsmen command their Seigneur? I am not finished with the young man and it is not my pleasure to surrender him to you.'' An uncertain muttering ran through the ranks of the townsmen, and Keprose held up his hand. ''The subject is closed.''

The invaders seemed disposed to agree, until Scrivvulch reminded them gently, ''The crimes? The murders? The pillage of the Egg House?''

''The Neraunci is right,'' observed Gyf Fynok. ''Laws have been broken and the criminal must pay. 'Tis only justice, and we'll accept no less.''

''You will accept my decision, whatever it may be.'' Four lips curled disdainfully. ''The Councilman forgets his place, I think.''

Gyf Fynok opened his mouth to reply, and Scrivvulch broke in diplomatically, ''The townsmen rely upon the renowned virtue and impartiality of their lord. They are confident that the Seigneur's celebrated probity will ensure a happy outcome. Fortress Gavyne harbors a notorious felon. Now that the situation has been directed to the Seigneur's attention, his loving subjects may no doubt expect fair dealing.''

''As you note, justice is impartial,'' returned Keprose Gavyne, somewhat mollified. ''Therefore, my apprentice here, although the object of universal contempt and execration, is no less entitled to protection than is the most blameless of my loving subjects, not excepting the Councilman himself.''

This assertion failed to reassure Relian. His melancholic dark eyes roamed the ranks of the townsmen who sought his life; rested for a moment upon the four indifferent and impatient Seigneurs; glanced out the windows to behold the fog once more concealing the Tyrant of Mists; and returned at last to the amiably earnest countenance of Scrivvulch the Stick. His sense of helplessness was almost intolerable; all the more so in that a relatively slight strengthening of his supranormal powers would have enabled him to defend himself most effectively. As it was, he found himself dependent upon the inconstant whim of Keprose Gavyne.

''What charges do you prefer against my apprentice?'' inquired a Self. ''And pray you—'' he addressed Scrivvulch, ''do not weary me with tales of multifarious outrages committed upon foreign soil. They do not signify. In what manner has this young man transgressed within my realm? Come, be quick about it.''

Clym Stipper chose to answer the query. ''First off, 'tis proved beyond all doubt that the young Equalist there was

poaching in the Miasm. 'Tis thought he bagged a mother
Wingbane. There's a capital offense right there, sir.''

"Bah," the Self near the window shrugged deprecatingly.
"He braved the Miasm upon my orders. In truth, the fellow
was unbecomingly reluctant to go, despite the protection I
furnished him. Not an enterprising spirit, by any means. As
for the Wingbane—does any here question the right of the
Seigneur to dispose as he sees fit of the birds within his own
forest? If any, speak; for him has my apprentice offended.''

Dubious murmurs arose, but no one responded.

"What more?" demanded another Self.

Clym Stipper's face turned dutifully to the new speaker.
"We know he stole the Fist of Zhi. We spotted him in the
Egg House the night of the explosion and fire on Tallow
Street—" Stipper broke off red-faced, suddenly mindful of
the delicacy of that particular issue, but the Seigneurs did not
seem unduly sensitive.

"Again, the young man acted on my orders," Keprose
explained. "I needed the Fist. I was within my rights as
Seigneur to commandeer it to my own personal use. I sent my
apprentice to fetch it. That is all. In any event, I have
returned the Fist, and that action must answer all complaints.''

"And so it might, Seigneur Keprose, if that were all there
was to it," Stipper replied. "But that doesn't answer for the
destruction of hundreds of our finest eggs one week ago.
Smashed for no reason, for the sheer pleasure of destruction,
it seems. And above all, it doesn't answer for the three Egg
House guards murdered the same night—two stabbed, and
one killed in a way I don't like to think about.

"I know nothing of the incidents you describe," the four
Keproses replied in unison.

"Maybe you don't, Seigneur Keprose. But I warrant your
apprentice does," said Gyf Fynok. "Your apprentice, the
Equalist, knows all about it.''

All eyes turned to Relian, who spoke for the first time
since the townsmen had entered the workroom. "I have
wronged you all, though not willingly. I regret it with all my
heart. But I swear to you that I am no Equalist, no criminal,
and never was. These tales are lies, and I can guess the
source. I ask you to judge the true worth of that source. I
never damaged your property, save for the locks upon the
Egg House door. And I have never killed a man in Vale
Jevaint or anywhere else. The murders you describe—

this is the first I have heard of them. I am not the culprit, and I can prove it."

Scrivvulch the Stick's brows rose in amused skepticism. The townsmen conferred in uneasy clusters. Some were impressed despite themselves by Relian's youth, bearing, the quality of his speech, and his straightforward manner.

"Where's your proof?" demanded Gyf Fynok.

"You mentioned that the murders and vandalism occurred one week ago?"

"One week exactly."

"But for the past several weeks—until this afternoon—I've not set foot outside Fortress Gavyne," Relian explained steadily. "There are several people—including a number of the servants, Mistress Mereth, the Seigneur himself and his Selves—who can attest to my whereabouts upon the day in question."

"That is true," Keprose confirmed after a moment's reflection. "I have seen the young man about the fortress, here and there, every day for a least a couple of weeks."

The corroborations of the Selves overlapped.

"He is generally to be found—"

"—Drudging in the Great Hall."

"He is singularly devoted to his studies—"

"—And I mean to observe his progress—"

"—When I find the time."

"A week ago today," Mereth spoke up, "Relian spent the day studying in the Great Hall. I was there too, from mid-afternoon until well into the evening. If you doubt my word, then you may ask Drist the footman, or else the new potboy. Both of them saw Relian when they brought food in."

"I believe that clears the apprentice," observed Keprose. "And that, I think, concludes the audience. You people have my leave to withdraw."

The townsmen did not appear eager to depart. The Seigneurs' disclosures influenced but did not entirely convince them.

"If Black Relian didn't kill the Egg House guards, then who did?" It was the first time that Clym Stipper—or any of them, for that matter—had seriously considered alternate possibilities. "And what for? What was there to gain? In the name of all reason, what for?"

"I have no way of knowing who murdered the guards," said Relian, and the others turned to him in surprise. "But you might arrive at the answer by starting off with this question: Who among you has anything to gain by attaching the blame to me?''

Scrivvulch did not wait for his companions to puzzle it out. "Ah, did I not tell you Black Relian is a clever young scoundrel!'' the Assassin exclaimed in apparent pleasure. "Plausible, is he not? Subtle and false as an evil spirit, and I cannot begin to name the poor souls deceived by his blandishments! But rest assured, my friends. Your original conclusions were wise and sound. Black Relian Kru is a famous cutthroat, and he is undoubtedly the man you seek. The evidence that appears to exonerate him of the Egg House murders is quite worthless.''

Keprose's impatience gave way to open anger. Four scowls darkened four brows, and several of the citizens instinctively drew back. "Worthless? How dare you, sir? You question the word of the Seigneur Keprose Gavyne in his own house, you spindling Neraunci malapert?''

"By no means, Seigneur!'' Scrivvulch performed a slight, graceless bow. "The word of the Seigneur is golden. You and your esteemed—others—state that you saw Black Relian about the fortress one week ago today. Yet I surmise from your description that you glimpsed him but fleetingly.''

"That is correct,'' the Keproses replied in unison.

"Then much of his time during the evening hours remains unaccounted for.'' Scrivvulch turned his benignant gaze upon Mereth. "And you, my child, spent the afternoon and early evening in Black Relian's company. I do not doubt your word for a single instant. But what of the later evening? I must assume for the sake of your honor that you did not spend the entire night with him. Was Black Relian still at his studies when you retired?''

Mereth nodded unwillingly. "But he was already tired, and it was too late for him to have considered going out—''

"Not at all. Not at all. A couple of hours would have sufficed,'' Scrivvulch assured her. "I admire your obvious loyalty, child, but alas—you have been Black Relian's innocent dupe, as was the tragic Lady Mayoress of Rendendil—''

"I have never been anywhere near Rendendil.'' Relian noted that the faces of the townsfolk, which had shown signs of softening, were once more hardened against him. "There is another witness to speak on my behalf, if the Seigneur will permit it.'' It was humiliating to sue to his hated captor's indulgence, but as usual, there was no other choice. "This witness has been with me throughout the days and nights that I have been held here. He can account for every moment of my time." Relian's bitterness was audible but restrained.

"Ah, Crekkid, you mean," replied Keprose. "I believe the little fellow is somewhere about, and it is to be hoped that he can put an end to this wrangling. My patience is great, but it is not inexhaustible." He clapped his hands sharply. "Crekkid? Come forth, my Crekkid, come forth!"

A swift flash of silver, and Crekkid shot from his station beneath the workroom table. Nurbo slithered beside him.

"Now, my Crekkid," Keprose addressed the serpent with a touch of sternness, "perhaps you would be so good as to explain why you and Nurbo have, without my leave, abandoned the throats of your humans?"

"Sssssssss! Crekkid doesss not know," the snake admitted, and exclamations of amazement escaped the townsfolk at the sound of the creature's hissing speech. "Crekkid sssleep. Wake up and human gone. Sssame for sssweet Nurbo. Ssstrange missshap. Crekkid isss assshamed."

His mate concurred. "Nurbo isss assshamed."

Relian could hear the whispers of the nearest of the townsmen:

"Listen to that—are they real?"

"Are they alive, or are they machines?"

"They talk as well as humans."

"Better than some I know."

Gyf Fynok was scowling suspiciously at the silvery creatures. Clym Stipper looked frankly perplexed. Scrivvulch the Stick's hand tightened briefly on his cane. For a moment his eyes narrowed, and then the expression of wary alertness relaxed. These were his only external manifestations of most unpleasant surprise.

"My Crekkid slept, and so did Nurbo? That is very interesting." The Keproses darted sharp glances at Relian. "Progress indeed, young man." They turned back to the serpents. Seigneur and Selves were ranged in a semicircle. Before them coiled the steel serpents, luxuriating in the multiplicity of their divinity, basking in the warmth of four suns. "Be at ease, my little friends. The Seigneur does not hold you responsible. You are forgiven." The serpents writhed ecstatically. "Now, my Crekkid, a question or two. You recall the night your human visited the town, entered the great building there, and came away with the living hand?''

"Yesss, Ssseigneur!'' Crekkid returned without hesitation.

Hostility stirred the ranks of the citizens.

"Since then, you've been with the human every moment, night and day, until this afternoon?''

"Yesss, Ssseigneur!''

"And now, think carefully. During that time, has the human ever returned to the town and the great building?''

"No, Ssseigneur! Never go back, for Crekkid doesss not let him leave fortressss. Crekkid, Ssscourge of Ssseigneur! Great Ssseigneur. Wissse Ssseigneur. Many Ssseigneursss!''

"Let that satisfy you,'' Keprose commanded his subjects. "My apprentice is not the man you seek.''

"It seems he's not,'' Clym Stipper agreed thoughtfully, "provided that little . . . snake, whatever it is—can be trusted.''

"And there you hit upon the crucial point,'' Scrivvulch interjected smoothly. "How can these good folk rely in so important a matter upon the unsupported word of a talking serpent, an animal devoid of human heart, human understanding, human morality?''

"Crekkid doesss not lie!'' the serpent broke in resentfully.

Scrivvulch ignored the interruption. "The creature is not even truly alive,'' he continued. "Clearly it is an automaton, a mechanical contrivance, and as such, its perceptions may not be trusted. A single gear in need of oiling—a wheel or spring out of alignment—a single sprocket worn or broken—and the well-ordered machine runs mad. My friends, we cannot rely upon it.''

Crekkid was vibrating with near-incoherent anger. "Crekkid livesss,'' he managed to hiss. "You think not? Ssstupid. Ssstupid. Ssstupid. Ssstupid.''

"I fear my little friend is correct in his assessment,'' observed the Keprose nearest Scrivvulch. "The steel serpents live. Your disbelief is the product of ignorance, and I cannot be troubled to educate you. Suffice it to say that the serpents are utterly devoted to their Seigneur and would not lie to him. I personally place far more faith in the word of Crekkid than in that of an officious Neraunci meddler. Events in Vale Jevaint are no concern of yours, sir. You sow dissension and discontent among my subjects, you undermine their loyalty to their Seigneur. Your motives are obscure and your methods highly questionable. My patience, as I have warned you, is not inexhaustible, and I suspect I have permitted you free rein too long.''

"Seigneur, it is not my desire to cause offense. If I, a stranger and a foreigner, have concerned myself with affairs in Vale Jevaint, it has been for love of justice. For in this violent and stormy world, Justice is the bulwark, the dam against which the tumultuous sea of Chaos batters itself in vain,'' proclaimed Scrivvulch the Stick. "Alas that love of Justice compels me to note the possible shortcomings of the reptilian automata. Consider the significance of the matter with which we deal. Three men have been murdered. Such a crime lacerates the hearts of those who believe—as I believe, as all men of conscience must believe—in the inviolable sanctity of human life. The criminal must be found and punished, and we must direct our best efforts toward that end. In view of the gravity of the issue, we cannot be turned from our purpose, we cannot accept the testimony of crawling reptiles, mindless automata, maladjusted machinery—''

Crekkid could stand no more, "Ssstupid!" the serpent hissed. "Ssstupid! Patriarch Crekkid livesss! And Crekkid doesss not lie to Ssseigneur! Ssskinny old human ssstupid!'' His rage could not express itself in words. The serpent darted forward. The anterior portion of his body lifted, curved into an S-shaped loop and shot forward as Crekkid struck. Short steely fangs sank into the ankle of Scrivvulch the Stick.

Scrivvulch started in sudden pain. His reaction was instantaneous. He kicked sharply and the serpent went flying. Crekkid hit violently against the leg of the table, and silver scales sprayed like drops of rain. The serpent dropped to the stone floor, where he lay hissing in pain, fear and rage.

"Patriarch Crekkid!" Nurbo's whistle of sympathetic anguish momentarily silenced all present. "Brave Crekkid!" She hastened to her lover's side, and her wiry tongue uselessly caressed his wounds.

"Enough!" The cry issued simultaneously from four seigneurial throats.

"Enough of—"

"—This, I'll have—"

"—No more! You wound my—"

"—Harmless creature!"

"It is unendurable—"

"—Insupportable!"

"You, sir—'' the nearest Keprose addressed Scrivvulch.

"You have gone too far. Hitherto I have tolerated your presence, though against my better judgment. I have been wrong to do so, but it is not too late to rectify my error."

The four Keproses lifted their hands. Their fingers wove arcane patterns. Chanting syllables dropped from their lips. Scrivvulch saw the gestures, heard the chant, and knew what they portended. He recognized his own mortal peril, and his response was based upon instincts honed to feral sharpness by twenty years' experience as High Court Assassin to the Dhreve of Neraunce. Without hesitation he lifted his cane. Hardly pausing to aim, he depressed the button in the handle, and the triangular blade flew to bury itself in the bosom of the nearest Keprose.

Keprose choked in mid-syllable. His limber fingers convulsed. He staggered and fell backward into the arms of his doppelgangers. They lowered him gently to the floor, where he lay still, blue eyes staring and breath coming in shallow gasps.

The Selves seemed paralyzed with horror. While the cries of the townsmen arose around them and Scrivvulch stood, cane in hand, looking on with an expression of bemused chagrin, the Selves could only repeat over and over in helpless unison, "The Prototype—the Prototype—the Prototype—"

The babble of human voices did not muffle the whistling shrieks that now burst from two tiny metallic throats. "Ssseigneur! Ssseigneur!" Crekkid and Nurbo arrowed to the side of their stricken master. "Great Massster, wissse Massster! Hurt! Hurt!" Their bodies writhed in unspeakable sorrow. Their whistles rose in hysterical grief.

The blade protruding like a thorn from the Seigneur's chest marked the center of a swiftly-spreading scarlet stain, almost invisible upon the black fabric of the robe. But Keprose Gavyne was still alive and aware. His lips moved feebly. He spoke with an effort. "Selves—Beloveds—Vanalisse—remember—attack—Vanalisse—"

The shocked townsmen pressed close to hear him. Their expressions reflected confusion, alarm, disbelief. The hum of voices all but drowned the Seigneur's whispered words. The close-packed surrounding bodies cut off his light and air. The Selves—any one of which might, in the eyes of the citizens, have been the true Keprose—were weeping and stupid with grief. Clym Stipper, accustomed to authority, took charge of the situation.

"Stand back," Stipper commanded. "Give him air. Bind up his wound. You there—Barber Hewdim—you know how to do it. Get over here right away and bind the Seigneur's wound. The rest of you, stand *back*, I say! Let him breathe! Someone—you, Finz Wooler—go to the stables, take a horse, ride down to town and fetch a surgeon. Someone go seek out the Seigneur's servants, tell them to bring water and linen, whatever salves or ointments there may be. Have them prepare the Seigneur's chamber. We'll carry him down as soon as we may. And some of you," Stipper concluded with a grim look at Scrivvulch the Stick, who stood watching quietly, "disarm and detain the Neraunci. There'll be a dungeon waiting for him, I doubt not."

Several townsmen sprang to do Stipper's bidding. Scrivvulch appeared unruffled and amiable as ever. "One moment, my friends," he advised. "Although I sympathize with your grief and outrage, circumstances oblige me to cite certain legalities that may have escaped your recollection in the heat of the moment. If you will recall, I am the fully Accredited Agent of the Dhreve of Neraunce, and I bear plentiful credentials to prove it. In view of my position, and of the conditions set forth in the treaties currently existing between the states of Neraunce and Nidroon, the Accredited Agent is subject to the authority of Neraunce alone."

"What are you getting at, Master Scrivvulch? Speak plain!" demanded Gyf Fynok with an air of frustration.

"You have no legal right to detain me, try me, or pass judgment upon me," Scrivvulch explained courteously. "No legal right whatever. If I have transgressed, you may, through proper diplomatic channels, demand that I submit myself to the judgment of the Dhreve of Neraunce. But that is all. I pray you do so, for the exercise may serve to ease your minds."

The citizens regarded him in bafflement. In the sudden hush that fell upon the tower workroom, the rasping, painful mutter of Keprose Gavyne was audible.

"Vanalisse—Fortress—Vanalisse—Unseen Hag—"

Perhaps Vanalisse could somehow sense the profound weakening of the supranormal defenses of Fortress Gavyne that came with the incapacitation of its master. Or perhaps it was mere coincidence that she awaited this opportunity to demonstrate her own recovery. Whatever the reason, it was at this moment that Vanalisse attacked. A great arc of blue force, a

bolt that burned the heavens, sprang from the mists, leapt th
valley and smashed effortlessly through the weakened shield
The air scorched and the fortress quivered under the impact o
a crushing blow. For a moment the air seemed to lose it
life-sustaining property. The occupants of the tower choke
and wheezed, their frightened voices temporarily stifled. A
few dashed to the windows, looked down to assess the dam
age. The southern extension of the building had been struck
A gaping hole pierced the wall of what must have been th
long gallery leading to the Great Hall. Blackened stone
strewed the ground below the ruined wall, and tongues o
blue fire licked about the opening.

The air was breathable again, but would not remain so. A
second bolt flew, unbearably bright, to wreak havoc upon th
fortress ramparts. Then four more came in quick succession
The first sailed harmlessly overhead. The second struck th
outer wall. The last two smote the Great Hall itself. Th
fortress shuddered. A split opened in the high wooden ceiling
of the workroom. A pair of the broad flags of the floo
buckled, and the men in that vicinity shuffled to maintai
balance. All of them choked and gagged on the burning air.

Terrified by the supranormal assault, the men of Val
Jevaint broke and ran for the door. The landing and th
staircase clear down to the floor below were clogged with
struggling humanity. There was movement, appallingly slug
gish movement; but for the moment, the occupants of th
workroom were trapped.

The Seigneur was speaking. His voice was excessively
feeble, and the Selves kneeling at his side had to bend low t
hear. His instructions completed at great cost to his strength
Keprose lapsed into a swoon. The Selves arose as one. To
gether they faced the window, and their hyperdigital finger
flew. Their lips moved, but the syllables that emerged were
inaudible amidst the townsmen's uproar. Presumably they
sought to strengthen the useless shield, but shock and grie
had much weakened their collective will. Even as they strove
Vanalisse's lightning flew. Once more the barrier was breached
and this time the target was the Cloudmaster itself.

The bolt struck the pinnacle of the tower, tearing most o
the six-sided, peaked wooden roof away. Cold gray light an
icy air swept in as the workroom was exposed to the sky
The few remaining rafters were wrapped in blue flame. Splin
ters of burning wood showered the chamber. Most of then

extinguished themselves at once upon the stone floor, but some scorched human hair and garments. Others drifted to the table, where they fell upon paper, parchment, and greasy napkins. Here and there, small fires blossomed.

The Selves continued their efforts. Their faces were bathed in perspiration, their gestures nervously jerky. From time to time their eyes dropped involuntarily to the still figure of their Prototype, stretched on the floor at their feet.

The next bolt struck the tower a high, glancing blow. The Cloudmaster trembled, cabinets overturned, and men were flung upon their faces. A short section of the workroom wall gave way, and the ruins clattered across the floor. Most present managed to dodge the tumbling stone blocks, but some were struck and bones were broken. Screams of pain and fear arose, and the exodus to the doorway became a shoving, scrambling rush.

Shrieks, flying rocks and a rain of blue fire broke the concentration of the Selves once and for all. As one man, they recognized the futility of continued resistance. For the moment, the supranormalcy of Vanalisse the Unseen was supreme. The shield was burnt and blasted. The fortress was crumbling, dying beneath the hammer-blows of the Unseen's lightning bolts. Her fiery missiles filled the sky, and where they struck unopposed, the stone walls toppled. There was no time to hate or to mourn. The only preservation lay in flight, and the way was still blocked by the last of the fleeing citizens, those who had stayed to help their injured comrades down the winding stairs.

Keprose Gavyne lay supine. His eyes were closed, his lips colorless, his breathing faint. Upon his bloodstained breast twined the steel serpents, their hisses soft with love and grief. The Selves stooped and tenderly lifted their Prototype. Keprose stirred and groaned without regaining consciousness. The movement dislodged the snakes, who slid to the floor and instantly sought the solace of each other's coils.

Together the Selves lifted their voices. "Townsmen of Vale Jevaint! Make way for the Seigneur Keprose! Stand aside—the Seigneur comes!"

Accustomed to obedience, the townsmen dutifully cleared the path, and as the fortress shook and disintegrated around them, the Selves bore their Prototype down from the Cloudmaster, through the galleries and out into the open air.

Hand in hand, Relian and Mereth moved to follow the

departing Seigneur. They found their way blocked by Scrivvulch the Stick. Scrivvulch stood before the door. His expression was untroubled, his appearance neat and soberly respectable as always. Carefully he detached the lower portion of his cane to uncover the steel spike. "Young Master Kru, I believe we've business to conclude," he remarked.

Relian's eyes widened in disbelief. "Surely not here. Not now." The tower shivered as he spoke.

"But yes. Absolutely. What better time, what better place? Who knows when another such opportunity will arise?"

"Scrivvulch, you must be mad. This fortress is falling apart around us. Let's get out, and then settle our differences."

"We have no differences. As I've often observed, young Kru, I like you. So high is my opinion of your resourcefulness, in fact, that I own I dare not permit you to leave this tower alive, for fear you might once again elude me. Never, in all my years of experience, have I been thwarted so successfully and for so long. Never before have I been forced to resort to such elaborate stratagems to gain my ends."

"You killed the Egg House guards, didn't you?"

"Alas." Scrivvulch inclined his head. "Those unfortunates may be seen as the victims of your success. No less a victim was the devoted lackey who sacrificed himself on your behalf."

"Trince? You're not speaking of Trince?"

"In seeking to protect you he died bravely, young Kru. His loyalty was superb, his death a grievous necessity. For in this heartless and indifferent world, true loyalty is—"

Relian's hold on Mereth's hand tightened so violently that a cry of pain was wrung from her.

Scrivvulch broke off and turned to the girl. "Pardon me, my child," he implored, "that my discourse touches upon matters no doubt obscure to you—"

"Less obscure than you imagine," Mereth returned coldly. "Relian has told me about you, Master Scrivvulch."

"Ah, famous. In that case, child, you would do well to leave the tower without delay. In view of the nature of the business that young Kru and I must transact, it is best that you avert your eyes. It is not my desire to distress the hearts of fair ladies—"

"I will not leave," Mereth returned, tight-lipped. "If you've no human conscience of your own, being something less than human, then I will be your conscience. I will watch you, and I will speak for the victims of your butcher's work—"

"A butcher—I?" Scrivvulch's air of gallantry dissipated. "You mistake the matter, Mistress. My work is dispatched with care and artistry, for that is my pride in life. Always I strive for perfection. Often I fall short of that mark, and the present instance is a case in point. Imperfections notwithstanding, Mistress—I do not fail. I do not fail."

"Mereth—go while you can," Relian implored.

"No."

"Happy youth, to inspire such devotion! Have no fear, I shall not harm her," promised Scrivvulch. The shock of the latest hit rattled the towers of Fortress Gavyne, and sparks shaken from the smoldering rafters glowed in the air like fireflies. Scrivvulch shrugged the cinders from his shoulders. "The hunt has been prolonged and exhilarating," he conceded. "But it must end at last. You have been a worthy opponent, young Kru, and I salute you as I bid you adieu."

The Assassin lunged like a fencer, and the steel spike drove at Relian's throat. Relian's quick reflexes saved him. He dodged, and Scrivvulch recovered himself at once. Relian backed away and Scrivvulch followed, his eyes studiously intent. He took care to maintain his position between his victim and the door. Relian's sudden feints to the right or left were deftly countered.

Relian continued to retreat. He noticed that he was being herded into the angle between the wall and one of the few tall bookcases still standing. Once trapped in that confining space, there would be no dodging the quick steel of his adversary. He feinted to the right, leaped to the left, and Scrivvulch's extended spike slid briefly along his jaw, leaving a trail of blood in its wake. Relian flinched, jumped back and collided with the bookcase. Turning, he braced himself against the wall and pushed with all his strength. The bookcase creaked, teetered, and toppled forward. Scrivvulch alertly sidestepped the descending shelves and an avalanche of books. He ducked as a couple of the heaviest volumes hurled by his quarry flew by his ear.

As Relian stooped for fresh ammunition, Scrivvulch lunged with the speed if not the grace of a bird of prey. His spike touched his victim's throat. "A creditable effort, sir," he observed. "And now, young Master Kru—"

A scrape, a rustle behind him, alerted the Assassin. He whirled just as Mereth, tottering a little beneath her burden, lifted one of the heavy chairs on high and swung it at his head. Scrivvulch dodged, and the chair whizzed harmlessly by, pulling the girl far off balance as it completed its descent. Scrivvulch shifted his grip on the cane, calculated instantaneously and struck. The blow landed behind her ear. Without a sound, Mereth crumpled to the floor and lay still.

Relian's face contorted. With an inarticulate snarl he launched himself at Scrivvulch, and came within inches of impaling himself. Balanced lightly, the Assassin stood en garde, cane extended. As his victim retreated, he thrust and once again drew blood. A spot of red appeared on the younger man's sleeve. A frown of concentration creased Scrivvulch's brow as he advanced.

A fresh shock rattled the tower, and chunks of mortared masonry plummeted from the walls. A tearing sound above, and one of the blackened rafters gave way. The smoldering timber crashed to the floor a few feet from Mereth, and dark ash covered her inert form. Scrivvulch shook his head in disapproval at the sight. "Come, come, Master Kru," he remonstrated. "Let us make an end. Submit to your fate and you have my word I shall carry the young lady to safety. Otherwise she is likely to die here, her death solely the result of your insensate obstinacy. Is this the behavior of a gentleman?"

Relian's eyes were fixed upon the fallen rafter. It was obviously too heavy to lift. He cast his gaze about the chamber in search of a weapon, any weapon. He saw the flames dance amidst the crockery, bones and debris that littered the table. He sprang to the table, seized the neck of an empty wine bottle and brought the bottle down hard upon the charred wooden edge. The glass broke jaggedly. Sharp points protruded from the fragment that Relian retained.

Divining his victim's purpose, Scrivvulch rushed forward. He did not expect the hitherto cautious prey to leap straight toward him. He saw Relian coming and thrust the spike forward a fraction too late—the other was already within his guard.

Relian stabbed for his enemy's eyes. Scrivvulch jerked his head aside and the glass ripped a gash in his forehead. The blood flowed freely into one eye and down the side of his face. Relian struck again and Scrivvulch, one hand pressed to his forehead, dodged, drew back a step and lifted his cane. There was no room to employ the spike. Using the weapon as a club, he struck cunningly at the broken bottle, and connected. A crackling of glass, and two of the points on Relian's weapon were gone. Only one remained. Scrivvulch struck, and the cane banged his opponent's elbow.

Relian's breath whistled with the pain of it, and it was with difficulty that he kept his grip on what was left of the bottle. When the cane rose again, he jabbed and slashed. The point bit deep into Scrivvulch's right wrist; ploughed along the forearm, severing skin, veins, tendons and nerve fiber as it went; and ended buried in the crook of the arm, where the glass broke. Instantly Scrivvulch's arm and hand were awash with the blood that gushed from torn veins. The quantity was remarkable; within seconds it was pooling on the floor.

Scrivvulch stiffened and the ebony cane dropped from his suddenly impotent grasp. For a hearbeat he gazed in disbelief at his mutilated arm, then abruptly plucked the glass shard from his flesh and tossed it aside. No sound escaped him, but the pain was dizzying. The Assassin swayed and caught himself on the edge of the table. His vision swam and he struggled for breath. His head soon cleared, but the weakness remained, and it was only with the support of the table that kept him on his feet. With his left hand he vainly sought to stanch the flow of blood. Despite his efforts, the blood continued to drip from arm to floor as he stood disarmed, helpless, and astounded.

For a moment Relian stared, unable to credit his most unlikely victory. Then he approached, and Scrivvulch automatically bent to retrieve the cane. His legs gave way beneath him and he dropped to his knees. His right arm hung useless and paralyzed. Determination intact, the Assassin stretched forth a shaky left hand. His fingers closed on ebony.

Relian stepped forward and easily twisted the weapon from the other's weakened grip. Without haste, he broke the stick across his knee and tossed the pieces aside. A faint exclamation of anguish, whether physical or mental was unclear, burst from the lips of Scrivvulch.

Relian met the eyes of his enemy. "You do not fail?" he inquired simply.

"You are bitter, Master Kru."

"I am, but it will pass. Bitterness gives way to pity."

"Such magnanimity must be applauded. But have I failed indeed?" Scrivvulch's left hand clamped down hard on his wound. "Are you certain, young Kru? You might ensure my failure by ending my life. That rare opportunity now presents itself, for you have been extraordinarily—almost miraculously—fortunate.''

It was true, Relian realized. *I was lucky. I—lucky?* The words of Vanalisse came back to him: ''Supranormalcy unmastered and unrecognized is the source of your misery. The talent unused will fester, poisoning all of life.'' *She was right, but today it has changed. The poison is gone.* The Assassin's voice broke in upon his thoughts.

''Fortune extends her bountiful hand,'' Scrivvulch continued, ''But I am confident you will reject the offering. My judgment is good, and I perceive you are not the man with stomach to dispatch a fallen adversary. Therein lies my preservation, and your inevitable undoing.''

''I'll chance it, and I don't think I'll lose.''

''Were I prey to vanity, my pride would be piqued. You despise the abilities of the High Court Assassin?''

''Far from it. But live or die, your title is lost.''

Scrivvulch's quick mind took Relian's meaning at once. His eyes dropped to his wounded arm.

''Yes.'' The lightning flashed overhead, but Relian did not see it. His blood raced as if he still fought, but now his weapons were words. ''Your wound is deep. The muscles and sinews have been severed. You cannot move your hand now, and perhaps never will again. Your right arm is ruined, and without it *you* are ruined. Your utility is at an end, and I don't believe your master is sentimental. The Dhreve of Neraunce can have no use for a crippled minion, and he will be swift to appoint your successor—no doubt a younger man. You will live on, and you will fill the idle hours as best you may. But your days as Court Assassin are finished.''

Scrivvulch's eyes emptied. He stared blankly past Relian, down the long corridor of purposeless, meaningless months and years that lay before him. Comprehension enshrouded his mind. He did not attempt reply.

Relian turned away. On the floor Mereth stirred and groaned. She was dusty with ashes and her garments were spotted with black scorch marks where the sparks had fallen. Relian hurried to her side. Her eyes opened and she looked up at him confusedly. A blue lightning bolt shot overhead, just barely missing the Cloudmaster, and Relian instinctively ducked. ''We must get out of the building, Mereth,'' he told her. ''I'm going to carry you.''

"I can walk." Her voice was scarcely audible. She attempted to sit up, raised herself on one elbow and fell back.

Relian lifted her as gently as possible. The motion was evidently painful, for she winced and pressed both hands to her head. "—Scrivvulch?" she inquired faintly.

"—Has failed," Relian replied. "Let him live with that. His fangs are drawn and he can't hurt us or anyone else." He glanced across at his nemesis. Scrivvulch, seemingly oblivious of the conversation, still knelt, leaning against the table. He had pulled the cravat from his neck and was now engaged in binding his wound. Red blotches marked the linen, but the flow of blood had finally abated. The Assassin's face was grayish. Perspiration matted his downy hair, and his movements were uncharacteristically uncertain. But his eyes were alive again, and he was undoubtedly capable of making his own way down from the Cloudmaster. Relian hesitated no longer. Bearing Mereth in his arms, he exited the workroom and hurried down the winding stairs.

Scrivvulch waited a moment longer. "Young Kru," he addressed his absent quarry, "you have committed a blunder. You should have killed me, for I am not defeated. A setback merely whets my determination." A whimsical smile touched his colorless lips. "For in this drab and ordinary world, 'tis Challenge that spices the tasteless meat of daily existence. Am I in truth Assassin no longer? All the more reason that the successful outcome of my final commission must put the period to a distinguished career, whose memories are all that ward off the chill of solitary old age. Ah, I must not think of it! We are not finished, you and I. I will cultivate the use of my left arm. Young Kru, I do not fail."

Summoning all his remaining strength, he dragged himself to his feet, squared his shoulders and walked toward the door. His steps were slow and wavering but his progress was steady, despite the occasional tremors that shook the tower. He was halfway across the room when a pair of silvery forms came slithering to intercept him. A double hiss of dire accusation arose—"You hurt Ssseigneur! You hurt Ssseigneur!" A steel snake swiftly encircled each ankle. Crekkid and Nurbo stretched to meet one another. The wiry tongues clicked briefly, and then the bodies intertwined to form a set of living shackles. Scrivvulch the Stick looked down to find himself effectively hobbled. He kicked, but the steel coils were not to be dislodged. The serpents hissed and tightened, drawing the captive ankles together and further lessening Scrivvulch's freedom of movement. His next attempted kick sent him sprawling. He fell upon his wounded arm and could not repress a gasp of pain. He lay a moment, breathing heavily. Blue lightning sped overhead, clipped the broken wall in passing. Loose stone pelted the workroom, and Scrivvulch scrambled from the path of the falling blocks as best he could. The snakes at his ankles did not permit him to rise. Despite his evasive efforts, a block of masonry smashed down on his thigh. He pushed the stone aside. The absence of pain was astounding. The leg was completely numb. Impossible to judge if it was broken or merely bruised; in either case, the member was temporarily unusable. For the first time, Scrivvulch considered the peril of his own situation, and for the first time in many a long year, he experienced significant uneasiness, even fear. The sensation was novel and disagreeable. However, all was not necessarily lost. If the snakes could be prevailed upon—

"Serpents," Scrivvulch appealed aloud, "what do you do? The tower is on the verge of collapse. You sacrifice yourselves. Release me or we shall all die together."

"You hurt Ssseigneur," came the grim response. "Perhapsss you kill Ssseigneur. You die."

"You die," Nurbo echoed.

"How could I kill the Seigneur?" Scrivvulch inquired. "Three of him remain."

"You hurt Ssseigneur."

"But three out of four went unhurt," Scrivvulch reasoned. "In the larger sense, he is therefore unhurt."

"Ssssssssss! Wordsss. Wordsss. Crekkid ssseesss you hurt Ssseigneur. Assssassssin! You pay."

"But serpents, so will you," Scrivvulch reminded them. "You will perish when the tower falls, as it must very soon now."

"Crekkid and Nurbo avenge Ssseigneur."

"Great Ssseigneur. Wissse Ssseigneur."

"Crekkid and Nurbo die together."

"For Ssseigneur."

"Gloriousss, ssshining death!"

"Gloriousss! Gloriousss!"

"Glorious indeed—but selfish, heartlessly selfish," Scrivvulch pointed out. "In dying, you deprive the Seigneur of your loyal and doubtless valuable selves. And in causing my death, you deprive the Seigneur of the pleasure and privilege of inflicting his own punishment upon me. Such self-indulgence robs the Seigneur of his rightful due.''

Silence for a time, while the serpents considered this logic. Silence broken by the crash of collapsing stonework, as lightning blasted the eastern face of Fortress Gavyne.

"Clever," Crekkid admitted at last.

"The simple truth, my friend."

Crekkid thought it over. "Sssssssssss! Truth? You hurt Ssseigneur. That isss truth," he decided. "Crekkid ssseesss, Crekkid knowsss thisss. You hurt Ssseigneur, and you pay."

"You pay," declared Nurbo. "Crekkid, Ssscourge of Ssseigneur!"

"Sssweet-ssshining Nurbo! Crekkid lovesss her for all time!"

"And Nurbo followsss Crekkid unto death. Avenge Ssseigneur. Nurbo and Crekkid—together!"

"Wedded at lassst in gloriousss death!"

"Death that consummatesss our passssion—"

"—Death that transssfiguresss our love!"

"Death! Death! Death! Death!"

Scrivvulch the Stick perceived the futility of further argument, and spoke no more. A few feet from him, the broken fragments of his cane lay where Relian Kru had contemptuously dropped them. Balancing upon his unwounded left arm, Scrivvulch dragged himself across the floor, his injured leg and shackled ankles trailing all but uselessly. When he reached the broken stick, he grabbed the spiked portion in his left hand; sat up and carefully worked the point of the spike between the two interlaced silver bodies that bound him. His efforts to lever the serpents apart were unsuccessful. The thin spike bent under the strain, and a particularly forceful twist snapped it. Scrivvulch regretfully laid the ruined spike aside and picked up the remaining fragment of his cane. It was the upper portion that carried the heavy ebony handle, with which Scrivvulch beat the unyielding skulls of Crekkid and Nurbo. He was thus engaged when a bolt of lightning struck the Cloudmaster dead on. The tower shattered. Its collapse crushed Assassin and serpents alike beneath several tons of stone.

*   *   *

Relian's descent from the Cloudmaster was taxing but swift, for stairs and corridors were now cleared of all humanity. The fortress was falling apart around him by the time he reached the foot of the central stairway. The entry hall was piled with rubble. Where the door had stood, a huge rent now yawned. Burning wooden fragments littered the floor from wall to wall, and the air was dark with smoke and cinders. He picked his way quickly past the obstacles. As he neared the exit, cold air blew in his face, and his lungs expanded in gratitude. The fresh air revived Mereth, and she spoke for the first time since they had left the workroom.

"Put me down, please, Relian. I'm better now, and you must be exhausted."

His arms ached from carrying her. "Are you certain?" he asked, and she nodded as vehemently as her aches would permit. He stopped to set her carefully on her feet. She wobbled a little and he slipped a supporting arm around her. Together they passed through the hole in the wall and out into the courtyard.

The courtyard was deserted. On the far side, the gate swung wide open. Relian and Mereth hurried toward the exit and as they went, they heard the thunder of a tremendous explosion behind them. They turned to behold the destruction of the Cloudmaster. Blue light flared and the tower seemed to bend and fold in upon itself. Stone blocks sprayed like shotgun pellets and the entire structure collapsed, its component stone and timber crashing down upon the lesser turrets below. Charred debris flew, and the two young people ducked under the arch in the wall. From that shelter they watched as falling rock crushed the lead-sheathed roof that peaked above the Great Hall. The roof crumpled like a piece of foil. The next strike took a supporting wall, and the Stargazer Tower went down. They waited no longer, but hastened through the short tunnel that led them through the wall and out of the fortress.

At the end of the clearing, where the Rising Road broke through the trees, a somber crowd had gathered. There stood the townsmen—those who had not already sought safety in Vale Jevaint. There were the frightened domestics who had long since fled the fortress kitchen. There was the Seigneur Keprose Gavyne, stretched out on the ground and surrounded by his sorrowing Selves. The heads of the Selves were bowed. Snowflakes powdered their pink curls.

Relian and Mereth approached. The Seigneur was unconscious or dead. His eyes were shut, his face waxen, and if his bandaged chest rose and fell, the motion was imperceptible.

As they drew near, Keprose's eyes opened. His gaze searched the clearing; skimmed the clustered townsmen and servants without interest; lingered an indifferent moment on Relian and Mereth; and came to rest upon the Selves. The blue eyes came to life, glowed softly. "Beloveds," Keprose whispered. "Beloveds."

The Selves, as always, shared sentences.

"Dear Prototype, do not try—"

"—To speak. You must—"

"—Conserve your strength until—"

"—A surgeon comes with leeches."

"My dearest ones, it is too late for that. I am dying. Far better that I die than live the conquered subject of Vanalisse the Unseen Hag."

Tears hung on the lashes of the Selves.

"Prototype, a momentary weakness quells your—"

"—Fiery spirit. Have faith. This—"

"—Weakness will pass, this—"

"—Dreary humor will subside. You will regain your—"

"—Wonted dauntless valor. Together—"

"—We shall overcome the Unseen Hag. We shall—"

"—Crush her and—"

"—Go on to greater triumphs. Courage!"

"Too late." Keprose shook his head weakly. "Too late. My fortress is destroyed. My wound is mortal."

Tears spilled down the cheeks of the Selves.

"I cannot bear it, Prototype. I cannot—"

"—Bear your anguish. It is as if—"

"—I saw myself bleed, and—"

"—Looked upon my own death."

"And for me," Keprose replied with an effort, "it is as if I saw myself whole and sound, alive and well, in all of you. Beloveds, you are the triumph of my life, the best and brightest, and my truest reality." He faltered, paused briefly to marshal the last of his strength. "In you, Keprose lives on. I die, but my Selves continue, and they are I. My fortress is destroyed, and so is my body, fortress of my spirit. But I have cheated death, for I have built other fortresses, which stand unscathed. Thus do I achieve my immortality. Do not weep, dear ones. I tell you I am content. I rejoice in your health and strength, for you are my fortresses. Build your walls strong. Fortify yourselves against the bitterness and envy you will encounter among lesser men. Go forth and thrive. Live, and wreak vengeance upon the Unseen Hag. Be happy, and be Keprose Gavyne. My Selves, I love you dearly and I know that love is returned. You will honor the dying wish of your Prototype?''

Three pink heads bobbed. Three sobs were simultaneously stifled.

''Beloveds, you must apply your supranormalcy to worthy ends. Thus it is my heart's desire that you strive to replicate yourselves. Create other Selves, other Keproses. There must be more of you; there must be more of me. Have I your promise?''

''Prototype—''

''—I—''

''—Promise.''

''Beloveds. Me. More . . . of . . . me.'' His strength exhausted, Keprose smiled and shut his eyes. He expelled his breath in a deep sigh, and smiling, died.

The sobs of the Selves broke forth uncontrollably. The citizens looked on in awe and wonder, but little grief. A rending crash signaled the complete destruction of Fortress Gavyne. The last of the standing walls fell, the last of the towers tumbled. The barrage of lightning ended, and fire faded from the sky. Silence reigned.

And out of the silence spoke a woman's voice—passionless, unimaginably old, and remote as the stars. *I am Vanalisse.*

Relian started. He knew the voice. It was the same that had once addressed him as he stood at the wall of the Tyrant of Mists. The same huge alien intelligence once again pressed upon his consciousness, and he shuddered at the contact. Had she spoken aloud, or did he hear her in his mind? Did she project her thoughts, or was she invisibly present among them? He could not tell. He looked around him and saw that Mereth was tensely poised, her eyes wide as she listened. The citizens and servants glanced in all directions, even up into the sky, as if they expected to find the speaker perched on a cloud. The tear-stained faces of the Selves lifted slowly. They froze, staring straight ahead. All present heard the voice of Vanalisse, vibrating in the air around them or—elsewhere.

I am the Unseen. I address the citizens of Vale Jevaint and the Selves of Keprose Gavyne.

The townsmen were clearly frightened. Only Gyf Fynok dared to raise his voice to inquire, ''Where are you?''

I am the Unseen. The attack of Keprose Gavyne upon the

Tyrant of Mists has engaged my attention, diverting my thoughts from matters of infinitely greater import. The Tyrant may be repaired, replaced, or dispensed with altogether. It is of no consequence. But the time that I have lost may not be recovered. The principle of universal fungibility does not apply to time. It is necessary to prevent the recurrence of this mishap. Therefore I banish the Selves of Keprose Gavyne.

The townsmen and servants whispered among themselves. The faces of the Selves were stony.

Selves, your creator is dead, your house is in ruins, and your presence is disharmonious to the point of diversion. Thus I exile you from this place. Go forth and never return. If ever you venture more upon these hills or the valley below, I will destroy you. Lest you doubt my ability to do so—behold.

As they watched, the dead flesh of Keprose Gavyne began to glow a pale blue. Citizens and Selves hastily drew back from the body. Brighter and brighter glowed the corpse until it shone like the moon at midday. A low crackling of energy preceded a sudden, blinding flash of blue light. The citizens instinctively shielded their eyes. The glare faded quickly. When it was gone and the spectators opened their eyes, the body of Keprose Gavyne had vanished. A powdering of blue-gray ash marked the spot where he had lain. Some men cried out in astonishment, but most maintained a near-stupefied silence. The Selves stared, motionless, wordless, shocked.

Selves of Keprose Gavyne, the uncanny voice rang out, *you are banished forever. Hear me and declare your submission.*

No response.

Selves, answer.

They spoke reluctantly.

"Vanalisse I hear you and—"

"—I must submit. I—"

"—Accept your doom."

"I—"

"—Will—"

"—Withdraw."

Nothing could have been more galling to the pride of the Selves than this admission of defeat. Their heads drooped, their faces were darkly flushed with bitter emotion.

A few men muttered. "Is it just that these—Selves—should be exiled for the offenses of their creator?"

"They *are* their creator. He said so himself. You heard him."

"That's impossible. When all's said and done, they can't be exactly the same."

"Technically true, I guess, but for all practical purposes—"

But some of the more pragmatic among the citizens were concerned with matters more mundane. Councilman Gyf Fynok hesitantly addressed the empty air. "One Seigneur's dead, and you've banished three others. Who's to govern the town now, Lady? The Council?"

In the name of my ancestor Honas Gavyne-Maveel, rightful lord of Vale Jevaint, I claim seigneurship. I am the Unseen. I am the Seigneur.

No one presumed to contradict her.

"But what are your intentions toward the town, Lady?" Clym Stipper inquired. "How will you rule us? What of the proposed tax on the imported batting used to wrap our eggs? What of our dispute with the Neraunci customs officials? What of our unfinished negotiations with the Port of Trisque merchants? What are your views on these issues?"

You shall know more hereafter. I trust these questions will not engage my attention unduly, nor divert my thoughts from matters of greater import. I will guard myself against such mishap. Farewell.

Silence and the listeners regarded one another in consternation. The alien presence had abandoned Relian's mind. Vanalisse was gone for the moment. Her departure left them all prey to aimless, anticlimactic confusion. The townsmen stood muttering in small groups. The Selves reverently collected the ashes of their Prototype. Relian and Mereth stood apart, conversing in low tones. The snow fell upon the clearing and the wind was cold. There was nothing to hold them there, and it was a long trek down to Vale Jevaint.

Master Gatherer Clym Stipper approached the kneeling Selves. "Gentlemen—lords—Seigneurs," he attempted, and gave it up. "I don't know what to call you."

"I am Keprose Gavyne," the Selves replied in unison.

"Gentlemen, I don't know what your plans are," said Stipper. "The rest of us, including your Lordship's—the Seigneur's—the fortress servants—are going back on down to Vale Jevaint now. Perhaps you'd like to come with us? It's late and you need a place to stay. You'd be welcome to spend the night in my home. And after that, you've plans to make and we'll help you as best we can."

The Selves rose.

"I thank you, my good Stipper, and—"

"—I accept your offer."

"I see that loyalty and a rightful sense of duty are—"

"—Not entirely extinct. We've many—"

"—Plans to make, my Selves and I."

"We go forth, according to the—"

"—Wishes of our great Prototype, to—"

"—People the world with Keproses. We require—"

"—Lavish provisions—carriages, money, meat, drink, bon-bons and the like—"

"—And it is naturally our expectation that the—"

"—Townsfolk, our rightful subjects, will—"

"—Furnish these necessities."

"We'll do what we can for your Lordships—you gentle-men," promised Stipper, accustomed to the high stateliness of the Seigneur Keprose. A useful idea struck him. "In order to make things easier for you, we'll even release your nephews—the Seigneur's nephews—the young men—to your custody."

The Selves considered it, arrived at a simultaneous decision.

"I consent to accept the nephews."

"They will be distributed—"

"—Equally. Each of me shall—"

"—Have one. They will—"

"—Serve to carry my burdens—"

"—Guard my persons—"

"—Deal with tradesmen and menials—"

"—Thus leaving me free to concentrate my attention—"

"—Upon the great work of self-replication—"

"—And hastening the day—"

"—Of my return and Restoration."

"Then that's settled, gentlemen," Stipper observed. "And we'd best be on our way. We've a long walk ahead of us."

"You did not own the foresight to bring a carriage, or even three sedan chairs?" inquired a Self.

"No, Seign—sir."

The Selves sighed impatiently.

"Well, I shall endure it, then."

"I must accustom myself to humility—"

"—According to my reduced—"

"—Circumstances. These privations—"

"—Are but temporary, after all."

The Selves paused for a last look back at the ruins of

Fortress Gavyne. Their eyes fell upon Relian and Mereth, still standing apart from the crowd.

"Ah, my apprentice," a Self observed. "He is not without some little ability, and—"

"—May conceivably prove useful. He—"

"—Shall come with me."

The townsfolk did not react with favor. Although it appeared that Black Relian could not be blamed for the murders and vandalism, he stood revealed beyond all question as the poacher of the Miasm and the despoiler of the Egg House.

"We want none of the Equalist," declared Gyf Fynok.

The Selves ignored the objection. "Young man," one of them commanded, "approach me, if you please. And you, Mistress Mereth."

They hesitated a moment, then complied out of sheer curiosity. If nothing else, Relian wanted a final close look at the doppelgangers. Under the hostile eyes of the townsmen, he advanced to face the Selves. He observed them minutely. Even under the closest scrutiny, each Self was absolutely indistinguishable from the original Keprose Gavyne. Keproses lived. Keproses spoke.

"Young man, despite the opinions of these good townsfolk concerning your violent and criminal tendencies—"

"—I have not lost all faith in you."

"I believe in your ability, limited though it may be—"

"—And I therefore offer you the privilege—"

"—Of continuing as my apprentice."

"I confess that we have had our differences—"

"—But I am willing to overlook them. As for you—"

"—No doubt you recognize the value of this offer that permits—"

"—Continuing development of your supranormalcy under my tutelage."

"Young man, what is your answer?"

Relian smiled and bowed slightly. "Gentlemen," he replied, "I recognize the value of the offer, but I reject it. Your Prototype held me against my will, and I did not grow to love captivity. I've no desire to share your exile. I've a life of my own once again, and it does not include the Selves of Keprose Gavyne."

Three massive sets of shoulders shrugged indifferently.

"A poor choice, indicative of—"

"—Frivolity and immaturity."

"Perhaps it is all for the best. I have—"

"—Always questioned your intellectual capabilities, and—"

"—This present declaration of yours confirms my worst suspicions."

The Selves turned to Mereth.

"And what of you, my pretty Mereth?"

"Do you accompany your benefactor?"

"You may yet strive for—"

"—Supranormalcy and elevation."

Mereth's response was suggestive of internal transformation. Her cheeks pinkened and she laughed—a natural, unforced spontaneous laugh. When her mirth had subsided, she replied, "No, all you Keproses. Now I may go where I please—anywhere I please. I will not go with you."

"Mistress, your folly and ingratitude—"

"—Reveals your unworthiness."

"My poor sister was not mistaken in you."

The Selves turned away, patently dismissing their apprentices. The three voices rose authoritatively.

"Townsmen! I have finished here—"

"—For the moment."

"We will leave at once."

The snow was driving in their faces, and the citizens were happy to obey. Without further discussion they filed from the clearing in a straggling procession quite unlike the orderly formation in which they had arrived a surprisingly short time ago. Most of them carefully ignored Relian. Only Clym Stipper paused to inquire somewhat grudgingly, "Coming with us? Maybe they'll find room for you at the Bearded Moon."

"No," Relian replied, and Mereth glanced at him in surprise. "I've belongings I won't abandon, and I've a good idea where to search for them."

"You can't very well stay here," Stipper objected. "It's cold now, it'll be colder yet by nightfall, and there's the girl to consider."

"The porter's lodge is still intact," Relian told him. "We'll be well enough."

"Suit yourself," Clym Stipper returned without regret. He turned and hurried after his companions. Relian and Mereth stood and watched them go, but did not watch for long. The lash of the wind soon drove them to the shelter of the porter's lodge.

The lodge had sustained no damage. The two small ston⸗
chambers were exactly as the porter had left them. There wa⸗
wood stacked up beside the hearth and food in the cupboard
While Relian built a fire, Mereth foraged for bread, cheese
apples and a canister of tea.

When they had eaten and sat sipping their tea beside th⸗
fire—a generous fire, most unlike the feeble flames that ha⸗
wavered upon the grates of Fortress Gavyne—Mereth turne⸗
to Relian and asked, "Why did you want to stay here
Relian? What are the belongings you must find?"

"Not mine, exactly," he admitted. "But no one else's
now. Books, Mereth. Keprose's library. You know—*Tw⸗
Thousand Greej Patterns; Kly's Theory of SupraVisual Flac
cidity; Index of Temporal Vortices*—"

"Of course. We *need* them. Do you think we can actuall⸗
find them under all that?" She waved her hand in the direc
tion of the ruins.

"Not all of them, of course. Not the whole library, not eve⸗
most of it. But many. Enough to give us a good start. I believ⸗
we'll have a couple of days before scavengers from the tow⸗
arrive. We might find hundreds of books in that time."

"There'll be so much to learn. So much knowledge—"

"Then you want to continue with supranormalcy?"

"*Yes*. Oh, yes! When I used it for the first time—when w⸗
used it together to free ourselves of the snakes, I felt as if I'⸗
been . . . cured, when I didn't even know I was sick. Do yo⸗
understand?"

"Yes. I've felt it."

"And now I want to learn so much," she continued in
tently. "So much. Everything I can stuff into my head
everything the books can teach me to do. And I want—"

"What?"

"To see the world. Some of it, at least. Today is the firs⸗
time I've ever left this fortress, and I only made it as far a⸗
the edge of the clearing, and then came back. I'd like to se⸗
towns—*cities*—mountains and seas—and the people, all thos⸗
different people—"

"Would you like to see them with me?" he asked.

"Of course." She smiled into his eyes.

Relian returned the smile and observed, "Then I'm a very
lucky man, indeed."

The End

Stories
✠ of ✠
Swords and Sorcery

✠✠✠✠✠✠✠✠✠✠✠✠✠✠✠✠✠✠

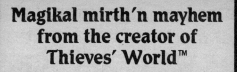